Ever This
Day

Also by Helen Moorhouse

The Dead Summer (2011)
The Dark Water (2012)
Sing Me To Sleep (2013)

Published by Poolbeg

Ever This Day

HELEN MOORHOUSE

POOLBEG
CRIMSON

Published 2017 by Crimson
an imprint of Poolbeg Press Ltd
123 Grange Hill, Baldoyle
Dublin 13, Ireland
www.poolbeg.com

A catalogue record for this book is available from the British Library.

ISBN 978-1-78199-854-0

 www.facebook.com/poolbegpress
 @PoolbegBooks

Typeset by Poolbeg in Sabon
Printed by CPI Group (UK) Ltd, Croydon, CR0 4YY

www.poolbeg.com

About the Author

Ever This Day is Helen Moorhouse's fourth novel. *The Dead Summer, The Dark Water* and *Sing Me to Sleep* are also published by Poolbeg.

As well as writing, Helen works as a freelance Voiceover Artist. Her interests include reading, cinema and TV.

Originally from County Laois (where she attended an only-slightly spooky boarding school), she lives in Dublin with her husband and four daughters.

For more, see www.helenmoorhouse.com

Acknowledgements

My enormous thanks go to Paula and the team at Poolbeg for their patience, guidance, faith and the opportunity to write the type of stories that I love to read.

To Gaye, my editor, for her knowledge, her observation, her thoughts and ideas and her dedication through all the late-night editing sessions. And for making my story make sense.

To my wonderful, patient and supportive husband Daryl; and Daisy, Florence, Holly and Bea – the four clever, funny, determined individuals that I am blessed to call my daughters.

To my family – sisters, brothers, nieces, nephews, in-laws and outlaws; and my incredible friends for all of your support.

To everyone – students and staff, especially the other five members of the Brat Pack – at the Brigidine Convent Mountrath (whose geography and routine I've borrowed a little of for Maria Goretti) for those five extraordinary, unforgettable years from 1985 to 1990. *Fortiter et Suaviter.*

To my readers for your time, your loyalty and for coming with me on my adventures.

Finally, to my parents for their encouragement and pride.

In loving memory of my parents, Claire and Sean Keenan

PART 1

Chapter one

BALLYKEERAN
August 1942

The child blinked and peered into the gloom.

"*Frances*?" she called. There was no reply.

She shivered, too late remembering that she'd tossed her cardigan on the ground early into their game. She'd have to find that, or Mammy would be very vexed with her.

But first, where was her sister?

"*Frances!*" she called, a little louder this time. There was no sound – no *human* sound. Just the eerie whine of a curlew in the distance, and the increasingly persistent drumming of thick, heavy raindrops against the ground.

The child looked around her, wrapping her bare, bone-thin arms around her body. She glanced up at the charcoal sky and blinked again, turning her face quickly away as the rain bounced off her cheeks and into her eyes. She wiped it away and again scanned the bog all around her. She couldn't see Frances anywhere. And it was so dark now. It must be nearly nine o'clock – they were out way past their bedtime, and in the rain too …

"*Frances!*" she called. "*Please come back! We have to go home! Mammy'll kill us!*" She pleaded with the empty night air. Frustrated, she stamped her foot against the moist ground. "*Frances, will you come on! We'll be killed!*"

She was angry now. This was a stupid game. Typical Frances.

1

Thinking her tricks were funny. She'd hide and hide for ages before jumping out and shouting, laughing like a drain if she made you scream with fright. It was never funny, this time especially.

The child looked around again, frowning. She trembled with cold under the thin summer dress which was plastered against her little body. She looked down at her feet, now streaked with greyish trails of liquid running between her toes from the dusty turf mold which had been kicked into her sandals. Her hair, which had come loose from her plait, was stuck to her face. She could feel thick drops tracking their way down through the roots, trailing over her scalp and down along her face and neck. She wiped one heavy drip from the end of her nose, only for it to reform instantly.

"*Frances!*" It was a whimper now, a pitiful cry into the dark that again went without a response. "*Frances, if you don't come out now, I'm going home without you! And you know that Mammy will double kill you if that happens ...*" It was less a threat than a plea.

The child looked around again, hoping, *praying,* that her younger sister's shape would loom at her out of the darkness.

Nothing.

Desperately, the child turned in a final circle, scanning as far as her eyes could see through the sheets of rain. Still nothing. She was entirely alone.

Why had she come out this far onto the bog again? They weren't allowed this far away from the house – she had told Frances not to come. She had wanted to see the machines that the fellahs had brought to cut the turf with, that Frances was afraid of ... but Frances had followed anyway. She hadn't wanted to be left alone. Didn't want to be called names like "sucky babby" and "Mammy's pet. Didn't want to be taunted for being timid, for liking to stay in the yard with the chickens, near the back door where she could hear Mammy sing and smell the fresh bread baking in the range. She should have just bloody stayed there, then.

Dada was always telling them it was too dangerous to come out this far, when they didn't know exactly where the dangerous bogholes were, didn't know where the ground dipped and rose, where it was soft and where it was safe to walk. It was too dangerous, he said.

She had thought that maybe they'd be safe together. But then they had fought. And now Frances was gone.

The child sniffed and turned, feeling very vexed indeed. *Frances was nothing but a louser*, she thought. Leaving her out here in the cold and the wet in the dangerous part of the bog. Leading her a merry dance. She was probably at home right now, warming herself by the fire, humming that stupid song she was always humming, eating warm batch loaf, leaving toothmarks in the butter, and drinking hot milk. Laughing at her.

Her feet sinking into the softening ground, the child turned for home, alone.

At least that's what she told everyone, at first.

Chapter two

Ria
LONDON
April 2015

There were two things that day that reminded me.

Two random, unexpected, unconnected incidents that jolted me right back to somewhere, to something that I hadn't thought about in years. Or so I told myself.

I was lying, of course.

I was a teacher, living alone in London, and I liked it that way. I liked peace and quiet, my own company. No alarms and no surprises.

Divorced once, currently single. Not quite Cat-Lady-of-Camberwell just yet, but who knew what delights the future held? I had a daughter, Emma, who was twenty-eight, some lovely friends but not too many, a very small mortgage on my own clean and modern flat and a Story. One that I told myself I hadn't thought of in years, as per above – the truth was, however, that it was a story that I had thought of *every* day since it happened, but had never once told anyone else. Why? Because, firstly, it was a joke without a punchline, a song with one verse and half a chorus – it had no ending. And who wanted to hear one of those?

And secondly? Because, even if I found someone who liked half a tale, I'd still never tell them. Never could, because no one would believe me – not up until *that* day, that is.

The day that started the end of the Story.

4

It was April 20th, my fifty-third birthday, and a Friday. I had booked a day off work and felt a little self-congratulatory – actually, downright smug – at my excellent timing. It seemed I had bagged myself one of those glorious spring days that just couldn't be ignored, because it wasn't spring, as in shivering-daffodils-in-damp-gardens, but finally spring, as in explosions of magnolia and cherry blossom, hyacinths and tulips dancing in flower tubs on the kerb. Sunshine, rich with actual, much-missed and longed-for warmth, inviting skin to be bared and faces turned upward toward a blue sky. London was glorious. It was lunch-outside weather, sweaters-around-waists weather.

I decided to make a day of it, to play tourist and take the bus into town before heading to my friend Jess's place, as planned. I'd normally have taken the Tube straight there, my route and its timings planned to the hilt, but on that day the thought of going underground was just plain wrong. I couldn't face the hot, still air of the stations, the crowds, the smells. The spring day stirred something primal in me, made me felt like an animal emerging from hibernation. Emma would have called me Punxsutawney Phil, the legendary groundhog, I'm sure, but I didn't want to miss out on everything gorgeous and light-filled that was happening on the streets I loved so much. Because I did – I loved – love – London, and everything in it, and everything it had given me.

So, I re-planned my route carefully, disembarked on the Strand and strolled through the nearby theatre-lined lanes, watching Londoners walk with light steps in the sunshine, some of them even daring to catch each other's eye here and there, mumbling an awkward hello while blushing. I smiled at a gaggle of tourists clustering noisily together into a clump and cheesing it up to an iPhone on a selfie stick, took my time checking out theatre posters, thinking that Emma and I were overdue a night out, and after a while I emerged onto the piazza outside Covent Garden Market to be greeted by the usual blaze of colour and noise – crowds gathered around a man on stilts, two jugglers balancing on unicycles while swopping knives in the air, hordes of people holding disposable coffee cups striding along, or chatting animatedly. From inside the market building, I could hear music – Bach today: 'Sheep May Safely Graze' – or The Birthday Cantata as it was also known. Just for me, I smiled. I loved Bach. And how beautiful it sounded. I would go to that overpriced shop that I loved to mock but which my friend Jess just loved, for some of the geranium and orange oil she used – a gift to thank her for the dinner invitation. And I'd get her some flowers maybe, they always cheered her up. Tulips … no, hyacinths …

It was then that I saw him.

I wasn't sure at first. It couldn't be. *How* could it be? How could he be *here*? He belonged *there, and then* – that's where he had chosen to stay. He didn't *exist* in my world – not since that last time I saw him from the rear window of the taxi as it pulled away. My stomach lurched.

I shivered, suddenly cold as I stared, unable to comprehend what I was seeing. That familiar, tall form, head held high. His hair, completely grey now – he'd be close to his sixties after all – was thick still, no longer skimming his collar, but short and slightly tousled. I could see his profile – it was unmistakable. And that walk – relaxed and confident. It feels like such a cliché to say it, but for a moment the world genuinely slowed, everyone and everything else in slow motion, a blur, with him the only thing I could see clearly as he strode across the square. The earth seemed to lurch a little under my feet. Indescribably, out-of-body strange, yet there was something so inherently familiar about seeing him, and something so terrifying about the possibility that he might see me.

Turn, I urged him in my head, some voice from somewhere buried suddenly shouting out, my every sense shooting electricity through my body.

Turn and look at me. See me.

But what if he did?

What if he turned and saw me, but looked through me? What if there was no recognition in his eyes? Or worse, what if there *was* and he simply looked away? Why would his feelings have changed, after all? And what if he looked and saw and his reaction was *disappointment*? After all, what would he see? A middle-aged woman, thankfully with make-up on, but probably not winning beauty awards with just a coat of foundation and a dash of blusher, her hair cut short – still roughly the same auburn colour, mind, thanks to good genes and a better hairdresser – wearing jeans, a shirt and a trench jacket with a favourite blue scarf and comfortable Ecco shoes for walking? There were wrinkles around the mouth that hadn't been there before, a tiredness in the eyes. In my own head, I looked nothing like I did when I knew him first.

A ripple of sudden fear rushed through me. My knees felt weak. I didn't *want* him to look now – and for an instant I was sure, terrified, that he *would* – that those brown eyes would lock with mine, and I'd see his face full on, and that his reaction would be … what? Could he still be angry after nearly thirty years? I supposed he could. If only I'd had the chance to explain, if only he'd listened to me back then.

I didn't see the woman until she stumbled against me, catching my arm as her ankle twisted in her high heels on the cobbles and gave way beneath her. In an instant, the world speeded up again. Noise and movement returned and I turned to her, instinctively grabbing her arm in return to keep her upright as she regained her footing. She began a typical English barrage of apology – "I'm so terribly sorry, my heel, I didn't mean to …" her face burning with embarrassment. I smiled and nodded, but turned away from her, unwilling to engage. After all, she had caused me to lose sight of him – and I had to find him again, if only to prove to myself that he was real. I ignored her, and searched the sea of passing people instead, but he was truly gone, absorbed into the crowd. For an age I stood there and still scanned the throng, and watched where he had been, overcome with something – drained, yet assaulted by memories that crowded around the edges of my brain but which I simply couldn't allow to come to the fore. My head felt foggy, my body odd – numb, slow, stunned.

And yet there was more to come.

I said there were two things that day that started everything again. The second thing was the newspaper.

After I saw him, I drank a coffee from a stall with trembling hands, trying to find meaning in the almost-encounter. I felt suddenly different. Rattled, deeply unsettled. In that instant, the joy, the sense of freedom and carelessness or, rather, carefully planned spontaneity disappeared from my day – I simply felt odd and discomfited, eager to be with someone. I was cold, too, unable to warm myself. My jaunt into town held no appeal for me anymore and I decided to take the Tube after all.

It seems pertinent to point out, at this point, that once upon a time I was Irish. I was more English now, of course, I felt, having lived here for longer than I'd lived there, teaching in English schools, marrying an Englishman, raising an English daughter. I have an English, or at least neutral accent now, where only touches of Dublinese seep through the cracks – *the craics*, Emma would splutter. The occasional Irishism here and there, but nothing serious. I wasn't one of the Irish who dream of going 'home', whose fantasies are soaked in an Atlantic mist rising off a surging sea. I'd never wanted care packages of Tayto sent to me, or Lyons Tea, or soda bread or what not – there was no one to send them anyway, as my parents were long dead since before even My Story happened. But an Irish newspaper? That was something different.

I saw the copy of the *Irish Independent* tucked on a stand just outside the station. It caught my eye out of habit as I passed – seeing the familiar masthead always triggered something in me – so did other things, like hearing an unmistakable Irish accent, or hearing Irish itself spoken, or seeing a pint of Guinness pulled. My ex-husband Joe had always joked that I got a 'look', rather like a puppy tilting its head to one side. "Have you had your diddly-aye activated?" he used to ask; or "Watch out, Mum's gone all Gael Force". Hilarious. And even nowadays, where every last piece of information I could possibly want and more was accessible on my smartphone, I was still incapable of passing an Irish newspaper by, especially today.

At first it had been to keep an eye on things. Things to do with My Story. Even with that consigned to a room in my brain marked 'do not open', I still couldn't ignore a newspaper. There was something comforting about it, familiar and reassuring. I bought the copy at the Tube station without thought or hesitation.

I flicked through it quickly as we rattled along the dark tunnels the couple of stops to Jess's. I never knew what I expected to find. Irish issues about mental health, and hospital beds, and an Irish model who had split up with her Irish boyfriend, and some Irish opinions on things that I couldn't really understand and, despite a deep-rooted sense of feeling that I *should*, couldn't care less about. And I didn't.

Until I came across the story about the man who had found the human remains. The scene was closed off ... the State Pathologist had examined it ...

And for the second time that day, time froze. Human remains in Ballykeeran Bog, County Laois. I felt instantly sick. *Don't let it be her*, I prayed. *Don't let that be what happened ...*

At my stop, I stumbled up the steps and out of the Tube station. It was still bright, but getting chillier now as the afternoon wore on. Taking a deep breath, I concentrated on putting one foot in front of the other, punch drunk and reeling from what I had seen and read. Why both of those things on the one day, my birthday? Was it fate? Was it somehow designed to happen? Or was it just a coincidence? I felt the shift again under my feet as I tried to stay focused. *First him ... now her. That place ... those people.*

I tried to push it away as best I could, but as I made my way down Shoreditch High Street in a complete daze, an overwhelming sense of dread washed over me like a slow tide, bringing it all back. Everything I had failed to put behind me, despite myself.

Chapter three

Ria
LONDON
April 2015

It was just after one in the morning when I woke in Jess's spare room. I pushed myself up gingerly on my elbows, waiting for the pounding in my head to subside. It was slightly better than when I had gone to bed, by which I mean that it felt like ten of the eighteen or so drummers who had turned up in there to practise earlier had left. By now, it was also probably compounded by hunger. I hadn't really eaten since a bowl of soup at lunch.

The meal that Jess had cooked in honour of my birthday had looked wonderful – tender salmon, with sweet cherry tomatoes and tart balsamic vinegar, baby potatoes, fresh beans – but I had barely managed a mouthful. The other guests, too – the gang – friends that Jess and I had accumulated since 1990 when we had met – were long overdue some of my time and attention but I had failed them. I had looked forward so much to my birthday dinner, and yet had managed only a sip of champagne and a nibble of birthday cake before I had apologetically retired.

I sat up in bed and listened. There were no voices from downstairs – the others must have left – an early finish by our standards but I had probably – actually, undoubtedly – made things awkward. A birthday party without the Birthday Girl. I could hear movement from downstairs, however, and concluded that Jess must still be up. Cleaning, most likely. She could never bear having to set-to and wash up the morning after a party. There was something comforting about hearing the gentle clink of plates and cutlery followed by the hum of the dishwasher starting up. She'd clean up, would Jess, but wouldn't damage her nails. Knowing she was still up made me feel much better, relieved that I wasn't at home alone in my own bed, even, and I liked my own bed. Really liked it. Tonight, though, being in Jess's felt safe somehow. Ordinary. It made it easier not to think about the other stuff. To keep that in the shadows, to try my best to render it irrelevant.

Except it wasn't, was it? It was a big part of everything. A big part that I had tried to keep tightly tied away all this time. Except today, when I could feel it start to unravel. I sat upright and took a deep breath. I needed to hold myself together and block it out. Just as I had strived to do for all these years. I simply didn't have the time, or the headspace, to dredge it all up again. To try to figure out what had happened, to try to understand any of it. I wanted – today, more than ever – as I had wanted then and wanted since – for it all to have never taken place. Well, most of it.

I swung my legs to the floor, pulled the knitted throw from the end of the bed around my shoulders, and made my way from the room out along the landing and down the stairs where a lamp was lit in the small hallway of her small, renovated Victorian terraced two-up, two-down. The door of the kitchen was slightly ajar.

I pushed it open gently, peering around it to see my friend filling a bucket to mop the floor, dressed in habitual black – to "keep her curves a delicious surprise", she always smirked – her glasses perched on her glossy black bob – we shared a hairdresser. I watched her, completely absorbed in her task, for a moment. Jess had always been a ball of energy. And was always busy with her hands – baking, cleaning, embroidering, crocheting.

She jumped and turned suddenly as I pushed the door slightly and it squeaked.

"Oh, Ria! Did I wake you? I'm so sorry," she began, but I shook my head.

"Not at all. Not at all. It's me who should be sorry for running off on you all earlier like that. You went to so much trouble for my birthday and I was so rude. My head was splitting, is all. Did everyone think I was really rude?"

She dismissed the thought. "Not a bit. Dave and Katherine are going hillwalking in the morning or some healthy nonsense, and were leaving early anyway. And myself and Eleanor had a killer of a week at school so things just finished up naturally about half an hour ago – I saw them all off into taxis. How does your head feel now? Did the paracetamol help at all?"

I nodded. "Much better," I lied. "Dinner was delicious by the way. Did you bake that cake yourself?"

"Just a carrot cake," she replied, dismissing it with her hand. "You must be starving – would you be up for a slice now? Or some toast and hot milk, maybe?"

I was hungry, I realised, and nodded eagerly. "Cake," I said. "And tea." So terribly British. And Irish, come to think of it.

Maybe we could chat for a while. We had always been night owls, Jess and I. I was warmed by the thought of just talking with her in her cosy kitchen. Anything to distract me from what that day had done.

I sat silently at the kitchen table as I watched Jess bustle about, warming the teapot – *scalding the pot*, it was called at home – retrieving mugs from a cupboard above the sink. She was so at home in the kitchen and had made it all so homely – cushions, curtains, the string of pink and red hearts that hung over the edge of the countertop, the Kilner jars filled with lentils and pastas that lined the worktop, the tall glass vase filled with lemons and limes, the jug full of deep purple and white tulips that rested in the middle of the table. Jess was good at getting just the right amount of clutter in place. I was not. I liked things simple and neat. Uncomplicated, modern and clean.

"Did anything ever happen with that bloke you went out with last month?" I asked as Jess handed me a steaming mug and served me a slice of cake on a hand-painted plate with a proper dessert fork.

She stood, cradling her own mug, with her back to the cooker opposite me. "Pukey Paul? Not likely," she scoffed. "There's something very unappealing about someone who takes you on the London Eye and then sits there with his eyes closed the entire time, breathing like Darth Vader, before throwing up in a bin the minute you get back down to earth. I guess anything's possible when you swipe right. Not that you'd know, of course – the internet being the devil and all that. Anyway, that's not what concerns me here. Now, what's up with *you*?"

I smiled, but squirmed in my seat at the same time. "Nothing," I replied casually, lifting my mug and blowing steam from the top of it. "I was just curious if you'd seen him again – or anyone, for that matter."

Jess continued to stare at me. "You just seemed awfully preoccupied at dinner."

I shrugged, suddenly uncomfortable. "I had such a terrible headache," I said. "I forgot town could be such a nightmare to get through – the Tube and all that." I studied the tulips again, aware that Jess's eyes were fixed on me over her mug.

"That's nonsense," she replied.

I turned my attention to my cake, popping a small piece of it in my mouth before chasing some crumbs with the fork.

"You could barely eat – even cake," Jess continued. "And you seemed completely distracted."

"There's *nothing* wrong, Jess. This headache's really awful – it just came out of nowhere, and I've actually a lot of class prep to get done this weekend – a lot of planning. I'm not distracted ... more ... preoccupied, I suppose." I didn't want to have this conversation. I wanted us to huddle together and talk about anything else – the weather, her work, my work, Pukey Paul and his panicked panting – *anything* to distract myself from the dark thoughts that lurked in the back of my brain, the dreadful possibilities that had presented themselves to me since I had seen the newspaper.

"So you heard me say that I'm getting a puppy, then?" Jess countered, stopping me in my tracks.

I squirmed again. "Fair enough, I missed that," I admitted, surprised. Jess was a lifelong cat lover. "But why are you getting a puppy when you're out at work all day?"

"I'm not," she said. "Getting a puppy. I never said that earlier, but I just wanted to prove my point. You're not listening. You're completely distracted." She fell silent, sipped her tea.

I looked at her, her flawless skin and perfect teeth, her cheekbones high and round. Her expression was deathly serious.

"Ria," she said.

13

I nodded.

"I'm going to ask you something and I want a straight answer. Do you understand?"

"Of course," I replied.

Jess cleared her throat, thought for a moment and swallowed hard.

"Ria. Are you ... is there something ... are you *ill*?"

I blinked, silenced for a moment as I tried to understand what she meant until it dawned on me.

"You mean *ill* ill? Good God, Jess, no! What made you think that?"

She rolled her eyes gratefully upwards, trying, I could see, to keep tears in. "Thank *heavens*," she said forcefully. "I was sure ..."

"No! I swear, I'm fine."

"I thought that's what you crept down here to tell me – why you couldn't eat, why you couldn't face everyone."

"Absolutely not! I feel so guilty now!"

We tripped over each other's words as we sought to explain and to reassure.

"So what the hell is wrong with you then?" Jess demanded, simultaneously relieved and again annoyed. "I've *never* seen you so preoccupied as tonight? You practically ran in the door, crushed me in a desperate hug and then didn't listen to a word anyone said the entire way through dinner and then suddenly disappeared off to bed with a ton of painkillers. Is it any wonder I thought you had terrible news for me?"

I looked at her vexed face, filled again suddenly with the worry that had left it moments before. My heart softened, and I longed to hug her again and reassure her that our friendship wasn't ending any time soon. Instead I looked at her kind, motherly face for a little too long. And as I did, the dam in my brain gave a little, and some of the darkness flowed in. I opened my mouth to release it without thinking.

"I bought the *Irish Indo* today ..." I began.

Jess rolled her eyes and grinned.

She was in on their joke, this exaggerated picture that they had all composed of me, where I grew maudlin when I spoke of Ireland, and anything Irish. They had a routine which left them helpless

14

with laughter where they put on terrible stage-Irish accents, and talked of "the old country" and would try to outdo each other with outdated stereotypical references. Emma favoured "turf sandwiches" while her father had a well-practised monologue about a banshee in a cowshed eating potatoes and being afraid of leprechauns.

"*Ochón, ochón*," Jess said drily.

"No – it's not one of the turf-sandwich stories." I paused for a moment to collect my thoughts. "There was a story in the paper about a body, or at least some *remains* ... some man walking his dog found it – it's always someone walking their dog, isn't it? That's another reason that you shouldn't get a puppy – you'd have to walk it and who knows what you'd find."

My attempt at humour went unappreciated.

"Is it Joe, then?" Jess asked.

"Is it Joe what? Who found the body?"

"Is *Joe* sick? You keep trying to change the subject!"

"No. Joe's fine. He's in Wales on a dig, has a new girlfriend I think ..."

"Well, who's sick then? Please tell me it's not Emma?"

"What? No-one's sick, Jess. *No. One. Is. Sick*. It was the remains ... in the bog ... the story in the paper ..."

"What *about* it then?"

I could see her frustration as she looked at me from where she still stood. Silence fell between us, filled only with the ticking of the wall clock. I knew it had to be getting on for two in the morning and that we should retire. But knew also that I was feeling weak, that the dam in my brain was close to bursting. With memories. With pain.

I took a deep breath.

"Do you believe in ghosts, Jess?"

Her shoulders sank, exasperated. "*Ria!*" she cried.

I waved my hands at her to get her to stop. "No, no, no, Jess. Please. You wanted to know what was wrong with me and I'm trying to tell you. Maybe that wasn't the best way to start ..." I paused for a moment, collected my thoughts. "It's late, I know, but I saw something today ... someone ... and then there was that story in the newspaper and it reminded me of something from long ago

... it's all very strange. It was then and it is now – after all these years. And suddenly ... all these memories ..."

"*Ria*."

Silence again. I didn't have to tell her, of course.

But then maybe it would make me feel better? And maybe it wasn't that big a deal – maybe sharing some of the story – not all – would diminish it, somehow?

I took a deep breath.

"I've never told you this – I've never told *anyone* this, not Joe, not anyone – but almost thirty years ago or so, before I came here to London, I had a ... job ... an odd job ... not as in 'get-a-man-with-a-wrench-in-to-help', but an actual odd job. An unusual line of work ... in an ... unusual place. And some weird stuff happened. Some truly unpleasant, strange stuff. And I never told anyone else about it because they quite simply wouldn't believe me. And they'd be right not to, because it's unbelievable. But I swear it's all true. And for a really long time I tried to put it out of my head, and out of my life. And I thought I'd succeeded. But of course I hadn't. And all of those things were just hidden away, like a little spark under some ashes. Until today, that is."

I hesitated. Then looked her straight in the eye.

"Have you ever heard me mention a place called Ballykeeran?"

Chapter four

Ria
DUBLIN
1987

I first heard about the job at the convent in the staffroom at work.

To explain, 'work' was St Theresa's – an all-girls' secondary school in Terenure, run by nuns, as most schools at the time were, with a complement of lay teachers, as most schools had. I was one of them. Fresh out of college, hot off the presses as it were, living alone in a small bedsit in Rathmines and barely scraping a living. My mother had managed to get through the small inheritance that my father had left her, and then some more money that the bank had lent her. Once she died of a sudden heart attack in my final year of college, what was left from their estate went to pay bills, and I was not only orphaned, but pretty penniless too. Very Dickensian.

At work, I taught English and History, and supervised a Creative Writing Club that the students had set up themselves. My pay was okay, my life quiet, and, despite the knocks that life had dealt me at that point, at just twenty-five, I was still possessed of that naivety that meant I thought I knew it all, and could do anything.

No one else was interested in the letter when it arrived. Sister Anne, the principal, pinned it to the noticeboard in the staffroom, and it attracted a small crowd which, on reading the contents, had a variety of reactions – mostly "pffs" and "don't think so's". I waited until the group had dispersed back to their sandwiches, their

17

marking and their little chats, so that I had the board all to myself. It was a job advertisement.

The letterhead was in cursive script with a sketch of a lily on it. The letter itself was typed on an ordinary typewriter. I soon saw why all of the other teachers had laughed at the notion – a live-in position in a convent boarding school. English and History teacher by day, Supervisor-slash-Matron – School Guardian, it was called – in the evenings and at weekends. One weekend off a month, accommodation and keep provided. Responsibility **"for the physical and spiritual supervision and care of young Catholic ladies"** at the Convent of Maria Goretti, Ballykeeran, County Laois.

"You might as well become a nun yourself," chortled Jim Mackey, the PE teacher, and a few of the others laughed.

I understood their position, in fairness. Some of them were married and settled with families, others just didn't want to leave Dublin – and, let's face it, the appeal of living in a convent full of nuns in a part of the country I was sure I'd never been to was pretty low. Except for someone desperately, desperately in need of money. The timing couldn't have been better for me – and neither could the salary which was outlined in small print on a second page, pinned underneath the first. You see, it wasn't just a normal teacher's salary – there was *extra* money for the supervision – evenings and weekends – it was, to me, *enormous*. And what appealed to me more was the fact that being a live-in meant that everything was included – meals, accommodation, electricity – it wasn't just money coming *in* – it was practically no money going *out*. I could save it all and barely spend – I wouldn't even need bus fare in and out of work. I was *dazzled* by how much financial sense it all made – so dazzled that I didn't spend too long thinking about the everyday of it other than that I could certainly cope with a year of it – eight months, in reality, when you took into consideration Easter and Christmas holidays. It seemed like winning the Lotto.

That evening, in the spring of 1987, I stayed late to use the typewriter in the secretary's office, typed out a CV, wrote my application letter and posted it on the way home.

A week later, I was interviewed by someone from an employment agency who said that they would submit their report to the Sisters, and I'd hear back soon. They wrote to me two weeks later to say I had the job and that was it.

I finished out the year in Terenure, and then spent the summer downsizing my life, as you'd say nowadays. By the end of August, I had only the bare essentials left – clothes, a few books, some memories. I gave up the lease on my bedsit – that was no hardship. It was all in place.

Step One of The Plan.

Chapter five

Ria
LONDON
April 2015

"So what was this Plan then?" Jess asked.

She had moved to sit opposite me at the table, her chin cradled in her hand as she listened. It was two in the morning and Jess had yawned once or twice but had shown no sign of wanting to leave. I eased myself off my seat to stretch my stiff legs, and limped around to the kettle. Time for more tea.

"It was 1987," I began. "Ireland was different to what it seems to be now – there were no jobs, no opportunities. Everyone emigrated if they wanted to get anywhere, it seemed. And that was The Plan. For me and Leonard to go to America, get married, and start a new life there."

Jess frowned. "Leonard?" she repeated, puzzled.

I smiled, nodding. "Leonard," I told her, flicking the 'on' switch on the kettle.

"But ... Joe?" she asked, puzzled.

"What about him?" I grinned as I rinsed out the mugs.

"I just thought ..."

"That there had only ever been Joe? I had a life before him, Jess. Even if I haven't had much of a one since ..."

Jess shrugged, but her expression was bewildered. All this new information after twenty-five years of friendship. I knew how she saw me. And why shouldn't she? She hadn't known me before

20

Ballykeeran – before I had been overtaken by an overwhelming urge to be *safe*. She knew on-time Ria, white-or-cream Ria, let's-go-to-the-same-pub-we-like-it-there Ria. She hadn't known how fiercely the desire had burned inside me back then to cross the Atlantic and get away from dreary old Dublin where I had grown up, gone to school and university; where my parents were buried and where my bedsit had damp patches on the bedroom wall. For a moment a feeling flooded back to me: a flashback to walking across O'Connell Bridge, hunched over against the sweeping cold rain of a February day, the wind off the Liffey slicing through me as I strode through the city centre. And the panic I felt, the sheer desperation at the thought of being trapped there forever. The burning need to get away, to start anew, to forget the cold and the boredom that threatened to engulf me.

"The Plan was why I took the job at the convent," I said. "I mean, I got a good job straight out of college. And I had a quiet life. I was a good girl, all round. Well brought up, well educated, hard-working, steady. But I was twenty-bloody-five and inside I wanted *more* ... so I came up with a plan. Boston. I had visions, you see. Visions of a house in the suburbs there with a deck and a porch and a big holly wreath on the door at Christmas, and friendly neighbours but I'd spell it without the 'u' ... and summers on the beaches from morning till night – all that stuff that you see on TV. Visions of my kids going to school in big yellow buses, eating peanut-butter-and-jelly sandwiches out of brown-paper lunch bags. Visions of driving a station wagon, and celebrating Thanksgiving. It was all-American goodness, fourth of July, land of opportunity stuff. I wanted it all so *badly*, even though you'd never have known on the outside ... would you prefer camomile, by the way?"

Jess shook her head.

"So I decided that Leonard and I should go there and I set about researching everything – a sort of feasibility study – writing away to people to see where we could work, where we'd live and, most importantly, how much it would cost to do those things. Leonard had a brother in New York and I gave him *lists* of questions to ask. I wrote to schools and employment agencies and letting agencies and everyone I could think of to gather the information that I needed. For months I couldn't wait to get in my bedsit door in the evenings to check the post to see if anyone had replied. I used to accost the postman if I met him on the street on my way to work, for heaven's sake! And I built a file, filled with brochures and addresses and facts and figures – so many figures. I had ledgers full of sums and calculations. Because it all boiled down to money. The money was key. It was the 80's – you lot in London were all Yuppies and City Executives and Car Phones!" I laughed and Jess rolled her eyes. "But in Ireland, it was different – we didn't do credit-card debt or even overdrafts or anything like that. We saved and paid outright if we were good little Irishmen and women. And you'll remember how expensive things were – flights were astronomical, for starters, even if they were one-way. And I knew that we needed X amount to live on once we got there, so I came up with a sum that we needed to save, each of us, to make The Plan happen. Because as well as all those other things I was, I was deeply determined. I was not going to have this plan go wrong on me – there was too much at stake. Leonard had his amount, I had mine. But straight away it became glaringly obvious that for me to save it on my salary was going to be impossible. So, clearly, I needed a new job."

Jess waved her hand. "That's all well and good, Ria, but rewind a bit … this … Leonard? You've never mentioned him before – whatever happened to him?"

I popped teabags into the cups while the kettle began to bubble and thought hard for a moment.

"Do you know, Jess, I'm not sure."

Her eyes widened. "But he was your boyfriend that you were planning to go abroad with?"

I shrugged. "I was engaged to him, actually – although we never got as far as doing anything crazy like buying a ring, or anything." 'Wait until we're in the States,' Leonard had said. 'We might get something better – a bit cheaper over there …'

Jess raised her eyebrows and rearranged herself in her seat. "So where did this Leonard guy come out of, then?"

"We just met – at a disco – in Dublin. There were a few of us at work who used to go out together and along the way we used to meet up with Leonard and his friends – a guy in our group and a guy in Leonard's were cousins, I think, and that was how the groups combined. At some point – I can't remember exactly when – Leonard and I started seeing each other – well, I say that but in reality we just shifted – *snogged* – each other at the Garda Club one night and that sort of defined us as a couple. We rubbed along nicely, we both liked our own space and we were desperate to get out of Dublin in the 80's – well, I thought we both were. He worked for his father's building firm, played GAA – Gaelic football – liked a few pints with his friends and a Sunday roast ... he was a simple sort of a chap."

"*Très romantique*," scoffed Jess. "So why couldn't you just marry him in Ireland and settle down there? Why the big urge to go to America?"

"It's how things were done then," I shrugged. "Like I said, there were no jobs in the 80's – Leonard and I were very lucky actually to both be employed. Thousands of people emigrated every day because they had to. They used to show it on the news at Christmas – one piece filmed at the airport before Christmas with the emigrants coming home, all happy and huggy and tearful and a second in the New Year at the airport again, except with them all going back – it was heartbreaking."

"It was hardly Mars," Jess remarked.

"It may as well have been back then," I said. "Travel was so expensive – and so many emigrants were illegal – had they left the US to come home for a visit, they might never have been able to get back in. Some people left, not knowing if they'd ever come home again – I suppose, there was no *hope* in Ireland – no opportunity. Everything was grim, and brown – there was *so* much brown in the 80's. Young people had the best education in the world, but nothing that they could do with it. They were filled with despair. This was before the Celtic Tiger, before technology, even. Computers – email – Facebook – Skype – all of these things were science fiction, for heaven's sakes. People wrote letters to each other – you weren't even guaranteed that everyone had a telephone, and the cost of calls was pretty damn prohibitive. It was a different world, Jess. And I had nothing to lose. No family or home, just a grotty flat, but I had plenty of determination and a good education. Those people on the news, going back ... well, I swore then that I'd never be one of them – because once I got out, I had no intention of ever coming home."

Jess looked taken aback. "So what happened then? Why aren't you a Desperate Housewife in Lexington or Cambridge? Why a divorced teacher in London?"

I paused for a moment and nibbled at the nail on my left thumb while I thought.

"You might need coffee instead if I'm going to explain all that," I said.

She raised her eyebrows. "You know where it is," she replied. "Two sugars for me. And the biscuits are in that jar."

Chapter six

Ria
BALLYKEERAN
September 1987

It was a Sunday afternoon at the beginning of September when I caught the 16.25 Heuston to Portlaoise. It was a typical All Ireland Sunday – the weather bright and sunny and the last heat of summer warming the city for the big hurling game. The Minor Final had been played already and the station bustled with buoyant Offaly supporters and downcast Tipperary fans.

I made my way to the station myself, waiting outside the Virgin Megastore for the 90 bus, and lugging my suitcase and handbag all the way upstairs and back down again when I got to the station. Aboard the packed orange-and-black train there was that distinctive musty, damp smell in the air, the green fabric which covered the seat rough against my bare legs as I sat down. I stared out the window as Dublin rolled by me, the city fading to countryside, hedges blurring past, the rhythmic rattle of the train loud through the open window which allowed a welcome breeze to kiss the top of my head. I settled back against the seat and watched. So this was finally it. The big change, the big opportunity.

A little over an hour later, I was hailed on the platform at Portlaoise by a round, possibly middle-aged man, although I couldn't tell. He could have been anything from forty to eighty. He wore brown trousers held up with braces, a checked shirt and a cap which he doffed to me, using the palm of his hand to then rub the

25

bald, round head underneath before replacing it. "Tom Gorman," he said, by way of introduction, and then nothing else, bumping my case down the stone station steps and out into the boot of a Ford Cortina parked outside.

The car smelled unpleasant on the hot day, like potatoes and old stew. I rolled my window down a little, but Tom Gorman kept his tightly shut and drove silently, the only sound heavy, thick breathing coming from between the long white hairs which peeked from his nostrils. He sat close to the wheel, hunched over it, eyes intent on the road.

Eventually, the town of Portlaoise – a lot larger town than I had imagined – gave way to countryside. In the distance, on our right, a row of low, blue hills ran alongside us. On either side, lush fields dotted with modern bungalows were interspersed with brown patches of bogland. The '*Fáilte*' sign for the village of Ballykeeran appeared about twenty minutes into the drive and I peered keenly out the window as we drove down its wide, deserted main street – typically Irish, with a pub, a small newsagent's and a brightly painted café called The Copper Kettle. A small drapery shop called Phelan's was hung heavy with baskets of petunias and, beside it, the undertaker's, attached to another pub named O'Neill's. Private residences stood either side of a supermarket called Raftery's, and opposite was a launderette. All of them were closed, silent in the sunshine as the people of Ballykeeran undoubtedly remained glued to their TV's for the big match. And then the houses grew fewer and suddenly stopped. We were through the village and back out onto the main road in a matter of minutes.

I had expected that my destination might be in the centre of the village somehow, but I wasn't sure why. In any case, I was wrong. Beyond the '*Slán Leat*' sign, Tom Gorman carried on for another mile or so, before taking another turning. To our left, a low wall topped with iron railings painted blue appeared.

My driver pointed to it. "That's it now," he said, without looking at me, before pulling in and stopping at a gate between two stone posts topped with a metal arch in the same blue as the railings, a simple cross in its centre.

I fumbled in my handbag. "How much do I owe you?" I asked, withdrawing my purse.

"That's on the convent account," he replied, waving my hand away, before letting himself out the driver's door. I followed suit on the passenger side.

Once my suitcase was retrieved from the boot, he bade me farewell with a "Good luck, now" in his deep, gruff voice, before he drove away, leaving me alone.

So here I was. Finally.

I stood in the evening sunshine for a moment, my shadow long beside me, and took it all in, taking deep draws of fresh air to counter the stale smell of the Ford which still lingered in my nostrils. The air smelled warm – different from Dublin, but then of course it would – there was no sea, no pollution. Instead, it smelled *green* – grass, with a hint of something agricultural – a city girl, I was entirely unsure what. Cattle, maybe, or silage. What *was* silage actually? I held my breath for a moment, taking in the stillness which was only punctuated by birdsong. Across the road and behind the hedge were fields stretching toward the same low hills I had seen on the way here. It was beautiful. And so, so peaceful. With another deep breath, I turned, and made my way under the arch.

I paused again for a moment to get my bearings. The entranceway was wide enough for a single car to fit through. On my left was a stone chapel with a few parking spaces marked out in front of it and well-kept flower beds running along its length. Opposite it, to my right, my destination. The place that now held all of my hopes and dreams inside its walls. The place that I had given up the life I knew for – the place that was to be the foundation stone for my future – the Convent of Maria Goretti.

It was, as was to be expected of such a place, a great, old hulking building. It looked just like I had thought it might – three storeys high and plain grey stone. In a recess, at the very centre of the front, between the top row of windows and the eaves, a tall Virgin Mary stood with her head bowed. I made my way toward the building and peered in through the front door of a geranium-lined porch with a brown tiled floor, inner double doors beyond with frosted glass panels to obscure the view within.

Ringing the doorbell required me to pull a chain which I did gingerly. Unsure whether it worked, or whether I should knock instead, I stood back for a moment and looked around, hoping that someone might have heard.

A rattle within signified that someone was approaching and I stood to attention as a figure appeared in the porch, making the Sign of the Cross as she did. The nun who opened the door was surprisingly young, a pretty, clear-skinned girl save for a small port-wine stain on her right cheek under her eye. She nodded as she opened the door and stood back for me to enter.

"Good evening," she muttered quietly. "Miss Clancy, isn't it?"

I walked inside, and rested my suitcase on the tiled floor, taking in the earthy smell of the plants around me.

"It is, Sister," I replied, and she nodded in return.

With a small sweep of her hand, she indicated that I should come into the main building. Once again, I picked up the case and stepped through, into the coolness of the convent beyond, into the darkness, into the silence. Into unknown territory. Behind me, I heard the lock click into place and a chain being pulled as the nun locked the outer door. We stood on a long corridor, which stretched away ahead and behind, leading to nowhere definitive that I could see.

"I'm Sister Ruth," she said, so quietly that I had to strain my voice to hear.

"Maria Clancy," I replied, thrusting out my hand in what I thought was a confident gesture. I didn't feel confident of course, but I had read somewhere that 'if you can't make it, fake it," so I did in an effort to impress. She didn't take my lead. A brief, cold, weak handshake followed. Clearly neither of us was comfortable.

"Mother Benedicta asked me to let you in," she said quietly. "She's our principal and Mother Superior."

"I've corresponded with her a few times," I smiled, wincing as I misjudged my volume and heard my voice boom around the hard walls and tiled floor. I coughed uncomfortably to cover up the echo.

The young nun ignored this. "Well, she's away at the moment. I'll show you to your room."

With that, she set off at a smart pace along the passage, gone before I realised. Taken aback at the brevity of our introduction, I grabbed my case and followed.

The passage was brown, of course. Partially, at least. Hard, cold brown ceramic floor tiles. The walls either side of me were a shade of pistachio green. It was stark, save for the occasional statue – St Anthony, St Martin de Porres, St Augustine – years of being educated and teaching in Catholic schools had taught me the names of these robed men. They watched us pass, as did St Thérèse of Lisieux and the Immaculate Heart of Mary. There was a touch of a Roman palace about it, except instead of the walkways lined with gorgeous marble figures, this passage was guarded by holy plastercast along either side.

I had worn low heels for the journey, to make myself look more professional when I arrived and as we walked I became painfully aware, not only of the fact that my feet were sweating in my tights and my toes were pinched together painfully, but of the loud '*clack-clack*' sounds that echoed around the hard surfaces, filling the silent space, like some unwelcome intrusion. The silence was engulfing, in fact, and I felt much too loud for it, wishing that I had worn something quieter. The nun, meanwhile, padded almost silently ahead of me in a pair of neat, leather slippers in dark blue, the same shade as her skirt and knitted cardigan which was worn over a white polyester round-necked top. Her veil was shoulder-length and wafted gently behind her as she strode ahead.

At one point, the passage was joined by another, more modern corridor, with long, narrow windows lining either side and brighter green tiles on the floor.

"The school is through there," mumbled Sister Ruth. "Mother Benedicta will show you around herself tomorrow before the students start back on Tuesday."

I nodded, and jumped suddenly as I looked ahead of me, temporarily dazzled from looking into the brighter space, only to see two shadows seeming to walk towards us in the darkness of the end of the passage. I quickly realised, however, that they were our own reflections in a large gilt-framed mirror that covered most of the wall ahead where the corridor darkened before turning left. We continued, passing through a small lobby with two closed doors either side of a tall, wooden cabinet. We then veered right, through an archway, and into a more open space – a large hallway, still tiled in brown and overlooked by an enormous St Brigid and – I did a double take – a wild-eyed, decrepit stuffed badger which stood on top of an upright piano against the wall, looking coyly over his shoulder.

To my right, a varnished wooden staircase wound its way upward through the building, Sister Ruth already at its base, indicating that I should follow. I lugged my case up the first few steps, noticing the closer I got to the landing that I was bathed in blues and yellows from the evening sun through the enormous stained-glass window that illuminated the space. We carried on up another flight before Sister Ruth stopped on the landing.

"Your room is down here," she said, before walking through a door off it to our right, down another, darker corridor. I followed meekly again, my heels a little quieter on the highly polished lino that replaced the tiles and wood here. I carried on, glancing to either side of me as we progressed down the passage, past a series of small rooms that lined it. They each contained two beds, sporting bare blue mattresses, and in between them, two bedside lockers, on each of which stood a plastic basin and cup.

"These are the Sisters' Rooms," Sister Ruth explained. "Not sisters as in the Sisters of Maria Goretti, but where students who have sisters also attending the convent sleep. The shared bathroom is here …"

She stood and let me look inside the last room on my right which was painted white, and contained two toilet cubicles and sinks and a single tiled shower space, its shower curtain pulled open.

"The shower is for your use only. The students, however, use the toilets and collect water from the sinks in their basins which they use to wash in the privacy of their rooms. And this is your room here."

She indicated the door straight ahead of us, at the very end of the passage – the bottom of it thick with layers of brown paint – what other colour would do? – the top half two glass panels covered in opaque contact to make them appear frosted.

The nun removed a large key from her pocket and inserted it into the keyhole below the brass doorknob, opening the door slowly to reveal what would be my living space for the next nine months. It was only as I saw inside that something gave within me. My stomach flipped a little, and my resolution wavered for the first time since locking the door of my flat in Dublin for the last time earlier that day – had it really only been that morning?

The nun stood back and I squeezed past her into the small space of my living quarters and put down my case. It was little more than a nun's cell – a bed dressed in flannel sheets and cream Foxford blankets trimmed with pale blue, a bedside locker with the same plastic basin and cup that I had seen in the students' rooms, a small table and high-backed chair with a shelf on the wall above, and a single wardrobe with a full-length mirror attached to one of the doors. Through the curtainless window I could, at a glance, make out Playing Courts and, beyond, the Laois countryside, separated from the school grounds by a row of evergreens – the view framed by grey-painted shutters. The floor beneath me was covered with blue lino, the walls cream. A change of colour scheme at least, I thought.

Above me, a single shadeless bulb was suspended on a long wire from the high ceiling. A crucifix hung above the head of the bed and on the wall over it, a small picture of the school's namesake, the martyr, Maria Goretti.

I suddenly felt as if I might cry, gripped tightly by an urge to turn and run. I tried to talk myself down. I had nowhere to go, for starters – my bedsit was gone, the keys dropped back through the letterbox for the landlord to collect – I had no close family – there was Leonard, of course, but that wouldn't work. And besides which, even if I fled, even if I turned at that moment like my gut told me to, and ran as fast I could from that place, even if I could manage to *get* back, somehow, to the train station and back to Dublin, then what? Where else would I possibly get work at this time of the year? I had no money – none that I wished to spend at least – and no means of earning. I was stuck here. Everything was invested in *this*. I swallowed hard, trying to quell the rising panic inside me. I stood as though nailed to the spot, afraid to move in case my knees gave way, my fists clenched, trying to regain control.

"I'll leave you to get settled." The nun's voice seemed far away. "Something to eat will be dropped up to you in half an hour or so. Lights out at ten o'clock. If you need anything else, it will have to wait until morning as we Sisters are holding a novena tonight for a blessing on the new school year. In the morning, you'll meet Mother Benedicta. Have you any questions at all?"

I shook my head. She answered with a nod and, without a further word, retreated into the dark of the corridor outside, pulling the door behind her. I held my breath, listening to the barely perceptible squeak of her leather slippers as she left. Soon it was gone and I was surrounded, *smothered* by silence.

With trembling hands, I unpacked and slid my empty suitcase under the bed. When my clothes were hung in place or folded neatly on the shelves of the wardrobe, I stored my toiletries in the locker and arranged my few books on the shelf, and placed a photograph of my parents on the desk, along with some writing pads and pens. That done, I sat down on the bed and slipped my feet out of my shoes, wiggling my toes free. I glanced around. It looked barely better than it had when the nun had first shown me in. Again, it washed over me that this was *it*. This was what I now called home.

And I had no one to blame but myself.

There was a sudden rattle outside the door. True to the nun's word, my evening meal had been delivered. Glad of something to break through the dark thoughts that were creeping into my brain, I opened the door with a smile to find only a tray on the ground outside and the form of a nun – I couldn't even tell if it was Sister Ruth – disappearing down the end of the corridor, out of sight. Resignedly, I picked up the tray and stepped back inside, placing it on the table. I wouldn't get fat on the rations anyway, I thought, making a small sandwich out of the white sliced bread and corned beef, spreading the salad cream on the hard-boiled egg, tomato and scallion and pouring myself a cup of grey tea from the small stainless-steel pot into the plain white cup and saucer. The meal didn't take long. What it did do, however, was make me aware of how hungry I actually was. I had eaten little all day between nerves and simply not having enough time. I rummaged in my shoulder bag and found a banana and a Mars Bar that I had bought for the train journey and ate both. I read for a while – a Sidney Sheldon thriller – until the daylight in the room grew dim and I switched on the light above, its bare bulb failing to cheer the room around me. With that light on, I supposed, I should have closed the shutters, but couldn't bring myself to do so. I couldn't block out the daylight, couldn't block out the outside world. Then I would be completely imprisoned.

At half past nine, I finally caved and pulled them tight. There was nothing for it but bed, I decided. Dressing in my nightie, I left the sanctuary of the room to step out to the bathroom outside to clean my teeth and use the toilet. It was eerie out there, dark and silent. I retreated rapidly to the room when I was finished.

Back in my bed, with its unfamiliar creaks and cold sheets, I tried to read again for a while, but couldn't concentrate. I stared instead at the four walls, not really seeing them. Could I really do this, I asked myself? Would I get used to this? Could I tolerate it? Could I last another second even?

But I'd have to, wouldn't I? I steeled myself. It was for such a short period of time in the bigger scheme of things. It wasn't forever – but it could make forever happen. I climbed out of bed and turned out the light at the switch on the wall by the door, making my way back to bed by the chink of remaining daylight just visible above the shutters. And there I lay, in the gloom. Away from what home I'd had, away from the city I'd grown up in and what few people I knew.

I forced myself to relax, visualising my goal as I did. I tried to ignore the flannel pillowcase against my cheek by thinking about getting on the plane, thinking about station wagons and snow, Thanksgiving pumpkins and the colour of autumn leaves – the *color*, I corrected myself, grinning ever so slightly, eventually feeling sleep make my eyes heavy and my thoughts fade. In the distance, as I drifted away, I thought I heard footsteps, someone running, and a door slamming, but I couldn't be sure if I was awake or asleep. Instead, I continued to force the thoughts and imaginings into my head that were my goal. The Plan. That was what mattered after all. This was merely a means to an end.

Chapter seven

Ria
BALLYKEERAN
September 1987

I was woken on my first morning by a sharp rap on the glass of my bedroom door, and a summons issued through it to make my way in twenty minutes to breakfast. I washed in a hurry in the empty bathroom, and dressed in a lemon cotton dress and sandals, brushing my permed red curls, cut short to just below the line of my jaw, into place, before leaving my room and making my way, as I had been instructed, back down the stairs, and along the Brown Corridor where I saw Sister Ruth standing patiently, outside a door marked 'Refectory'.

The meagre meal was set for me at a table for one, which stood on a dais in front of a fireplace overlooking the room. Eight long tables, four places each side, were set before me. Each was topped with a fawn-coloured oilcloth, each place set for breakfast with a white bowl on top of a white plate. At the head of each table, eight white teacups were lined up, in two rows of four, waiting to be filled. On a small table alongside my dais, a Burco boiler stood idle, two large teapots beside it waiting to be filled from the small tap on its front, a tin of tea leaves alongside them.

I observed the room as I ate the small bowl of cornflakes and a slice of white bread smeared with a scrape of butter and marmalade, washed down with a cup of weak tea. Once again, so much brown. Brown lino, tan walls, three small, square windows to my left looking outward toward the chapel and its flower beds, and three on the right looking inward over the Brown Corridor. Between the windows hung various religious artefacts – a St Brigid's Cross, a picture of the Sacred Heart, a plain, black crucifix. At the opposite end of the room was a door on which hung a long mirror in which I could see myself, rather disconcertingly, at my table for one, eating as quickly as I could, and slightly to its right my companion, the silent Sister Ruth, standing just inside the door. I stole a glance at her as I finished and saw that she seemed deep in prayer, her hands folded across her stomach and her eyes closed. It didn't seem like a beatific, peaceful prayer, however, but a desperate terrified one, her knuckles white, her eyes screwed shut. She glanced up as I pushed away my cup and saucer and replaced my knife on my plate and nodded.

"Very good," she said. "I'm to show you around now."

She took me first down the modern corridor that we had passed the previous night, toward the School Wing, as she called it, as opposed to the 'House', which was how she referred to the older part of the building. The school itself was surprisingly bright and new – there were language and science labs, rooms for art, cookery, geography, a huge, parquet-floored Assembly Hall. It was well-equipped and clean, walls and whiteboards bare, awaiting the start of another academic year. Through the windows, she showed me the grounds – a section of hard-surfaced Playing Courts for tennis, basketball and volleyball, bookended by two greens which were marked out as pitches of some sort, all encircled by a path which she called The Walk. With all that taken in, we returned to the House, back to the main artery that was the Brown Corridor, and plunged into the gloom of the old wing. There were more classrooms here, in altogether a more confusing muddle. Sister Ruth opened doors and barked out the names of all the rooms and areas leading off the hallway with the main stairs. "This is the Study Hall … the Classroom of the Holy Family … the Boarders' Cloakroom …" And everywhere we were watched over by more religious effigies – a weeping Virgin Mary, a crucified Christ bleeding bright red from freshly painted wounds. I noted that I had been so distracted by the coy stuffed badger the previous night that I had somehow missed the terrifying painting of a life-sized, greyish-green St Sebastian that he guarded, the saint's expression one of unparalleled agony from the arrows which pierced him, bright crimson blood flowing from him. At the bottom of the main stairs a Judgement Day, which I hadn't noticed the night before either, lined another wall – grey wraiths rising from open graves to be judged by a stern celestial figure on a glowing throne, some wafting heavenward while others were cast to hell, their faces filled with horror.

Sister Ruth suddenly glanced at her watch, and then at me, an expression that neared panic crossing her face.

"Twenty past eight," she informed me. "Mother Benedicta wishes to see you in her office in ten minutes and we still have to see the dormitories. Follow me, please."

We briskly charged up the stairs, past the floor where my room was, and up another flight. At the top of that, the nun pulled open a swinging door marked 'Dormitory'.

It was a single room – vast – stretching the length of the building. The walls were pale blue, the ceiling high, with long, fluorescent light fittings suspended along the length of it.

Before me stretched rows of beds, dressed uniformly in the same sheets, blankets and striped pillowcases as were on my own bed on the floor below. Also suspended from the ceiling was a system of metal curtain-runners, from which hung pale green curtains, pulled back now, but which would grant the girls privacy, creating little cubicles once pulled, each containing a bed and a locker topped with the obligatory plastic basin and cup for washing and tooth-brushing. At regular intervals, there was a gap between cubicles, where moveable metal clothes racks stood, plastic clothes hangers dangling on them, awaiting uniforms, I assumed, as there was nowhere near the beds where anything could hang.

"This is where the girls who have no sisters attending the convent sleep," Sister Ruth informed me hurriedly. "Through that door," she indicated a white door to our left, "are toilets and handbasins for collecting water to wash in their cubicles and for washing their teeth. There can be queues at night-time and in the morning, so one of your duties will be to keep them moving quickly and silently. Mother Benedicta will explain all of that to you anyway."

"And that door?" I asked, pointing to one opposite the

washroom, another of the moveable metal clothes rack pulled in front of it.

"It's not used," she said. "We should go back down right away now, so that you're not late."

With that, she turned and pulled open the door through which we had just entered, ushering me out and down the stairs again. At the bottom, we entered the dark lobby which led out onto the Brown Corridor and stopped outside the door to the right of the cabinet, which I could now see contained pigeonholes with names on each, including my own. Gingerly, Sister Ruth knocked on the door, which was marked 'Mother Superior', before suddenly scurrying away without a backward glance or goodbye.

There was no immediate answer. I noticed that the door the other side of the cabinet had the words 'Staffroom' painted on it and I was contemplating peering inside when suddenly I heard a voice behind the first door bidding me sharply to enter. It startled me and I flinched, taking a deep breath before slowly twisting the brass knob and pushing the door open.

The first thing I noticed was that it wasn't brown. The room was bright and comfortable, looking in fact plush by comparison with the other rooms in the old part of the building. It had a cream carpet patterned with clusters of pink roses, and pale blue walls, and at its centre stood a polished wooden desk before a fireplace over which hung a painting of Maria Goretti. The alcove to the left of the fireplace was lined with books, and a coat rack stood in the alcove to the right.

Mother Benedicta was in the process of hanging a navy-blue blazer on a clothes hanger. She didn't turn as I entered, closing the door as quietly as I could behind me. Instead, she continued to smooth the garment, brushing the shoulders with her hand, picking a piece of lint from the collar. It was only when she was satisfied it was straight and clean that she hung it from the rack, and turned to face me.

She wore the regulation navy of the Order: soft, sensible navy loafers, tan tights, an A-line skirt and a white polyester top. Her veil was shoulder-length, held back from her face with a white band. None of her hair was visible. She was smart – her stance ramrod straight, shoulders erect, head upright. She stepped silently back toward her desk and took a navy-blue cardigan from where it had been hung on the back of her chair, slipping her arms into the sleeves and pulling it around her.

She watched me as she buttoned the cardigan from neck to hips. Her grey eyes studied me closely from behind wire-rimmed glasses, unblinking, cold. Her skin was waxy, pale and clear. The nose was aquiline and sharp, the cheekbones even sharper, leaving shaded hollows beneath them which caved in to thin, small lips held in a firm line. She was bone thin. Her handshake was brief – listless and detached, the fingers icy cold.

"*Miss Clancy.*"

The voice matched the appearance. Cold ... *sharp.*

"Good morning. Please sit down."

The nun indicated that I take the seat opposite her at the desk. Her movements were efficient and measured as she slid her hands down the back of her skirt to smooth it before sitting herself, on the edge of her chair, back rigid, those knuckley hands, tinged purple, folded, one covering the other, on the desk between us.

"I'm Mother Benedicta," she said. "We have corresponded by letter prior to now."

"Good morning, Mother," I replied. Flustered, I pulled my chair clumsily closer to the desk. I felt my cheeks and neck flush red, and felt childlike.

She stared at me silently for a moment while I settled myself awkwardly, her lips in a thin line, her expression veering between disapproval and disbelief. Eventually, she spoke.

"Now," she began, her tone businesslike and efficient. "I hope your whistle-stop tour made the layout of our school and House clearer to you?"

I looked directly at her and saw there an odd expression: the thin lips curled back over straight teeth – an attempt at a smile. I attempted to return it.

"It's as clear as mud now, I'm sure," the nun continued, the smile flickering off as quickly as it had appeared. "But you'll figure your own way around soon enough. I suggest that you take what time you can today to familiarise yourself with the school and grounds before the boarding students return. I trust you slept well last night?"

I nodded, but she wasn't looking at me. She had instead diverted her attention to a small pamphlet in front of her on which she now rested her bony fingertips.

"You'll need to be familiar with the day-to-day living that you'll be supervising. As you know, your role is twofold, Miss Clancy – hence the substantial recompense which accompanies it. As per our correspondence, not only are you our English and History teacher, but you are also our Student Guardian, which is a very important role in the lives of our Boarders and in running the school efficiently and effectively. It is a role to be taken seriously, and with thought and prayer as guidance."

She folded her hands again and fixed me with a firm stare.

"The school day begins with prayerful assembly at nine o'clock and then classes run throughout the day until ten past four. Your supervisory role, however, begins before that and continues beyond it. Your day begins before the student rising bell rings at seven twenty. You will rise and dress respectably ..." She paused to study me over the desk. "You do own a pair of tights, don't you, Miss Clancy? And perhaps something to cover your arms?"

I blushed even deeper and nodded, folding my bare arms across my chest.

She pursed her lips. "You will supervise the students as they get up and dress. Orderly supervision of the dormitories is essential, Miss Clancy. *Complete* control is required because misbehaviour in such an environment causes delay and disruption to the day's events for everyone – a cumulative, butterfly effect of disorder, if you will – do you understand?"

I swallowed and nodded.

"There is *silence* at all times in the dormitories. *That. Is. Essential.* Chit-chat leads to ... *messing*, which leads to delays. Also, more importantly, when the mouth is closed, the mind and the heart are open to Jesus. On a practical note, we need to be efficient at all times – and the discipline is vital for young girls. You will find the outline of a typical day, and your duties, in this pamphlet here."

She passed the small booklet across the desk and laid it in front of me, smoothing it with her hand as she placed it down.

"Each day starts with Mass in our very own chapel of St John

39

the Baptist across the grounds but we also open the doors to welcome some of the local people from the surrounding houses and farms. Then breakfast, then Assembly where we gather together our Boarders and our Day Pupils before they head to classes. From nine in the morning, you are a teacher first and Guardian second, although you are expected to still maintain your authority over the Boarders during this time. After school, at ten past four, your duties resume as Guardian primarily. Games are organised outdoors, weather permitting, immediately after lessons have finished. The Boarders have time after classes end to return their books to their desks and to change into games gear. They are not allowed to linger around indoors during the time between half past four and twenty past five in the evenings – do you understand, Miss Clancy? Fresh air and sporting activities are vital to their well-being and to keeping them occupied – idleness is unacceptable. For this reason, part of your duties will be to ensure that the changing rooms are clear by four thirty at the latest, and that any girl found inside the school building without permission receives appropriate punishment. Do you understand?"

My mind reeled. It was becoming difficult to keep up.

"In adverse weather conditions, of course, games are held in the Assembly Hall but we do our best to ensure that this happens only when strictly necessary. A spot of rain or snow never hurt anyone, we believe. Our girls are not made of sugar. At five twenty, you will ring the teatime bell and they will change and make their way to the Refectory for tea – silence is again observed until after Grace, and then resumed during clean-up time toward the end of the half-hour tea period. Once they are finished, then they line up in an orderly fashion, oldest classes first, and make their way in silence to the Study Hall. You will then supervise silent study until eight o'clock when they break for tea. Study resumes at eight thirty and continues until ten o'clock when they make their way to the Prayer Room on the Brown Corridor for ten minutes of night prayer and from there, once again line up for bed. As per morning times, silence is observed at all times. The girls wash, dress and have a few moments for reading and reflection until you lead them when they are in their beds in a final night prayer to lights out at ten thirty. Is all of that clear?"

I blinked and studied the nun for a moment, unable to think of what to say.

"That's a lot of silence," I observed suddenly, only half-joking. I immediately regretted it.

The nun's response unnerved me.

Mother Benedicta breathed loudly through flared nostrils, slowly and deeply, all the while staring at me over her glasses. When she spoke, her tone was low.

"I've explained the need for it, Miss Clancy. Through silence we reach our thoughts. When pure in thought we reach our inner prayer. Through prayer, we reach God." She paused for a moment. "Everything that we do – sister, teacher, student – at Maria Goretti, is done to serve, honour and to please *God* Our Holy Father, Jesus His Son and Mary His Blessed Virgin Mother. We strive for *purity*, Miss Clancy. As Maria Goretti did. Purity of spirit, of heart, of thought and of deed. Our work and our leisure alike is offered up for the Greater Glory of the Lord. You will have Wednesday afternoons, Sundays and one weekend per month off – I've made that clear, yes? – to do with as you please, but always in keeping with our motto: *In Deo, Puritas*. In God, Purity, Miss Clancy. God is Purity, Purity is God."

She fell silent, but continued to glare at me. It seemed like an age before she resumed her speech.

"That in mind, we aim to protect the students with whom we are charged from an ever-changing, often … *wicked* world. For that reason, students are banned from having electrical devices on the premises. If you have any with you – a hairdryer, Walkman music-player, digital clock radio etcetera – then I advise that you lock them away and out of the way of temptation. Books are permitted, but it is part of your duties to remember that they must convey a certain tone – it goes without saying that they must be respectable and decent. Our library contains a good amount of suitable reading material and I recommend that you take time there and select some. As part of your duties, I will also require you to observe that the students do not attempt to use such devices or read unsuitable material – you will confiscate any that you find and bring them to me so that the owner can be appropriately punished. Any books must be deemed decent by our standards. Magazines are not permitted."

She paused suddenly and I watched, squirming slightly as the attempted smile played again on her lips.

"There is no room here for blasphemy and its like, Miss Clancy – no salacious novels filled with filth or written to the denigration of God and His Holy Name or the Holy Catholic Church, do you *understand*?"

I swallowed deeply and nodded.

"There is a payphone under the stairs that the students are permitted to use when necessary," she said, nodding toward the door of her office. "You can also use it, but discreetly. Are you close to your family, Miss Clancy?"

"My parents are dead but I–I like to keep in touch with … my … fiancé," I replied.

The nun's eyebrows shot up suddenly, and she peered over her glasses. "You are engaged to be married, Miss Clancy?" she asked.

I gave a fleeting grin. "I am." I smiled, a smile which wasn't returned.

She again glared at me for a moment before selecting a sheaf of papers from the front of the desk and moving them directly in front of her and starting to leaf through them.

"You will eat in the Refectory at the same times as the students – dinner is served at one o'clock and, as I said, tea at five thirty. Your room in the dormitories should remain locked at all times, of course, Miss Clancy. It goes without saying that you keep it neat and tidy – we require beds to be made and night attire to be stored neatly out of sight. With regard to your classes, you'll find your timetable in your pigeonhole in the cabinet outside later today. Please try to allow time for some reflection also. Visit the chapel and take a moment to pray for the year ahead." She looked up at me again. "Pray for yourself, Miss Clancy. That you will have the strength and the fortitude to be a good teacher and Guardian, and an obedient servant. That will be all for now."

With that, she nodded, and flicked her hand in the direction of the door.

I stared at her for a moment, but it was as if she had immediately forgotten me. I rose quietly and made my way from the desk to the door. When I glanced back, she was absorbed in her work. Silently I slipped from the room and back to the cool darkness of the hallway.

I had been dismissed.

Chapter eight

Lydia
BALLYKEERAN
September 1987

I hate the first night back.

Going to bed at half nine feels like the middle of the afternoon for me. It makes me feel like a kid. And I'm not. I'll be eighteen before Christmas – an adult.

It wasn't a bad summer, I guess. I've spent it like I do every school holidays – watching TV till the early hours because that's when all the good films are on, and not getting up until at least eleven or noon. There's nothing to do during the day for me anyway, at home in Dublin – it's not like I'd be hanging out with Uncle Neville, even if he wasn't at work. And I don't have any friends there anymore because anyone I knew in primary goes to secondary somewhere in the city and I go here. We've all pretty much lost touch – or just lost whatever childish friendship we had.

I mean, I'm aware of the benefits of going to boarding school – I really am – considering what my life is like. There's no one here lives a life like mine. No one. The rest of them all come from farms, or small towns, or normal houses in the countryside. They have at least one functioning parent, some siblings – they all probably have a *normal* life. They even get to go home every weekend. I wouldn't even know their version of a normal life if it came up and smacked me in the face. So it's probably best that I'm here – it's so bloody hard, though. Facing into another year of no freedom. It feels like

43

being sent back to prison after having a taste of release.

This is the last one, though. The last first night back after the summer holidays. This is finally almost the end of my sentence. Sure, there's the Leaving Cert at the end of it, but after that – next June – I'm free. I can go to college, maybe even move out and live in a flat, with flatmates and parties and a social life. I can stop wearing white knee socks and house slippers and wear ripped jeans, and my Docs every day if I want. I can start to live. Only nine months left of this – nuns everywhere you look, with their stupid silence and ridiculous rules and punishments and prayers.

Like now – this going to bed early on the first night back. Surely no one is ready to go to sleep – it's even still bright out – just not bright enough to read by. So frustrating. I'd take out my torch only sometimes they can come back on purpose to surprise you, first night back. That's what I mean about being in prison – they take away your freedom by not allowing something as simple as light. I mean, why wouldn't they sort the dorm areas by year, say, and leave the Sixth Year lights on for an extra half an hour even? We're practically adults after all – so why do they mix us all up and treat us the same as the little kids in First Year? Why wouldn't they move us seniors up to the old First Year dormitories upstairs, even? Give us a teeny bit of our own space?

It's odd that there are no new students starting this year. No little kids, the poor things, saying goodbye to their mams and dads for the first time, eyes a bit watery, either trying to be brave or weeping silently as they watch them go. There's always the ones who are full of chat and noise too – they're the ones to watch, because they cave eventually, and it's generally bad. Not for this year, though. No more Boarders at Maria Goretti, ever. They're phasing us out. *Goodnight, Mary Ellen.*

It was weird seeing the door leading up the stairs to the Baby Dorm closed tonight – they even put one of the uniform racks across the door to block it off. I can't help thinking of what it must be like – twelve empty beds, tonight and forever more. I remember I liked it up there myself. It was cosy. I didn't even mind when there were mice and we had to dodge the traps everywhere. Still, not much demand for boarding anymore, it seems. And rightly so. It's time this country got itself into the twentieth century and out from under the fists of the Catholic Church. Maybe they'd phase out nuns and priests while they were at it.

No First Years means less work for the new Guardian too. She was there tonight, shadowing Sister Ruth who did bedtime duty. She looks like … not too sure, actually. Molly Ringwaldy, maybe. Had a nice summer dress on but I could see that she was freezing, even though she was doing her best not to show it. She didn't say much, and you couldn't tell much from her expression so I hope she's not a bitch like Miss Butler was for the last two years. Wonder where she went? But who cares?

Not that it matters to me anymore anyway – whoever likes can patrol these floors for the next nine months – I don't care. I'm keeping my head down and serving my time, studying as hard as I can so I can get into college. And come next summer, I'm gone. Gone from this place with its cold, brown walls and the big grey heating pipes. Gone from lights out and prayers before bed and prayers before meals and stand back for your elders when you meet them in the corridor. Gone from yes sister, no sister, three bags full sister. Finally free.

Chapter nine

Ria
LONDON
April 2015

Jess frowned. "So what was the deal with that place anyway? Was it like ... exclusive? Were they the kids of millionaires? Or religious nuts or what? Here ... give me one of those."

I leaned over and handed her back the packet of Hobnobs, taking one for myself as I did. I turned it over in my hands as I thought back.

"Goretti's Daughters, they were called," I began. "Although to the locals it was always 'Greta's Girls'. It was meant to single them out as a privileged few, the daughters of a martyr, a sacred child of God who would always remain pure. It was an aspirational thing. Made your daughter stand out, made her someone special, untouchable. By the early 80's, though, just before I started there, it became time to make some dramatic changes if they wanted it to survive. Numbers had started to dwindle as far back as the 60's, so even back then they had to take steps to keep the place going – they had to allow Day Pupils to enrol for starters, then they had to offer more scholarships and finally they were reduced to accepting 'ordinary' folk – anyone who could pay the fees could attend as a Boarder. There was still something about the place, though. They were still seen – and, deep down *liked* to be seen – as being something 'above' the locals of the area, so that naturally caused a divide of sorts. The Boarders were subtly – unconsciously, even –

46

separate from the Day Pupils – a hangover from the days of their parents and grandparents who remembered Maria Goretti for its closed gates and stink of money. For example, in the glory days, the Greta Girls were driven to and from the convent, once a term only, in grand cars or a special bus which took them to the train station to return home. There wasn't open animosity, mind – I mean, all the girls seemed to get along, but there was an invisible divide, the Day Pupils and the Boarders just keeping to themselves. I often wondered why a parent would want to send their child away from the age of twelve. It wasn't for me when the time came to send Emma to school, but I suppose some wanted their offspring to be able to concentrate exclusively on their studies, away from the family farm or younger siblings for example, or the distraction of the opposite sex. Some boarded their daughters for logistical reasons – it was easier to drop them off on Sunday night and pick them up on Friday afternoon than to manage daily runs – a lot of the students came from agricultural backgrounds so it suited better. Some even still had the superiority complex that meant they thought their daughters were simply better than other girls – others liked the religious aspect. Whatever their reasons, however, they were dying. Whereas once there had been three hundred Boarders exclusively, there were only sixty-four when I started there and those numbers were dwindling – the decision had been made the previous year that no more would be taken, so there were no First Year live-in students enrolled, for the first time. Boarding, as it was, had four years left at Ballykeeran."

"So what was it like, then? As a job? What was the day-to-day like?" Jess sat forward in her seat, her expression less curious than genuinely baffled.

I realised that I still held the biscuit and nibbled at it for a moment to provide distraction for myself while I made it look like I was thinking hard. I remembered well how it felt, however – could recall the emotions in an instant.

"It was lonely," I replied. "For someone who was an only child, with no parents or family left, I was used to being *alone* – I quite liked it that way –"

"You're still a weirdo loner," Jess interrupted.

"I prefer *introvert*, Jessica. But at Maria Goretti I felt like I'd never felt before. Surrounded by people day and night, but *lonely*, like I had *no one* – no one who cared about me at all.

I mean, I got used to the whole routine quickly enough, and I got on fine with the rest of the staff – the lay teachers used the Staffroom, the same as I did, so we met between classes, or at break time. You'd have a cup of tea or coffee, or a cigarette if you smoked. They'd be pleasant, say hello and that, remark on the weather, but no one ever asked about *me*, ever bothered to get to know me. It was as if they all existed inside a room within the room – chatting about their weekends, their kids, what they did on their holidays, the students, the weather even. But with me, it was as if I was hovering around the edges, like the invisible barrier that existed between the day students and the Boarders existed in the staffroom too. The teachers and the nuns didn't mingle, you see – and I was a teacher, but I also lived there, so in a way they saw me on a level with the nuns. Sometimes, I felt like I was a shadow that they caught sight of out of the corner of their eyes."

"Oh, it's all *me me me* with you introverts!" interrupted Jess again, giggling. "But seriously, that must have been difficult. What about the old veiled vixens themselves?"

I snorted. "There were seven or eight nuns who were on the teaching staff and they were all polite nods in the corridor, or the odd 'good morning' but nothing more – they didn't even use the Staffroom. The convent nuns kept to their end of the building so I barely interacted with them except for maybe the occasional encounter with the kitchen nuns or to exchange pleasantries with the elderly ones who'd appear every now and again to shuffle around the grounds for a bit of fresh air while the weather was still warm enough. But, as a whole, the sisters stayed to themselves – with the exception of Benedicta who ruled the roost. They were all ... shall we say, *respectful* of her ... if by respectful you mean *terrified*. Even the lay staff would go quiet, like children, when she appeared on the scene. So I kept to myself mostly. Kept busy when I was in the Staffroom, pretending to read or prep the next lesson. Or I just didn't bother to go in and would head straight to my next class a few minutes early. It soon became the way things were. And I could cope with that, just fine. I was lonely, yes. But I did my jobs and as the weeks wound on, even though it wasn't a day at the funfair, I felt that time – *life* – was progressing in a way that satisfied me, like I was doing what I had come there to do."

I sighed and paused for a moment.

"But it didn't stay that way for very long," I said.

"What do you mean?" Jess asked when I fell silent.

I looked at her. And then looked away. I was about to break a promise I had made to myself almost thirty years previously. I hesitated for a moment, before I closed my eyes slowly and took a deep breath. For the first time, I was allowing myself to do something I had sworn I would never do.

Tell someone what happened.

"Life was different there from what I had known before," I began slowly. "It was tiring, monotonous, dull, silent, lonely – all of those things. But at first, like I said, it was predictable, straightforward. I knew I could get through it."

Jess watched me as I fell silent again. "At first?" she prompted.

I nodded. "At first. But it wasn't long before things began to change. I had a small period of grace, to get used to it – the routines, the bells, the silence, the prayer, the early starts and late finishes. The nuns everywhere. But that was all. Because after that – once the autumn term really kicked in – that's when things grew different."

I looked Jess in the eye, unsure if I should begin to tell her what I was about to tell her, but at the same time unable to stop myself.

"It was around the time that the evenings began to shorten and the weather started to turn cold, and damp. That's when it happened. When all the strange things began."

Chapter ten

Ria
BALLYKEERAN
September 1987

By my third week there, I found myself dreading the weekends. Without the purpose of classes, and the bustle of the Day Pupils and, indeed, most of the Boarders, the days seemed interminable, despite the general relaxation of rules – by Maria Goretti standards. Most Boarders went home for the weekend, collected by parents on a Friday afternoon and returned on Sunday night or very early Monday morning. It hadn't always been the way – as recently as five years ago, Boarders came back in September and stayed until Christmas.

Those who still stayed at the school for weekends out of necessity enjoyed certain freedoms which weren't permitted on weekdays. They were allowed to forego their bottle-green tunics and cardigans in favour of their own clothes on Saturdays, for example – and while a certain amount of study hours, varying per year, was mandatory, they were also flexible, and students were allowed a special dispensation on 'wicked' gadgets – some TV or a school-approved video in the library – usually something religious, a musical or an adaptation of something on the syllabus like Dickens or Shakespeare on a Saturday night as a reward, once the hours were done. They were even trusted to study mostly unsupervised, at hours that suited themselves. On the surface, it seemed like a brief snatch of autonomy for them. Whether the girls noticed the covert supervision which I was instructed to carry out, complemented by surprise visits from various nuns at various stages, I wasn't sure, but the self-regulation of study was quickly revealed to me as a test in seeing what the girls got up to when left to their own devices.

Because of it all, Saturdays became structureless, apart from mealtimes, and I found myself with a limited freedom that left me alone, as always, adrift and bored. There was only so much class-planning for the week ahead that I could do, after all.

Sundays were no better with an obligatory long Mass to endure in the morning, taking up half of what was meant to be my day off, then a dreadful attempt at a Sunday roast from the convent kitchen and the dismal prospect of a free afternoon – something I should have relished, but which, without transport of my own, I had grown to hate.

So far, I had walked as far as the village of Ballykeeran to find everything closed. I had taken an aimless stroll around the fields that surrounded the school on another – a dreary, solitary exercise that I had undertaken purely to get through the afternoon before heading back for tea which, on Sundays, was invariably revolting rissoles – a leftovers recipe from the Inter Cert Home Economics textbook. Forcing them into me – I had to be seen to eat everything as an example to the students 'not to waste food or develop eating disorders' – I longed, in as much as I could, for the bustle of Sunday nights when the returning Boarders would require supervision again, and it was back to work, as exciting as trudging quietly around and around the dormitories could be. From Sunday night to Friday, I felt, at least, like time was passing constructively. But from Friday afternoon onwards it stood still.

On my third weekend there – had it only been three? – a total of five Boarders were on the premises. They were all Leaving Certs, who stayed in some weekends so that they could 'remain in the school environment to study rather than be distracted by the comforts of home'. Toward the end of the year, as the exams loomed, apparently most of the Leaving Certs would spend *all* of their weekends in the school, many voluntarily, but for now it was still only the dedicated – or disadvantaged – few. That day, the girls had knuckled down straight after breakfast to get homework finished and make a start on revision. There had been talk of them being allowed a film that night although I reckoned the appeal of that reward was somewhat limited. The previous week we had sat through a grainy copy of *Song of Bernadette*, although I had caught a glimpse of Sister Ruth with what looked like *The Sound of Music* under her arm the other day which would be a definite improvement.

After breakfast, I made my way to the Study Hall, just beyond the stairs, passing through the territory of St Sebastian and the Coy Badger, as I had come to call it. On weekdays, the Study Hall was divided into three classrooms by huge wood-and-glass accordion-style partitions, which were then pulled back after school hours and at weekends to make one large room which accommodated every student. I settled myself quietly at the teacher's desk in the Senior section, watching the group who were working hard – so hard, in fact, that it soon became apparent there was very little need for me to be there at all. They were actually a diligent bunch, and all heads were down. Had it been a group from any other year, I'd have had to stay or, at least, separate them out throughout the study hall to make communication between them more difficult, which would have been something to do, but the Leaving Certs knew better, had a certain sense about them, an awareness of the importance of the year that was in it.

I eased myself from the desk after a time, crept across the long room and closed the door behind me silently. For a moment, I contemplated phoning Leonard before checking my watch and realising that there was no point. At ten o'clock on a Saturday morning he wouldn't yet have surfaced after Friday-night drinks with work. And when he did, it would be for just enough time to throw on his tracksuit, grab his kitbag, and head out to training. No better way to sweat out the Guinness, he always said. I sighed. I'd have to go for a walk instead.

I let myself quietly out the back door which led outside from the Boarders' changing rooms at the rear of the building, and walked past the back windows of the study hall, a couple of prefabs and the rusting fire escape towards The Walk. I would do a couple of rounds, I decided, and then see where the mood took me.

It was a grey, damp September morning. Not raining, but not

not raining either. The air smelled dank and moist and it felt as if the world were bearing down around me. The chapel sat silent in the dull light of the morning, the mossy lawns and rose bushes glistening with dew, leaves and blooms dripping with moisture. The branches of the Leyland cypresses that formed a border between the school grounds and the surrounding fields to the rear were also heavy with droplets of moisture, like tiny baubles dangling precariously on each branch. In the distance, I could just about make out the shape of the grey hills rising into an equally grey sky. Around me, I could hear water dripping from the lintels of the study hall windows as I passed. It felt like being inside a grey bubble, a cloud. I walked silently and slowly, thinking about Leonard.

He'd thought I was mad, of course, to go "upsetting the apple tart", as he said. He liked the way we had things in Dublin. On Wednesdays, he'd come around to my place after work and I'd cook, or we'd pop out for an early-bird meal, watching a video together before he headed home on the last bus. Our Saturday nights were spent with our group of friends in town, going to the pub, then the Garda Club, sometimes even ending up in Sucsey Street or one of the other Leeson Street clubs. Those places seemed very far away, all of a sudden. Like something I had seen on TV, in fact, not places that I had actually been to.

On Sundays, it was lunch at Leonard's house. The four of us – Leonard and I and his parents – would sit around their dining-room table with its white lace tablecloth eating roast beef followed by trifle, and talking – usually about Leonard's brother Robert – the one who was already in New York, but who still had a place set for him at the table – and how proud they were of him. I remembered the time that Leonard's mother had a glass of Blue Nun too many and became nostalgic, and regretful – chastising Leonard for not having joined the priesthood like she wanted him to, but reassuring herself that at least he'd be there to take care of her in her old age, like it was his duty to do as the youngest. I had thought that he might be embarrassed at that, but when I glanced at him across the table I saw that he was impassive, shovelling his trifle into his mouth like a small boy, clutching the spoon in his fist. It was his dad who had interrupted her, suggesting that she might like a lie-down after all her hard work, and helping her from the room. Leonard was just used to that sort of thing, I supposed, having grown up with it. He might want to set her straight at some stage, of course, heading as he was to a new life in Boston once we had the cash together.

Which would be a lot sooner now with the money from my job, I thought to myself as I sauntered along the damp path, kicking the first of the fallen leaves as I went and allowing myself a hopeful little smile. I did that sometimes as a form of reward to myself – totted up the figures in my head – what I'd be saving, and how that calculated into *T.U.D* – Time Until Departure. It gave me a little boost inside, to acknowledge the purpose of this job that I was doing.

"*What if you get all influenced, and holy and decide you want to be a nun yourself?*" Leonard had wailed, dismayed, when I'd told him about it first.

I'd laughed at him, and quickly laid out my plan and my goal, and shown him the figures. "You can't argue with that amount in the bank, Leonard," I'd told him. "We both have to make sacrifices if we want our dream to come true, and this is going to be mine. We'll be there before we know it."

And with that, he'd shrugged his shoulders and pressed 'play' on *Top Gun* which he'd reserved especially at Xtra-vision. I'd settled down happily beside him, my head on his shoulder, to share a bag of Minstrels. If Maverick and Goose and motorcycles on highways and fighter jets didn't get him fired up about going to America, then nothing would.

It might have been nice to talk to him on the phone though, I thought to myself as I strolled. He was a useless correspondent, but he was just going to have to improve – it was simply the only way to communicate with each other. I had written off using the telephone under the stairs for a number of reasons – firstly, with my schedule, I was never available to talk when I knew that Leonard would be with his; secondly, the queue of teenage girls waiting at it with their tenpence pieces was offputting, to put it mildly, and I wasn't sure that Benedicta would find it seemly of me to join them. Plus, they could hear every word that was said when anyone was on a call so I gave it up as a lost cause. I was proud of myself, however, for not missing him too much. In fact, I was so busy that on some days he didn't even enter my head. It was difficult, and unusual, I knew. But it would all be worth it in the end, of course. I just had to keep telling myself that.

I took a deep breath of the moist country air, and continued along the path, strolling along beside the long, low yew hedge that separated The Walk and the Playing Courts from the chapel grounds – tracing in reverse the route that the students took to file into the chapel for Mass. On impulse, I stepped through the gap in the hedge that led to the side entrance used by the convent girls – the Goretti Door, as it was known. There was a small cemetery through there that I could see from my bedroom window, and through which I passed each morning as I led the girls to Mass, which I had been meaning to explore since I'd arrived. This was the perfect opportunity. I stepped off the path that led from the yew arch to the Goretti Door and walked among the graves.

I liked graveyards. Not as some sort of ghoul, but as a history teacher. I loved what – who – I might find in them. An interesting headstone or monument here, or an epitaph that hinted at a life, or death, worth learning more about there. Usually the older and more disordered the graves, the better I liked it. Standing in the burial ground outside the chapel, however, I felt a little disappointed. There were no hidden treasures to be found – I could tell that at first glance. This was a typical Nuns' Graveyard, simple and almost military in style. No grave had a border, or a stone surround, there were no tombs, no interesting inscriptions. It was simply grass, and crosses. Everything was neat and precise, the engravings on the headstones all exactly the same. A nun's name, and her dates of birth and death. And that was it. Sister Assumpta O'Brien, 1900-1975; Sister Margaret Harris, 1870-1965; Sister Claire Murphy, 1920-1967 – only forty-seven years old that one – next door to one who had lived until her mid-nineties. Although, as I stepped slowly through them, I felt a pang of something. All of them were women who had given up their lives for God, who had lived and died inside the stone walls behind me. I stared around me at the crosses. The last resting place of these women was together, with each other, far from family and home. It was a sort of sadness that I felt – not at their passing, but at the waste. I couldn't understand wanting to be a nun. The more time I spent among them, I really couldn't see the point in giving up every chance, every opportunity, every possibility that life could throw at you to live, cloistered, with the same company and same routine day in and day out.

My eyes scanned over the crosses. There was nothing of interest here for the historian in me. I had missed nothing passing through this small burial ground every morning as I ushered a crocodile of schoolgirls in through the door to Mass.

Until, that is, I turned to get back to the path and something caught my eye, something I hadn't noticed before. A marker that was entirely different from the others. I watched my step on the wet grass as I tried to walk between what I guessed were the boundaries of graves, but I couldn't be sure. I gave a whispered apology as I lost my balance and stepped near the head of where Sister Alice Cotterill lay. Another couple of steps and I had reached my destination. Curious, I crouched down at a small, grey rock which rested there.

The wording was different from the others, and it was in Irish: *Prionsias Ní Faolain*, it read. There was no indication that it was a nun either. I soon spotted why when I looked at the date. *1936-1942.*

It was a seven-year-old child.

I did a quick calculation in my head. She had lain here for forty-five years, in this cold, wet earth. A poor little girl. *Prionsias.* What on earth had happened to her? A shiver ran through me suddenly and I stood up, folding my arms about me, still staring at the stone.

"Morning, Miss!"

I jumped and swung around.

Two girls approached through the gap in the hedge from the school, both with arms filled with roses, one of them wielding a large key.

"Martina, Lydia," I said, standing upright, recognising two of the Leaving Certs. "Have you finished studying?"

Martina Nolan, thin and sporty, taking English but not History for her exams, shook her long blonde hair which was loose – something else that wasn't allowed on weekdays. "No, Miss. Sister Anne asked us to bring these over to the chapel for the ladies doing the flowers."

"Is that the key to the Goretti Door?" I asked, nodding at her hand.

"It is, Miss. We're to let ourselves in, come straight out again and lock up."

She beamed as she told me and I almost smiled back until I realised that it was a smile of planned mischief, not of friendly intent. Her companion looked at her from under a long, dark fringe disapprovingly. She was in both of my Leaving Cert classes – Lydia Madigan. A small, silent girl. Observant, but disinclined to participate, shying back on the edges of everything. She was dressed in a long black skirt and Doc Marten boots, holes in the sleeves of her black jumper. She tilted her head to one side and her fringe fell away from her face which was pretty but blighted with acne.

"Make sure you do that," I warned.

"You're visiting Little Frances, Miss?" Martina asked suddenly. I frowned. "Who?"

"Little Frances." She pointed towards the small rock. "Have you not heard of her?"

I shook my head and walked over to join the girls, stepping back onto the path. "No. Who is she?"

"The Day Girls say that she was murdered. Some local kid." Martina shrugged.

I looked from her to Lydia and back.

"And do they say why is she buried here in the Nuns' Graveyard?"

Martina shrugged again. "There was something dodgy about it – one of the Sixth Year Day Girls told me about her when I was in First Year, but I've forgotten. There was something about a rumour she's not in there at all …"

"Martina!" I was surprised to hear Lydia interject.

Martina ignored her. "They say she's too busy running around the school"

"What do you mean, Martina?" I asked.

Martina's smile grew wider, and she cast a sideways glance at Lydia. "She haunts the school, Miss. Our very own House Ghost!" There was a mischievous glee in her voice.

Beside her, Lydia rolled her eyes. "It's only a story, Miss," she sighed.

"That's not what the rhyme says!" Martina was clearly enjoying this. "You don't know the rhyme, Miss?"

I played along, shaking my head. "No, Martina. What rhyme?"

She cleared her throat and began, whispering for dramatic effect.

"Blessed Frances slams the doors
And runs around the upstairs floors.
She'll steal your pen or touch your hair,
When you're sure there's no one there.
The nuns are meant to keep her safe,
But she gets out of her own grave
So pull your covers over your head,
Little Frances isn't dead!"

There was silence as she finished, both Lydia and myself staring at her. Lydia looked embarrassed suddenly, and fidgeted with her armful of roses.

"Did you make that up, Martina?" I asked.

She shook her head. "No, Miss. Everyone knows it. They teach it to the kids in the village even. Some people have seen her, you know …"

"Girls!"

All three of us jumped as another voice rang through the hedge. An elderly, chubby nun dressed in an old-style habit, wearing her rosary looped onto her leather belt – one of the non-teaching convent nuns, a generation who blended the old ways into the new – stood in the gap this time, glaring.

"I thought I told you two to get those flowers inside the chapel and get *straight* back to your books, did I not?"

Sister Anne's face was red and she was a little breathless as she stood there, hands on hips. The girls glanced at each other, shamefaced at being caught out, Lydia more than Martina.

"Yes, Sister, sorry, Sister," Martina mumbled.

"It's my fault they were delayed, Sister," I piped up.

The nun frowned. "Well, get on with it, then!" she barked at the girls. "And no dilly-dallying in the chapel either. I want that key returned to me at the front porch in *five minutes*. And I'll time you."

She watched, glaring, as the girls hastened toward the chapel door and fumbled with the key, then disappeared inside.

She turned to go, but not before pausing to scrutinise me for a moment. "You'll catch a cold in this damp," she said, finally, before disappearing behind the hedge.

I heard her busy footsteps retreat back to the school building. And shortly afterwards the girls emerged from the chapel, locking the door behind them.

"Bye, Miss," Martina mumbled as they rushed past, stepping back through the gap onto the school grounds and out of sight. Muttered words and Martina's giggle floated back through the still air as they ran.

I shivered.

Chapter eleven

BALLYKEERAN
August 1942

"I've found her."

Silence. A long silence.

And then a great, trembling cry. It is anguish. It is despair. They are the most unwanted words. They are words that end all happiness, forever. There will never be another smile, another laugh, another moment not longing for death, not longing to be with her.

"Is she ..."

The mother speaks at last. There is more silence. Then more deep cries of soul pain.

The child should not be listening, but she is, her ear pressed to the bedroom door.

Dada was dirty when he went into Mammy's room. Soaked to the skin. The child saw him through her bedroom window returning through the rain, leaving his shovel by the back door, the sheepdog, Setanta, running low at his heels. The dog whimpered outside now, giving the odd bark, looking to be left in.

Mammy is crying now too, in an unstoppable flood. The child cannot see but she can picture her. Mammy looks like a granny, her once-black hair threaded through with wiry silver, unbrushed. Her skin is grey and her cheeks hollow. Her lips are always turned down at the corners. She has not left her bed in three nights, not since the child returned in the storm without her sister. It hasn't stopped raining since then either.

Stupid, lousy Frances, the child thinks. Always ruining everything. And now everything is strange – Mammy locked away in her room, her prayers rising and falling day and night, Dada always out, looking and searching – and now this. The child pictures her mother's bony fingers clasping each individual bead of her rosary, sees in her mind's eye the furrowed brow of concentration. As if words can bring her sister home. Eventually the wailing recedes and there is silent whimpering for a while.

The child lolls against the doorpost.

"Will you bring her home?" she hears her mother gulp.

"I did already." Dada is weeping too, but quietly, like a man does.

"Will you keep her safe now?"

"The nuns will take her, Evelyn, like you wanted," he says, his voice breaking a little. "She's safe now."

"And the other one?"

Mammy's voice is suddenly cold. The child presses her ear back to the door.

"I'll make sure they take her too, when she's old enough."

"I wish it was her, Liam."

"Ah now, Evelyn!"

Bitterness and rage have overtaken the tears.

"No, I swear. God strike me down but I do. I wish it was her was gone and my Baby Frances beside me. I want her gone, Liam – gone! Out of this house! I never want to see her again – I want the devil to take her down below where she belongs!"

"*Shhh*, Evelyn … she'll hear you …"

"She's the *Devil's* child, Liam. Not mine. Not yours. Not like my angel Frances. From the day she was born, I knew there was something not right. I don't want her anymore, Liam … I *don't want her!*"

The child slowly backed away from her parents' door, her eyes narrowing, turning and making her way into the kitchen to quietly open the back door and let Setanta in. He was an excitable dog. Grateful to be let inside, but wary of his little mistress, the one who liked to pull his tail. He, too, was confused at the absence of the other little mistress, the one who kissed him and hugged him and threw a stick for him. The child stood back and watched as he jumped about the kitchen, coated in muck from the bog all over his paws and coat which he shook vigorously and his tail which he wagged at top speed. Someone might need to clean up that mess, she thought. She decided to leave the back door open, just in case he needed to get out again. The rain would get in but it was better to let Setanta have a bit of freedom.

The wind gave a long, low whistle through the keyhole of her parents' door as she made her way back to her bedroom. Mixed with her mother's keening, it sounded like there was a ghost in there. She shut the door of her room tightly against it, and climbed, alone, into the bed under the hard, grey blanket and lay her head down on the bolster that she normally shared with her sister, her head ringing with her mother's words.

Chapter twelve

Ria
BALLYKEERAN
October 1987

The insistent trilling of my alarm clock at seven o'clock made me jump, worsening my already foul mood. I leaned back towards it in my chair and slapped it silent, suppressing the urge to open the shutters and throw it through the window. I had no need for it to wake me up. I had been up for at least an hour and a half now, and unable to sleep for an hour before that. I had slept fitfully all the previous night, unable to stop my thoughts. I hated everything.

Especially Leonard. He was the main cause of my dark mood – thoughts of him like a blister on my heel. Everything had suddenly changed.

It was the Tuesday after I had been back to Dublin for my first full weekend off, an event that I had longed for. As the last week of September crawled toward its conclusion, I thought Friday would never come, but finally, impossibly, the bell rang at ten past four and I was free to return to my life. Another lift with Tom Gorman to the station, the reverse trip through the countryside and into glorious, dirty civilisation. A return to what was normal, what was known, and among it all my fiancé.

It had been a disaster.

I was excited about our reunion – not butterflies-in-the-tummy, double-checking-for-lipstick-on-my-teeth excited – that was the reserve of a Maria Goretti girl on a secret assignation with a local

63

Christian Brother boy, after all, I felt. No. Leonard and I were grown-ups. We were going to emigrate and get married and spend our lives together. I looked forward to having what I liked to call a 'planning meeting' over the weekend.

My first pay cheque, sitting in my pigeonhole that morning, bolstered my mood considerably too. I had made a mistake in my careful calculations and, to my delight, it was *more* than I had expected and seeing it, holding it in my hand, had made me want to punch the air with satisfaction. I couldn't wait to show it to Leonard – he'd be as excited as I was.

On reaching Dublin, however, there was no sign of him. I searched the crowd on the platform at Heuston, but he was nowhere to be seen. In fact, I didn't see him until almost nine o'clock that night, when he arrived home to his parents' house. At that point, I had been waiting for two hours, two awkward hours of conversation with his mother – a woman who, it turned out, I didn't know very well, and to whom I had never been allowed to mention The Plan. She couldn't know yet, Leonard warned me – it would break her heart to know that her second boy was going across the Atlantic. He'd tell her in "his own good time", he assured me. It left our interaction awkward, as the woman clearly couldn't understand why I now lived in a convent in Laois, instead of staying in a good, pensionable normal job in Dublin, and I couldn't explain to her my real reasons. At least she had been expecting me, however, and had served up a fry with stacks of white, crusty bread and butter which, after a month of convent rations, I devoured gratefully. Leonard's father, on the other hand, a man who spoke little, seemed surprised to see me and slipped into the living room where he read his paper.

When Leonard finally arrived, he smelled of Guinness and was loud, having gone to the pub after work "for one or two". He claimed he knew I was due to arrive, but not that he was to meet me at the station, and he "didn't think I'd mind" making my own way to Rathfarnham. "Sure didn't it give you and Mam time for a girlie chat?" he'd said before devouring the meal his mother prepared for him on the spot, and promptly falling asleep during the *Late Late Show*.

I left him on the couch at ten o'clock, excusing myself quietly to the spare room.

I was disappointed that my envisioned reunion hadn't gone to plan, but woke on Saturday feeling warm – which I hadn't felt in a month – under a cosy duvet in a bright room, and filled with a renewed hope. His parents had gone to the shops first thing, so Leonard and I shared breakfast together – me showing him my cheque, him nodding approvingly before returning to his cereal and the sports pages. I looked at the top of his head as he ate and read and felt a thrill of hope for the future, that this was how it could be when it was just the two of us, far away. Except we'd share bacon and eggs and read the *Boston Globe* over breakfast, or have pancakes or bagels or one of those strange and exciting-sounding things that Americans ate. Like biscuits maybe, although I couldn't understand why they ate them with gravy.

It did niggle at me a little that he had arranged to train with his football team in the afternoon, but I soon brushed it off as an opportunity to go shopping in town – I needed new clothes.

It felt wonderful to stroll around Grafton Street for the first time in so long, to feel *alive*, the air filled with chat and *sound*, snatches of song, and drumming and performance coming from the buskers I passed. I bought some new, suitable clothes for school and then treated myself on impulse to a new dress, knee-length, royal blue, wide at the shoulders and cinched in at the waist. On a whim, I popped into Peter Mark and had my hair blow-dried, and had my make-up done at the counter in Switzers. When I stepped back out into the autumn evening sunshine, it felt good, like I was slowly transforming back into *me*, even if only for one night. I was sure that Leonard would appreciate it.

It became apparent soon after heading to the pub, however, that he didn't. I had naively envisioned dinner for two in town with him, where we'd catch up over some pasta and a bottle of wine in a wicker holder perhaps, followed by a couple of quiet drinks somewhere classy – I'd even have gone to a nightclub if the mood had taken us. Instead, however, I found myself sitting in Leonard's local. He stood with his teammates in a huddle at the bar, while I sat in a row along a banquette with their wives and girlfriends, all of them dressed in jeans and casual tops, all of them chatting in twos and threes, and no one to me. I nursed my 7UP, staring into space, feeling that same loneliness that I felt every day of the week in my work.

Sunday couldn't pass fast enough. I cried off Mass, saying that I felt ill. Leonard's parents were sure that I had a hangover. I simply felt angry and disappointed. I lay in bed and listened to the front door slam as they all left. Without having to calculate, I knew that I had already attended Mass close to twenty times that month, and, despite what Leonard's mother said, figured that there was no way God could be as angry at me as I was at Leonard. And his parents. And his GAA team. And at my life.

His dad dropped me to Heuston on Sunday afternoon for my return trip – Leonard had to meet up with some friend of his who worked in Belfast and was home for the weekend, he said. The farewell with my fiancé was cursory. I mentioned writing or trying to ring him in the next week or two and was rewarded with a "Sure, whatever". I sat in silence, staring out the window of the train all the way back, wondering what next.

It was the question that I was still asking myself on the Tuesday morning, the cold of early October creeping in, the morning grim and dark. I stood and opened the shutters a little and peered out, the unfinished letter on cerise pink notepaper on my writing desk behind me.

Darling Leonard, it began. *It was so lovely seeing you at the weekend – I knew that I missed you but didn't realise just how much until we had some time to ourselves again – it had felt like forever since I'd last seen you. It was so difficult to get on that train on Sunday and leave behind everything that felt like normal in Dublin but, if anything, it gave me the impetus to keep going. Every day that I'm here, away from you, is another day closer to being able to execute The Plan. Another day closer to getting on that plane and making the magical future for ourselves that we both deserve. Another step closer to creating our dream home in Boston, having the family and the life that we dream of. Sometimes it feels like time stands still here without you, but I cannot wait to fill a house with love and children and happiness – our own little kingdom ...*

I looked back at the paper and pen, useless in the morning light. The letter which I had worked on for over an hour now was meant to repair what had happened over the weekend, was meant to reconnect Leonard and myself, to rekindle the romance that had been so lacking in our time together. But it didn't feel right. The language … it was meant to be filled with words of love to make Leonard realise that what we had was important and wonderful and worth working for, but it wasn't how we spoke or showed affection. It was all wrong – the notepaper was childish, the words forced and insincere. I sighed and turned back to the desk to pick up the letter which I folded roughly and stuffed in between two books on my shelf. I would read it again later but I was sure now that it wasn't the right way to repair things between Leonard and myself.

My eyes returned for a moment to the window. Another grey drizzle permeated the dawn. I glanced at the chapel next door, to where it was my duty to get sixty-four schoolgirls to Mass in the next hour and a half. I scowled at the thought, and tramped out of my room and into the bathroom. I ran my hand under the hot tap at the handbasin. No hot water, again. I washed my hands and face and swiped under my arms in cold, and stormed back to my room, seething silently while I dressed in the new navy-blue suit that I had bought that weekend in Dublin, being careful to choose a red polo neck to wear under the smart jacket to distinguish myself from the nuns. What had I been thinking, I asked myself. And not just about the suit.

As the Morning Bell was rung in the corridor outside by a Fifth Year rostered for the task for a week, and then taken upstairs to wake the dormitory, my head was filled with black thoughts of rage. At my suit, at my so-called fiancé, and at this place with its freezing walls and water. But underneath the rage, however, was a niggling worry.

What now? What future for myself and Leonard? What exactly was I trying to save with that ridiculous letter? Did I really want to spend my life being wife to a man who didn't think I'd mind sitting with his mother while he went to the pub? Who ditched me to go banter with his friends at the bar? And more to the point, what did *he* actually want? Because I was beginning to feel that, despite what his mouth said, his heart wasn't truly on the same track as mine. It struck me for the first time that perhaps he wasn't as serious about The Plan as I was. He hadn't been bothered to talk about it when we were together – had minimal interest in my cheque, hadn't even wanted to be alone together, come to think of it. And *still* he hadn't told his mother he was moving to America with me. Would he ever, I asked myself, finally acknowledging the doubts that had slunk around my brain since the weekend. Was there any future in this? Was my biggest dream ever going to be realised? And if not – if I was destined to stay in Ireland, with or without Leonard – then what was the point in all of this? Of being here in Maria Goretti? Nothing but icy cold, dark mornings pacing silently around a roomful of sleepy teenagers barking at them to stay quiet, to hurry up, to dress faster; then herding them downstairs, out across a cold yard into an even colder chapel to chant prayers with a handful of locals, and a doddering priest.

I took it out on the girls. I was normally controlled. Stern, but controlled. But this morning I barked at them, and yelled at any sign of dawdling or delay. They were taken aback. I noticed a few glaring at me with shock on their faces but I could only glare back at them. I hated myself for acting that way, but couldn't stop.

They filed past me in silence out through the locker-room door, having changed into their outdoor shoes and gaberdines, and with the last of them gone I slammed it shut behind me and locked it noisily before pocketing the key and storming after the unusually silent crocodile of green.

I had barely taken a few steps when the light caught my eye. It had been left switched on in one of the rooms in the Sisters' Corridor – third window along – Catherine and Becky McGovern's. I swore under my breath. Benedicta would go nuts if she saw a light left on unnecessarily. *Damn* them. Why couldn't they just have turned the bloody thing off?

I glanced at my watch and gave a groan of frustration. It was close, cutting it very fine this morning to make sure that everyone, including myself, was in their seat for Mass. Late arrival was classed by the nuns as a 'disgrace' to the school in front of the priest and the locals and would mean a dressing-down from Benedicta. Like I needed that on top of everything. I paused, observing how the line of girls progressed towards the chapel, and then looking back at the window of the McGoverns' room. I hesitated for a moment, and then turned to run as quickly as I could up the stairs to angrily flick the light switch to 'off' before flying back down the stairs and out into the mizzly morning again.

Breathlessly, I rounded the side of the school and saw to my relief that there appeared to be, initially, no sign of any student left outside. It looked as though they had all entered the chapel themselves, and I uttered a silent prayer that they had gone to their seats quietly, without realising I wasn't present. I hurried faster, as the chapel bell suddenly began to peal the first of the eight bongs that signified the time – it was also the cue for the barely comprehensible Father Mack to shuffle onto the altar to begin proceedings, led by the two nervous pre-teen altar boys who would blush furiously under the scrutiny of the girls sitting in the front few rows before them.

And it was then that I saw the girl as I passed through the arch in the hedge. There was always one, of course. A straggler. Someone who just couldn't follow the pack, but who was distracted by something – a flower, a dewdrop on a leaf, her own shoes. I couldn't tell who it was as she stood with her back to me, looking across the gardens at the school. What frustrated me more was that she had strayed off the path between the yew arch and the Goretti Door and stood instead directly in the centre of the Nuns' Graveyard.

"Get inside *now!*" I barked, my words drowned out by another loud peal of the chapel bell. She didn't hear me, or if she did, she didn't move an inch, just continued to stare at the convent, oblivious to the time, or where she should have been.

I fumed and glanced at my watch again in panic. It was really nothing in the bigger scheme of things. But in my universe, one late girl wasn't just a late girl – it was a Guardian who could not keep control.

I looked up, opened my mouth to bellow at the errant student again, and then I stopped completely in my tracks.

She was gone.

Confused, I looked around. There was no girl standing there. Perhaps she had heard me after all, and run into the chapel? But surely that was impossible – I had seen her mere *seconds* before. There simply hadn't been sufficient time for her to get from where she stood and in through the chapel door past me. Perhaps she was hiding? But how? The headstones were all small, narrow markers, too small for anyone to crouch behind. Where had she gone? And who on earth had it been?

Another loud ring of the bell sounded through the air, bringing me to my senses. There was no sign of her out here – I'd have to check inside. I sped in through the chapel door myself, distracted immediately by the smell of incense, my cheeks burning as I slipped into my seat in the front row under the eyes of the Sisters of Maria Goretti, and the villagers of Ballykeeran.

As we stood for the entrance hymn, I glanced around at my charges, at the sea of faces that filled the rows behind me. I couldn't be fully sure, but it seemed that they were all there. *All dressed in green*. But the girl outside ... she hadn't been. I tried to recall exactly what she *was* wearing as I sat back down and Father Mack began to drone his greeting. Something grey – I hadn't really taken it in in my panic. So she wasn't a Goretti Girl after all? She must have been local? Relief washed over me. At least my charges had all been 'under control', as the nuns liked to say. I was in the clear. I joined in the recitation of the Confiteor and focused on looking devout, shivering in the chill of the morning.

Chapter thirteen

Lydia
BALLYKEERAN
October 1987

The summer seems so far past now. It's only a few weeks, really, when you think about it, but it's October already – The Walk is all 'kicky-leafy', as my friend Carmel calls it, and now that the evenings are too dark, we can't go outside to the Playing Courts for Night Break at eight o'clock and have a stroll or knock-about with a ball. The doors are locked at half five and they stay that way till morning. I hate that. I hate being kept indoors all the time. And it means I have to be around other people – it's easier to get a bit of time to myself when we're spread out outside.

When it's Night Break and we have to all go the Assembly Hall, like tonight, I can't get any peace, even if I curl up on a windowsill right down the back with a book. There's always someone trying to sit down near me, or the First Years playing stupid kid games – running around and squealing like six-year-olds at a party. And as for the record player – that stupid old record player we're allowed that's in the three-legged cabinet that someone rolls out of the games equipment room night after night. There's only one 7" single with it, for God's sake. If I ever hear 'Pride' by U2 again, I might kill myself, but the Fourth Years *love* it and jump up and down to it, eyes closed, punching the air as if it means something to them, over and over again. I think I might hate them more than the song, in fact.

71

The alternative is to look out the long windows of the Hall, but that's even more depressing. Even if they didn't have mesh over them to protect them from balls bouncing off them, they just look over the horrible, grey pebbledash of the old wing and the disused prefabs. And it's raining tonight, so it's even darker and murkier and grimmer than usual. To make it worse, two Fifth Years are skipping around the Assembly Hall, closing the heavy green curtains that hang over each window, blocking out every last shred of remaining daylight, going on about how it's "cosy". If one of them comes near my windowsill, I'll fight her, I swear. If she closes those curtains, I might just suffocate.

Most of the time here, I tolerate it, especially now that the end is in sight. But there are times when I just can't help but hate it. Especially on nights like these, just after I've had my once-a-month deluxe weekend in Dublin. Bad and all as it is at Uncle Neville's – I can never really call it 'home', of course – at least my own bed is there, the one I had since I was a child; and I like getting up when I want with no bells controlling everything and no praying practically every five minutes.

It was a nice, peaceful weekend. I went to the cinema in town on Saturday afternoon – it feels like a lifetime ago now – to see *Withnail and I*, and then for a big mug of white coffee in Bewleys on Westmoreland Street. I found a marble-topped table and surrounded myself in the red velvet of the seating and read for a while before going home to Uncle Neville's. He was gone out, of course, so I had the house all to myself. I had cheese on toast with HP sauce for dinner and watched some videos. I could watch *St Elmo's Fire* forever, and *Out of Africa* made me cry. It was perfect. Complete peace and solitude, my thoughts and my time my own. The only fly in the ointment was the niggling guilt I felt about the video tapes. It had felt so good to walk out of Golden Discs with them in my bag without anyone noticing me, but I have to stop. I swear, I won't do it the next time I'm in there. I'll pay for them. That's the last time. I'll be good from now on.

On Sunday, I walked the short walk to the Garden of Remembrance and sat in the sun for a bit, staring at those sad Children of Lir, but then it was time to come back here, and I had to get home and be ready to come back to school because Uncle

72

Neville had arranged for his friend, Ron Whatshisface, the travelling sales rep, to give me a lift back and save on train fare. What a pleasant trip that wasn't. Ron never spoke to me, not once, apart from 'Hello, Linda' and 'Bye then, Linda' – like how could he not know my name, after five years? But hey, who cares? I don't. Not anymore.

I can't wait to get away from everything next summer. I'll be eighteen in a few weeks, and no matter what he says or does, Uncle Neville can't keep me there forever – nor does he want to – so as soon as I have my Leaving Cert under my belt, it's 'Adios, Uncle Neville', 'Adios, Maria Goretti' and 'Hola, Freedom!'

I think if my mum knew what sort of a substitute parent her brother was going to be, then she'd have taken his name off her will, but as her only living relative he sort of got the job by default. He was the entitled one – my grandmother's favourite. He inherited their house, after all, when Mum should have as the eldest, and then it should have been mine after her – not that I want the poxy thing with the damp and the draughts and the mouldy attic, and the dodgy location, but still. Instead, because Neville was male, and Granny's little pet, he got the house on George's Street, dump that it is, and then when Mum and Dad died I had to move there too because it was now Uncle Nev's responsibility to look after me. A job that he didn't want any more than I wanted him to have it.

I mean, I resented him so much at first. Living his life – his glam job making loads of money, his never-ending supply of 'friends', going out all the time, doing everything that they wanted, while I was under lock and key down in Laois, in boarding school. Safely out of the way, no harm to anyone. It needn't have been that way. I was perfectly capable of getting myself to and from a day school in Dublin – I had been for years. After all, I was allowed to wander where and when I wanted up there one measly weekend a month, so why couldn't I go to school there and just live in Neville's? It's not like I cared to impinge on his lifestyle one little bit. But no, that plea had fallen on deaf ears, and here I was, stifling, smothering in this place, surrounded by noise and nuns and nonsense and yet completely cut off from everything that mattered in the world. It's what my parents wanted, Neville told me, for me to go to the same school as Mum had, before flouncing out again to some social engagement. It wasn't. It was what *he* wanted, more like. Me out of the way by sixty miles or so, locked up safe where he didn't have to concern himself in the slightest with me.

"Hello, hello!" The familiar scent of White Musk perfume fills the air as a shape plonks down beside me.

Carmel's back, still wearing her gaberdine, like she's only just come in the door. I wondered where she was last night alright – she's normally back on a Sunday night without fail – but there was no sign then or today either. She's got her Night Tea snack – a triangular corned-beef sandwich in either hand. I ate mine standing up, with a lukewarm cup of tea served by two Fifth Years who were thrilled to get out of study ten minutes early to wheel up the Night Tea trolley to the top of the Brown Corridor at the big mirror and pour cups for everyone, making sure everyone got just the one sandwich each. Carmel got lucky – if you could call it that – with her two.

"Where were you today?" I ask her, swinging my legs off the window ledge to allow her sit down beside me. She's a good laugh, Carmel. The closest thing to a friend that I have here, really.

"Dentist," she replies, her mouth full as she squeezes in a whole sandwich. "Got the day off to go get my metalwork seen to. Want one?"

I can see the corners of the white bread squeezing out between her train-track braces and I look at her hand instead. Carmel's a comforting presence, but not big on table manners. I shake my head.

"Had mine," I reply. "How the hell did you get two?"

Carmel swallows the half-chewed sandwich. "Said I was starving! Sure, I had my dinner at six before Mam dropped me back," she giggles. "You have to stockpile, though, in this place."

"What was for dinner in your house?" I ask, almost lustfully. We're all always starving. Food is a constant topic of conversation, what anyone else gets at home, what we might get in an ideal world, what our last meals would be. It's the stuff of fantasy.

"Stew, potatoes and a big bowl of trifle for afters," Carmel replies. "What was it here?"

I snort derisively. "Chicken for dinner," I respond. "Managed to sneak my fork in to bagsy the breast bit before we said Grace, though, so it wasn't too bad. Mash and cabbage, and then suet pud for dessert. Potato cakes for tea though."

We both grimaced.

'*Eurgh*!" says Carmel. "Who got the manky legs of the chicken?"

"Joanne!" I snort, and both of us dissolve into giggles.

"Serves her right," sneers Carmel, as we both stare out across the packed Assembly Hall at a blonde girl, her hair loose about her shoulders, wiggling her hips with her hands raised in the air as 'Pride' gets its third play of the evening.

"She'll have had a secret tuck bag full of Rolos to make up for it," I observe.

"Oh, my mam sent some goodies for you," says Carmel, finishing the last of the second sandwich. "I left them in your locker."

"Thank her for me, Carmel," I reply gratefully. "She's very good."

Tuck from home is worth its weight in gold in here. Sweets, crisps, a bottle of Lemon and Lime – they need to be rationed, need to last until our next trip back. Most Boarders go home every weekend so if they finish their stash by Wednesday then it's not the end of the world, but that isn't the case for me. Carmel's Mam knows this, and remembers it – she actually cares, which blows my mind. Calls me a "poor starving *cratur* " and sends a few Mars Bars or Moros back with Carmel to keep me going every week.

The sandwiches finished, Carmel dips into the deep pocket of her cardigan and fishes out a Crunchie. "Do you want this, actually?" she offers, passing it to me almost surreptitiously, glancing around to see if anyone's watching. It's like we're in prison sometimes. "I'd swallow it whole, but my braces are killing me after today and the dentist warned me about eating stuff like this. Crunchies are the natural enemy of the train-track brace."

I accept it gratefully, and slide it into my pocket. I plan when I'll have it – half at small break tomorrow, and half after school maybe. I ration things when they're thin on the ground. It's important to keep something to look forward to, even if it's just half a chocolate bar.

We sit in silence for a moment, watching the room heave with people. Miss Clancy is here too, somewhere, patrolling silently, like the nuns have taught her. I don't think she's like them, though. She watches us, but not in the same suspicious way that they do, always trying to find fault with the most innocent thing. She's nice, Miss Clancy. Quiet. Doesn't shout or give out very often and, somehow, no one pushes it with her – well, apart from that time the first week when Imelda Hannigan hid in the cupboard behind the lectern in the Third Study and fell out, just as Miss Clancy was going past. She was cross, of course, but it felt like only because she had to be. In fact, I'm sure I saw her laughing at her desk later. Imelda had looked really stupid, after all, and Elizabeth O'Connor had screamed so loud that we all jumped out of our skins.

"Oh, c'mere, I've something else for you as well," Carmel whispers, so I have to lean in to hear her.

The volume's gone up as we hit the chorus of 'Pride' and Joanne and her cronies are well stuck into it tonight, singing at the tops of their voices, their expressions earnest. I hate Joanne Murphy. She loves to go on and on about injustice in the world – Nelson Mandela and all that – she's heard about Steve Biko too now, thanks to that movie *Cry Freedom*, and she's unbearable. But she's actually a bully, making fun of people, telling the nuns on them and that. She used to be a dab hand at making the First Years cry, and then teasing them about being homesick. Last year, she stole a pair of knickers belonging to that poor overweight girl in Second Year, Aileen, and hung them up on the Virgin Mary's head on that statue in the library so that everyone could see and then laughed herself sick at how upset Aileen got. The poor kid cried and cried and rang her mam to go home on a Thursday night because she was so upset. Joanne and her friends still snigger loudly behind her back when she walks past – a whole year later. She's poison, Joanne Murphy. She deserves every manky piece of chicken in the world, and then some more.

I smile as Miss Clancy makes a beeline toward her group and orders them to turn the volume down. They comply, eventually, but not without making stupid faces behind Miss Clancy's back when she walks away. Such a pack of bitches.

"Here. Have a look at this," Carmel hisses, and I turn to see what she's handing me.

It's a book. I glance at the cover and immediately I feel my face go red. I look up, panicked, to double-check where Miss Clancy is.

She can't see this – in fact, no one can see this. We'd be in so much trouble.

It's a slim book, sort of like a Mills and Boon. *The Secret Passion of Sister Claude*, it's called.

"*Carmel!*" I hiss, pushing it back at her, but she sits there with a stupid grin on her face, and her arms crossed, refusing to accept it. Her face creases with hilarity at my shocked expression. "I found it in my nana's over the weekend – she loves this sort of thing!" she giggles. "It's filthy, isn't it?"

She's not wrong. The cover shows a young woman surrounded by flames – a nun, clearly – you can tell by the veil from which jet-black curls escape – in the throes of passion – her head thrown back, exposing about an acre of milky white chest, two heaving bosoms straining to escape from a completely immodest habit which is a little ripped over the right boob and ... is that ... yes, it is, the faintest hint of a pale-brown nipple escaping from the black fabric. Her eyes are half closed and her lips open – her hands raised in half-hearted defence against a dark attacker who lunges for her open neck with his lips. His own hands are clearly just about to grab her in the chest area and his expression is one of fierce concentration. And he has a dog collar. Yes. Sister Claude is clearly exploding with secret passion for a horny priest and it looks like she's about to give in. "*He longs to violate her vows,*" reads the cover. "*Even God Himself cannot quell their lust ...*"

I glance up to see Miss Clancy coming toward us and immediately, without thinking, slip the book inside *The Hobbit*, which is open on my knee and slam it shut. It's a weak hiding place, but hopefully ... please, God ... it'll keep the filth hidden and we won't get into trouble.

Miss Clancy's not stupid. She knows we're up to something. She can see that I'm puce, and nervous, and Carmel is doubled over with helpless laughter. I slide *The Hobbit* as casually as I can off my knee and slip it down beside me, pushing it gently under my leg, out of sight. I don't think I could be any more suspicious if I tried. I shake my head slightly, out of habit, to shake my hair over my face, but it's clipped back, of course. Uniform rules. I feel exposed.

She looks at us for a few moments, smiling a little at Carmel who is crying she's laughing so hard.

"Everything alright, Lydia?" she asks.

"Yes, Miss," I reply. Too quickly.

I'm waiting, just waiting for her to ask me to hand over my book. There's silence between us. We're in direct eye contact with each other ... she's going to ask now. And then she's going to take the book, and say nothing. But later ... or in the morning ... or when I least expect it, I'm going to get the summons to Mother Dick's office. Maybe me alone, or maybe both of us. Whatever way it's going to work, this is bad. Mother Dick goes nuts at this sort of thing. It contravenes her purity laws, and upsets the Baby Jesus, or whatever.

Suddenly, there's a blast of sound: "*In the naaaame, of looooove!*" Thank you, Bono!

Miss Clancy swings her head around, tutting loudly as she sees Joanne covering her mouth in laughter. All around her, the bitchy friends snigger and exchange glances. For the first time ever, I see a teacher unnerved. It's weird. But it saves my skin.

Miss Clancy says nothing more to us, just gathers herself, glances at her watch and strides toward the Bitches.

"Who turned that up," she demands firmly. "I specifically told you to turn it down. Now who was responsible?"

Needless to say, no one answers directly. The four of them glance at each other, smirking. It's Joanne who replies. "Must have been Little Frances, Miss."

I roll my eyes. They pull this Little Frances crap on new teachers all the time. It's not funny.

Miss Clancy doesn't answer them. Instead, she points to the hall door.

"Break time's over," she says. "Back to study for you."

She reaches behind the record cabinet and pulls the plug out of the socket. Commanding a nearby group of Second Years to roll it back in where it belongs, she strides out after the troublemakers.

Relief washes over me. "That was bloody close," I sigh.

Carmel is wiping her eyes with the heels of her hands, still shuddering with occasional laughter. "*Oh, Jesus!*" she wails. "Your face! But isn't that the funniest cover for a book ever? Wait till you read the dirty bits – the nun and the priest go at it in a confession box and then later on out in a cornfield. You'll *love* it!"

"Not if I get caught with it!" I hiss.

But Carmel's unstoppable laughter is contagious and before long I begin to see the funny side and laugh too.

"Take the bloody thing back!"

"Not until you've read it." She shakes her head, her eyes wide as saucers. "You *have* to read it – I command you! Sure, it'll be safe inside your goblin nonsense there till I can take it home on Friday. Have you got your torch with you? You can read it after lights out. Inflame your passions and all that!"

From the doorway, the bell rings to signify the end of Night Break.

I jump up, eager to get back quickly so that I can hide Sister Claude inside my desk and possibly transfer it to a folder, or a bigger textbook to carry to bed with me where I can then hide it somewhere safer.

"You're taking it back as soon as I've had a look through," I warn Carmel, walking backwards across the hall away from her, wagging my finger as I go. *The Hobbit* is clutched tightly across my chest with my other hand.

She smiles, waving her own hand dismissively. "Yeah, yeah – c'mere, did we get any new Maths today?"

We file back to the study hall, walking back into the warm, stagnant air of the room for the final hour before bedtime. Before I can finally get this thing hidden.

Chapter fourteen

Ria
LONDON
April 2015

"Why did you stay?"

Jess leaned back in her chair and stretched, folding her arms to study me, her head to one side.

I reached over for another Hobnob, and shrugged.

"I mean, it was 1987? Not 1887, and, as far as I'm aware, you hadn't popped a veil on and taken vows yourself, and no one was holding you against your will – it was just a *job* after all, wasn't it? A job that made you miserable with living conditions that, frankly, sound Victorian. And am I right in thinking that despite the absolute *glory* of your royal-blue shoulder pads and court heels, Leonard wasn't up for your Big Plan anymore? So what on earth were you staying there for?"

I smiled and shook my head. I *had* looked fab in that outfit, no matter what she said. I thought about it for a moment.

"Because, I suppose, I didn't know what else to *do*. I'd been so focused on The Plan for so long, I didn't know what else to focus on. Plus – there was the practicality of getting another job in the middle of the school year – it would have been impossible. I had to figure out what to do next and, with my future slowly crumbling down a cliff in front of me, I couldn't think of anywhere to go except to stay on the edge."

"I can think of more comfortable cliffs," snorted Jess.

I smiled. "Me too," I agreed.

"And what about the kid in the graveyard? Who did she turn out to be? Did you see her again?"

A chill crept over my back and shoulders and I put down the biscuit. "Yes. But lots of other things happened too. Other things to make me stay. Because, believe it or not, some of the best days of my life were coming. There – in the convent."

Jess cast me a sideways glance. "Really?"

"I told you weird things happened to me. Really. Genuinely. As the song says, *'Days I'll remember all my life'*. At the least expected time, in the least expected place, I met someone."

"The handyman with the stew-scented car!" exploded Jess.

I smiled again, but didn't laugh.

"No. It was the man ... the one I thought ... no, I *saw* today in Covent Garden," I stammered. "Him. I met him. And everything changed. It all went horribly wrong, of course, but for a brief while it all changed. And it was wonderful."

Chapter fifteen

Ria
BALLYKEERAN
October 1987

I remember it so vividly.

I met him during my free class on a Tuesday morning in October. It was the first class period, ten past nine to ten o'clock, on a dry and bright morning. A gloriously, autumnally bright morning. I can still smell it, if I try hard enough.

The sun bathed everything golden – from the ochre, russet and yellow-brown leaves on the horse-chestnuts along The Walk, to the cold grey stone itself of the chapel. It was as if the world had a glow about it that the dull walls of Maria Goretti couldn't keep out, even though it tried its hardest. Snatches of sunlight just kept filtering in, unfettered, through windows here and there, casting sunbeams along cold, tiled floors and the dusty crimson and blue-patterned carpet of the staffroom. I sat in a long beam of light which lay across the big oak table around which we had our breaks.

I was alone, notes on the first World War spread around the table, and a cold cup of instant coffee at my elbow. But I couldn't concentrate. Instead, I raised my face to the light and sat there, feeling it on my face, seeing inside my eyelids kaleidoscopes of colours against the brightness.

I felt more at odds with the convent that day than usual. Uneasy. Out of my depth, out of place. I could normally suppress it, but I was filled suddenly with a longing to be elsewhere – to go *home*, wherever that was, to be comforted and cared for. Except such a place didn't exist. The reality of the end of things with Leonard sat heavy with me. I hadn't bothered to send my letter – to finish it, even. There was no point. How could I have pinned all of my hopes on him when, the more time went on and the more I reflected, he had been humouring me all along? His ambition had never been the same as mine, his desires and wants different from my desires and wants. The Plan had been nothing – a notion. But a costly one for me. I had given up my life and my freedom to make it happen, and now I was giving up The Plan itself with no idea what would become its replacement. I felt alone, disappointed and foolish.

The room was pleasantly warm, but I had a sudden longing for fresh air – a stroll around The Walk in that crisp sunshine would have been bliss, but I knew that the nuns would see me, and that they wouldn't approve during class time. Instead, I got up from my seat and pulled open the sash window a little, closing my eyes and allowing the fresh breeze that drifted in caress me. The air smelled clean and crisp, and I took a deep gulp, hoping to somehow cleanse myself from the darkness that seemed to have crept into me.

In the distance, suddenly, I could hear music. A piano. The still air carried it so clearly. I cocked an ear: 'The Entertainer.' Of course it was. Music exams approached and 'The Entertainer' seemed to be the go-to practice tune for all the students. Night after night, I had to prise girls away from the upright piano at the bottom of the stairs – Brock's Piano, they called it, after the Coy Badger that stood guard on its lid – as they waited in turn to play as much of it as they could fit in before it was someone else's turn. Catching the familiar, plonking air through the staffroom window, I tutted loudly, and turned to go find the culprit. If they were caught by a nun during class time they would be in serious trouble. But if I could just get to them first ...

The tune changed as I turned, however, slowed down in pace, grew more sorrowful. I paused, and lifted my ear again to the window. Debussy's *Clair de Lune*. And not on the tinny upright in the porch either, the quality was too good. It was coming from somewhere else – it had to be the baby grand in the Assembly Hall. The Steinway. *Sister Cecilia's Steinway*. My stomach did a nervous flip. If a student was caught so much as touching the Steinway, it meant expulsion. I had to stop whoever it was before they lost their place in school for such a ridiculous offence.

I hurried towards the Assembly Hall, grateful and relieved to encounter no nuns headed in the same direction. Most would be in class now, I reckoned. And Benedicta simply couldn't have been in her office, because she'd be striding along the Green Corridor already if she could hear what I was hearing. I prayed silently that it wasn't a Boarder that was playing. If it were a Day Girl, at least, then it would be exclusively Benedicta's territory. If it were a Boarder, however, then somehow some of the blame would be shifted on to me. A surge of nerves coursed through me and I quickened my step.

The player was good. I had to say that for her. *Clair de Lune* segued into *Für Elise*, another music-exam favourite, and then seconds later, as I turned into the passage that led to the Assembly Hall, into the *Moonlight Sonata*. It made me pause. The playing ... it was perfect, *exquisite*, even. It wasn't the plonking, mistake-filled delivery that I heard from so many of the students – not that I was one to talk – I could barely tell which was the ebony and which the ivory – but it was note perfect, and smooth, and had *feeling*. I reached the Hall and peered around the open door, just as it speeded up again into something livelier, something bluesier. The name of it came to me just as I peered in and my mouth fell open in shock as I saw who it was, seated at the keyboard. It was, in fact, its rightful owner – Sister Cecilia, a small, stern, neat nun, only in her early forties, who presided over the music department like a queen. And she was playing, of all things ... David Bowie. The intro from 'Oh, You Pretty Things' to be precise. And watching her, tapping his foot, was a man, dressed entirely in black, at whom she looked up and grinned, her feet dancing on the pedals, her fingers flying deftly across the keys. My eyes widened as I watched her – she was relaxed, and clearly enjoying herself, her eyes twinkling as her audience-of-one raised his eyebrows and burst out laughing.

"*Bowie*, Sister?" he guffawed as she played the intro again and laughed back.

"I wasn't always a nun, you know, Mr Flynn," she laughed back, before turning her attention to the keys and finishing the piece with a flourish.

Grinning, she swivelled in her seat and folded her hands in her lap, as if waiting for praise.

The man rewarded her with applause and more laughter, shaking his head as he did.

"And you know all the lyrics as well, I suppose," he smiled.

She nodded. "Of *course*," she answered in her brisk, businesslike tone. "*Make way for the Mother Superior,*" she misquoted, grinning, and set him off again, laughing in disbelief and joy.

Beaming herself, she turned back to the piano and gathered up the sheets that sat on the music stand, sliding them into a small leather folder and, standing up, smoothed down her skirt. She was in charge of uniforms, as well as music; always impeccably turned out with her neat A-line skirt and fitted navy jacket, and ready to admonish anyone and everyone for a rolled-up sleeve, a hanging hem or a sagging sock. She even had her own music rooms which were down in the convent section of the building. She had always come across as aloof, prim and proper. To see her laugh like that, to hear how she played, and *what* she played, was a revelation. For the first time since arriving at Maria Goretti, I actually found myself looking at a nun as a person, as someone who had previously, possibly, been just like me, with a life outside the service of God; as someone who was actually capable of *enjoying* herself. It washed over me that I had never seen any of the other nuns smile, or laugh in pleasure.

Sister Cecilia tucked the folder under her arm. "I've enjoyed your company, as always, Mr Flynn," she addressed the man, "but I have lessons to prepare, a Mass to organise a choir for, and a musical to produce – so if you don't mind, I'll get going."

The man swept his arm out before him in a theatrical bow. "The pleasure is all mine, Sister," he replied.

She nodded, smiling again.

"I'll see you for the auditions then?" he asked.

She grimaced, and clicked her fingers. "Oh … the *auditions,*" she replied. "Would you believe I forgot all about them! I'll see you at ten past four then, Matthew. Will you see your mother before then? Tell her hello – I'll look forward to seeing her on opening night, as always."

"We've a long road to go before then, *pardner,*" he answered.

Sister Cecilia giggled and swatted her arm in his direction. "We *shore* do," she answered. With a small wave, she started toward the door where I stood, still unseen, and I ducked back around the corner onto the Green Corridor, bending to pretend to tie my shoe. The nun sailed past gracefully, tapping her hip with her folder in time to a tune in her head, and walked off in the opposite direction, back toward the convent, without so much as setting eyes on me.

I watched her go. She moved gracefully, her figure trim, her back straight. I had never visited her music rooms, but suddenly burned with curiosity to see what they were like. She was the only nun, other than Benedicta, who had such a thing – a space to call her own, other than wherever it was she slept. I wondered if it were full of impersonal religious artifacts, like the principal's office, or if something – anything in there – would give an insight into who Sister Cecilia was as a *woman*. The notion of it overtook me for a moment, until suddenly I could once again hear piano music come from the Hall – a scale, this time, which turned into 'Chopsticks'. Intrigued, I crept back around the corner and down the short passage to peer once again in the Hall door. The man was sitting sideways on the piano stool, idly picking out the notes with two fingers, staring directly at the door. He couldn't have missed my face, peering around the door frame, like one of the Three Stooges.

I panicked, tried to duck back again but I wasn't fast enough.

"Can I help you?" he asked.

I entered the room gingerly, aware that I had blushed pink.

"Come for the *Oklahoma* auditions?" he said, smiling.

I smiled shyly back, shaking my head.

I've never forgotten how he looked at that precise moment, the sun streaming in through the window behind him, flooding the piano with warm light. I can still see him framed that way, and hear the sound of the notes echoing around the empty space of the Hall. He was in his early thirties, his face rough with a little stubble. His eyes were brown, with long, thick eyelashes and his hair shaded his face, in need of cutting. *He's beautiful*, I thought, and blushed.

"Sorry," I replied. "I don't mean to intrude – I heard the music from the staffroom and thought it might be a student, messing about ..."

He looked taken aback for a moment, and then arranged his

features in mock outrage. "Did she sound that bad?" he asked. "Like a student?"

I blushed deeper. "No, not at all." I stammered. "The playing was ... excellent ... I just heard it from the staffroom ... I couldn't be sure ..."

"Don't mind me," he laughed suddenly. "I'm Matt Flynn, by the way. And you are ... new, obviously?"

He extended his hand and I tentatively reached out to take it.

"What's your name?"

"I'm Maria ... *Ria*," I replied. "Ria Clancy. I teach English and History here ... and I'm the Boarders'... Supervisor."

He made an 'oh' face, eyebrows raised. "The new Guardian? Interesting job."

I studied him for a moment, unsure if he was sincere or not.

A silence fell between us for a moment.

"I'm here for *Oklahoma*," he announced suddenly, realising that he still had hold of my hand and releasing it. "I help to direct and choreograph the annual musicals here. At least I have done for the past three years or so."

I nodded.

"Auditions today," he explained. "I always give Sister Cecilia a hand with them. Although, truth be told, she knows well who she wants in the parts already. She just gets me to be her back-up through the process. And makes me reject the hopeless ones ... not that they're hopeless, of course ... they're all great ... in their own ways ..." he gave a bark of nervous laughter; "which I hate, but there you go. It's what I get paid for, I suppose."

I grinned at him.

The conversation ran dry again for a moment, and we studied each other awkwardly. I was trying desperately to think of something to say, when a sudden, shrill noise filled the air. At first, I thought it was the end-of-class bell, but after a moment or two realised that something wasn't right about it. It was the wrong bell, and it was far away – much further away than the school building. Anyway, it wasn't time ... no, what I was hearing was ... it was the *dormitory* bell ... which meant that ... someone was in the dormitories during class time, which was *strictly* forbidden. Someone was up there, and had taken the bell from the cubicle of the Fifth Year in charge of it and was ringing it, incessantly, during class time. I felt the colour drain from my face.

Matt Flynn, however, was still smiling. "Is there a fire or something?" he asked.

"What? *No* ... someone's got the ... have to go ..." and with that, I fled. This was trouble. And, unlike the piano incident, it was most definitely within my jurisdiction. I retraced my panicked steps along the Green Corridor, silently praying that Benedicta wouldn't hear the bell, as she hadn't heard the piano.

I was out of luck. To my dismay, she was already standing at the foot of the stairs, looking upward, waiting for me. The bell still pealed, shrill, from above.

"Who is *that*, Miss Clancy?" she barked. Her hands were twisted together tightly, as if she was gripping herself for control, and her face burned with cold anger.

"I don't know, Mother ..." I began, trailing off as she charged up the stairs ahead of me.

"This is *not on*!" she barked back at me.

Meekly I hurried behind, listening to the bell, trying to pinpoint the source. It was coming from the main dormitory, growing louder as we climbed higher and closer ... and then stopping just as Mother Benedicta reached the dorm door.

She paused, her hand on the handle, and turned back to glare at me. "I will search," she said through gritted teeth. "And you will wait here in case our culprit tries to escape."

With that, she flung open the door and charged in, her cream leather shoes squeaking against the pine floor as she disappeared.

I could hear her calling out, "*Who is there? What girl is responsible? Come out now and hand me that bell*!"

She emerged after a few minutes, her face red and her breathing heavy. "Has any girl emerged?" she panted.

"No, Mother –" I began, but was suddenly cut off by a loud clanging noise and a thump. Benedicta's head whipped around and she let go of the door, storming back into the dormitory.

The nun was even redder when she emerged the second time, her hand inside the bowl of the bell, holding the clapper. I stared at it, noticed that it trembled slightly, and frowned as I looked at her face which I was sure would be incandescent with rage.

But it wasn't.

There was something else there, another emotion which I couldn't quite read, couldn't quite discern.

Discomfort. Confusion ... *fear?*

I looked in her wake to see who would emerge from the dormitory, whatever girl had been foolish enough to pull a stunt like that – waited also for a rage-filled tirade from the nun – to be questioned on my earlier whereabouts, on who had responsibility for the bell this week, on why this had happened, how I wasn't to allow it again, how being in the dorms outside of allocated hours was a grave misdemeanor, how it made theft possible, how it was a severe disobedience ... all of it I expected.

What I didn't expect was silence. And for her to brush past me abruptly, and walk down the stairs, one hand holding the bell silent, the other gripping the bannister, her knuckles white. And for no one, no culprit, to emerge from the dormitory behind me.

"Back to class, Miss Clancy," I heard her say as she disappeared below me.

With a final glance back at the empty silent dormitory, I followed her, too confused to be relieved.

A small group of girls stood at the bottom of the stairs peering up, who scattered like birds as Benedicta appeared. Behind them stood a couple of the lay teachers – Miss Connolly the Geography teacher, Mr Reilly the Maths teacher ... and with them, Matt Flynn. He stood there, a little apart from the others, hands in his pockets, observing the small disruption, watching Benedicta as she stormed past to her office, and then turning his attention to me as I came behind her. For a brief moment, we made eye contact, and he winked. I smiled, in a sort of odd shock. It was such a simple thing, but enormous at the same time because, in the midst of the confusion, for the first time at Maria Goretti, I didn't feel entirely alone. I felt like I had an ally.

I could have cried with gratitude.

Chapter sixteen

Lydia
BALLYKEERAN
October 1987

I'm Stage Crew again! *Yessss!* Exactly what I wanted to do! Loads of time out from lessons and study to build the set, painting and hammering and all sorts of stuff. And a trip into Portlaoise to buy supplies – nails, and paint and what have you. And none of the stupid prancing about on stage – those ridiculous dance routines that Mrs Carbery comes up with – or wearing silly costumes and that awful panstick make-up that they put on you, that you can't get off for a week. No learning songs, or lines or entrances and exits, just lifting, carrying, painting, making things – the real fun stuff. I can't imagine why anyone would want to be a principal or a dancer or anything. If I wasn't Stage Crew, I'd have just about put up with being in the chorus but I must have done a good enough job last year to get picked again this year. Happy days!

Carmel is Stage Crew as well so we'll have a bit of fun. There're five others – only seven of us out of the whole school get the gig, and they always choose Boarders because the work can get done at night-time and weekends then. Thank *God* there's something to do at the weekends between now and Christmas.

I love Musical time. It's all so different from normal. Between October and the week of our Christmas holidays, this place is actually fun – we have rehearsals, choreography sessions, the choir learning all the songs, the principal cast being announced, costume fittings – it's like a *real* theatre company. And we get to rehearse during study time, and sometimes get called out of classes and we all gather in the Hall and sit on the floor and do our homework on the windowsills and the benches – that is, if we're not on stage or on call. It's so exciting – people learning lines, talking to each other in character – and Sister Cecilia relaxed about stuff, banging away on the piano and teaching people songs.

It doesn't hurt either that there's plenty of time to stare at the magnificence of Mr Flynn. Wow, but he's changed so much, with his long hair – well, longish, we're not talking Michael Bolton or anything embarrassing here – more Michael Hutchence. He's changed so much from when he came to direct first, when I was in Second Year. Back then, he was just really weedy, with his side-parting and his skinny arms and that awful jumper he used to wear. He dresses cooler now, with his stonewash jeans and that sweatshirt covered in paint that he uses. And his stubble and all – he's a bit of a ride – no, scratch that – total ride actually.

He's really easy to talk to as well – he just chats to us like we're normal people. I suppose I'm not used to that, maybe. Nuns and teachers talk to me – well, like nuns and teachers do. And Uncle Neville still treats me like I'm seven on the rare occasion that he does actually talk to me. Mr Flynn though – he keeps telling us to call him Matt, but that feels so weird – he treats me like I'm the same age as him, even though he has to be, what, thirty-something? And he's really cool for his age – he likes The Cure and The Smiths and Prince and hates all that chart stuff like Mel and Kim and Wet, Wet, Wet. He brings in music sometimes if we're working at night-time and plays tapes for us, although not everyone shares our taste in music. Last Thursday, Joanne – she's got the part of Ado Annie, of course – just happened to have the tape of Tiffany's 'I Think We're Alone Now' and she played it seven times in a row while Sister Cecilia went to Nun's Night Prayer or whatever it is they do between eight and nine on Thursdays. Anyway, Mr Flynn – Matt – looked like he was fit to kill her, but he kept his cool while she danced and performed up and down the stage like she was onstage at Live Aid or something. And all her gang came over to the Hall during Night Tea break and stood below the stage, like they were in the front row at Wembley, clapping and cheering her on – if she was made of chocolate, she'd have eaten herself.

It was so funny then when Mr Flynn just walked over to his stereo and stopped it mid-play. The Bitches were booing him and everything, but he just ignored them and snapped the tape deck open, and just dropped the Tiffany tape and left it sitting on the floor of the stage while he unplugged the stereo and put it away and went back to work. Joanne was raging, and she had to go back to learning her lines then. And then I accidentally-on-purpose gave the Tiffany tape a little kick with my foot and sent it sliding off across the floor under the steps to Aunt Eller's house when she was in a huddle with her gang, giving out about Mr Flynn. She'll have a job finding it under there, I can tell you. Mightn't even get it back till we take the set down. It also made me feel better about the Boost bar that I took from her locker last term when she was out at games.

Mr Flynn tells us stuff too – like what's happening in the news and that – he even lets us listen to the news on his radio sometimes. The nuns get us Leaving Certs and the Fifth Years a newspaper each day – we're meant to read it for Bus. Org., for stock prices and that, but it's difficult to get time with study and everything. And if the Fifth Years get it first – they're such a crew of messers, they cut stuff out and colour it in and draw beards and willies on all the pictures and that – it's just like reading a rag by the time it gets to our section of the Study, so I don't often bother with it, even though I know I should.

There's another nice thing about the Musical every year. How Mother Dick acts while it's on. She loves how it looks to the audience during performance week, but something about rehearsals repels her. She stays away from them as much as possible, although she does float in every now and again because she feels she has to and finds fault with stupid stuff like the angle you might be sitting at – "Back straight, at once, if you don't want to be a crooked old hunchback!" or a bit of dirt on your uniform – "God doesn't love slovenly little sluts!" and stuff like that. She blows Mr Flynn's mind, I'm sure of it. When she called Deirdre Brennan a "layabout and a thug" for giving Orla Kelly a little punch on the arm when they were messing instead of doing homework, he just stopped what he was doing and *stared* at her, like she was mental. Which

92

she is, of course, but that's beside the point. I think he blows her mind too – she doesn't know what to be doing with a total ride about the place. She knew he was staring at her, and she got really flustered and stormed out that night. We all rolled about the place laughing. Mr Flynn barked at us to get back to work – and we did, because we like him, but I could tell he was totally freaked out by her.

The best conversations that I have with him, when we're working or just painting a piece of set or something, are about movies. He loves them as much as I do. He's actually a proper actor, of course. I couldn't believe that when he told us. Went to theatre school in Dublin after he finished university. He even acts in plays in Dublin when he's not down here – I don't know why he wants to help us out every year to put on our tiny little musical when he's been on proper stages like the Gaiety and stuff, but he says that he takes any work that comes his way and that he likes doing this job. He's great at everything, mind – directing and the stage and stuff. And he must be a pretty good actor too seeing as how he even acts like he gets on well with Sister Cecilia. I just don't understand how anyone could do it. Get on with a nun, that is. I don't understand them – don't understand what it is they get out of being a nun in the first place, and I don't understand why they'd give up real life and step out of it, step away from the chances to meet someone and fall in love and get married and have kids and travel the world – except for the Missions, maybe. I cannot understand someone who would want to live a life where they'd give up music and movies and freedom and fun. I mean, what do they contribute to society, locking themselves away when they could be doing good things like nursing, or working with animals or something? I mean yeah, the teaching nuns – I guess they're doing *something*. But why become nuns to do it?

I would *never* in a million years want to be a nun. No. I want to go to college and study movies and stuff. And then maybe work in them – in the background – be a set designer, or something like that. Mr Flynn says that the Irish movie industry is growing all the time and to follow my heart. He says that it's not an easy path to take, but that I'll be happier if I do it. Poorer, but happier, he said. I'm not sure about the poorer bit, mind – I don't want to live at Uncle

Neville's in the Ancestral Dump forever – but it seems like a really exciting life.

Mr Flynn is so sound. And I fancy him, but I don't, if you know what I mean? Joanne's always flirting with him – so's Karen Dunne who's playing Aunt Eller and the two of them try to outdo each other, acting up to him, and asking him questions in these sweet little voices. I'm sure that they think he's going to suddenly sweep one of them up in his arms and kiss them and tell them that he loves only them forever and take them away in his dirty old Citroen – his car is *gross!* So yeah, he's a total ride, and yes, he's lovely, but I just can't think about him in a romantic way – I tried, but it didn't feel right, so I went back in my head to Judd Nelson and Johnny Marr.

Anyway. Happy days are here again – my last Musical is working out just peachy for me – my favourite job, and some sound people to do it with. Couldn't be better.

Can't wait for the next couple of months now. It'll be the best craic. As good as it gets here, in fact.

Chapter seventeen

Ria
BALLYKEERAN
October 1987

It felt like spring had come in October. Even though the days were getting shorter and colder, the whole place was *transformed*. The walls that had made me feel so trapped and helpless were suddenly completely different because now *he* was within them. I never knew when he'd arrive, so every day was filled with opportunity – I just tingled with the mere *chance* that he might be there when I turned a corner, or looked up, or walked into a room.

He became my North Star and I set my daily course by him – what I wore, how my hair looked, the route that I took to classrooms, my afternoon stroll as I supervised games, what I did with my time off – just in the hope that I might catch sight of him. Some days we chatted, briefly; others, we simply exchanged a smile before carrying on about our business.

Every morning when I woke, he – and the mere chance that I might *see* him – was my first thought; at night, he came into my head and fell asleep with me. All day long, I daydreamed about him, his glorious smile beaming back at me, across a room where it was forbidden. It was all so delicious.

At first, I chastised myself – I was a grown woman, but I was acting no better than the girls, many of whom were completely infatuated with him as well. If he passed in the hallways, they'd blush and giggle as he went by, peering over their shoulders to watch him go, nudging each other and exchanging looks. Around him, they talked a little louder, laughed a little harder in an effort to be noticed. I knew it was stupid, but when they flirted, I felt *jealous*.

I knew that he went to bed with them every night as well, their fantasies soundtracked by the music that they listened to on their forbidden radios and personal stereos to which I turned a blind eye – there was a group of Fourth Years who would break into Peter Cetera's 'Glory of Love' when they knew he was around. Some just stared at him from behind books as they attended rehearsals, others blushed and stammered when he spoke to them.

Pretty soon, it became evident that he needed to spend a lot of time about the place, usually in the Hall, working on the stage every afternoon, directing at night-time, taking the principals out of study to work through scenes. Then I began to see him during the school day, often on the corridors between classes. Then he started using the kettle in the staffroom to make himself a coffee – he always seemed to be just about to leave when I arrived in for small break in the mornings, but would stay long enough to exchange pleasantries. Some days, I'd find him in there, reading a book, or scanning a newspaper, ready with a smile when I walked in; others, he'd be perched on the long oak staff table, a coffee in hand, chatting with a group of the other teachers – and charming each and every one of them. I'd go about my business when he was there, always listening. Listening to how he'd talk football with Ted O'Connor, who taught Irish, flowers with Miss Connolly, who was a keen gardener, athletics with Ellen Morris, the PE teacher. I'd watch them – him, leaning into the conversation, head bent and listening before speaking, and then after a while both of them throwing their heads back in laughter at whatever he'd said. They'd leave him with a smile, a 'See you later, Matt' or 'I'll keep an eye out for that' or something … something *comfortable*. Around him, you couldn't help but feel valid, interesting even.

He'd always smile at me across the staffroom. More than the others. And then we started to chat more, talking easily about everything and nothing. And sometimes, I imagined he leaned in to my conversations closer than the others, touched my arm against his as he spoke. Sometimes he'd offer to walk with me "as far as the

Hall", or "down to class". Once or twice, he'd appear beside me as I did my afternoon circuits of The Walk, supervising outdoor games. He'd complete one round with me, saying that he had to clear his head, before slipping away again as we passed the back door of the school, back to work, back to his cast and crew.

Sometimes, I'd hear music come from the Hall – all sorts, jazz, classical, pop – songs from other musicals. That was when he was alone, playing the piano. Often, I contemplated going in – I'd fight with myself, one part of me urging myself to go and be with him for a few moments, to see his smile, to feel that *feeling* that being with him gave me. I fought it every time, however – as it was, the other teachers had started to look at us in the Staffroom, and the students would giggle and whisper if he and I so much as walked in the same direction. One night, when rehearsals were in full swing in the Hall, the door of the Study had squeaked quietly open and in he strode. A wave of giggling and whispers rippled through the desks as, one by one, each girl looked up and saw him walk along between them. I, in my usual seat on the teacher's dais in the Senior section, couldn't help but grin – at the sight of him, but also at the way he was acting – grinning at them, doing a stupid, exaggerated walk and shushing them before reaching my desk and asking, whispering *"Please, Miss, could Ailish Conlon and Vanessa Doherty come out to rehearse for their scene?"*

My stomach flipped. There were dried paint spatters in his hair. I fought the urge to reach up and touch it, blushing deeply as a low '*Wooooh*' started with some of the Leaving Certs, and spread to the four corners of the room. My face turned to thunder. Panicking, I tried to silence them. He managed it with a single frown, before turning back to me and grinning: that stupid, handsome, gorgeous grin. I nodded, only permitting the faintest smile to cross my lips as he beamed back at me before waltzing out with his actors. I watched him leave, dressed in jeans and a black T-shirt, leather bands around his wrists and holes in his trainers. He smiled again from the door as he closed it behind him and I felt my head spin and my cheeks burn. I was embarrassed and delighted at once. Completely and utterly infatuated.

Chapter eighteen

Ria
LONDON
April 2015

"I get it," laughed Jess, covering her ears and leaning back in her seat. "I get it so much that I think I just did a little sick in my mouth!"

I bit my lip. "I'm sorry," I said. "I forgot myself for a moment there – I haven't thought about this stuff in almost thirty years – it was like I had forgotten completely up until now ... until ..."

I was lying again, of course.

"Sounds like you had completely forgotten about Leonard too." She smirked at me and flicked her empty cup with her forefinger, making a small 'ding' sound.

"I had. I confess I had indeed." I laughed. "He was so far away ... not just physically, not just because our contact was limited to calls that he was never there to answer, or letters that he'd never write but ... he ... Leonard didn't make me feel ... the way I felt about Matt ..."

I took a deep breath to clear my mind.

"What I've just described, to your mortification – that stupid, childish, schoolgirl thrill – I had *never* felt that way before. In my life. Which sounds stupid, because by the time you're twenty-five, *everyone* should have felt that tingling, crazy, excited sense of infatuation at least once. Leonard might have been the plan for the rest of my life but he had never ... *excited* me, which sounds ridiculous, but meeting Matt … it was like *waking up*, like I had been asleep my whole life, going through the motions, plodding along, and here I was, with all of these feelings coursing through me, my every move governed by thoughts of him … it was like tasting *champagne* after a lifetime of drinking dishwater. It was *wonderful*. It was *delicious! Exhilarating*! So I hardly even thought of Leonard anymore – there was no room for him in my head because Matt filled it, and I didn't want it any other way."

Jess gave a low whistle. "I have to say, Ria – you're the *last* person on earth that I'd have said would have been feeling *delicious* in a *convent* of all places!"

"I know," I replied. "It went against everything that I had planned for myself. Occasionally, that would cross my mind – why was I there, being a lackey for a bunch of nuns, freezing cold, eating terrible food, surrounded by giggling teenagers, twenty-four hours a day? I may as well have been in prison and for what? Was I still going to go through with it? Go to Boston? Go live the life that I had planned so meticulously? With someone who I suddenly realised was becoming a fading memory? When those thoughts came, I just shoved them away, to be honest. Just put them back underneath everything else – the excitement, the daydreaming – it was foolish, I knew. And I also knew I was going to have to face up to my future at some stage soon – after all, this dream, this fantasy, nothing could really come of it, could it? And it would have to end – come Christmas, when the musical was over, when the curtain had finally fallen on everything – when Matt would go back to his life – whatever or wherever that was. You see how stupid this whole thing was? I barely even knew the guy, yet here he was, occupying every second of my life."

"But it was wonderful, right?" Jess smiled kindly.

I nodded. "It was, yes," I replied, smiling, but it faded quickly. "But winter was on the way – the place was getting colder, the evenings darker – there were shadows that always danced at the edges. It was like Matt gave off a light that illuminated everything I did, but it couldn't quite reach the corners. And that's where the bad stuff was. There was so much bad stuff to come – I just didn't know it."

Chapter nineteen

Ria
BALLYKEERAN
October 1987

My job, first thing in the mornings, was to patrol. To walk slowly, and quietly, around the dormitories like some sort of jailer, to '*keep silence and order*', the handbook told me. There was hardly any need for me there, however. The Goretti Girls, whether it was through habit or fear, more or less kept silence and order for themselves. I, used to kids who took any opportunity in the slightest to giggle or make mischief with their friends, found it odd that they complied so blindly with the rules, yet they did, appearing from their cubicles in their dressing gowns first thing to queue silently for the toilets and to fill their plastic basins with – probably cold – water. Once this was done, and they were dressed neatly behind the privacy of their curtains, they'd emerge for a second time to empty the basins in which they had washed, returning to fix their beds and tidy their cubicles before pulling their curtains open wide and making their silent way down the stairs to change their shoes and put on their coats for Mass. They'd make someone perfect Stepford Wives some day, I was sure.

I often pictured myself as a snail, my progress slow and direct, while surrounded by ants, bustling about at efficient speed, carrying their loads, minding their own business. I was one species, and they another and we didn't – couldn't – understand each other. I supervised both floors of girls alone – making the occasional check down to the Sisters' Corridor but mostly I paced the polished wooden floor of the long dormitory above.

Which is why it came as such a shock to come across the nun one Tuesday morning while I did my rounds. Deep in thoughts of Matt Flynn, I rounded the corner at the top of the room, and had to stop suddenly, as she blocked my path, standing as she was, silently staring into the cubicle of one of the girls.

It was Benedicta. She stood with the curtain of the girl's cubicle held wide open. I took a step forward so that I could see what the nun was looking at, and at once stepped back, ashamed at my intrusiveness. The girl stood with her back to the nun, wearing only a pair of flannel pyjamas bottoms, the top flung on the bed while she washed herself with a sponge at her basin of water, completely topless. I itched with discomfort at the intrusion, the girl's semi-nudity on show to anyone who cared to pass. I turned suddenly as I heard the gentle slosh of water behind me, and silently redirected the student carrying her washbasin to be emptied in the sink to go back to her cubicle. I couldn't allow the poor, exposed girl to be seen like this by her peers. I turned back again to Benedicta, expecting her to drop the curtain and leave the student in peace, but she showed no signs of doing so. Instead, she remained where she was, watching – what was she doing? What could she be waiting for? Or was she simply *watching* a teenage girl perform private bodily functions? Anxiety bubbled within me and I just couldn't bear it any longer, but as I opened my mouth to speak so did the nun.

"*Miss Madigan!*" she barked sharply.

I flinched at the tone of her voice. Around me, the bustling sounds of the girls at their morning ablutions in the neighbouring cubicles, all protected by their curtains, suddenly stopped. The air grew still and silent, permeated by unease. There was no sound from the girl in the cubicle. Unable to hang back, I stepped forward again. *Miss Madigan* – Lydia Madigan, the girl who always looked apart, as though she had a carefully maintained shell constructed about her. It made Benedicta's violation of her privacy even more discomfiting.

"*Miss Madigan!*" This time it was louder, and harsher.

It startled me, and most likely all of the silent listeners in their cubicles. It also startled Lydia Madigan, who turned suddenly, and shrieked at the sight of her observer, jamming her arms against her body to hide her breasts, and turning to scrabble at her pyjamas top on the bed. There was another loud clatter, this time from inside her cubicle as something fell to the floor. I glanced down, as much to avert my eyes from the poor girl's embarrassment as anything. My stomach flipped as I saw what had bounced onto the floor. It was a Walkman. I glanced back at Lydia's face in horror and saw her fumble to remove the headphones which had remained on her head when the Walkman fell and disconnected from the jack. Her expression was also one of horror. Horror at being exposed naked, horror at being caught with something that was entirely forbidden. She stared at Benedicta, her eyes wide, and gulped, her skin burning red from her chest up. I looked away again.

And still the nun stood in the same position, staring at her, completely silent. It was unbearable, like waiting for a gunman to open fire, or an animal to attack. I braced myself, waiting for the tirade to begin. But nothing came. Instead, her eyes still fixed on Lydia, Benedicta bent slowly at the knees, her back straight, and picked up the personal stereo with one hand. Once she stood again, she extended the other for the headphones which Lydia, shaking, gave her, all the while pressing her pyjama top against herself for protection.

Sharply, Benedicta's hands closed around the device. "I am disappointed in you, Miss Madigan," she said. "Four o'clock," and with that she turned, allowing the curtain to fall back into place, fixing me with a stare so ferocious that I stepped backwards. "And you, Miss Clancy ..." her tone was the same as that she had used on the student, "You will be in my office after assembly. Immediately. Do not be late."

With that, she brushed past me and left.

I wasn't late. I was too afraid to be late. But she was. So while I waited, I was left standing meekly and nervously outside her office door while the students filed to their classes past me.

The Day Girls stared, some of them nudging each other at the sight, and giggling. There was even an occasional "You in trouble, Miss?" and some tutting and finger-wagging. It was humiliating, for sure, but not half as unnerving as the reaction of the Boarders who passed me by in uncomfortable silence, none of them catching my eye, some of them looking downright fearful. I felt sick with nerves.

It was a full ten minutes before Benedicta strode around the corner and, without any acknowledgement, brushed past me and into her office, leaving the door ajar for me to enter behind her. I approached her desk nervously as she opened a drawer and pointed down into it at Lydia Madigan's Walkman before slamming the drawer shut.

"I was wondering, Miss Clancy," she bit, "where the rest of the *confiscated items* might be?"

She fixed me in her stare and I stared back, my mind blank. I opened my mouth to speak, but nothing came out.

"The radios," she prompted. "The tape-players and whatnot. Unsuitable reading material. Sometimes even food? I've noted that you haven't passed any of these items on to myself, as head of the school, and I was wondering where they might be?"

I shook my head, unable to think of a response.

"You see, usually, by this stage of the year, our appointed Guardian will have collected some items – *distractions* – that the students have brought back with them. Like this one from Lydia Madigan which slipped through the net. You know that there are strict rules in place about the possession of such things. Did I not speak to you about this?"

I struggled to respond. My tongue felt huge in my mouth. "Yes, you did, but ..." I managed before the nun calmly interrupted again.

"Then where are the items that you have confiscated over your first month in your position here? Or are *all* the students especially well-behaved this term? Are you so wonderful a Guardian that there are no infractions under your guidance?"

I took a breath to calm myself. "There aren't any ..."

"Oh no, Miss Clancy." The nun gave a short, bitter laugh as she shook her head. "There most certainly are. Do you mean to tell me that you haven't taken any such items into your possession?"

"I ... I didn't find any ... there were none ..."

I felt my cheeks flame red as I spoke. The nun didn't respond, just continued to glare at me. My heart raced, and I could feel my blood rush through my body in the silence.

"There was this one," she eventually answered. "And there were the others which were retrieved yesterday afternoon when I had the dormitories and all rooms thoroughly searched."

I flushed deeper.

"We found a number of items – among them, those I've listed previously. Also, a magazine down the back of a locker – sweet wrappers in the bin – all items to which I should have been alerted. To which *you* should have alerted me, Miss Clancy. Appropriate punishments will be carried out. A number of students will be required to keep their cubicles ready for spot-check examination for the remainder of the year – which *you* will carry out, Miss Clancy. A number of parents will be receiving telephone calls over the coming weekend, requesting that the girls not return Sunday evening ..."

"*Expelled*?" I couldn't help myself, but I was horrified – yes, rules were rules, but to expel a teenager for having a *magazine*?

Mother Benedicta closed her eyes for a moment, almost as if counting to ten, before answering. "For now, suspended," she replied. "Although if the transgression takes place again, expulsion is certainly warranted. Unfortunate, of course. But a girl who is expelled, is a girl who has expelled *herself*." She allowed this to sink in. "Now to what was found in Miss Madigan's cubicle this morning. You will be with her at four o'clock, Miss Clancy."

I frowned. "So she's not allowed to participate in after-school activities ..."

The nun twitched violently. "I don't mean four o'clock as in after school, Miss Clancy," she said.

I looked at her, puzzled for a few moments before it finally dawned on me what she meant. "You mean four o'clock in the *morning*?"

There was neither yay or nay from the nun, just a twitch of her lip, and a tap of a finger on the desk.

"She is required to be at her desk in the Study Hall at four thirty, is that understood? She will use the time and solitude to read through a list of the school rules which will be supplied to her – and that done, to *think* about what she has done and resolve herself, through contemplation and prayer, to not do it again. You will ensure that she does this, Miss Clancy, is that understood?"

I nodded in disbelief.

"She is *not* to use the time to revise, or complete homework of any sort. It is not a time to benefit her. It is a time of punishment and reflection. She will also be required to write a letter of apology to the school, with a promise not to bring such items onto the premises ever again. I will not expel her on this occasion as she is due to complete her Leaving Certificate in June. However, as a Leaving Cert student, Lydia Madigan knows what is required of her. However, I find her ... *challenging*."

She paused and sighed, finally looking away from me and down at her desk.

"Miss Clancy, I have thought long and thought hard about *your* actions in this situation – or your inaction, such as it is. I am disappointed in you."

She paused to allow this to sink in, to sting.

"However, as it is your first term here, I will give you a chance." She fell silent again.

I realised it was my turn to speak.

"Thank you, Mother," I replied.

She nodded, still avoiding eye contact with me.

"On the understanding," she continued, "that from now on, you will improve. As is expected of you, we require that the students be ... *controlled,* be observed more prudently, and that confiscated items, along with the names of the girls who owned them, are brought to my office. Spot checks will be conducted – that is your fault, Miss Clancy, so I warn you, we will know if you are doing your job or not. We are taking your poor performance in this area so far as due to a lack of understanding – I assume we are correct in that? Because ..." she caught my eye again, fixed me in a cold stare, "be warned, Miss Clancy – there is no room here at Maria Goretti for teachers who somehow think that they are *more* than the rules. Who think that they can be cohort as well as mentor, conspirator as well as disciplinarian, to run with the hare and hunt with the hounds, as it were. You are their Guardian – an *authority* figure – and you must act accordingly. You are on the side of right, Miss Clancy. Not the side of rule-breaking, transgression and wrong. The girl who is allowed to break the rules, to bring what she likes where she likes or do what she wishes today, is the girl who is fallen tomorrow. Strength in Purity, Maria. To be strong, they must be pure. To be pure, they must *keep the rules*. I trust that you can deal with Miss Madigan for now. A written report on this incident will go on your file, and you will start afresh tomorrow morning."

She locked the drawer where she had put the stereo.

"Remember what you are paid to do, Maria," she warned. "And always remember who is in charge. You are dismissed."

I left, pulling the door closed silently behind me, back out into the silence of the corridors, emptied of girls and teachers as a new class period got under way, wondering if what I had just been told to do was really an order? Was she serious? Was she even allowed to punish a student like that?

And it was only later that day that I finally figured it out, that it finally dawned on me, that the morning's events had not been to catch a student out – after all, if the cubicles had been searched the previous afternoon, then why had Lydia Madigan been allowed to keep her Walkman overnight? Why hadn't it been taken away yesterday? Why hadn't Benedicta dealt with her in private, like the other students?

Because it wasn't Lydia Madigan who was in trouble, was it?

No. Benedicta's presence in the dorm that morning hadn't been to catch out an errant student. It was to make an example of *me*. I was the one who needed to be caught out, who hadn't behaved according to Mother Benedicta's wishes. *I* was the one who was really in trouble. *I* was the one who was being taught a lesson.

Chapter twenty

Ria
BALLYKEERAN
October 1987

It was dark outside, the October morning made bleaker by the storm which had risen in the night and whipped the building outside. Rain drummed off the windows and, when the wind gusted, they'd rattle loudly in their old frames. It sounded for all the world like someone was beating on them, demanding to be let in.

I dressed quickly, running a facecloth over my face and a brush through my hair. My eyes stung. The alarm had gone off at half past three. I couldn't be late. I wondered if I was being observed to make sure that I carried out this punishment. Lydia was on my mind from the second I awoke and I hoped that she was getting ready above me in the main dormitory. Girls being punished were given a special alarm clock to wake them to ensure that they were up on time. They had to dress in darkness and silence, however. I thought of poor Lydia alone in the dark upstairs with the rain pounding the windows while her peers slumbered on around her, cosy in their beds.

It was just twenty past four when I locked my door behind me and crept along the Sisters' Corridor as fast, and silently, as I could in the darkness – turning on lights anywhere, other than my own small room, was prohibited – feeling my way along by counting the doorframes with my hand as quietly as I could – then out onto the pitch-black landing, and down the stairs. The back of my neck prickled as I made my way, the wind flinging a torrent of rain at the stained-glass window on the landing as I passed. It was freezing, too. The central heating wouldn't come on for another two hours. Finally I reached the bottom step where I flicked on the hallway light, finally able to see my immediate surrounds, although the darkness still pressed against the glass panels in the doors that led off it into the locker rooms and through the arch to the staffroom and Mother Benedicta's office. I shivered suddenly, and turned the handle of the Study Hall.

When I opened the door, I was surprised to see that Lydia was already there, sitting in total darkness, her shape illuminated in the light from the hallway behind me, already hunched over her desk. How odd, I thought, and felt with my hand along the wall beside me for the light switch. Surely the up-at-fours didn't have to sit there in the dark too, did they? Surely not? Part of their punishment was to read the school rules, so they would have to be allowed some light.

I was just about to gently call her name when I heard the footsteps behind me, coming down the stairs. Heavy, steady footsteps. I froze, for a second, before starting an even more frantic search with my hand along the wall for the light switch – *where was the damn thing?* As if on cue, the wind's screech began to strengthen and ascend unstoppably. A bolt of fear ran through my entire body as a powerful gust battered the walls, rain pelting against the window like stones, a great screech rising through the air, causing every window frame in the dark Study Hall to beat a thunderous tattoo as they rattled. I was sure that I whimpered as I turned finally, unable to stop myself, desperate to see what it was that had followed me down the stairs. A nun, surely? Who had been sent to spy on me? But in my terror, in the electricity of the air, I felt sure that it was something else ...

Blessed Frances slams the doors, and runs around the upstairs floors ...

My fingers found the Study Hall light switch at the moment that I turned and I was suddenly bathed in glorious, comforting light. The great gust of wind subsided as quickly as it had risen to a crescendo, and momentary relief flooded through me as I recognised who it was that had come down the stairs. Only momentarily, however. A look of puzzlement and relief also crossed the features of Lydia Madigan, who stood on the third-from-last step, clutching her chest.

"Miss …" she said, her voice trembling. "I got a fright there."

"Lydia," I replied, feeling my heart hammer in my chest, "it's you … but …"

I swung around, taking a step into the Study Hall, searching, for who … what … I was certain had been there moments before.

Except now there was nothing. The room was empty, the desks neat and bare, as they had been the evening before when I had wrapped up Sunday Study. Every desk was unoccupied, even Lydia's – the desk where I had seen a figure only moments before.

Chapter twenty-one

BALLYKEERAN
August 1942

The child shouldn't have been watching – shouldn't even have been in the kitchen. She should have still been in her room. On her knees, in prayer for repentance, if she was truly obeying her mother's orders. But she was hungry – so hungry. Mammy had barely left her room these past few days and Dada – well, he'd hardly been around at all since the night he came home and told Mammy he'd found her. Even Setanta wasn't around. He must have run off that night she'd left the door open for him.

Dada looked tired, she thought, from her hiding place at the base of the hot press in the kitchen, where they kept their good shoes. She watched him through a crack in the door. There was someone else with him now – his friend, Ned Gorman. The undertaker. She'd seen him arrive earlier, carrying the small white coffin.

"Does she know, James?" she heard him ask.

Dada stood at the sink, washing his hands. He turned to look at Ned and for a moment she could see that the water that ran from his hands was pink. He must have cut himself.

He shook his head. "It'd kill her," he replied. "As it is, she's taken to the bed with her rosary. I'm fearful there'll be another episode. I can't let that happen, Ned." His voice dropped to a whisper. "They'll take her into the Mental and I won't get her back

again – and who would look after the little one? She has to be …
watched …"

The child's blood felt cold as it ran through her. She knew that
she was "the little one". And now she was all that was left. She bit
her cheek hard.

"You'll have to tell her, James," Ned urged.

Dada looked around, and shushed him. "Don't let her hear you,
Ned."

"But you can't lie to her …"

There was silence for a moment. Her father moved from her line
of vision so the child couldn't see him. But she heard the sob. He
was crying again. She hated that. Dadas weren't supposed to cry.

"She *can't* know, Ned. She can't know the truth – and you can't
tell anyone either – *you* shouldn't even know."

Silence again.

"Well, is there something to go in it?"

Dada stepped back to where he had been. He looked downcast,
miserable. He nodded.

He cried again.

And so did the child. Silent tears coursed down her cheeks. She
didn't know what he meant, but she knew it was bad. Knew it was
the worst. Knew that no one wanted her anymore

Knew that she was completely alone.

Chapter twenty-two

Ria
LONDON
April 2015

Jess stared at me, her head tilted to one side, her expression confused.

"So let me get this straight … first of all, as punishment, you had to get up at *four o'clock in the morning*?"

I nodded. "It was when the saints rose to pray, or something. The most meditative, thoughtful time to think about your transgressions. It was seen as a blessing to rise early, believe it or not."

"Oh yes," Jess nodded vehemently. "That's what I always say when the beagle next door kicks off at a fox *at four am*, or when my back wakes me up and I have to take painkillers *at four am* or when the dawn chorus starts chirping *at four am*. A blessing, I say! Why would I want to, I dunno, *sleep* when I could be up *at four am!*" She shook her head in disbelief.

I smiled.

"No wonder you hallucinated someone in the bloody room," she chuckled, looking at me, expecting that I would join in.

But I didn't.

I took a deep breath and thought for a moment. Here it was again, that feeling that I was sounding ridiculous, unhinged. This, I remembered, was why I had never shared this with anyone before. Anyone.

"At the time I put it down to an optical illusion," I began. "When I looked back, the overhead light had flickered on and the shape was gone. I thought I was seeing things because I was tired, it was dark, unfamiliar, stormy, all that jazz."

"At the time?" prompted Jess, frowning.

I shrugged, trying to appear casual. "It was a creepy old place. And October brought with it more darkness. We closed the study shutters before study time began at six o'clock, instead of later in the evening, and in the mornings the light was still dull and murky when we opened the dormitory shutters before making our way out into the wind and leaves for Mass. A gloom seemed to hang over the place, making it greyer and colder and murkier. I wasn't used to this sort of environment. It made me ... jumpy, I guess. It would have made *anyone* jumpy, come to think of it. And I grew jumpier – I began to dread walking through the place on my own, nervous of what waited around dark corners for me, jumping at shadows."

"Sounds like it really got to you," said Jess, looking at me funny.

"There were sounds too. In the evenings, when the other teachers and lay students had gone home, when I was alone with the Boarders and the nuns, the place was silent, but still *filled* with sounds – the shuffling from slippers and soft-soled shoes, forbidden whispers, occasional escaping laughter. From locker rooms that should have been empty, from dormitories where girls were forbidden to go except at bedtimes, from hallways and echoing passages and empty classrooms. I could never tell if the noises were from girls who were somewhere that they shouldn't have been, or my imagination, or something else. I began to think I was imagining seeing things too – shadows where they shouldn't have been, moving shadows – once, I was so sure that a girl had run from one room across the Sisters' Corridor into another that I chased after her, calling her ..."

"Except there was no one there, right?"

"Right. Not a living soul. I might have been going mad, of course. Another morning I could hear singing ..." I sighed. "My room was at the end of the passage and my routine was to check each room as I made my way out to the stairs, once all of the girls had gone down to the locker room to get their outdoor gear on to go out to the chapel. So, as I left my room, I could hear this ... humming ... like, you know that sort of preoccupied tuneless humming that a kid does when they're lost in a game? Well, when I left my room and locked it, the humming sounded as if it were coming from the rooms nearest the door out onto the landing – the opposite end of the corridor to my room. I thought there must have been a girl left behind – probably just a slowcoach who'd come dashing out any second and leg it off down the stairs. But when I got to those rooms, there was no one there. And the weirdest thing was that the humming seemed to have … *moved*. It sounded now like it was coming from *behind* me."

Jess crossed her arms. "The wind? Old rattly, draughty windows?"

"Could have been," I replied. "Except for one thing … the humming happened while I was moving, while I was locking the door, checking the rooms, walking. But when I'd stop – pause to listen, or try to figure out where it was coming from, it would stop too. Like someone was doing it on purpose."

There was silence between us for a moment while Jess simply stared at me. I felt goosebumps rise on my arms.

"I became aware, too, that I was being watched. For real, I mean this time. By the nuns. My room was searched a couple of times, as I'd been warned – I'd come back up after class to change for afternoon games and find things moved around. Not subtly either." I paused to laugh. "Once, they'd even folded my pyjamas and put them under my pillow, instead of where I'd left them at the end of the bed, as if to show me up as the slattern I was. I suddenly found myself under constant supervision – a nun, not necessarily Benedicta, would suddenly appear when I was monitoring the dormitories at night or in the morning. Or I'd be paid a visit in the Refectory during mealtimes, or I'd look up during study time from my reading or corrections and see a nun peering around the Study Hall door."

"Jesus!" exclaimed Jess.

"Benedicta started studying me too – telling me off for wearing shoes that weren't quite right, or reminding me that silence had to be observed at Mass at all times – little, incongruous things, undermining me, niggling at me. It was clear that since I hadn't been complying with the rules on monitoring forbidden items, that any trust the good Sisters of Maria Goretti had in me was gone – or dwindling, at least. They were putting me in my place.

Reminding me that I had no more power there than one of the students, as far as they were concerned."

Jess adjusted herself in her seat and shook her head. "Still don't know why you stayed there. What did the lovely Matt have to say about all this, by the way? Your newfound ally?"

I shook my head. "I didn't tell him."

"*What?* You have one individual in the world that you can talk to, and who'll talk to you, and you don't tell them that you're being killed by a thousand paper cuts from a religious nut who wears cream soft-soled shoes?"

I chuckled. "So many crimes! No, I didn't – I mean, I was infatuated, but I didn't think … I didn't want to … look – I was twenty-five years old. You know when you meet a new guy, and you really like them and you don't want to put a foot wrong?"

"I remember it from the distant past," Jess smiled.

"Well, it was *that*. I didn't tell him about being under supervision because then I thought he'd start to look at me differently – like, wondering what was wrong with me that I couldn't do my job right. And besides which, I didn't want him to think I was too much in cahoots with the nuns because – well, that's not very fanciable, is it? And I didn't want to tell him about being permanently freaked out over shadows because – that's just nuts. So I sort of preserved myself as this girl who didn't say much that meant anything – I thought he'd like me better that way. Keeping it light, keeping it flirty."

Jess rolled her eyes. "The start of every meaningful relationship, eh?"

"It helped me get by, too. That October was … *dark* for me. Dark outside, dark inside – the convent, and *me*. It was such a struggle, and I didn't want to ruin the one bit of light that there was in my life. So I knuckled down and pretended that none of the bad stuff was happening and tried to focus on Matt and my – thus far – imaginary relationship with him. But it was only imaginary for a short while."

"Which bit – the bad stuff, or the relationship?"

I rubbed my hands over my face and blinked. The night had drawn on, and tiredness was beginning to work on me.

"Both," I replied. "Both."

Chapter twenty-three

Ria
BALLYKEERAN
October 1987

I found her outside at the school gates on the Friday evening of the Bank Holiday weekend. She startled me, stepping out from the shadows as I made my way toward the front gate. It was five o'clock – it had taken me an hour after school had finished to pack a weekend bag and organise my books in the Staffroom, and I could see Tom Gorman's battered car with its engine running waiting for me, parked just inside the main gate. A part of me was filled with relief at getting out of Maria Goretti for three days. Another part, however, was filled with dread at the thought of heading back to Dublin.

My plans for the long weekend were uncertain. Instead of going to Leonard's, I had asked a friend, a former colleague from Terenure, if I could stay with her and she, surprised, and polite, had said yes. I regretted asking as soon as I had put the phone down. The truth was that we weren't exactly friends – we had worked together and socialised a few times, but she had another circle entirely. It would be awkward landing in her flat, not really knowing her, without any real connection. I felt that I had already outstayed my welcome before even arriving.

Of course, I'd have to see Leonard at some point too. That, I was dreading, but it couldn't be avoided anymore. The more time went on, it became clear that we had been over for months now. This

116

weekend, it would have to end formally. Both of us had to be set free. And instead of saddening me, a strange excitement filled me at the thought of it.

Maybe, of course, that was because of Matt. I started to drift off into yet another of the million daydreams that flitted around my mind every hour of the day but stopped myself suddenly. He, too, was another reason why I had to get out of the convent for a time. I had grown slightly, unrealistically, obsessed. He got me through the day, yes, but solely in my head – and there was certainly an attraction, but I had to be honest with myself and acknowledge that any connection between us was probably because I was the only unmarried lay teacher under the age of forty-five in the place. I needed the distance from both him and the impossible environment that made it all the more appealing. I had been incredibly naïve with Leonard. I was determined not to be that way with Matt. I needed to come up for air, to detox. I needed perspective.

The light was fading, and a steady rain had begun to fall by the time I encountered her. Lydia's fringe was already damp where it hung down under the great hood of her gabardine coat.

"Lydia!" I jumped at the sight of her. "What are you still doing here? You should have been gone an hour ago?"

"I know, Miss," she replied. "I was supposed to get a lift from my uncle's friend but he's late – I'm sure he'll be here in a minute though."

The rain became more persistent as we spoke, and a wind suddenly rose, whipping our coats up violently. We turned our backs against the gust as it drove rain against us.

"You'd better wait inside," I told her, but she shook her head.

"I'm grand, thanks, Miss," she shouted against the wind. "He won't be long."

For a second, I believed her – believed her because I wanted to go myself. I glanced at Tom Gorman sitting patiently staring out his windscreen, his engine running, waiting to take me to the train and then glanced back at the girl whose face was damp and, despite her bravado, whose eyes were filled with concern. I didn't really have a choice.

I dashed over to the old man's car, gesturing for him to roll down the window and told him that I'd be another while.

He nodded, good-naturedly. "You'll be tight for the five twenty though," he responded. "Next one's not till seven twenty-five. I'll come back for you at seven, that alright?"

My heart sank. Two hours more of waiting, and I was impatient now to get gone. I glanced back at Lydia, getting more soaked by the minute and nodded.

"That's fine, Tom, thanks very much," I replied.

He nodded and waved, and drove off into the rainy evening. I watched his tail-lights disappear through the main gate, under the blue metal arch, my heart heavy.

I helped her carry her bags to the convent porch, which was unlocked, and we stood there for a moment, surrounded by the smell of the geraniums, shaking the rain off our wet selves. We surely wouldn't be there long.

There was silence between us as we waited, Lydia chewing on her sleeve at the wrist, as she leaned against the door, keeping an intent eye on the gate. I stood on the other side of the porch, arms folded, rocking back and forth on my heels, our weekend bags on the floor between us.

"Thank Crunchie it's Friday," I quipped, to no response. "Have you something nice planned for the weekend, Lydia?"

Lydia glanced at me and then back out the window, in case she might miss the arrival of her lift. "No, Miss," she replied quietly.

"No getting dressed up, or heading to a disco? All the Day Girls seem to be going to the one in the town hall in Ballykeeran," I offered.

Lydia remained expressionless. "Just going home, Miss," she replied.

"And where's that exactly?"

"Dublin, Miss?" She answered in the form of a question, looking at me with raised eyebrows, as if I was an idiot.

"Oh," I replied, "I didn't know you were from Dublin too – what part?"

She seemed to squirm a little, as if she didn't want to answer. "Near town, Miss," she replied.

"I used to live in Rathmines," I said. "Anywhere near there?"

"North Great George's Street," she answered.

"In a flat?" I knew that I should stop quizzing, but I was curious now. She shook her head.

118

"In a house. My mum – my uncle owns it now. I live with him."

It came back to me suddenly that someone had told me that both of Lydia's parents had been killed in an accident when she was a child. I looked at her with concern.

"And you come to school here. Would you have not have preferred to go to school in Dublin?"

She shrugged again. "It's fine," she replied. "I've only got another few months here anyway. I'm eighteen just before Christmas, so ..." Her voice trailed off and she continued to stare out the window, avoiding eye contact.

I glanced out at the gates myself. There was no movement out there, other than the rain, now lashing against the glass porch, raindrops flinging themselves against it in long streaks, distorting the darkening view outside.

I studied her for a moment, her dark hair damp against her head, her eyes dark too, her skin marked with teenage pimples. Her coat was worn, as was the uniform underneath it. It was a little too short – I figured that it might have been the same gabardine and pinafore that she had worn for the past four and a bit years, never replaced. The girl looked just the right side of scruffy – unmothered, I supposed, and I felt sad for her.

"Are you going to apply to college?" I changed the subject to something that I thought would elicit a response. She was a bright student. Her English was excellent, particularly her creative writing. "Have you thought about your CAO form yet?"

She remained silent and impassive for a moment, as if considering whether or not to answer.

"I want to do Communications in the College of Commerce in Rathmines," she replied eventually. Then silence again. Watching hopefully for headlights to sweep the building as a car turned in the gates.

"Excellent. Have you been home since September at all?"

She shook her head and blinked. For a second, I thought I saw tears glisten in the corners of her eyes, but she suddenly looked down at her feet and back up again, and they were gone. My heart contracted sharply in my chest for her.

"What *will* you do so, for the weekend then?" I changed the subject again, eager to get her onto something that she might enjoy talking about, eager for my own reasons to learn more about her. "I'm planning to relax myself," I lied, aware how dull I sounded.

"Not much," she replied, shifting her weight from one leg to the other, glancing at the sleeve which she had been chewing. "I'll watch some movies, maybe. Go into town for a look on Saturday."

"Your uncle will be delighted to have you home, I'm sure."

She suddenly looked at me straight in the eye, a fierce glare. "He's not that bothered," she said forcefully, before looking away again.

In the dim light from the single bulb which hung down into the porch, I thought I saw her cheeks redden. A strained silence lay between us for a few moments. The wind howled outside suddenly, driving more rain against the glass.

Suddenly, without warning, the door behind us leading from the House burst open. We both jumped and turned to look at the shape that stood there in the darkness beyond. My heart sank.

"What are you doing in here?" Mother Benedicta demanded angrily.

I took a step backward to make room for her to step down into the small space as she peered over her glasses, glaring first at Lydia, and then frowning at me.

"Miss Clancy," she snapped. "What is the meaning of this at almost six o'clock on a Friday evening?"

"Lydia's lift home hasn't arrived yet, Mother Benedicta," I explained. "I thought it best that she waited indoors, rather than outside in that weather, and that I wait with her for a while."

The nun was hugely displeased. She glared from Lydia to myself and back to Lydia again. The wind whined loudly outside again, whistling suddenly through the large lock in the old porch door and the rain drummed on its roof.

"Miss Clancy, could you come through here with me for a moment, please," she snapped. She turned abruptly and stepped back into the convent building onto the Brown Corridor. Reluctantly, I followed.

"*Miss Clancy*," she whispered loudly, "who exactly was it gave you permission to keep a student on the premises for so long after school hours? Everyone should be gone home by now. There are no Boarders permitted to stay here for the Bank Holiday weekend. The place should be *empty*."

"No one, Mother," I replied in a low voice. "I thought it was only kind to make sure that one of our students wasn't left standing in the cold and the dark out at the gates. It's dangerous to leave her outside. I'm sure that her lift will be along presently and then she can leave. Tom is coming back for me so I can catch the seven twenty-five train.

The nun breathed heavily through her nose. I noticed that she twisted her hands around each other as she did so, glancing at the porch door and then back at me, her lips thin with barely concealed anger. Her entire body trembled very slightly.

"Is it her uncle that's coming for her?" she demanded.

I shook my head. "No. It's some friend of his who is giving her a lift back. I suppose he might have been delayed in traffic or something."

"Where is he coming *from*," she demanded, growing angrier by the second.

"I'm not sure," I replied.

This enraged her more. "This sort of arrangement is *unacceptable*," she hissed.

"I didn't *make* the arrangement, Mother," I retorted sharply, regretting my tone instantly. I was sure it would be perceived as insolence. "That has nothing to do with me. I simply wanted to keep a deserted student safe out of the rain."

She inhaled sharply, in a thinly veiled attempt at keeping whatever raged within her contained.

"And how long will he be?"

I frowned. "I don't *know*, Mother. But I do know that we can't send her outside in *that*." I was growing more exasperated.

The wind whistled obligingly through the keyhole again.

The nun clenched her hands into fists and tore her gaze away from me, thinking.

"You can't wait here," she said eventually, shaking her head vigorously. "Bring Miss Madigan to the Refectory for now. I'll try to telephone her uncle. We'll have to try to sort this out."

With that, she turned abruptly and stormed away in the direction of the convent living quarters, while I instructed Lydia to follow me and made my way, my heart heavy, back along the deserted Brown Corridor.

Lydia and I sat at the top table in the Ref, Lydia looking forlorn and yet annoyed. I glanced at the clock continuously, as the time for Tom's return grew closer. There was still, clearly, no sign of Lydia's uncle's friend. I wondered had he genuinely been delayed, or was he, himself, halfway to Dublin, his friend's niece in her countryside school forgotten along the way?

Mother Benedicta returned half an hour later and summoned me to join her at the door. She seemed to have calmed a little, but she remained inwardly agitated, I could tell, her eyes darting into the Ref and back to myself, then to her watch.

"This is really most exasperating, Miss Clancy," she began. "I have been ringing that man's house over and over and there's no answer at all from him. I simply don't know what to do."

"Might the uncle be at work, Mother?" I suggested. "Although at this time on a Friday evening … perhaps he does shift work, or works in a hotel or bar?"

"He is a *sales representative* for a *radio station* of all things," the nun spat back, disgusted at that for some reason. "The only number to contact him on outside his work is that house and, as I said, he's not answering." She fell silent, thinking, for a moment, punctuated by more agitated checking of her watch and glances at the student who sat, still, at the Refectory table. "We'll have to feed her now, I suppose," she remarked. "Your lift to the station will be leaving soon, Miss Clancy."

"I've been thinking," I began. "I didn't know until just now that Lydia lived in Dublin. Perhaps I could take her with me on the train and drop her home in a taxi – she doesn't live far from the city centre and –"

"Certainly not!" barked the nun in a disparaging tone.

I was taken aback. "Why not?"

"The uncle," she muttered almost to herself. "If he is not at home … I am familiar with him of old. He is an unreliable man. An *unreliable* man." She stared at me as if I were stupid. "Firstly, her lift doesn't show up. And then there is no one at home to receive my calls. I *cannot* allow a student to leave if I'm aware that there's the slightest possibility of no one to look after her. Although … could you take her with you to your home if there's no one there for her at her own?" She brightened momentarily.

I shook my head. "I'm afraid not, Mother," I replied. "I'm visiting a friend this weekend."

The nun's face blackened with anger and frustration. "Well, *then* ... Miss Clancy," she hissed and suddenly turned, striding away from me.

I watched her, baffled, as she disappeared from sight. I stared after her for a time, unsure what to do, whether or not she would return. When there was no sign of her after a few minutes, I stepped back into the Refectory and lowered myself into the seat opposite Lydia.

She was clearly distressed, gnawing on the tip of her thumb, her face pale and tears pricking at the back of her eyes.

"I'm awful sorry, Miss," she whispered, her voice fragile.

"Don't be, Lydia," I replied, in what I hoped was a reassuring tone. "There's nothing to be sorry about – we'll get this sorted for you in no time."

My words didn't seem to calm her in the slightest.

"He did this once before – when I was in Inter Cert, and I had to stay the whole weekend and Mother Di ... Mother Benedicta ... was raging with me."

"Why with you?" I asked. "It's hardly your fault."

"She's right when she says that my uncle is unreliable – I could hear her. He was my mum's younger brother – much younger – and he's single and he likes to go out and sometimes I think ... well, he's not all that bothered about me being there and sometimes he forgets ... it's his job, you see ... it's very ... *social*, and sometimes he's gone for the whole weekend at parties and going out with work and stuff ... like he takes clients places, to restaurants, or they go racing on a Saturday, or to a big game in Lansdowne, if there's one on ... he might not show up at home for ages, and Mother Benedicta won't let me leave now until she's spoken to him."

I placed my hand on hers, which pressed down on the table, the knuckles white. "I'm sure he hasn't forgotten you, Lydia," I said. "And I'm sure there's an explanation for why your lift hasn't arrived."

She snorted in response. "He's *definitely* forgotten me – the lift, that is," she said. "There's no use pretending at this stage that he's on his way."

"Look, Lydia," I said, patting her hand, "it will all be fine. Your uncle will be home soon, I'm sure, and we can get you on the train with me …"

"No, he won't," she replied, exasperated. "It's Friday – he goes out after work on a Friday – *every* Friday. And he might not get home till one or two in the morning – sometimes not at all!"

"And he leaves you alone in the house by yourself, all night?"

She nodded. "Yes. And that's fine – I'm almost eighteen, I can take care of myself – probably better than he can take care of me, but the nuns don't need to know that sometimes I have to. You won't tell them that, will you?"

I shook my head. "Have you no idea where he might be?"

"Never. He could be in a restaurant, a pub, then a nightclub, or a house party – you may as well go, Miss. They won't get hold of him." Her voice wobbled again. "It looks like I'm stuck here."

"Oh Lydia, please don't worry," I begged her, feeling tearful myself at the sight of her, trapped. "We'll sort something."

We were interrupted by a familiar sound coming along the corridor outside. The meals trolley, rattling over the tiles. It stopped outside and Sister Ruth appeared into the Refectory, carrying a large tray with a covered dish in its centre and a small teapot.

"Mother Benedicta says that you're both to have your tea," she mumbled quietly. "She'll be with you in a moment."

We ate in silence, thinking, the clock ticking toward the time when Tom would come to pick me up. The meal was sparse – the same small salad as I'd been given the night I arrived. All the while we ate, the wind howled outside, and the rain dashed against the Refectory windows.

When she returned, Mother Benedicta looked furious.

"Why didn't you tell me, Miss Madigan?" she barked at Lydia as she entered.

Lydia's hand, her cup raised halfway to her mouth, began to shake and it rattled on its saucer as she put it down. "Tell you what, Mother?" she replied, terrified.

The nun's eyes were ablaze.

"I finally spoke to someone in your uncle's place of work – why didn't you tell us that your uncle departed on a week's holiday earlier this evening? Why didn't you tell me that?"

I looked at Lydia, who had turned completely white. She had

been about to stand up, but sank back into her chair.

"I didn't know," she managed, before the tears suddenly spilled silently down her cheeks.

It seemed to infuriate Mother Benedicta even more that Lydia cried. "There's no use in tears, Miss Madigan," she snapped. "So you're telling me that there is no adult to receive you at your place of residence, no matter who brings you there?"

Lydia shrugged her shoulders, helpless, and Benedicta inhaled sharply – I wasn't sure if she saw Lydia's shrug as what it was, a simple 'I guess not', or some sort of act of defiance. I thought it best to intervene; the nun looked as though she were about to explode.

"Lydia wasn't aware of any situation, other than that her uncle's friend was to come pick her up, Mother," I said, calmly. "None of this is her fault."

"But it is *most* inconvenient, Miss Clancy!" the nun snarled. "I *cannot* allow a student to leave the premises unless they are accompanied by an adult and being received by a parent or guardian whom I trust. This has not happened with Miss Madigan – her parents are *dead,* her guardian is overseas. There is *nowhere* for her to go. And it would be inconvenient at the best of times for her to stay at Maria Goretti for an entire Bank Holiday weekend, but it is additionally *impossible* this particular weekend as myself and the Holy Sisters are away on Retreat tomorrow. At least that was the plan, now *someone* is going to have to remain behind to take care of *that girl!*" Her face had grown red, and spittle rested at the corners of her lips as she raised her arm and pointed at Lydia while still looking at me. *That girl* ... the contempt ...

"I will take responsibility for her then," I blurted suddenly. "I will take care of her."

"*But you said yourself that wasn't possible!*" the nun shouted.

Her body was rigid and her eyes on fire. I half expected her to stamp her foot.

"You said that you were staying with a – a *friend*. What do you mean, Miss Clancy?"

"I could take care of her *here* is what I meant, Mother." I lowered my tone in contrast to the nun's. "If it was permissible. I cannot take her to Dublin, but my plans are not firm and I can stay here and do what needs to be done."

Lydia looked at me hopefully.

"But ... *but* ..." the nun spluttered.

"I cannot see any other way of making sure that Lydia is taken care of for the next couple of days, until school opens again. I'll tell Tom that I won't need my lift to the station after all."

I watched the nun's facial expressions – the fury turned to a sort of desperation, to confusion, and in a matter of seconds, to something that might have been a reluctant acceptance. She looked from Lydia to me and back again. I could tell by her that she wasn't satisfied, that she wanted desperately for another option to materialise out of thin air to take the problem at hand – myself and Lydia – away, and out of her responsibility, but she simply couldn't fathom how to do that.

The wind screamed suddenly, a noise that made us all jump. It sounded for a moment almost human, and seemed to come from everywhere, inside and out.

The nun went pale and flinched, Goosebumps crawled along my own arms and legs.

"*Fine.*" Her tone was low, but not calm. Instead, it appeared as if she was physically suppressing rage. Her voice and body still trembled. Her hands were rolled into fists, the knuckles white. "*I* will telephone Tom Gorman and tell him that he has been inconvenienced and apologise accordingly. I will review the situation, and reflect on it. For tonight, you can follow regular schedule. I'm sure you have plenty of study and then revision to get on with, Miss Madigan..." Her eyes flicked behind me to where Lydia still sat at the table. "And you, Miss Clancy, could use the time to perhaps ..." She glared at me, her mouth searching for the words, but nothing came out.

Abruptly and suddenly, she turned and marched from the room.

Neither of us moved for a few moments. I remained standing, watching the door to see if she would return. When she didn't, I turned slowly back to Lydia and realised that my legs had turned to jelly during the exchange. I sank down on the Refectory chair opposite the girl who was pale and wide-eyed. She stared at me, looking for some sort of guidance, it seemed, but I didn't know what to say to her. Instead, I took a deep breath, studied the table with the remains of our meal still on it, and then removed her empty plate from where it sat and stacked it under my own. There was a clink as Lydia took my lead and stacked the two teacups one into the other. Together, we cleared the sparse table. It served to calm me a little.

I sat back in the chair for a moment and looked at her. "We'd best get to the Study then," I said softly, smiling at her.

She managed a weak smile back, before frowning and looking worried again. "Your plans, Miss ..." she managed, before I shook my head and raised a hand to silence her.

"Nothing that couldn't be changed, Lydia," I said. "Now can you take the tray out and place it on the trolley outside the door? I'll bring the bags." I smiled again and nodded toward the door.

I watched as she carried the dishes out to the trolley.

It gave me a few moments to reflect on what I had done – the commitment that I had just made, on the spur of the moment, and out of fear of the nun. Bank Holiday Friday. And here I was, still within the walls of Maria Goretti.

The place felt cold, and empty. Our footsteps echoed as we trudged to the heart of the House, down the Brown passageway in the dark toward the Study, which was lit only by occasional dim emergency exit lights high on the walls.

I watched Lydia slope along ahead of me, carrying her sack of schoolbooks which she had intended to take home with her. Her shoulders were slumped under the weight of it. She, too, looked worn down, I realised. She couldn't have advocated for herself to Mother Benedicta back there – she was too painfully quiet and shy. And what could I have done? I wondered what might have become of her if I'd left her standing out in the rain at five o'clock. If I'd just nodded and bid her a good weekend and carried on my way? Might she still be out there? Or would she have eventually had to knock on the convent door to beg re-admission? Would she have even been let in? And what would Benedicta have done if she had? She'd have taken out all the rage and fury that she clearly felt towards Lydia's feckless uncle on the poor girl. And then, begrudgingly remained behind for the whole weekend to supervise her every move. What hell that would be! That poor child – having to suffer for three whole days in the company of a bitter Mother Benedicta, alone. I sighed. I needed to be gone from here, I knew. For my sanity. But, much as it filled me with despair, Lydia needed me to be here even more. It was best that I stay after all.

Chapter twenty-four

Ria
BALLYKEERAN
October 1987

We reached the Study Hall door. Meekly, Lydia entered before me and turned on the lights. I followed her in and glanced around nervously to ensure that it was empty. It was gloomy and uninviting, a stale smell of earlier classes still lingering in the air, that typical classroom odour of mandarin orange peels, banana skins and pencil parings.

Lydia trudged resignedly the length of the room toward the Leaving Cert section. I put her weekend bag down on the floor beside me and glanced around. Even with the lights on, the long room remained gloomy and the large sash windows rattled in the gusting wind. "We'll close the shutters," I said decisively. "Keep some of the heat in."

"Yes, Miss," Lydia replied humbly, setting her bag down at her desk in the middle of the Leaving Cert study area.

"You take that side, and I'll do this side," I said. "Study's not a bad idea for tonight actually – may as well get your homework done, eh? And then we'll figure something out in the morning. These things happen."

I almost believed myself, and I felt slightly encouraged as we went from window to window, closing the big, grey wooden shutters and clasping them firmly shut. It blocked out some of the sound of the howling storm outside, and there was soon a familiar

128

clank from the old radiators along the walls, and a rattle in the huge pipes that ran underneath them and around the room, indicating that Mother Benedicta wasn't going to freeze us out at least.

"Heat's on," I remarked. It gave me an idea. "Why don't we both sit at the desks along the wall? We can put our feet on the warm pipes then. May as well make the best of the free seats."

Lydia looked downcast as she nodded her head and picked up the heavy bag to move to the area I had suggested. I felt so sorry for her then, stuck in the last place that she wanted to be, with nowhere to go. I also knew how she felt.

"Should we turn the lights off back there, Miss, where no one's sitting?" she said, turning and indicating the empty Study Hall space behind her. "Only Mother Benedicta ..."

I grimaced at the thought, my mind flashing back suddenly to the last time I had peered into this room in the half dark. "You're probably right, Lydia," I said. "We should. But we won't. Alright? Just this once – it's too dirty a night outside to sit in the half-dark in here."

Lydia managed a weak smile, and slid into a desk as she did, opening the flap of her rucksack. I sat into one of the student desks myself and reached into my handbag for my book.

"It'll be break time in no time anyway – if we're following regular schedule to the letter, right? And the rest of the night will fly."

We settled. The room warmed up, the old pipes clanging and clanking as it did. As was the habit of the lucky students who claimed these desks as their own, and sat there every night, we both slid our feet between the top and bottom pipes which ran along the wall beside the desks we had chosen, and fell silent. I saw Lydia was working on some Maths, while I read a Rosamunde Pilcher that I had found in the library. It passed the time.

I roused when I heard the chapel bells ring for half past eight, their clanging distorted as the wind carried the sound in odd directions. I told Lydia to stretch her legs around the room for a bit, and took the opportunity to nip out to the payphone under the stairs to ring my friend in Dublin to tell her that I wouldn't be arriving that weekend. I could tell that she was relieved and, despite how grim my situation was, I was too, in a way.

I made the call brief, keen to get back to the warmth of our end of the Study Hall – the storm seemed to have worsened even more, and a screaming wind ripped around the building, rain drumming against every window. Out in the dark corridor, keyholes whistled, and gusts blew through open cracks, under doors and in through the tops of windows. On the way back to my desk, I was surprised, and pleased, to find that I had missed a tray on the floor outside the Study Hall door – a flask of coffee, two slices of jam sponge, and two Club Milks. It made a pleasant change from the usual cups of grey tea and limp corned-beef sandwiches that constituted supper on a normal week night. I smiled as I carried it back to Lydia, closing the door firmly behind me, and we ate gratefully in silence. Clearly, some nun had taken pity on us. Sister Ruth again, I imagined.

Heartened by the break, and the heat in our bones, Lydia plunged back into work – this time, an essay that I had set her class – and I took out a notebook of my own, to make some lesson plans for the coming weeks. We worked in silence for fifteen minutes or so when, suddenly, the wind gusted loudly outside, and the lights in the Study Hall began to flicker. Both Lydia and I glanced around, but returned to work when they settled, only for them to go again – off and on quickly, then off again, but this time for a little longer, before flicking back on. We carried on as best we could, but after a few moments the flickering became constant. I caught Lydia's expression as the light came and went – she was unnerved, as was I, becoming increasingly panicked that the lights would go completely. I had no idea where I might find candles or a torch – the staffroom, I presumed, but I couldn't be sure. And the thought of making my way there in the pitch dark filled me with dread. The light came back again for a moment as the wind abated, but soon my worst fears were realised when we were plunged into complete darkness.

Lydia and I sat silent for a few moments.

"Looks like it's finally gone properly, Miss," Lydia said quietly, through the dark.

I sat there, my nerves tingling, dread gnawing at the pit of my stomach at the prospect of what I had to do. And then, suddenly, the lights came back on again. But not as they should have. I looked up at the fittings, confused.

The long room, normally divided into three classooms during the day, had six large fluorescent light fittings per section, and we had left all of them on. Now however, only the lights over the section where we sat had returned. I looked at Lydia, who looked around, puzzled.

"*That's strange,*" I remarked, glad that we had light again, but discomfited by the fact that it was only over part of the room, and nervous at the notion that it might go again any second.

Then very slowly, almost imperceptibly at first, the light that we had began to dim.

And then the banging began.

Suddenly, the shutters behind where we sat started to rattle. We both turned to look at them – and then across the room, where the shutters opposite had also started to bang, joined by the remaining shutters back through the Study Hall, first on one side, and then on the other. The noise grew deafening, and we watched, as well as listened in complete horror, able to *see* them move, but also clearly able to see that there was nothing physically *there* to move them. Lydia jumped up from her seat and stood there, turning slowly as she looked from window to window. I, on the other hand, was frozen, unable to stand. Goosebumps swelled all over me, and a coldness ran the length of my spine as suddenly the lights began to malfunction again, going from brightness to dark as the rattling persisted. It felt like being under attack.

It carried on for minutes, but felt, of course, like forever. And then, as unexpectedly as it had all begun, it stopped. The lights reverting to normal, the shutters still. We stood there, our shallow, panicked breathing suddenly audible, along with the rain outside.

"What ... was that " I managed breathlessly. I noticed I was gripping the desk where I sat, my knuckles white.

"Maybe ... maybe it was the lads, Miss ..." Lydia's voice trailed away, as if she realised mid-sentence that her suggestion had no more substance than air.

By "the lads", I knew that she meant a small group of five or six pimple-faced teenage boys who lived in the village and attended the local Tech. On occasion, they appeared at the windows of Maria

Goretti's Study Hall at night-time, peering in at the girls, giving us all a fright before becoming an annoyance, as they popped up at different windows, occasionally shouting something in and waiting for a response of some sort from the girls. The girls always found the distraction amusing at first, but soon grew tired of it. It made no sense tonight, however, that "the lads" would pay a visit on the Friday of a long weekend when they knew that there should be no one there, particularly in this weather. And besides, even if it were them, how were they manipulating the lights? How could they make the shutters *move* from the inside?

"It might have been a sort of ... I don't know, a mini hurricane or something?" I suggested, trying to sound calm. "A tornado! Yes, a tornado – or a twister – you see them on the news sometimes. That would explain why it hit all the windows at once."

Lydia nodded. "Maybe," she replied, but without conviction.

We stayed there, in silence, for a few minutes, the sound of the rattling still in our ears, but the room still and calm again. Lydia sank to her seat after a few moments, and we tried, for want of a better idea, to return to what we had been doing, but we couldn't manage it. I knew that we were too unsettled, too terrified of it happening again. My mind raced – I was the adult, the teacher – I had to remain calm and responsible – but I was shaken to my core. I began to plan what I could do, should it happen again.

I knew that I had to source light – candles, a torch – anything – in case the electricity went again. I wondered if the same had happened in the convent wing? And if a nun would come to check on us, perhaps? I couldn't take the risk, however, of waiting for that to happen on the off chance that we were plunged into darkness again.

A loud gust against the windows made us both jump, and Lydia looked to me, pale-faced, her anxiety clear to see. I had to make a decision.

"I think we'd best head to bed, Lydia," I managed, eventually.

If we were tucked up in bed, then at least we could just stay there – we wouldn't have to move until it was light again. It seemed like the only logical answer, and the safest bet. It was just the prospect of getting there terrified me.

I stood up, shakily, while Lydia tidied her things and picked up her rucksack and overnight bag. We made our way out of the Study Hall as quickly as we could. With shaking hands, I turned off the study lights, and pulled the door shut rapidly behind me, closing it with a bang. I paused for a moment and thought, before instructing Lydia to follow me as nervously I crossed the hall at the base of the staircase, instead of heading straight up, then through to the lobby to the staffroom where my trembling hands fumbled with the key that was left in it. I entered, switching the light on immediately. Lydia waited outside for me. Even in moments like these, her conditioning was strong. Students were not permitted in the staffroom for *any* reason.

I emerged a few moments later, a torch in hand, delighted at having found exactly what I sought in the supply cupboard. My joy soon dissipated when I saw Lydia's face, however, her huge brown eyes staring at me in complete terror.

"What's the matter, Lydia," I asked, feeling the colour drain from my own face.

"*Listen!*" she urged in a whisper.

The roots of my hair prickled as a chill spread across my scalp.

I did as I was told, but there was nothing, no sound, save the steady gusts of wind and the pounding of the rain.

"What for, Lydia?" I asked, feeling my hands begin to tremble. "I can't hear –"

"*There!*"

Her voice was a terrified whisper. I held my breath. Still nothing. Lydia looked at me, exasperated.

"Didn't you hear that?" she managed, breathless.

I shook my head. "Hear what?"

She paused again, looking into the darkness and straining to hear something that I couldn't hear.

"There was someone … *singing* … or *humming* or something …" She sounded as if she might burst into tears.

I shivered, and stared at her alarmed face. She wasn't making it up.

We listened again. Nothing.

"Most likely the wind and your imagination – this storm is making noises come out of keyholes and everything." I managed a small, forced chuckle in the hopes of reassuring her. I failed, however. I swallowed deeply. It was imperative that I stay calm, I thought. Imperative that I hold it together for her, even though my knees trembled and my heart raced. "We'll get up to the dorms and get cosy in bed and under the covers and before we know it, it'll be morning." I tried to make my voice chirpy and positive.

Lydia said nothing, but frowned. She knew that I was lying. To myself, and to her. And, although the urge burned within me to just run as far from the place as I could, I knew that I would continue to lie. To tell myself that it was the weather that was making this happen. Anything else was just too ridiculous, too inconceivable. Even though she had just described something I'd heard myself before. I couldn't think about that now, I told myself.

We ascended the first flight of stairs in silence, the torch clutched in my hand, our weekend bags over our shoulders. I tried to believe what I had told Lydia, that focusing on getting into bed, pulling the covers around our heads and sleeping through would make it all better. I was fooling no one, however. I saw Lydia's face fall, as we reached the first landing and, off it, my room. Nervously, she glanced up above her at the remaining stairs to the Big Dorm where she would have to sleep. Alone.

"I'll go up with you," I offered, turning on the light that illuminated the last two flights of stairs for her. It was dim, but better than nothing.

She glanced upwards again. "Thanks, Miss," she said quietly, but half-heartedly.

I felt cruel.

We carried on the rest of the way. The dorm was chilly and uninviting, with every shutter in it still open and the absence of the students keenly evident. As we had downstairs, I set to closing the shutters along one side and Lydia dumped her bags on her bed and followed my lead along the other. Down the rows we went, past the empty beds with their open surrounding curtains. It was grim, a far cry from the usual bustle and gentle noises of girls preparing to sleep or rising for the day. I worried as I worked, worried about Lydia alone up here. I had a door that I could close behind me and lock, after all, but she had nothing but a curtain to pull around her bed – in this vast, empty room, icy cold and bereft of company.

We were halfway down when we first heard it. Both of us looked up at the same time because that's where the sound came from. Above us, clear as day.

The sound of footsteps.

They were slow at first, hesitant, heavy, like someone stamping slowly. Lydia and I froze in disbelief. My mind raced again as I tried to understand what I was hearing, what it could possibly be and where it might actually be coming from. Because it couldn't be ... it simply *wasn't possible* that someone was now above us, stamping around. The fear grew in me, however, as the steps speeded up gradually and then began to run. They pounded over our heads, from the end of the room where we had just entered, to the far wall, stopping for a moment before turning around and running back again. My eyes widened as I looked at Lydia who stood stock still, breathing heavily and following the progress of the unseen feet with her eyes. She whimpered, a stifled scream.

"What's up there again?" I asked her. "What's above us?"

She shook her head, gasping, "Nothing," she managed. "We're not allowed up there ... it's the old Baby Dorm and some attics for storage, but it's not used ... no one sleeps up there ... it's locked ..."

"It must be one of the nuns up there," I said.

Lydia shook her head. "It can't be," she replied, stiff with terror.

"No, no, Lydia – that must be it," I said reassuringly.

It had to be – it was the only logical explanation. It was easy for us to feel that we were alone in this big old building, but the nuns were all nearby. It had to be one of them ... *Running like that?* Never ... why would they? I quelled the thought.

Unless there were an intruder? What if someone had broken in, somehow? Someone reckoning that they would be undisturbed in a building deserted for a long weekend? What if they were a danger, and came down to us?

"I don't think so, Miss," Lydia's voice trembled as she spoke. "The door leading up there is locked ... and the clothes rack is pulled across in front of it, to block it ... "

I spun around to where Lydia pointed to double check that she was right. Sure enough, the unused door remained locked, and blocked by the clothes rack, as it had done every day since the first time I had seen this room.

My mind went blank, but soon revved into gear as the running began again above us. I looked up. How could someone have got in there? Because it was most definitely a person ... it had to be.

The running suddenly stopped, and everything fell silent, save for the steady patter of rain on the windows. We remained still, looking above us, unable to move.

Gradually, the violent fear that had grabbed me began to subside a little. "It could be an animal," I said quietly.

Lydia flinched at the sound of my voice.

"A rat, maybe?" I said. "They can get in through all sorts of places – if you're telling me that no person could get up there, then that must be it – a rat – or – or – a badger or something ..."

The noise proved me wrong, however. Louder than before, the running suddenly resumed, but this time from a completely different position to where it had stopped. We swung around, still staring at the ceiling, at the new location of the noise. Lydia whimpered as it pounded, louder and faster above us, down to the end again, back to where it began. I stared in disbelief as a light fitting suspended from the ceiling *moved* with the vibration of its passing. The sight of the movement spurred me into action. Anger suddenly overrode fear in my mind. How *dare* someone do this? It had to be an intruder – or a resident, one of the nuns – there had to be some other entrance to the attic rooms above. But why? Why would someone do that? And had they been responsible for the activity downstairs?

What if ... what if someone was *squatting* up there? Some tramp or homeless person? What if they had access to the dormitories that we didn't know about? Up the fire escape, perhaps? What if they were up to mischief? The bell ... who had been ringing the Morning Bell that day? It began to make sense in my mind. But what if the person was dangerous?

"Get your things, Lydia," I barked. "I'm not leaving you up here with this nonsense going on. You can sleep on the Sisters' Corridor tonight." And then, adrenalin coursing through my body, I lifted my head and roared at the ceiling. "And you can *cut that noise right out! Stop it! Immediately! I'll call the Guards!*" I don't know why I yelled, what I thought it might achieve. For a brief moment, I was sure it had, actually, achieved something as the footsteps fell silent again.

I walked over to where Lydia stood and, together, we retraced our steps to her cubicle and I waited as she gathered up her belongings – together with her duvet and pillow – and I picked up her overnight bag where everything else she needed was packed for the weekend. It had worked, I was sure, as silence remained.

Until we were on our way out. Until we had just reached the door that led out onto the stairs. That's when the banging started again. Not just from above us – that was bad enough – the running had stopped, but had been replaced by the sound of someone – something – *jumping* up and down, over and over, in the same spot. But the shutters we had closed began to imitate those we had left downstairs – rattling, as if being blown by a strong wind. Except there was now no wind – it had completely died down. We paused for a moment, again uncomprehending. Until the flight instinct over took.

"Come on!" I ordered Lydia, and we fled as fast as we could manage, out the door of the Dorm, and down the stairs.

We stumbled down the first flight of stairs as fast as we could, and then the second, through to the Sisters' Corridor where we scurried as quickly as we could to the door of my room.

My hands shook as I fumbled in my pocket for the key. I heard Lydia whimper as she glanced behind her, into the dim light of the passage. The air felt electric. I found the key, then the lock, then fumbled as I tried to make them meet. Eventually, it yielded under my hand and I pushed the door open as quickly as I could and we fell in, slamming it behind us and locking it. We both gasped in gratitude as I found the light switch and filled the small room with what light came from the overhead bulb. Outside, the storm had stopped. We could no longer hear the noise from above either. The only sounds were our breathing, and the occasional drip from the gutters outside.

I spoke eventually. "I should go get Mother Benedicta," I said, trying to compose myself.

Lydia looked at me, wide-eyed with panic. "Don't, Miss," she said, her voice filled with fear. "I mean … can you not tell her in the morning? She might be annoyed?"

I breathed deeply and thought for a moment. I should, of course, have informed her. If there were an intruder, then she needed to know about it. But to find her would mean leaving and walking all the way down the stairs, through the shadowy corridors and halls, then searching in the convent for her – I had no idea where to look, having never been permitted into the convent wing – and Lydia was right, what if she was – *annoyed*? She had been so enraged earlier, verging on volatile … I decided to pause for a while, to think it through, to recover.

I was sure of one thing, however. Lydia was not going back up there alone.

I looked at her frightened, pale face. My intention upstairs, when the panicked thought had hit me to remove her from the dormitory, had been to instruct her to sleep in one of the rooms along the corridor. But looking at her, her trembling body and eyes on the verge of tears, I decided that wasn't an option either.

"It's an unusual course of action, I know, Lydia, but I think that you should sleep in here tonight."

Her eyes widened.

"I know," I smiled, "Sharing a room with your teacher is the last thing that you want to do, but under the circumstances …"

I was taken aback when she nodded enthusiastically.

"Thank you, Miss," she said, gratefully, the relief in her voice palpable.

Truth be told, I was relieved myself.

"You take the bed and I'll have the floor. No arguments," I insisted, raising a hand to counter her. "In the morning, we'll sort out what we're going to do, but I'd imagine we're safe here. If she's got an early start in the morning, Mother Benedicta might well be gone to bed anyway, so I'll find her in the morning before she leaves and see what she wants to do."

We prepared for bed in silence, each of us undressing nervously and shyly. That done, I removed my own bedding, and replaced it with Lydia's before making myself a makeshift bed on the floor beside her. A couple of times we paused, sure that we could hear something from outside, hearts racing as we imagined something coming down the corridor, waiting outside the door – but that was all it was, our imaginations. After a while, we relaxed a little, felt reassured with the shutters tightly closed and the light on. I left it that way when we both lay down to sleep, a prospect that I felt was distant and unlikely.

"What do you think that was, Miss?" Lydia's voice came from the bed above me, timid and scared.

I couldn't think of what to say to her. The whole thing had seemed so terrifying, so unbelievable at the time, yet in retrospect, there *had* to be a reason, *had* to be something tangible to explain it all. I thought for a long time before answering.

"I'm not sure, Lydia," I replied, trying to keep my voice steady, to sound brave and reassuring. For a moment, I contemplated telling her it was nothing, to go to sleep and forget about it. But I couldn't. I couldn't dismiss her fears like that, nor my own. "A combination of things, I think … it might have been the boys from the village after all …" I pushed up on my elbows and looked around the room again as if reassuring myself that it was empty save for myself and the frightened girl who lay in my bed. "I don't think there was any malicious intent – after all, the place is supposed to be empty. Strikes me that they have some way in – up the fire escape, maybe, and they were just up to devilment in the storm – taking shelter, perhaps, and then messing about. Chances are they didn't know we were even there …" My voice trailed off. The ideas borrowed from one other and they were plausible enough.

Lydia didn't respond.

"I'll tell Mother Benedicta in the morning, and she can look into some security perhaps …"

"Or maybe the stories are true."

I stopped dead at Lydia's interruption.

"What was that?" I asked, pretending that I hadn't heard her.

She knew I had, but repeated herself anyway.

"Maybe the stories are true."

She didn't budge, remained lying under the covers, still.

"What stories are those, Lydia?" I asked.

"The stories about Little Frances, Miss." Now she leaned over the side of the bed and looked at me, wide-eyed.

I shook my head dismissively. "That rhyme that your friend Martina recited? That's just childish local nonsense, Lydia. There is no such thing as … that *sort of thing*."

We fell silent and lay back down, waiting, and listening, until Lydia's breathing grew steady and soft.

I was right, wasn't I? That there was no such thing as that sort of thing? I urged the voice inside me that said it to speak louder.

Until it was drowned out, however, by the voice that chanted in my head.

"So pull your covers over your head
Little Frances isn't dead ..."

Chapter twenty-five

BALLYKEERAN
1942

Frances' funeral was held on a Friday morning.

The child remembered it most for the silence, except for the crunch of boots across the Nuns' Graveyard outside the convent as Uncle Mike and Dada carried the coffin of her sister to be buried. That sound stayed with her for a long time afterward. Forever, in fact.

There was hardly anyone there. Dada and Ned Gorman, Seamus who worked for Ned and who helped him while Dada stood to one side for the prayers, holding her hand to keep her from falling in. There were two old nuns from the convent, who the child didn't know, and the priest who had said the early morning funeral Mass. Mammy hadn't come. She was too sick, Dada had said. They'd have to be very quiet now when they went home so that she could sleep.

The child stayed close to him, drawing a little reassurance from his bulk, but not much. He had been cross with her earlier, shushing her loudly when she had asked him if being dead made you smaller because Frances would never have fit in that coffin? He'd told her that when you died, you lay down like you did when you went to sleep. When she thought about it, Frances had always slept on her side, her knees tucked up against her chest, hadn't she?

So that must be it, then.

The prayers were quick, and even though she had promised Dada she'd be brave, the child couldn't help but start to cry softly when Uncle Mike removed the boards across the top of the hole and he and Seamus lowered the coffin down on two strips of cloth. It made her feel a panic rise inside her, an urge to run and go get Frances back. The child gave a little sob as the coffin went down so far that it was out of sight. She hadn't thought she would, but she missed her sister. Missed having her to run about outdoors with, down to the river to catch pinkeens with, missed the bulk and the heat of her in the bed beside her at night.

"She's safe with us now," one of the old nuns said to her as they left.

The child stared up into her face, which was wrinkled and yellow, framed with her wimple and her white collar. The nun terrified her – her appearance mostly, but also the other thing she said.

"Just like you'll be safe when you come to us."

The child stared back at her as she walked away. What did that mean? Was she going to die too? And be put in the ground with the nuns like Frances? Was that to be her punishment?

Her heart pounded all the way home, the words ringing in her ears. She was going to die too. And she'd never grow up, and she'd be in the ground with Frances and all the nuns – and she didn't know what to expect from a dead person, because she'd never seen one, had she? Dada had explained that usually you'd see the dead person at their funeral in their coffin, but that Frances' coffin had been closed so as not to upset Mammy.

So, if she was going in the ground, what would happen to her down there? Was it hell? Was she going to hell for being a bad girl?

Because of what had happened to Frances?

Chapter twenty-six

Saturday morning dawned gloriously bright. It surprised me that I had slept, but at some stage, obviously, I had fallen into a slumber. Lydia was asleep still – I could hear her steady breathing from the bed above where I lay on the floor. I checked my watch. It was already late, past eight. Time to get up, before a nun arrived to wake us and the questions would begin as to why we were in the same room, a student asleep in her teacher's bed and the teacher on the floor, all reports going straight to Benedicta. That was, of course, if Lydia's empty bed hadn't already been discovered in the dormitory. If that were the case, however, someone would have been pounding on the door of my room already. We remained undiscovered, I felt sure. For now.

I sat up quickly and flung the covers off me. We had no time to waste if I was to get Lydia back to her cubicle upstairs and make everything look as it should be.

The events of the previous night streamed back into my mind. I wondered if, perhaps, unnerved by the storm, Lydia and I had overreacted. If perfectly ordinary occurences had been blown out of proportion because of … atmospherics? Surely that had to be the case?

Although what if I was correct and someone had made a temporary home inside in the attics on the disused top floor,

143

someone who knew to be quiet and unobtrusive when the students were in the school, but who had thought they had free rein the previous night? What if they were a threat to the students? It was certainly something that I wouldn't investigate alone.

No. Whatever had taken place, I would have to talk to Mother Benedicta. And although the thought filled me with dread, I knew that she would have the answer. She knew the place, knew the access points and probably knew what went on there better than I.

Lydia's eyes opened wide as I shook her shoulder to wake her and she, too, leaped from the bed and dressed as rapidly as she could.

We spoke in hushed voices as we gathered our belongings and left my room as quickly and quietly as we could, hiding her bedclothes in the Barry sisters' room next door under Aideen's bed, and pulling their door over as a precaution.

An idea had come to me as I dressed. Checking for nuns as we made our way down the stairs, we headed straight for the payphone.

Within half an hour, Carmel's mother – an earthy-looking woman with short black hair – had arrived in a mud-splattered Toyota, Carmel beaming and waving at Lydia from the passenger seat, ready to whisk her away in a cloud of kindness and 'why-didn't-you-call-us-last-night?'. The woman was kind, and clucked around Lydia who smiled weakly and resisted attempts at huge, enveloping hugs, anxious to leave and embarrassed by the whole chain of events. But relieved. We both were. Why hadn't we thought of Carmel indeed? In the stress and strangeness of the previous night, it hadn't occurred to either of us that Lydia staying with a pal might be an option. And despite the fact that Carmel boarded, she lived close enough that her mother could be there to quickly collect Lydia and take her home with them.

Despite the brightness of the day, Lydia still looked pale and nervous. I watched her as she left, sitting alone in the back seat of the car, turning to look back – and up toward the dormitory windows – as it pulled away. She was gone and safe, and in a way that should satisfy the rules I hoped. I had assured her that I would take responsibility for informing Benedicta. I closed and locked the door of the convent porch behind me, leaving the key back on the lintel, and wondered where, in fact, the Mother Superior was?

Lydia and I had executed her escape plan without the presence of a single nun, which struck me as odd. And while I dreaded the prospect of having to face Benedicta again, it would have to be done, and soon. She would rave, of course, at my audacity in daring to make a decision without her, but at that point I didn't care. I just wanted that poor girl out of that dreadful building. Perhaps, if I was lucky, Benedicta's rage might be diminished by a measure of relief that the problem had been satisfactorily solved.

I set off in search of her.

It wasn't to be, however. On passing the Refectory, I glanced in, and there saw two breakfasts set out – one on my Guardian's table, the other on the student table nearest to it. From the door, I could see that a note was set on my saucer under my upturned cup. I frowned as I read it.

Miss Clancy,

I have been unable to speak with you this morning as I cannot delay our departure. You alone are to enter the convent kitchen to retrieve meals for today only which have been refrigerated for you and the student. I have arranged that a nun will return to the convent tomorrow, Sunday, and will take care of meals from there on in. Normal weekend schedule regarding study, sleep, recess times and, most importantly, prayer, is to apply. Please be vigilant and sparing regarding use of electricity as usage this weekend is unscheduled. Tell the student that she is to use her time wisely and to take some for prayer and reflection as well as additional study for exams. Take time for reflection yourself. I will speak with you on Monday morning.

Mother Benedicta

So, she was already gone. They were all gone. No wonder Lydia's departure had been so easy and undisturbed. It meant, however, that there was no one to speak to about the previous night's activity. And I was alone.

I ate the small bowl of cereal that had been left for me, followed by the slice of bread and stewed tea and then had the breakfast that was left for Lydia, too. I was hungry, and figured that no one would have to know that Lydia had left before eating it. It seemed such a stupid thing to worry about, I thought. Having to cover myself for eating a paltry handful of cornflakes and two slices of white bread.

But that was my mindset now. What Maria Goretti had done to my way of thinking. I realised that I really needed not to be here. I needed to get out. I pondered what to do as I finished the second cup of tea. I couldn't really ring my friend in Terenure again, having told her yesterday that I wouldn't be arriving.

I briefly thought about heading to Leonard's, but abandoned that plan quickly. I couldn't honestly have tolerated time with him, especially when I knew that I was going to end our relationship for good.

So where could I go? My brain suddenly flooded with possibility – where *couldn't* I go? Who said that I'd even have to go to Dublin? Why couldn't it be a B&B somewhere? Anywhere? I had all that money in my bank account that wasn't going to get used now – surely I could withdraw a little of what I had saved and head somewhere by myself for the weekend – three whole days of freedom ahead of me. I could go to the West, maybe? Or south, or north? All I had to do was get a train or a bus and *go*. I felt emboldened by the idea all of a sudden. The freedom – the idea of the independence to do this, free of nuns, free of rules, free of Leonard, free of another living soul, was liberating.

I drained the last of the tea, and looked around for something to write with, spotting a pencil sitting on the mantel under the mirror at the top of the Ref. Grabbing it, I turned over the page on which Mother Benedicta had written her neat note, and scrawled a response.

> *To whom it concerns*
>
> *Myself and Lydia Madigan will now not have to spend the weekend at Maria Goretti. I have resolved the situation and personally released her into the care of Carmel Peake's family and she was collected by Mrs Peake this morning (Saturday). Without having to care for Lydia, I will, myself, be leaving this morning also and will return on Bank Holiday Monday evening, as scheduled.*
>
> *Regards, Ria Clancy*

No doubt about it, Benedicta would be unimpressed, most likely enraged again. At the very least she'd be annoyed now that the 'refrigerated meals' wouldn't be used but what should I do? She had nearly blown a gasket in the first place at the thought of unwanted weekend residents on the premises, and was clearly annoyed that someone would have the audacity to need electricity over the weekend, so wasn't it preferable that the 'refrigerated meals' should remain uneaten and the school building remain empty? But what about the nun who was being sent back to take care of us? What should I do about her? I had no way of contacting Benedicta which, come to think of it, was ridiculous. Where was this bloody Retreat even taking place? Why hadn't she given me a contact number for emergencies? That was entirely her fault.

I frowned as another thought crossed my mind. What if there *had* been intruders the previous night? What if it had been the presence of Lydia and myself that had thwarted them? I had failed to tell Benedicta straight away when we heard them, so what if they came back and there was no one here, or just one person here? What if there was a break-in over the weekend, the possibility of which I had been aware of, but had left to happen anyway? Should I call the Guards, maybe? But surely that would upset Benedicta even more? Guards called in her absence? Rummaging through the dormitories? I rubbed my hands along my face, overwhelmed by thoughts, all sense of the freedom that had washed over me moments before gone. What should I do? Should I stay in case the intruders came back? Man the ship, as it were? But if I stayed what on earth would I do for three whole days? I'd go mad, surely? And in practical terms, what use would I be? Could I stop them? Unlikely. And what if they were dangerous? What defence did I have? My mind went blank for a moment, overloaded. I grabbed the pencil again and held it over the piece of paper, contemplating writing a postscript. But again, what could I say? That I had heard banging noises around the school building on Friday night – possibly intruders – but was leaving anyway? No. That could cost me my job. I chewed my lip and put the pencil down.

I just had to get out of there.

That was the plain and simple truth of it. I couldn't stay – for my own sanity and protection. If intruders were able to access the school, then they'd do it with or without me. And no matter what I did, it would displease Mother Benedicta.

I looked out of the window at the bright day outside – proper winter would arrive soon and there would be fewer and fewer days like this. The urge to go out in it – to be *out* there, to be far away, to be myself again, burned within me. I would leave, catch a bus from the bus stop in the village, and whatever would be would be. I hastily grabbed the dirty breakfast dishes and rinsed them in the pantry across the way, leaving them to drain, and then flew upstairs to my room to grab my weekend bag, still packed from the previous day.

I had removed a few items – toothbrush, toothpaste, hairbrush – the jeans and top that I was wearing. I repacked quickly, urgently, driven by a quiet underlying panic that surely something would stop me now that I had made a plan of escape. I tidied hurriedly, hanging, folding and putting away. I had no doubt that the room would be somehow scrutinised in my absence, probably doubly so if my leaving was seen as some sort of insubordination. And then it hit me. Lydia's bedclothes – I hadn't thought of them earlier. I didn't want Lydia getting into trouble when they'd be found missing from her bed, or rolled up under Aideen Barry's. I'd have to return them to her bed. Upstairs. In the Big Dorm.

The thought made me anxious. For a moment, I thought about just leaving them where they were and hoping no one would notice before Monday night, but I shoved it aside. It was too risky and, if found, no way would Benedicta allow it to go unpunished.

But going up to the Big Dorm again – after last night. For a second, the sounds of running footsteps from the blocked off attics replayed in my mind and I felt my legs weaken. Before allowing myself to think too much, I took a deep breath, stormed out to the Barry's room, grabbed Lydia's pillow, threw it into the centre of the duvet and vigorously rolled them up together. It was only the Big Dorm. I went there every day without incident. And it was broad daylight. What was there to fear?

I forced myself to walk quickly and intently, however, along the Sisters' Corridor and out onto the landing, up the stairs and through the door that led to the Dorm.

It smelled of yesterday's deodorant – most of the girls still used aerosols, even though a small group of Fifth Years preached about the hole in the ozone layer and urged them to stop, citing chlorofluorocarbons as the cause. I found the smell clean and pleasant, and it comforted me a little as I glanced around and sighed. Some of the shutters were still closed, of course, from where Lydia and I had stopped working through them the previous night. A flash of irritation ran through me at the thought of having to open them all and delay myself further, but it would have to be done.

I hurriedly replaced Lydia's duvet and pillow on her bed and got to work, making my way around the room, opening what shutters we had managed to close. By the time the last shutter was flung wide and light streamed in across the room from the windows either side, I felt much better and braver. In the distance, I could see the hills purple against the clear sky and felt a ripple of joy at the thought that I would be out there soon. I turned and left the room, my step light, and made my way back toward the door that led down the stairs.

I paused for a moment, my eye drawn, as I passed, to the metal clothes rack that stood in front of the door to the disused Baby Dorm. I had never paid much attention to it before. Now I suddenly couldn't stop myself going over to it for a look. I had to check the door at least, to make sure it was secure, to see if there was anything at all that meant potential intruders in the attic could come down to the dormitories. If I was sure it was secure, then my mind could at least rest a little as I left.

The rack was the type found in a drycleaner's or clothes shop – white-painted metal, a single pole across the top and bottom, held together with a pole at either end, with castors beneath so that it was mobile. I rolled it out of my way, stepping behind it to get a closer look the door behind which had dark wood panels, and a round, brass doorknob, like the old doors to the Study Hall downstairs. I tested it, rattled it gently. It was locked. Underneath the handle was a brass lock – I reached my hand up to the lintel and felt for a key, but there was nothing there. At least if this door was secure, then it would make an intrusion into the dorm more difficult. I pressed my ear against it, listening for anything that I might hear from above, and absent-mindedly knocked it with my knuckles, making a hollow *tap-tap-tap* sound which echoed gently around the dormitory, dying away to silence.

The last thing I expected was a response.

A thump. Then two more in rapid succession. Three booming

knocks. I screamed and leapt back. There *was* someone on the other side. They had been there all along … the whole time that I had been in the Dorm, replacing the duvet, opening the shutters … someone there, listening to me …

I jumped back from the door, and turned to run, to get out of the Dorm as fast as I possibly could, forgetting about the clothes rack which I had rolled straight into my own path of escape. In my haste, I tripped over the bottom bar, crashing through it to the ground, twisting my knee and falling with such force that my head bounced against the pine floor. I winced with the pain, but, terrified, looked back at the door in case something … someone … would emerge through it, in case they were coming for me.

And then, from my position on the floor, I watched in a state of paralysed terror, as the curtains of the cubicles, all the way along to the end of the Dorm, all open and hanging straight and still, were suddenly whipped up by a wind, as if someone were running at high speed past them. One by one, they blew upward, all the way down to the end of the room – toothbrush mugs clattered as they fell over inside plastic basins, some of which were knocked to the floor, all as if a tiny tornado had blasted through the long room. And then, as suddenly and silently as it had begun, the wind was gone again. The curtains hung limp again, the air was still, disturbed only by a single plastic beaker rolling from side to side to stop on the wooden floor somewhere.

For a moment, I was sure I was concussed, that the blow to my head had done this, that I was seeing things, imagining things in my fear. I stayed there for a moment, my brain trying desperately to process what had happened. I was calm – *stunned,* more like – but for just a couple of seconds. The panic seized me again then, however – a ferocious urge to get out of there, in case whatever it was – the wind or the footsteps, whatever had pounded against the other side of the disused door came back for me.

Blessed Frances slams the doors
And runs around the upstairs floors …

Clumsily, I staggered to my feet, my heart pounding, my mouth dry, fear and confusion coursing through me. My knee throbbed as I put weight on it, but I didn't care. I flung myself as quickly as I could toward the door that led out to the stairs and, whimpering, I ran from there, terrified to look back, in case something was coming behind.

It was from in front of me, however, that the next sound came, as I reached the bottom flight of stairs.

A man's voice. "Hallo!" it called, not unfriendly, but cautious.

I turned the final curve in the stairs, unable to stop myself, and ran straight into Matt Flynn who was coming up.

"Ria?" He was completely confused, catching me by both arms to stop me as I frantically struggled to keep moving forward, looking up and behind me.

"Let me go!"

I pushed against him, but he held me firm.

"Ria, what's wrong?" His voice was calm and concerned. He looked up. "Is there someone there?"

I stopped my struggle and closed my eyes for a moment, taking a deep breath. "There's someone … something … up in the Dorm … a wind … someone in the attic …" I knew that I was talking gibberish, that I should slow down, but what if…a sudden surge of fear coursed through me again and I tried to bolt, but Matt wouldn't let me.

"Calm down, Ria!" he snapped, glancing up the stairs again. "Is there someone up in the Dorms? Do you want me to get one of the nuns?"

I shook my head. "They're not here. I'm alone … it's not someone … it's … like a *wind*, and a noise and movement, but no one …"

Matt rubbed my arm and tried his best to look me direct in the eye, gently pushing a strand of hair behind my ear as he did so. "Do you want me to go up with you and check?"

"*No!*" I barked. "I just want to … go … get away …"

He held me firm again for a moment and then, noticing that I had calmed, stepped back and down a couple of steps. It made his face level with mine. I managed now to look at him. Relief flooded through me at the sight of him – those kind dark eyes. His expression was calm, if concerned.

"Okay. Let's go then. Come with me, you've nothing to worry about."

"My bag …" I remembered it suddenly. It was still in my room, the door open and unlocked.

"Where is it?" he said. "I'll get it for you."

Hesitantly, I explained where it was – a part of me nervous about allowing him go to my room alone in case ... in case somehow the nuns found out. Another part, however, wanted my possessions badly – my Pass card, my purse – even in my addled state, I knew that I couldn't leave without them – and I wanted out. Outside that building, outside those gates, preferably never to return. I stood, terrified and alone, as he disappeared up the stairs at my bidding. Fearfully, I kept glancing upwards as I stood there, only allowing relief to creep in when I heard steady approaching footsteps as he returned. He handed me my handbag, and carried my small case for me all the way out, his other hand at the small of my back as he guided me along the Green Corridor, past the Assembly Hall and out the Day Pupils' door which he locked behind him. His old Citroen was parked on the Playing Courts. I noticed that it smelled of pine air freshener, paint and timber as I sank into the passenger seat. Moments later, having placed my case on the back seat, he settled into the driver's seat beside me.

"Are you alright?" He sat there in silence beside me, studying me with furrowed brows and an expression of grave concern.

The strangeness of it all swirled around my brain. It was still early in the day, gloriously bright, the House bathed in the late autumn sunshine, the leaves of the trees around The Walk the most brilliant oranges and browns. It was a perfect day to be outdoors, a day filled with possibility. What had just happened ... it was too unreal, too unbelievable, now that I was outside, safe, with the familiar lemon-and-musk smell of Matt so close beside me.

"I'm such an eejit – I fell upstairs," I managed. "Tripped over a rack ... I bumped my head ... there was a noise ... I thought that there was someone there, but there wasn't ... there couldn't have been ..."

No. There couldn't. It hadn't really happened. What I thought had happened ... It was clear now – I must have knocked myself out for a few moments and dreamed it – the thump against my cheek, the curtains whipped up by an invisible passerby, even the door banging ... it had to have been a muddled dream. I was nervous after last night, tired. My brain was addled – there had to have been a million reasons for what I had just experienced. It wasn't real. Couldn't be.

"Where are you off to? Can I give you a lift somewhere?" Matt asked.

Could he, I wondered? But where was I going … what was I going to do?

He sensed my indecision.

"Or would you like to just come for a drive maybe?" he offered.

I turned and looked at him, managing a brief smile, noticing for the first time that his hand rested on my arm and his thumb rubbed gently against the sleeve of my sweatshirt. I nodded. He hesitated for a moment, and we looked at each other, before he turned the key in the ignition and put the car in gear, driving slowly out through the gate and along by the front of the school and convent, and out the main gate onto the quiet road outside, and away.

Chapter twenty-seven

Ria
BALLYKEERAN
1987

We drove in silence for a while. I could tell that Matt was confused, but I didn't want to speak, to tell him what had taken place. I needed to process it. I watched the countryside slip past – I wanted to soak in the brightness of the day and the newness of the view – the vivid green of the fields either side of the road, dotted with tidy bungalows and farm buildings – and in the distance the purple hills which grew closer as we drove along.

"I didn't think you'd still be there today … I thought it would only be the nuns …"

His voice was hesitant as he tried to begin the conversation. It calmed me a little and I turned to him and managed a smile.

"They're all gone on Retreat," I replied. "There was a mix-up over one of the girls being collected and she and I had to stay last night. She went off early this morning – I was just about to leave myself when … I fell …"

"So you were heading home for the weekend?"

I looked away again. "I had no plans actually," I said. "They had to be cancelled. I just didn't want to stay behind when … well …"

"Did you hurt yourself?" His voice was tender. "I mean, if you need me to take you to a doctor or anything … only you seemed very confused and agitated back there."

154

Back there. It felt like a different place and time. I shook my head and grinned sheepishly, rubbing my head where I had hit it to see if there was a bump of any sort. There wasn't, and my knee had stopped throbbing.

"Not at all, I'm grand," I smiled. "I feel a bit stupid actually. What were you doing in there on a Saturday morning anyway?"

He slowed down at a crossroads and looked left and right. "I went in to get my script that I left there ... *shite!*"

I jumped. "What is it?"

"I left the fecking thing behind me again!" he declared, carrying on through the crossroads. "The whole point of me coming out this morning, and I completely forgot it – I heard you scream, you see, so I went to investigate. It's still sitting on the stage. Mother Dick will surely find it now, and it'll drive her mad but instead of coming to me about it, she'll hand it to Auntie Eileen like it has the plague or Protestantism on it, and give her a lecture about it, to be passed on to me, instead of actually coming and talking to me cos I'm a *man.*"

"Auntie Eileen?"

He glanced at me and grinned. "Didn't you know? That's Sister Cecilia – she's my aunt – well, not exactly, she's my mother's cousin, from Monaghan. Cecilia's her nun name. It's how I get the job on the musical every year. Sheer nepotism."

So that explained that scene in the Hall that day, the informality between him and the nun.

"I wondered why you got on so well. I just thought you had a way with the ... more ... *godly* ladies." I grinned.

He chuckled. "I *am* good with a woman in a wimple, all the same. Thanks for noticing!"

I looked out the window for a moment, smiling. "Sorry about the script," I said, turning to glance at him again, to find him glancing at me already.

"Doesn't matter. I think I know the damn thing in my sleep but I wanted to go over some stage directions. No matter – sure, didn't I find something nicer instead?" He glanced again at me with a grin.

I blushed and looked back out my window, intently studying a copse of trees perched on the side of a hill in the distance, orange and red in the sunlight. We drove on in silence.

After a while, the landscape grew flatter, and I realised that we were driving through bogland. Stretching out either side of me, black and pockmarked where turf had been cut and harvested. Here and there, the occasional pagoda of footed turf remained where it hadn't been bagged and taken home. Grasses and heathers danced in the breeze and puddles filled by last night's rain glistened in the reflection of the sun. Matt took a sharp left, growing closer to me as he leaned into the turn. My nostrils filled with the clean scent rising from the checked flannel shirt that he wore over ripped jeans. I made no effort to move away.

The road grew narrower, the surface rough and we were jostled from side to side as we drove along, finally reaching a space which seemed to serve as a parking area.

Matt stopped and pulled the keys from the ignition. "Bit of fresh air?" he said, smiling at me.

I nodded. "Oh, I've no coat, though." I realised that my trench coat still hung on the back of my bedroom door back at Maria Goretti.

Matt raised a finger to stop me and, reaching to the back seat, handed me an item of dark clothing. "Sure, give this a go – it'll be a bit big."

I took it gratefully. It was an American varsity-style jacket, black and white, emblazoned with the number 27 on the sleeve, chest and back. "Thank you," I said. "I'm sure it'll be fine, but what about you?"

He opened the door and stepped from the car as he responded, "I'll be grand – there's a parka in the boot. Now, come on, it's a lovely day."

He retrieved his parka and slid it on and we set off. We strolled in silence for a while, trudging onto the bog which spread out flat and far around us. I paused for a moment to take it in, the sheer *difference* of it from the fields and farms which we had passed along the way. It was bleak, yet oddly beautiful. Empty and silent as far as the eye could see, dotted with heathers and ferns and odd little lichens. It even felt different. There was something about the air, about the gentle wind that gusted along – something clearer and purer than normal. I took a deep breath.

"I've never been on an actual bog before," I explained.

Matt had turned to squint at me – the sun was in his eyes and his head was tilted to one side.

"It's really beautiful up here," I said. "Peaceful."

"I'll have to bring you up here in the summer then," he replied. "The air is delicious and the bog cotton is everywhere, bobbing around in the breeze. We'll get you footing some turf – flask of tea and ham sandwiches for lunch. You'll have a tan like you've been in Mustique!"

I laughed and pointed to my red hair. "With my colouring, I doubt it!" I replied.

There was something about what he had just said that warmed me more than the sun on my face. The prospect of a summer with him. Of still being around him, after the winter, months ahead.

"Is it hard to work on a bog?" I asked.

We fell into step side by side and continued to trudge along over the black ground through the dancing grasses.

"It'll hurt your back, for sure," he remarked. "And you have to watch your step as it can be deceptively dangerous, but there's nothing like it. Repetitive, physical, silent. It's quite rewarding – and it's great for clearing the head. I did all my mam's turf last year for her – there's a local fellah has a machine so he'll cut your plot for you, but I did the rest. Evenings, weekends – footing it to dry, like this ..." He bent and made an arrangement of sods that were left scattered on the ground – two down, two across, two more across that – sods of turf arranged in a small tower. "You arrange them so that the wind can get through them," he explained. "You can't burn wet turf so the drier they are, the better. We had a couple of good spells during the summer so I really knuckled down then and got the whole lot home. The best bit though is stopping for a big swig of Club Orange every now and again – and a bag of Tayto! You really work up an appetite in this fresh air – and you sleep like a baby!" He stood up again, smiling.

"And then you pack up your Club Orange and go off and do a musical with a bunch of teenage girls and some nuns?" I grinned.

He threw back his head and laughed. "Exactly!" he replied. He kicked at the small tower of stray, wet turf sods with his dirty canvas runner and walked on. "If you put it that way, maybe I need a proper job."

"What exactly *is* your job?" I asked, before regretting the question. He might not have one. And that could be a sensitive subject.

He didn't flinch, however. "I'm an actor," he replied. "Not a very good one, mind, but it's sort of … my calling, or my destiny or whatever you want to call it. I take work where I can – I've been living in Galway since the summer – I did a play there. Before that, I was in Dublin – I go where the work takes me, so every year in October, in the absence of something more lucrative, I come and help out with Auntie Eileen's – sorry, Sister Cecilia's – musical. I'm the closest to a professional director that the nuns are comfortable to allow around the girls – they reckon that, even though I'm a man, I'm sort of safe because I'm related to one of them, and while the work is pretty strange for an actor, it helps to pay rent for the next gig I get, wherever that is. You can say what you like about the nuns, but the money is bloody great."

"I know," I replied.

He turned and smiled at me. "Is that why you do it? The job that you do? Being the Guardian?"

I blushed and nodded. He had me pegged as money-grabbing now, I was sure.

"Because I wouldn't do that job for love nor money."

"The job's a tough one, alright," I answered. "But the money … it's not to buy clothes or go on a holiday or anything. I'm saving really hard for something." I suddenly stopped.

"For what?" Matt asked.

I was suddenly unsure. It had been for The Plan, of course. Myself and Leonard. Going to America. Getting married. The kids, the peanut-butter-and-jelly sandwiches, Thanksgiving. It suddenly hit me like a brick that I actually didn't want that. Not anymore.

"For what?" repeated Matt.

I shook my head. "I want … to … travel. I'm saving up to travel. Saving for the future. To go away somewhere. Out of Ireland. What do you want to do in the future?" I deflected the conversation back to him. I needed to think.

"I'm going away too," he replied. "As soon as the musical is done, in fact. After Christmas."

My heart sank. "Where?" I asked.

"London," he replied, bending down to pluck a blade of grass.

In the distance, a bird gave an odd, lonely cry, and a gust of wind caught my hair. I pulled the jacket tighter around myself and slid

158

my arms back up the sleeves so that my hands were covered.

"I'm going to try my hand over there – there's loads of lads that I went to school with over there, working on building sites and stuff. It's funny – there's fellahs that have degrees coming out of their eyeballs working as brickies and sparks wherever they can get the work. I'd pick something up easily enough to pay the bills – quicker than here, God knows. And while I'm there I can do auditions or get involved in a theatre group or something. It's the opportunities, you know? The excitement. It's time I grew up, you know? Finally do what I should be doing with myself. Can't live with Mammy your whole life now, can you?"

"You live at home now?" I asked, only half listening to my own question. What Matt was saying, about growing up, getting where he wanted to be in life – it all rang in my ears as I slowly realised that I hadn't a clue what I wanted to do – to actually achieve for myself.

"Between jobs, I come running back to my mam and the home-made soda bread and Mass and the *Late Late* and *Glenroe* and getting her turf home and what have you. What about you?"

The question made me giggle. "You know where I live! With twenty nuns and seventy-odd teenage girls. No home-made soda bread, but plenty of stew and potato cakes and tiny bowls of cornflakes. Not much *Glenroe* – lots of Mass though!"

He smiled back. "We should get together there sometimes," he drawled in a mock-American accent. "Hang out? Let's do Communion – I'll find a window in my diary!"

We looked at each other, laughing, until I stumbled on a small hillock underfoot and fell against him. Matt grabbed my hand to steady me, and then didn't let go. Instead, as I shyly watched my feet, I felt his fingers twine through mine. A small firework of joy burst in my stomach.

"When you're not living with nuns and teenage girls and praying though, where do you live – *Number One, what's your name and where do you come from*?" he said, impersonating Cilla Black perfectly and I burst out laughing again, a nervous laugh, much bigger than the joke deserved.

"Nowhere," I replied, once I had settled a little. I felt giddy. "I used to have a flat in Rathmines but I got rid of everything when I got this job ...”

Without warning, he pulled me toward him and kissed me.

I froze at first, but then I sank into it, into him. When we broke apart, he cupped my cheek in the palm of his left hand and made me look at him directly. He was flushed and smiling. “I'm sorry,” he whispered. “For doing that ... I should have asked.”

I shook my head, unable to speak. My breath came rapidly and I was afraid that I would stammer, lose the words – could I think of the right thing to say in the first place?

“Actually, I'm not really sorry at all.” Matt still whispered, still held my cheek, still held my hand with his other hand. He started to giggle, as did I. “I'm not a bit sorry, in fact.”

He kissed me again.

“I've wanted to do that since I saw you in the Assembly Hall that first day ... *Jesus*, but I need to work on my lines ... that was awful, wasn't it?”

My body shook with laughter, as did his. We were still pressed together. I nodded, but lifted my head for another kiss. This time he wrapped his arms around me as we kissed and laughed. When we stopped kissing, he pressed my head into his neck.

“You make it worthwhile ... going in there every day,” he whispered, releasing me so that he could look at me again.

“More than ‘Oh, What A Beautiful Mornin”?” I teased and was silenced with yet another kiss.

“More than ‘Pore Jud is Dead’, even!”

We laughed again. Kissed again.

I inhaled the sweet, clean smell of him, the feel of stubble against my chin, the smoothness of his cheek when I ran my hand over it and then into his tousled hair. The broadness of his back, his shoulder blades ... I wanted to never stop kissing him, laughing with him. It felt as though time had stopped – the stillness of the bog surrounding us, cocooning us. We were entirely alone, save for twittering birds. At some point, somehow, we walked back to his car, hand in hand, pausing now and then to kiss again – laughing all the time. I felt free, released, calm.

“So what's your plan for the weekend, then?” he asked as we reached the car and he pulled me close again.

I shrugged. “Not sure. I was going to head to the village – get a bus somewhere – stay in a B&B or something." I looked at him and grinned. "Have an adventure!"

He smiled, and studied me for a moment. "How about having an adventure with me, then? Would that be an idea?"

I studied him back for a moment, then nodded, suddenly unable to think of being anywhere else but with him. Where everything was suddenly bright and funny and special, where it felt *safe*. I had no thoughts left of what had happened the night before. Even the school itself didn't exist in my brain anymore – there was no room for it.

"I suppose," I pretended to sigh, settling for what he offered.

He bellowed with laughter.

"What'll we do, then?" I laughed back.

He stepped away from me, and gallantly opened the passenger door of his car with a flourish. "I was headed to Galway myself," he grinned. "Fancy a lift?"

I climbed into his car, smiling.

Chapter twenty-eight

Ria
LONDON
April 2015

"You need to get to bed," I said softly as Jess opened her eyes.

I had broken off my story to watch her drift off toward sleep for a while now.

"Did I fall asleep?" Jess's voice was thick as she roused herself, blinking and looking around the room as though she wasn't quite sure where she was, or what she had done. "What did I miss? You went to Galway – was there more kissing? I feel like the kid in *The Princess Bride* except I'm not going to bed until you tell me there *was* more kissing!"

I smiled at the memory. "You didn't miss anything and there *was* more kissing."

"And?"

"And it was wonderful. And we went to the King's Head and listened to a trad band and got tipsy on Guinness ... and we drove to the Burren and walked on the rocks, and saw a dolmen, and strolled down the Claddagh in the moonlight – we did all the Galway stuff you're meant to do, I guess."

Jess stood up and stretched. "That wasn't the meaning of my '*and*'," she said sternly.

"Not the first night," I replied coyly. "But the second ..."

"And again ... *aaand?*" prompted Jess.

"Good God, Jess, how much detail do you want?" I laughed. "It

162

was wonderful. It was romance-novel good – I'm not sure what else I can say."

"*Plenty, I'm sure!*" Jess screeched. "*You had a fling with this guy and I can tell that you're still in love with him, thirty years later What the hell happened?*"

I paused, swallowed, and thought for a moment. If only it were that straightforward.

"And if he was so out-of-this-world, what happened that it ended between you? And what did he think of all that spooky stuff that was going on? What did he make of all that?"

"It was really complicated … and I never told him," I replied. "In the long run, what could I say? He'd think I was insane, I was sure of it – and I was having too much of a good time to let that happen. And I wasn't sure myself what had happened – and I was afraid that if I told anyone that something had happened, and I'd still jaunted off to Galway with the musical director for a dirty weekend that I'd be in deep waste up to my neck, *vis a vis* my *job,* so I said nothing."

"But what *was* it all?" Jess was caught out by a sudden yawn as she spoke.

I looked her in the eye and shrugged. "*It was what it was,*" I whispered.

We looked at each other in silence for a while, Jess in disbelief.

"And you're sure it was him you saw today?"

I nodded. And there, for an instant, I saw him again. "Knocked me for six. It just all reminded me of then – seeing him here like that. It was like another lifetime coming back to me and I realised I had never told you."

She regarded me in silence for a while. "So why tell me now?"

I looked away from her and shrugged. "Not sure. Getting old, I suppose, just wanted to … remember it, maybe."

She snorted. "You're fifty-three years old. Younger than Madonna. I hardly think she sits up all night with … with Gwyneth Paltrow in her kitchen rambling on about the 80's because 'she's getting old'."

"Getting *older*, then," I replied. "And yes, I'm rambling. So go on to bed for yourself."

"We'll have a lie-in and a lazy day tomorrow," she said, opening her mouth wide in a yawn. "Maybe you can finish your story then, eh, Ree?"

She padded past me to the sink and filled a glass with water. She patted me on the shoulder as she passed me again, mumbling "Goodnight" without turning as she trudged from the room, exhausted. I heard her footsteps, heavy on the stairs, the click of her bedroom door above.

I sighed as I slipped off the stool where I sat, rubbing at the base of my stiff back as I crossed the kitchen and twisted the blind pull so that I could see out. It was heading toward dawn already, the sky grey through the slats of the blinds as I stared out into Jess's tidy garden and up into the sky.

I remembered doing this out over the gardens of Maria Goretti, after Galway, peering out the window in the mornings, looking up into the darkening winter sky and visualising him, tingling as I remembered him asleep in the dawn light of that B&B, my stomach gently rolling with excitement at the thought of a forbidden glance, a formal conversation, a snatched kiss later that day.

After Galway, every moment was a moment of opportunity. A glance that we thought no one else could see, or his hand brushing against my sleeve or my back as we passed each other somewhere. A smile, a look of longing, one of his notes.

Whatever had happened to him? Where had he gone when I left? And where was he now?

Was he close by, in fact? Had he been here – in London – all along? Had he married, divorced, like me? Did he have children like me? Did he know that I lived here? What if he had seen me before? Did he even remember me?

And if I hadn't seen him in Covent Garden, would I just have carried on living that life as before or would I have ever thought of all this, ever felt like this again?

Tomorrow, I could finish my story, Jess had said. Could I though? Could I really?

Sure, I could tell her what happened next. Could tell her what had stirred all of this up in my mind, seeing Matt like that in Covent Garden – a man who had become so much part of the past that I wasn't sure if he were real or not. I could tell her why that newspaper story about the remains in the bog unnerved me so, and why. I could even tell her the truth about Emma, I supposed. But could I truly tell her the end of my story?

I shook my head. Of course I couldn't, I realised.

Because you can't finish a story that has no ending. And suddenly, that bothered me more than anything I had ever known, it started a ringing my ears and an alarm in my head. It had been a story that had lasted for almost thirty years, without an ending. And there would probably be none. Ever.

Chapter twenty-nine

BALLYKEERAN
January 1943

The child and her father walked in silence.

He held her wrist, rather than her hand, giving it a little yank every now and again to keep her apace with him. By the time they reached their destination, she was breathless, her little-girl legs carrying her at Dada-speed. Before, he would have slowed for her, waited patiently while she stopped to blow dock seeds into the air, or watch a Hairy Molly make its way across her path. But not today. With one hand, he firmly kept her at his side, with the other he held her grey suitcase. There wasn't much inside – she could tell by the weight of it – but it was "all she'd need". At least that's what Mammy had said when she'd kicked it across the kitchen floor at her with her foot before disappearing back into her room from where the child soon heard crying that turned to prayers, then back to crying.

She was used to that now. It was almost half a year since Frances had gone and her mother had slowly gone madder and madder. She had grown thin, so thin that her bones seemed to be in danger of poking through her skin. She didn't go to work at the convent to clean anymore, didn't clean or cook at home either – just stayed in her room and prayed all hours of the day to get her "baby back", pleading with God to tell her what she had done wrong, what she could have done better, demanding to know why he had taken

Frances, and not "the other one". She didn't even try to keep her prayers silent or private. Didn't care who heard.

As her mother had grown louder, her father had grown more silent. Gone were the hugs, and the piggybacks, the long, patient walks over the bog and around the fields. There were no more tickles, no more invitations to touch the ceiling when he would lift her high above his head and laugh as she tipped the beams above her. Instead there was quiet, as if he had grown back inside himself and could only look out. He went to work on the farm all day, then came home and made the dinner and swept the floor when he had time. He tended to her raving mother, and late at night he drowned his sorrows in porter or whiskey or both if he had them – and sometimes, from her hiding places in the house, she watched him weep, rivers of sorrow tracking down his cheeks. Always silent.

In Frances' absence, the girl heard all of her mother's heavenward pleas, and watched her father's noiseless grief and she felt the hunger and the cold and thought about how they neglected her, even though she didn't know the word 'neglect'. And sometimes it made her sad. But more times it made her angry, an anger that made her feel as though she had been lit on fire, and she clenched her fingertips into her palms until they left marks and made her mind go somewhere else where none of this could really be happening.

And then came the day after that miserable Christmas, when she had just turned eleven, when her mother kicked the suitcase across the floor of the kitchen and disappeared again. And her father took her by the wrist, and they walked together across the fields. Until they stood outside the familiar door where she had sometimes come with Mammy, when she had still been Mammy, and watched her polish and mop, proud of the gleaming parquet and speckless wood. She recognised the tall woman in the long, black gown who answered the door, the gleaming white wimple framing her face. She recognised the smell of soil and earthy plants that surrounded her as she stepped into the porch, and her heart filled with ice and hammered against her chest as she turned, expecting her father to be close behind her, but seeing him instead take a step backward from the door through which she had entered, and nod his head reverentially to the nun who said, without emotion: "We'll take care of her from here, Mr Phelan."

She didn't see her father turn and go because the nun ushered her inside the main door, into the dark and cold corridor beyond which she had once helped Mammy mop clean. She didn't see his shoulders sag as he headed home to right what had been upset earlier, to pick up the overturned chairs and sweep up the broken china. To make dinner that would be left uneaten by her mother, and to spend another night crying silently into the flames of the fire.

And neither did she see the other child. A cold little girl with damp hair and ragged clothes. Who watched her from between the headstones of the Nuns' Graveyard. Who watched the man retreat, and the child disappear into the darkness with the veiled woman.

The nuns had charge of both of them now.

PART 2

Chapter thirty

BALLYKEERAN
October 1987

The nun laced her fingers together and pressed her hands against her bowed forehead. It was time for her private evening prayer just after tea, when the students were studying and the sisters about their business. She had made her way, as always, through the darkening gardens and in through the Goretti Door of the chapel. At this time, she could be completely alone, could give herself over totally. If she began now, she might have lost herself in the words by the time her visitor was sure to arrive. She began the Rosary in her head. She had no beads, but it didn't matter. She knew the rhythm of the prayer like a song, knew by the very feel of it when it was time for a 'Glory Be'. She would lose herself in its familiar cadence, the soothing mantra repeated over and over again. She would go inside her head with it, *become* it.

She adored solitary prayer. The sweet release of it from her burdens. Like handing herself over to God, inside her own head. When she prayed, she forgot everything – the running of the convent and school, her own moral state, the heavy weight that she had carried around inside herself for all of these years. There was a headiness to it, an absolute state of ecstasy to be achieved – she often felt giddy when she reached the end of her prayers and had to sit quietly on a pew until the spinning sensation had passed and her senses had calmed. She wondered sometimes if this was what others

171

felt when they engaged in acts of pleasure? And then she immediately discounted the notion. There was no state that the body could achieve to equal or surpass the peaks that she reached inside her own mind. Indeed, as she prayed, she often forgot that she had a body and as she reached the pinnacle, the climax of her prayers, and began to wind down, the very feeling of her hands against her face felt strange. She often returned to herself to find her cheeks damp from tears that she had cried in her elevated state, a state that she could never have described to anyone because there were no words to explain the utter bliss and peace that it gave her, no description fitting for the plane onto which she transcended. And no one other than her could reach it. Sometimes she felt sure that this was heaven itself. The sheer, sweet, solitary escape into her own mind where God was waiting. She wished that she could be there forever.

Often, she felt like Jesus in Gethsemane. Her path that she had chosen – that God had chosen for her – was difficult and tiring. She wished that someone would take the cup from her, that someone else would take on the heavy load of the moral guidance of the students, the well-being of the nuns in her care, but if God had wanted someone else to do the job, then he would have chosen them. It was fitting that it was her load to carry. To set young girls on the right path through life, to teach them to value God and themselves, to stay pure and strong, to be steady-footed on their path, with Jesus as their companion. To do the right thing.

That was what she tried to do all the time now. The right thing. She had made that decision the day she was old enough to enter the convent. To atone, to make amends, to prove that she could do right, that she was deserving of the love of God.

She had carried it with her throughout her novitiate, to the missions in Africa and Mexico, and back to inner-city Dublin. She tried not to think about Dublin. About the fallen girls. The girls who had not tried their best to remain pure. The girls who had the audacity to cry when their mewling spawn was taken from them. Didn't they realise that they were being given a second chance? That their slate was being wiped clean for them? That they had a whole life to live, and dedicate to God now? She hadn't been able to stay there for long, had prayed and wept and begged her Lord to take her out of there, away from their round, fecund bodies, away from their tears, and those of the infants in their cribs at night, the product of sin. Why should they be comforted? The stain of original sin on their souls so bad that they would have been better off in Purgatory.

So when God had sent her here – had sent her home – in one way it was an enormous relief. Away from the horrors of those Dublin girls – it had been easier to teach the heathens in Africa – their godlessness was through no fault of their own, and Jesus was waiting for those who took the right path to him. But the girls in Dublin, with their weaknesses and stupidity, making the conscious decision to go down the wrong path – that, she could not abide.

In another way, however, to return to the place where she was born and made, to come back to Ballykeeran, that was the most difficult challenge of all that God could have sent her.

Because here, she could never be alone.

She began to pray harder, whispering the words now instead of just thinking them. *"Holy Mary, Mother of God, Pray for us sinners, now and at the hour ..."*

She forced herself to whisper them louder, harder, faster, trying her best to accelerate the process, to reach her state of bliss, where nothing from the outside world could enter, where she was protected.

But she was too late. She wasn't protected. As hard as she tried to force the barrier of prayer between herself and the inevitable, she could not. Because there was that feeling in the air that prayer could not override. The nun whimpered as she heard the door of the chapel close behind her. Yet there was no sound of footsteps padding across the polished parquet floor, no dull thud of a choir stall being pulled down and used as an elbow rest for a kneeling nun, no creak from a wooden kneeler as someone sidled into a pew. There was nothing except the sensation of the cold draught that wafted past her before the candles on the side altars were extinguished in one sharp gust of air. The nun didn't – couldn't – open her eyes to look, but she knew by the smell in the air that tendrils of grey smoke wafted upward like wraiths from their blackened wicks, before dissipating. She knew that the chapel would be dull now, dusk taking the light of the day away, leaving only black and grey shadows in the small chapel, not all of them still.

The nun felt the cold air pass her again, returning in the opposite direction to which it had passed at first. *Now* there was a noise – a gentle creaking of wood as an unseen weight pressed down on it. Behind her, always behind her. At her left shoulder. She felt the cold against her ear, and rubbed the side of her head against her shoulder to eliminate it. But it didn't work. It never worked.

In desperation, the nun separated her fingers and placed both palms flat against her face, muttering the prayers now, the words flat against her hands as they rose in volume and speed. If only she could stop what was coming. If only God would hear her this time, if only God would take this remnant of her past and put it to rest. Why her, Lord? Why her?

The breath was icy against her cheek as the voice began to speak in its unnatural whisper. "*Evelyn,*" it said. She tried to block it out. She was not that girl anymore. She hadn't done anything wrong, had she? And she had said sorry a thousand, no, a million times. She had begged for forgiveness. Through Jesus and his Holy Mother and the saints and angels, through the offerings of the living and the souls of the dead. And still nothing worked. "*Evelyn,*" the voice hissed. Always in her ear, always reminding her that no matter who she thought she had become, she was still no one. She was still a child listening at doors, a child abandoned and bereft of love.

"*Holy Mary, Mother of God …*" the nun's prayers trailed away as she began to weep. Not in prayerful elation this time, however, but in deepest grief and remorse.

"*What did you do, Evelyn?*" the voice hissed. "*Why did you leave me? Why do you still leave me? Why am I alone when you are so near?*"

Everything grew dark as the nun was forced to listen, her bones chilled, her heart in darkest sorrow. This was her punishment. This was what God had decided for her. Her own private Purgatory.

Chapter thirty-one

Ria
BALLYKEERAN
November 1987

When we returned to Maria Goretti, I knew we had until Christmas.

Till the final rehearsal was done, till the last applause died away on the last performance of *Oklahoma*, till the set was placed into storage in the cellar underneath the stage to be recycled and reconstructed the following year. Then school would break up for Christmas. And after that, for Matt and me, who knew?

Being with him – in our glorious, secret, stolen love affair – made me different – different than I had been with anyone before.

It gave me a transcendent feeling, as if I rose above the daily grind, the long hours – the freezing cold afternoons as the light grew dim, standing there with a whistle around my neck, refereeing another game of volleyball, until it was time to usher the girls in to change back into their uniforms to troop in silence to the Refectory for another sparse meal. I'd watch them eat it excitedly, chatting animatedly, for the fifteen minutes that they were allowed – the remaining fifteen minutes spent clearing up in silence. Occasionally, I'd look up to see Benedicta standing outside, her face thin and pale, against the glass of the door – or, worse still, peering through the glass of the internal windows that overlooked the Ref from the Brown Corridor outside. Her frown was always disapproving, before she sped away in her state of perpetual troubled silence, like a living ghost. Often, her gaze was directed at me, and not at the girls. It made me feel like an insect under a microscope; made me burn with discomfort, and, oddly, something close to shame. I feared she could see inside me – see my secret. More than once, I wondered if she knew? If she was toying with me in some way, perfectly aware of what Matt and I were doing, yet observing me, biding her time before dismissing me. But it never came. And I kept vigilant in my secret-keeping – no diary entries, no outward signs of happiness. I could *not* lose my job. Whatever became of us when Matt left for London, I felt sure that I would have to stick out the remainder of the year here at Maria Goretti.

The idea of being here without him filled me with dread. Apart from the illicit joy of being near him, the simmering temptation of being so close yet unable to so much as touch, his being here made me feel *safe* – which was silly, because there was absolutely nothing that he could do to protect me from whatever it was that I had experienced here – I wasn't even sure if I *needed* protecting from it. But while he was there, it was like being in a room with the light on. Without him, or, at least, the promise of seeing him the next day, I felt I was in darkness – vulnerable and defenceless.

I hadn't mentioned that night with Lydia to him, ever. And, as time went on, and no questions were asked of me by the nuns about the events of that night, and no conversation passed between Lydia and myself about it – and, most importantly, nothing else odd happened, the fear of it lessened in my mind. Thinking about it, in retrospect, I could apply logic to the events with the distance of time, and my fear subsided. There had been a storm and a power cut, we had been frightened, old buildings can make odd noises, particularly in harsh weather. I wasn't fully aware of how this building reacted when under pressure from heavy winds and rain, and also, practically speaking, there simply couldn't be someone living in the attics. How would they get in and out to get food? Or use the toilet? No. None of what I imagined made any sense. It was simply my imagination jumping to conclusions in the dark of a storm. Silly, really.

So I kept silent. If I told Matt, I knew I would sound irrational and alarmist; if I told the nuns – and they clearly weren't concerned about anything – then I would be considered insane, and probably sacked on the spot.

So I carried on and did what I had to do in the way I always did it.

I was used to it all now – used to the bed in my small room, used to the constant silence. I had grown accustomed, too, to the cold that pervaded everything, to the ringing bells dictating my routine. I even confiscated the occasional item – only when it was unavoidable, however. A hairdryer here, a magazine there, the occasional small radio. I hated myself for doing it, but it seemed to keep Benedicta off my back.

So I carried on, teaching my classes during the day, supervising study at night-time, watching all of the heads bent low over books, or turned to the ceiling, eyes closed as they wordlessly recited information they wished to retain, testing their own memories in silence. I wondered how these girls saw me – as a subordinate of the nuns that they despised, their age predisposing them to a hatred of authority, I had no doubt. And while a part of me would feel cold at the thought of it, the idea that they saw me as an emotionless lackey would ignite something else in me. The part of me that kept my own secret. I would retreat into my own thoughts, memories of touching and kissing and laughter, and that *energised* me, fed my soul. It made me feel alive again, like *me* – but a hidden me, a *new* me discovered in the most unlikely of places.

Matt and I agreed that it was sensible to create a distance between us while inside the House or school. His forays to the Staffroom for coffee when he knew I would be there ended, as did my visits to the Hall during rehearsals to 'check on progress'. When we did meet, or even converse in passing, I'd feel the delicious panic of possibility rise in me, studying the faces of anyone who happened to be nearby for a sign, some indication that they knew, that we had given ourselves away, yet feeling almost disappointed when no one noticed. A part of me wanted to scream at them to look at me, to see how incredible this was, to see that I *wasn't* a servant to the sisters of Maria Goretti, a nun-in-the-making – I felt sure that the other teachers had come to view me this way also – but an exciting, vibrant woman, desired and different, set apart from the rest of them. And another part of me wanted to keep the secret in a tiny, perfect ball in my pocket, so that no one might ever know, in case an outsider's knowledge would taint it in some way. I wonder how

I ever actually managed to teach classes, my head reeling from the secrecy and the excitement.

So Matt and I managed to conduct our affair, if you could call it that, outside school walls. I began to actually take my afternoons off on Wednesdays, my days off on Sundays. I would leave the convent on foot, and we would meet somewhere, he in his car, driving as far as we could in our allotted time together to walk in private and talk, or share a quick meal; we drove to the nearby mountains and walked along scrubby grassland, sometimes white with hoarfrost as winter settled in. We kissed in his car overlooking the countryside, made hurried love in the cramped space of the car before sitting huddled over a pot of coffee in a café or restaurant of whichever large town was nearby in the hope that we would be anonymous there, nervously watching others lest we should be caught out. We talked, laughed, debated, fingers laced together, or tracing the line of the other's profile – did everything that young lovers are supposed to do, living in a forbidden dream world that couldn't have been further from reality.

Chapter thirty-two

Lydia
BALLYKEERAN
December 1987

I'm starting to wonder if I shouldn't put carpentry on my CV as a skill. I've pretty much single-handedly built the Surrey with the Fringe on Top, and Aunt Eller's porch. Finally, the whole set is almost finished and the cast is in full-on rehearsal mode. I *love* this bit. Excused from classes and study whenever Mr Flynn or Sister Cecilia need us – which is most of the time.

It's mostly Mr Flynn's doing. He calls us his 'crew' and even if we're not practising scene changes and prop shifts, he has us watching the rest of the cast – being his eyes and ears, he says. It's such a doss. We'll pay for it after Christmas when we have to do our Christmas exams the first week back instead of before the holidays like other schools – and it'll be a nightmare with the mocks starting at the end of March – although we'll have a ton of the revision done so maybe it'll balance out ... either way, between now and Christmas, I'm going to make the most of things. Because after that it's hard, hard work. It's my CAO form, and revision and study every hour that God sends – Christmas Day even.

I'm not big on Christmas. Sometimes I envy the others when they talk about their Christmas Day – Carmel's family, with their big, cosy, dirty old farmhouse teeming with massive dogs, and all her younger brothers and sisters. Her mum is permanently cooking, it seems. She says they have a massive turkey, roast and mashed potatoes, six different kinds of veg, stuffing and even little sausages – chipolatas, they call them. Carmel says they eat Milk Tray for breakfast and have as much plum pudding and trifle and ice cream as they can manage, and they all go for a long walk after Mass to make room for dinner and play Monopoly afterwards. It sounds really cool.

Her mum invited me actually, that time I stayed for the Bank Holiday weekend. After all that … weirdness. That really strange night with Miss Clancy. I try not to think about it too much – I mean, what exactly happened? Who knows? Miss Clancy's never brought it up to me, and none of the nuns ever asked me what happened, so I've put it out of my head. There's been nothing more, after all. It's all been calm for a few months so maybe it was just that strange storm? I dunno.

Anyway, I told Carmel's mum that I was really grateful for the invite but I'd best go home to Dublin and spend it with Uncle Neville, although I don't know why. He cooks a roast chicken and we eat it in the dining room – which is always cold, but less damp than some of the other rooms in the house, which is a Brucie Bonus. I hate it actually. He makes frozen roast potatoes and peas, and allows me half a glass of wine while he polishes off the rest of the bottle. Then, afterwards, he tells me he's "popping out" for a bit before disappearing until the small hours, off to some party his friend in Clontarf throws every year, and leaves me with a Marks and Spencer trifle and a box of Maltesers. I sometimes wonder what my mum would have made of it all – how Uncle Neville takes care of me. I remember Christmas with her and my dad, before the accident. I remember our house in Raheny being cosy and warm and bright. And I remember a big tree with coloured lantern-shaped lights – reds and blues and yellows and greens – and one time opening a parcel wrapped in paper with Christmas wreaths on it to find a big dolly inside – with blonde curly hair, and a green dress and little white shoes and socks that you could take on and off. Her eyes opened and closed, I remember. And she had tiny, pale pink lips. She was called Mia – I remember it said so on the box. I sometimes wonder where she went afterwards?

Anyway, Christmas Day will be as good a day for revision as any. As will Stephen's Day, and every other day of the break. It's not like I have anything planned. I might take one day off. Maybe go to the cinema, get a coffee in town or something. Treat myself to an album in HMV. Or maybe Uncle Neville will take the opportunity to host a big eighteenth for me, seeing as I won't be home for my actual birthday, which was yesterday? As if. I doubt he'll even send a card. Or remember, for that matter.

I wasn't expecting Mr Flynn to remember either. I mean, he's nothing to me, but he's so kind. There I was, yesterday, painting away, listening to The Smiths on the tape deck, when next thing I heard the rest of the crew singing 'Happy Birthday' from offstage, and I turned round to see them all with a Swiss Roll on a plate and a heap of candles stuck in it all round. Mr Flynn called it 'The Flaming Hedgehog', which we agreed was a good name for a pub, and we sat around and the seven of us ate it. He even had cans of Lilt for us – I love Lilt – and we all did a big 'cheers'. It was a good giggle, all of us sitting around doing nothing for a bit, until Sister Cecilia arrived in with her sheets of music and the principals trailing behind her like exhausted ducklings and we got back to work while they warbled out 'It's a Scandal! It's a Outrage!' over and over again.

I was a bit surprised that we had time to do that, because Mr Flynn has reached busy mode with opening night coming up soon. He gets in a sort of bad form at this stage of things – not 'giving out' bad form, but sort of quiet. Not messing like he normally does, or chatty.

We've had some really great chats about films while I've been doing Stage Crew. He knows his stuff – I guess he would, being a director and an actor and all. It's cool chatting to him. And working with him. He's really patient about showing you stuff and when you do something right, he really makes you feel like you've done a great job.

Miss Clancy is a bit like that too, in fairness to her. Although since the October weekend I've sort of steered clear of her. And I think she's steered clear of me too. It's like, somehow, we have this *bond* because of something that happened – like the whole sleeping in her room thing – but neither of us really want to talk about it. I don't anyway – it's really embarrassing actually – I haven't mentioned it to a single soul for fear they'd slag me about it forever, and I can only guess that she doesn't because she hasn't been popping into the Hall to see how rehearsals are going since then. In fact, she's steered clear of everything, which is really noticeable because before she was always coming in to say hi or chat to someone about something, always having a little laugh with Mr Flynn – we were all sure they fancied each other for a while actually. But then that all just stopped. *C'est la vie*, I guess.

Whatever. One more month to the Christmas holidays, then six more months till exams. In the bigger scheme of things, that's nothing. And then I'm free. Out of here for good. And on to a whole new beginning. The first day of the rest of my life, and all that.

Chapter thirty-three

Ria
BALLYKEERAN
December 1987

There's a quality to the light on a sunny December afternoon – an intensity, that reaches a point where it turns to evening, and suddenly dims, as if someone has turned down a switch very slightly, or as if daylight has suddenly got tired and lost power.

It was after school had finished on a Monday, just as the light dimmed, on the cusp of daylight and dusk, as I strolled slowly around The Walk. Slowly, because I was coming down with something. My limbs ached, my appetite was gone and I longed for sleep. The day had been a struggle, from Assembly that morning where the second candle on the Advent wreath had been ceremonially lit, to the ringing of the bell at ten past four when I gratefully downed tools and let the students go. Back in the Staffroom, I took some paracetamol and bundled myself up in my coat, hat, scarf and gloves before reluctantly heading outside to supervise the Boarders in their afternoon activities. There was hardly anything to supervise – just a couple of girls shooting basketball hoops, and one girl running laps of The Walk. Organised games and training had finished for the term, as most of the girls were involved in the musical. It was compulsory for boarders to participate, and most of them were currently at work in the Assembly Hall, running lines, practising songs and dance routines – all supervised by Matt. I knew that I had no right to, but watching

183

him concentrate on the work, watching his way with the students, watching him turn his hand from wielding a drill to belting out a chorus of 'Oklahoma!' with them made me proud. I had peeped into the Hall on my way out for my walk. It was warm in there, and it smelled of paint and freshly sawn timber. I longed to sit down on one of the wide windowsills amidst the excitement and just watch, but knew that was unwise. We had promised to be careful, as exciting as it was to be in such close proximity to each other.

Excitement was high around the school. There was much talk of Christmas – of plans and gifts, of when 'the tree' was going up at home, of going Christmas shopping, all mixed in with the excited chatter about the musical which would run for six performances over the last week of term – only a little over a week away now. It would start on the Friday night – all boarders stayed for the final weekend – with two performances on the Sunday and the final show on the Tuesday. There was then a half day Wednesday – which consisted of tidying up the classrooms, a school Mass in the Assembly Hall and then a short party before everyone broke up at lunchtime. It sounded like an informal week, filled with excitement.

I was dreading it.

It was the last week when Matt would be here every day. And the thought of him not being around me in my orbit and I in his, made me feel awfully alone.

We hadn't discussed exactly when he would depart for London, but I knew that it was early January, after he had spent Christmas at home with his mother. He'd be gone in the New Year, and I'd be here, still, returning to two weeks of post-Christmas in-house exams and then heading into the Easter term, and the intensive pressure of the Inter and Leaving Cert mocks. I disliked the spring term. Hated the cold, damp weather that lasted well into March or April, hated the pressure that sat on my shoulders. And that had been in my previous school, where I could return at night to the sanctuary of my little flat in Rathmines and my own life. What on earth would it be like here with that pervasive cold that never lifted, the dark evenings filled with shadows, the only relief the few minutes that I had alone in my little room at night before lights went out. The fun of the musical, the release valve for the students, would be over, and there would be nothing left but hard work, early cold mornings and long dismal days.

"Miss Clancy."

Matt's voice behind me came as a total surprise. I turned suddenly to see him approach along the section of the walk that ran under almost-bare horse-chestnut trees. He scuffed through the damp leaves on the ground as he made his way toward me, his parka hanging open with his Aston Villa scarf flung over his shoulder. He smiled, his breath puffing out into the afternoon chill.

"Mr Flynn," I replied, glancing around. "What are you doing out of rehearsals?"

I continued to walk slowly as he fell into slow step beside me. "Just taking five, Miss Clancy. Mind if I join you?" he replied loudly.

"Not at all," I answered, looking down as a broad smile crossed my face. "I feel like I'm in a Jane Austen novel, taking the air and that," I whispered.

"I saw you go past the window of the Hall and I couldn't stop myself," he replied in a low voice. "It's a bit tough sometimes, not being able to talk to you when I want."

I stole a glance at him and my heart lurched to see him smiling back down at me. His hand crept to the small of my back and he pulled me ever so slightly closer to him. I resisted a little, checked again to see if there was anyone around, but didn't pull away. The sensation of him being physically close was too irresistible.

"We'll get caught," I whispered, looking again at the ground.

"I don't care," he whispered back.

"Well, I *do,*" I retorted. "I'd like to keep my job, thank you very much."

He tutted and sighed. "Why? What's so special about this job. Do you know, I think you're some sort of masochist who actually *likes* it here. Who *likes* all the shit that Mother Dick dishes out. Am I right?"

I giggled again, shaking my head. "No, you're not. But I don't fancy setting to and finding another job in the middle of the school year with the sort of reference I'd get if I was caught *in flagrante* with the school musical director."

He squeezed my waist. "I'd hardly call this *in flagrante,*" he giggled. "Even though I *am* finding it really difficult to stop myself just *grabbin' you and kissin' you right thur on your purty li'l face.*"

He said it in what he called his Curly McLain voice.

I feigned cringing, and smiled again. I would have liked nothing more. "Don't," I said instead. "You might catch whatever dread lurgy I've got at the moment and we can't have you coming down with the flu so close to opening night."

"You still not well?" His voice was filled with concern. "Why don't you go to bed? I can come tuck you in once I've dealt with Aunt Eller and the gang. Bring you some Lucozade."

I elbowed him away, both of us laughing. "I wish," I said, looking up at him. "Really, I do. I wish we could be like that ... just normal again, like it was in Galway."

"Normal? Is that all I am to you?" He wore an expression of mock disbelief. "I'd prefer to be exceptional – quite good, at the very least!"

I laughed again. We turned with the path and began to descend the slope that led onto the courts, away from the canopy of the horse-chestnuts. I grabbed his arm instinctively as my foot skidded on a wet leaf. "You're ... oops ... *immaculate*, how does that sound?"

His face was aghast. "*Terrible!*" he retorted. "That makes me sound like I've been scrubbed with bleach. Can't you come up with anything else?"

"Let me see," I grinned. "Outstanding?"

"Better."

"Excellent?"

"*Comme ci, comme ca.*"

"Extraordinary."

"Now that's more like it!"

We smiled at each other, falling silent suddenly as the jogger passed us. I recognised the girl as a quiet Fifth Year. She breathed steadily, her face red and her hair slicked with sweat as she passed. She was entirely focused on her run. Nonetheless, Matt had tucked his hands into the pockets of his parka before she reached us.

We walked on in silence for a moment.

"We've only got about two weeks left," I said suddenly.

"Until what?" Matt asked. "Is one of us going to die? Is your lurgy more dread than you've led me to believe?"

I grinned, but fell serious again. Around us, the afternoon had turned grey and hazy.

"You know until what," I said. "Until *Oklahoma*'s over and you're not here anymore. Until Christmas. Until you're gone."

He didn't reply. I glanced again at his face, hoping to see a funny expression, a joke brewing there, mock disbelief. Hoping that he'd suddenly tell me that he wasn't going. I didn't find any of that there, however. Matt was solemn. My heart sank.

"I can't stay ..." he began.

"Of course not ... I wouldn't expect you to ..."

"But I did want to talk to you about that."

We stopped and faced each other.

"It's *okay*," I said. "I'm fine with you going – it was your plan, before ever we ... we met ..."

I didn't mean a word of it. But I didn't want him to know that. I didn't want him to think I was clinging to him, expecting something that he might not want to give, even though I hoped desperately that he did. I took a deep breath.

"I understand that you're going to have a new life in London – I mean, that's my plan too – getting out of Ireland for a new life somewhere. I understand that you need opportunities. And when you go to London ... then that's great, isn't it? New job, a new chance at your acting, new people ..." My voice trailed off and I looked away from his face, terrified that my own would betray the insincerity of everything I was saying.

"New girls? Other girls?" he said.

I bit my lip, still looking away. A sudden sting of tears hit the backs of my eyes and an unexpected surge of slight nausea rose in me. I shrugged my shoulders.

"But what if I don't want one?" His voice was soft, confused.

I blinked and managed to look at him. He frowned and studied my face intently, grasping my shoulders suddenly. "Because I don't. Do you think I do? Do you think that this ... that what's happened here ... between us ... do you think that's just been a *diversion*? A *fling*?"

I shrugged. Still unable to speak, fearful of either crying or being sick, I wasn't sure which. I shivered suddenly.

"That's nonsense," he said. "Here, we'd better keep moving, you're getting cold."

He took my arm and we carried on slowly, down toward the Rounders Green, and around the bend that took us into the shade

187

of a solitary fir that grew on the edge of the path. Once we were partially hidden, he touched me, pulling at my scarf and rearranging it around my shoulders.

"I wanted to talk to you about me going to London – not because I was trying to arrange some *goodbye*, or trying to break it off or anything. Ria, I'm seriously falling for you. I … actually wanted to ask if you'd think about coming with me, or at least after me, when the school year's finished, if you want to see it out … or are you still planning on going to America?"

"No," I blurted. "I mean, yes – yes, I'd like to come with you. Or at least to think about coming with you, if that's okay? Do you really want me to?" My breath puffed small clouds out into the dampening air.

Matt rolled his eyes and nodded, as if it were the stupidest question that he had ever heard. He looked relieved.

"What we had in Galway, Ria – I want that *every* day. I want to be with you, to learn all about you – all the little things, to see you laugh, to see that big, messy, gingery head of yours on the pillow next to me in the morning and last thing at night."

We laughed.

"I'm not meant for here," he said. "And neither are you – I mean, I'm grateful you *are* here, because we wouldn't have met otherwise – but I hate leaving you. I hate going home at night because all I can think about is you, here, alone in this miserable place. And I long to get in here to start the day just in case I might catch a glimpse of you. I can't imagine what my days would be like without you all the time – I'm dreading Christmas as much as you are – but if I knew you were coming with me, or at least coming *after* me – that's entirely up to you – then I have something to live for. I think I just want to be with you, Ria."

I interrupted him by suddenly, impulsively, standing on my toes and planting a kiss on his lips, wrapping my arms as tightly as I could about his neck. It was reckless, and we sprang apart again briskly, in case anyone saw us. Smiling, we started to walk again, back toward the House. I felt alive, electric with excitement, and as we strolled in step beside each other, it suddenly didn't seem to matter so much if we were seen. We began to babble excitedly, Matt relaying suggested plans – me, interrupting them here and there, exhilarated. Because now there was *something* – something to look forward to, to live for.

It was only when I heard the voice calling me as we passed the Nuns' Graveyard that I realised we were being watched.

The confidence that had filled me seconds beforehand drained from me as I stopped and turned to face where it came from. She stood there, in the dusk, in a heavy navy-blue coat, tall and straight amongst the graves. Watching.

"Mr Flynn. How are rehearsals today? Surely they're not over?" Mother Benedicta said calmly, her voice cutting the air. It was clear that it wasn't a question, but an order.

Matt, glaring at her, stood his ground.

We waited as she approached us. What exactly had she seen, I wondered? How long had she been there? Was there any way that she had seen us kiss? Had she been somewhere nearby and in my distraction I had missed her? Had I been too open in my body language? Would she question me on the spot? Dismiss me? She could hardly dismiss Matt. Would she set me a punishment, tell me that I had to get up at four in the morning or something worse? The queasy sensation returned to my stomach.

She reached us and for a few moments stood silent.

I quailed while Matt met her eye to eye.

"I won't delay you, Mr Flynn," she then said brightly. "I just want to let you know that I'll be leaving an envelope for you in the usual place later this evening."

Relief crossed his face. He clearly understood what she meant – his pay cheque, I assumed. She left it for him in an empty pigeonhole outside her office each month. We had joked how she could never bring herself to hand it to him personally in case she was overcome with lust. Matt nodded his understanding. "Thanks." He hesitated then, obviously at a loss, unsure of the situation. "Well, I'd better get back to rehearsals."

"Indeed," said Mother Benedicta drily.

With a nod to me, he turned and walked away.

As he did, Benedicta turned her attention to me.

"I meant to ask you, Miss Clancy," she began loudly, casting one look at Matt's back as she raised her voice, setting in motion the end of everything. "How is your fiancé in Dublin this weather?"

Loud enough for him to hear.

Chapter thirty-four

Ria
LONDON
May 2015

I felt my handbag vibrate as I pulled the Staffroom door closed behind me. Much to my annoyance, it stopped just as I located it in my bag. I took it out, and was taken aback to spot five missed calls, all from Jess. She answered on the second ring.

"*Ria!*"

She was out of breath, and annoyed, I could tell.

"Jess, I'm sorry – I missed your calls!'

"And then some!" Her tone was indignant. "Why don't you ever answer your phone?"

I smiled. "Because I'm usually standing in front of a class of thirty-five teenagers and I'm sure it's best practice *not* to?" I replied.

"You must get breaks occasionally?" she barked.

"I'm sorry!" I exclaimed, smiling. "We've finished up for half-term, so I didn't get a chance to even *look* at my phone. We had cake and coffee at break time and –"

"Lovely for you all," she interrupted. "Have you seen the *Metro* today?"

"No," I replied, pushing open the main door of school and stepping out into the fresh mid-May sunshine. The day was glorious – a long walk on the Common was in order, I reckoned. Clear the cobwebs out. I fancied a coffee, and reading my book on the grass for a while. A delicious sensation of freedom washed over me.

"Well, I think you should – actually, no – you shouldn't."

"What are you on about, Jess?" I asked.

"Look, I think there's something in it that you should see – I've got a copy – do you want to meet somewhere in town?"

I frowned. No. I did *not* want to meet in town, not when I had a half-holiday and the weather was like this. What I wanted was to be as far away from the hot air, the smell of warm tarmac and exhaust fumes of the city as possible.

"Not particularly," I replied. "I'm planning on taking my book up onto the Common for the afternoon – it's such a nice day – and I can pick up a copy of the *Metro* anywhere – just tell me what I'm supposed to be looking for in it."

Jess sighed. "There's just something – why don't I come and meet you, eh? I can show you then."

"Well, okay."

"Perfect. Same spot as we had that picnic last summer. Don't look at the *Metro* between now and then – have you got that?"

"Yes, Cap'n!" I said.

"See you in a while." Her tone was abrupt and serious.

I ended the call, puzzled.

An hour and a half later, I could see Jess's copy of the freesheet rolled up and sticking out of the top of the tote bag she carried as she strode briskly to where I sat on the Common, fifteen minutes from my flat. I smiled as I saw her, shielding my eyes from the sun and waving.

"Hallo, lady," I greeted her as she flopped down beside me, breathless.

Her cheeks were flushed and her hair slightly damp with sweat. She threw her head back and grimaced as she caught her breath.

"Did you run all the way?" I asked as she pulled a bottle of water from her bag and took a deep swig. I replaced my bookmark in my book and laid it to one side, turning my full attention to her.

"Well, if waddling quickly counts as running," she said. "Have you seen it yet?"

"The *Metro*? No. But what is it? Has someone printed nude pics and put my name to them? Or worse – has Rod Stewart died?'.

She gave me the side eye "*Do. Not. Joke. About. Such. Things,*" she replied sternly. "But there *is* something. Sorry for making such a drama of it, but I thought … I wanted you to see it … *with* me. In case it upset you or something. I mean, it might be nothing …" She pulled out the copy of the *Metro*, unrolled it, and flicked through to find the page she wanted. "But … you know all that stuff about Ireland? The stuff I keep begging you to finish telling me about but you keep changing the subject?"

I stiffened. She was right. I had woken the day after beginning my story with another headache and had rushed home as fast as I could. Since then, Jess had pleaded with me to tell her more, to reveal the outcome, but I had fobbed her off. I was too busy with something else, or heading off to see Emma, or prepping lessons. I had even told her that I couldn't remember the rest which she had dismissed as the rubbish excuse it was. Over the past week or so, she had stopped asking, and I hoped that might be the end of it, but I should have known better with Jess. I felt my cheeks burn, wished for the millionth time that I had never begun the story. I had got so caught up in it again – told her so much. Now, I didn't want to go back to it. I wanted to leave it there, bury it all again, and the pain with it.

"And that guy – Matt? Remember him? Why of course you do – vividly!"

I blushed deeper. It was all such a mess.

"Well, your period of grace is up – you're going to have to spill. I spotted this today – and it's so odd. A coincidence maybe – or not – I don't know. I just didn't want you to see it without someone there."

Now I was getting nervous. I took the proffered tabloid from her, scanning first her face and then the words.

It was the *Personals* page. I scanned down the column of comments from people looking to meet the girl that they saw on the Tube each morning, or say hello to the barista with the lovely smile. And there it was. At the very bottom.

MaRIA Goretti, it read. **Will you see me? I have info. And I've never forgotten.**

Beneath it was an email address: *Rodgers&Hamm@yippee.co.uk*
Underneath me, the earth felt as if it shifted slightly.

Chapter thirty-five

Ria
BALLYKEERAN
December 1987

Matt was avoiding me.

Every time I thought of Benedicta's face, her words, said aloud so that he would hear them, that afternoon on The Walk, I burned. She had seen us. She must have. Had seen us steal that kiss, had watched us as we laughed, as Matt asked me to go to London with him, had spied on that moment where life was changing for both of us. We were breaking the rules on a massive scale. And she would *not* allow that to continue.

She was a calculating woman. I knew that already. Her punishment methods, the constant suspicious eye on everything. I had called her 'Sauron' once to Matt and he and I had laughed as he looked at me with exaggerated blankness and pretended to watch my joke fly past him, miming seeing it disappear past his shoulder before laughing himself.

We had been so close. And now, he couldn't even look at me.

On the night after Benedicta had thrown her spanner in the works, he had passed me on the Green Corridor as I supervised Night Tea, his face like stone. I tried to catch his eye, mouthed his name – '*Matt*' – as he passed. I watched, stunned, as he avoided eye contact and stormed back to rehearsals. I contemplated going after him, but a sudden squeal from a Second Year as she upended her cup all over the floor put an end to that.

193

I had forgotten that Benedicta knew about Leonard. *I* had almost forgotten about Leonard, to be honest. And if he had forgotten about me, I didn't care a jot. Our communication had been nil since I had returned from that weekend in Dublin what seemed like a lifetime ago. What an engagement, I thought to myself. One moment we were planning a life together across the Atlantic, and the next we didn't even call or write. And it bothered neither of us, certainly not me, and if it bothered him, I simply didn't care.

Yet there he was, suddenly thrown into my thoughts again, and how. With one sentence, that witch of a nun had made sure her job was done. Matt now thought I had a fiancé; her rule-breakers were dealt with.

He spoke to me long enough the following day to growl at me that he was busy. The day after, with the thought that the frustration might eat me alive, I finally caught him, following him as he strode to his car which was parked around the back of the Assembly Hall, in the part the nuns called the Farmyard.

"What do you want?" he said gruffly, without pausing in his step as I struggled to catch up with him.

"I need to talk to you, Matt," I huffed breathlessly.

He didn't turn.

"Go back to your ... *wedding* plans," he barked, dismissing me with his hand as he did so.

The gesture brought tears to my eyes. How could he be so cold?

"I'm not getting married," I replied. "Will you please hear me out?"

He stopped, reluctantly, scanning the buildings around him – small sheds and disused storage. Here, we were overlooked by the back of the convent itself. I wasn't familiar with this part of the grounds, but I knew we were at risk of being seen again. I didn't care. I had to explain.

Matt turned, and glared at me. It was an expression I had never seen on his face, and it stung. How I hated that he'd look at me like that, after so many glances of longing, so many smiles.

"Mother Benedicta ... what she said ... I don't have a fiancé."

"So you were lying to her and not me, then?"

I shook my head and paused. I was starting to feel nauseous – I was still carrying the bug that had hit me over the past week or so, and it seemed impossible to shift. I took a deep breath.

"I'm not lying to anyone. I did have a ... sort of ... fiancé when I got here first, but I don't any more."

His eyebrows shot up. "So you've broken up with him?"

He spat the word '*him*'. It made me feel both ashamed and hopeful.

"Yes. Well ... it's sort of just died out ... I haven't seen him in over a month, nearly two ..."

"How restrained of you," said Matt through gritted teeth.

"I don't love him," I pleaded. "I don't think I ever did ... I think it was more an ... *arrangement* ... than anything else ..."

"An arrangement?" he said, incredulous. "An *arrangement*? You know, the more I hear about this, Miss Clancy, the more pleased I am that I found out so early on exactly what you're like!"

I gulped back a wave of bile. "I'm not like ... I'm not like anything ... I'm not like *that*. I love you, Matt – I know it's been quick but –"

"Well, you seem to work quick," he bit back, hands on his hips. "And I'm glad I've found out what I was getting myself into. You seem to have a fiancé when you want to, and no fiancé when it suits – like when you were with me, lying through your teeth to me about wanting to follow me to London. Promise me you'll come along when you can, is it? When you've finally decided whether or not you actually want that poor sod you're engaged to, or you want to follow a–a fling you've had down the country out of his sight? How long have you been engaged?"

"I wasn't properly engaged – a couple of years – but –"

"Forget it, Ria." His eyes flamed with rage. "Forget it. I was really falling for you – I really thought that something good could come out of this, but I've had a lucky escape. You've lied to me, you've maybe lied to him, I don't know – but you're just a *liar*, sneaking around stringing two of us along at the one time to see what's the best deal you can get at the time. Well, I'll do you a favour and *un-complicate* things. I'm out."

He turned and stormed away.

"*Matt!*"

My tone had turned from pleading to anger. For a moment, I

thought that he would ignore me, but suddenly he stopped and turned back, his face red with rage.

"Why?" he demanded.

"Why what?"

"That's all I want to know – why? What was the point in telling me that you were going to come with me to London when you had no intention of it? What did you get out of it? Was it some sort of joke with him? Or were you so weak that you couldn't tell me the truth? That you were going to string me along until I left, all the time believing that you were going to follow me when in fact you had no intention of it? Were you just not bothered in being straight up with me? Was it a case that I'd be out of sight, out of mind, and you'd be off to America with whats-his-name? Were you kidding me or him?"

"Matt, I don't understand ..."

He fumbled in the back pocket of his jeans as he stormed closer to me, thrusting a folded-up piece of paper into my hands as hard as he could. "Maybe this will help you!"

There were tears in his eyes. I frowned and shook my head as I looked from him down into my hands at what he had given me. Suddenly, my stomach dropped as I recognised what I held there. It couldn't be ... but it was ... the same cerise pink paper.

My hands trembled and my heart thudded against my ribcage as I opened it.

Darling Leonard, It was so lovely seeing you at the weekend ...

I glanced from the letter back to Matt. "This is ludicrous," I said. "I can explain this – it's from weeks ago – months, even. I never sent it ..."

He responded by flinging his arms up in the air and walking a few steps away from me before walking back. "Jesus *Christ!*" he roared. "You just can't stop yourself! *Months* ago?"

"Yes! It was stupid, I didn't mean a word of it!"

"Look at it!" he hissed. "Look at the damn date on it!"

Frowning, I did as he asked. This was laughable. This letter, the exercise – it was nonsense, it meant nothing. If I could just get Matt to calm down and listen to me, he'd see ...

I frowned as I scanned the sheet the paper, my blood chilling as I saw something at the top of the sheet, something that I hadn't put there. A date. November 3rd 1987. Except, unlike the rest of the letter, it wasn't in my handwriting. It was stamped there. I looked from the paper to Matt in disbelief.

"This wasn't me – I don't have a date stamp – I didn't date the letter. I didn't even write it then, I wrote it before. This date was just after Galway, for God's sake! I wouldn't –"

"Would you just stop! Anyone could have a stamp. There's a date stamp in the Staffroom, Cecilia has one in her music rooms, Benedicta has one in her office –"

"But why would I *use* one?"

"Well, evidently you *did*!"

Someone had deliberately put the wrong date on my letter ... the idea was so preposterous he would never believe me ...

"Hang on, where did you even get this?" I managed. "I threw this away!"

But had I? My mind flashed back to the morning when I had written it and had given up in disgust and anger at both Leonard and what I was trying to achieve. I hadn't thrown the letter away, I remembered. I had, at the time, had a half-hearted notion that I might return to it, that I might magically make it better, say the right thing ...

So I had put it away. Folded it in two, and slid it in between the books on my bookshelf. I remembered now ...

"They took this when they searched my room!" I blurted out. "They made no secret of being in there – they rubbed my nose in it. Who gave it to you? Was it Cecilia?"

"It doesn't matter where I got it from," he retorted bitterly. "What matters is that you wrote it, and you *admit* you wrote it. What matters is what's in it. It must be so hard for you, missing Leonard as much as you do. Such a hardship. But at least you've got your *Plan*, whatever that is!"

I opened my mouth to speak again, to explain, but he silenced me by lowering his face to mine, and speaking in a low, harsh tone.

"I just can't, Ria. I can't do this. All this stuff I don't know, that you're hiding from me, making a fool out of me, or using me or whatever it is you're doing. Whatever I am, or was to you, I don't even want to know anymore, because I'm out – I can't even get my head around you anymore. And Jesus knows, I couldn't ever trust you again. Good luck, Ria. I'm gone."

With that, he turned and walked away, his back straight, his gait determined.

I watched him go.

There was no question of me following him. In that moment I felt I had no defence. Even to reason that I had never *sent* the stupid letter seemed weak and futile.

A tightness gripped my chest suddenly and I swallowed down the urge to vomit. I knew that I couldn't quell it for much longer so I turned and fled back to my room, biting back tears and nausea as I passed a group of girls heading out of the Locker Room toward The Walk. They stared as I passed, but I ignored them, and made no effort to speak to them lest I should cry or vomit. Once in the sanctuary of my cold little room, I sank onto the bed and did the former – wept tears of rage and frustration, of the injustice of it all, and of desperation at the thought of how this could happen, of what was disappearing before my very eyes.

I cried until my throat and chest ached, until my eyes were sore, and my head thumped. The nausea rose in me again and this time I knew that it wouldn't pass. I bolted from my room suddenly, hand over my mouth, and dived into the bathroom next door where I brought up the entire contents of my stomach, retching loudly and uncontrollably as my body emptied itself. When I finished, I sank to my knees in front of the toilet bowl and rested my throbbing head on my arm for a moment. The pressure in my head made it feel as if it were about to explode, and I waited for it to subside.

Moments passed, and the sensation inside my head began to abate. I sighed, drained by the argument, the crying, the being sick, by my stupid life. How had I got here? To this point, where I was completely out of my depth, miles from anywhere that I had ever called home. How was I alone again? And was that how things would always be for me? No family? No true friends, only acquaintances? Colleagues? Would I ever make a good decision or would I forever sabotage everything positive that might happen to me? Would I have been better off just sticking with Leonard? Abandoning The Plan if that was what he had really wanted and maybe settling in Dublin instead? Would that have been so bad? If I hadn't wanted so much – some impossible American dream – then could I have been happy just like everyone else? A normal suburban housewife, in a normal semi, with normal kids and a normal marriage? Coffee with other mums in the mornings, Jane Fonda workout videos, the odd night out with my husband – safe and secure all the way? Why couldn't I have settled for that? Why go chasing what was out of my reach? Why take on this ridiculous job? And why allow myself to fall so hard for the first good-looking male – the *only* one in fact, that I had encountered in four months? Was I that *stupid?*

I closed my eyes and sighed deeply again into the crook of my elbow, feeling entirely overwhelmed.

A sudden sound from outside the cubicle disturbed me and I lifted my head. There was someone there – I tensed. Had someone heard me being ill? I had been unable to restrain myself but I'd been full sure that I was alone. Worse, had someone heard me crying? Was it Benedicta? Had she seen Matt and me argue and come for me – to do what this time? To lecture me or to finally give me my notice? I stood as hastily as I could, smoothing down my skirt as I did. I quickly reached for a piece of toilet paper, blew my nose and wiped my mouth before flushing the toilet and taking a deep breath.

"Who's there?" I called, trying to insert a tone of authority in my voice. There was no answer.

I held myself as straight as I could as I emerged from the toilet cubicle into the empty bathroom. I frowned. There had definitely been someone directly outside, but I hadn't heard anyone leave. I looked left to right, pushing the door of the other toilet cubicle open gently, and then checking the handbasins where no one stood. I paused for a moment and listened. Nothing, just the distant sound of a few girls outside, on a break from rehearsals; laughter and shouts of 'Mine!' as they claimed a volleyball. My heart began to beat faster.

Slowly, I stepped out of the bathroom and back on to the shining lino of the Sisters' Corridor. "Hello?" I called, my voice reverberating around the empty space.

There was no movement at all from any of the small rooms, and I began to slowly creep along the passage, peering into them as I passed.

"Is there someone there?" I called again.

Then, suddenly, a rustling came from one of the rooms to my left. I shrieked as a figure stepped out in front of me. Lydia Madigan stood there, red-faced and worried, as she stuffed something up her sleeve.

"Lydia!" I gasped, my body jolted by fear. "You gave me a fright."

She had. It had looked at first as if a shadow was emerging from the room – it was nothing more than a trick of the light, of course. She was dressed in paint-splattered black jeans and a plain hooded sweatshirt, her hair tied back from her pale face with a black bandana – her Stage Crew clothes.

"I'm sorry, Miss. I know I shouldn't be up here but one of the girls said I could borrow something and I really needed it and it was an emergency and it won't happen again, I promise."

Her words were jumbled and rushed with fear, and I realised that she thought she was in terrible trouble. By Maria Goretti rules, she should have been – in another girls' room, especially in an area that she didn't sleep in, and during the day.

"What are you doing?" I began, more out of curiosity than to admonish her. Then I recognised what was sticking out of her sleeve – a sanitary towel. "Oh," I acknowledged.

She looked from my face to her arm and blushed deeply, stuffing the towel further up. "I'm sorry, Miss."

"For what? For having your period?" I smiled.

She winced at the word. Periods were a big deal at Maria Goretti. The girls referred to them in hushed euphemisms – 'Aunt Flo', 'having the painters in', 'my *friend*'. Some even bullied others if they showed an outward sign of it being their time of the month – if a pad fell from a schoolbag or a sleeve, if the sanitary towel bin banged shut and was heard outside the privacy of a toilet cubicle. I had heard girls sneer at others about how 'gross' they were, and 'disgusting'. It was a shameful thing for most of the girls, an embarrassment. To be caught out was sheer mortification.

I smiled at her. 'Don't worry, Lydia,' I whispered. "I won't tell if you don't. Are you okay? Do you need any … supplies?"

She cringed again. "No thanks, Miss," she said hurriedly. "One of the Day Girls is getting me some. I know I shouldn't do that either, but I completely forgot to bring any this month – I was at Carmel's for my last weekend home …"

I shook my head to show her that I didn't care. "So long as you're not stuck, Lydia. Do you need a painkiller or anything or are you okay?"

She didn't blush this time, but rubbed her hand over her stomach. "My stomach's a bit sore alright," she said.

I indicated that she should follow me to my room. She walked down the corridor behind me in silence, and waited at the door for me to emerge with a handful of capsules.

"Take two now," I said, "and keep the rest for later if you need them. They might come in handy."

She accepted them gratefully.

Just as she did, however, something on the floor caught my eye. "What's that?" I asked, leaning to get a closer look.

Confused, Lydia turned and peered at the floor herself.

In the light that spilled from the open door of my room, it looked like a small spillage: a tiny pool of water glistening in a patch of afternoon sun.

"I didn't do that, Miss." Again, Lydia's tone was defensive.

The poor kid, I thought, so browbeaten that she expected to be blamed for everything. "I know you didn't ..." I replied, my voice trailing off as I saw a second puddle a bit behind it and to its left, and then another, the same distance beyond, to the right.

I stiffened as I realised what they were.

"Has anyone been up here using my shower?" I asked Lydia.

"Not me, Miss," she replied quickly.

I glanced quickly at her feet to see her wearing her Doc Marten boots – another black mark against her if she were caught. The Dorms were slippers-only for students.

"I don't think anyone else did either though?" she replied.

I peered further along the corridor – the wet patches continued along as far as my eye could see, visible now that I knew what I was looking at, in the light that came from the open doors of the bedrooms either side.

"You'd better head downstairs, Lydia," I said. "Before you get caught and we both get into trouble!"

I smiled, and she returned it, her expression warm and grateful. It transformed her usually pained, unreadable face. She was really quite a beautiful girl underneath it. I watched her turn and make her way back along the corridor, before turning to look back at what I had seen on the floor.

A chill ran down my spine at the sight of them. There had to be a logical explanation, of course, I reasoned with myself. The wet footprints were fresh – why hadn't I seen them when I emerged from the bathroom before?

"Miss Clancy!"

I jumped at the sound of my name being called, and looked up along the corridor to see another shape standing there, except this time it was clearly a nun, Benedicta was watching me, of course. As usual.

I straightened, and cleared my throat which was sore from vomiting, aware that my eyes were red and swollen. I hoped beyond hope that she wouldn't notice, in case she somehow knew she'd won.

"Yes, Mother," I replied, and walked towards her, following Lydia's example and sticking close by the doorways to avoid walking on the prints. My stomach sank as I grew closer to her. What had she seen this time? What did she know? How long had she been there?

"Did I see Lydia Madigan coming down the stairs a few minutes ago?"

My heart beat faster as I thought how to respond. Should I lie, then she'd catch me out – she obviously had seen Lydia. What she wanted was my reply. I decided the truth, or a version of it, was best.

"You did, Mother," I replied. "Lydia was feeling unwell so I asked her to accompany me while I got her some tablets from my room. She wasn't here unsupervised."

Benedicta didn't respond. Instead, she looked me up and down, her eyes filled with a strange look. A sort of victorious disgust, I thought. Until suddenly something behind me caught her eye. She gasped as she looked along the floor.

"What are those?" she said, pointing at the floor.

I didn't let on that I knew what she was talking about. I feigned surprise, and instantly regretted it, unsure that I'd be able to carry off innocence.

"I don't know, Mother," I responded and then braced myself for the attack that was sure to come, like a dog cowering in fear of its master.

However, no attack came. Instead, the nun fell silent as she anxiously looked from one footprint to another, up and down the length of the corridor.

When she finally spoke, her tone was flustered. "I'll – I'll send Sister Augusta with the mop immediately to clean that up," she said. "In the meantime …" She didn't finish her sentence. Instead, she swallowed deeply, looked at me and abruptly walked away.

I followed her to the end of the passage, and saw her grab the bannisters for support as she reached the stairs. I watched her hurried descent, stunned at the manner of her departure. She had made no attempt to correct me, to order me about, to pull me up on something – instead she had simply *fled*. It was just like the day when the bell had rung in the dorm. Like she knew something. Something that frightened her …

I looked at the top of her head as it disappeared down the flight of stairs below me, and then back at the wet patches on the floor.

And admitted what my mind had been trying to deny.

A child's footprints. A small child, by the looks of them.

A child smaller than any student currently at Maria Goretti.

A familiar chill gripped me as I looked at them, and suddenly couldn't bear to be next to them anymore. For an instant, the sadness, nausea and exhaustion of the afternoon's events were forgotten and replaced by something completely different. Terror. Like the nun before me, I turned and fled.

Chapter thirty-six

Ria
DUBLIN
1987

FILE OF MOTHER AGNES DE BRUIN
REGARDING THE CARE OF EVELYN PHELAN
CONVENT OF MARIA GORETTI, BALLYKEERAN,
COUNTY LAOIS
YEAR OF OUR LORD 1944

Transcript (with notes) of Interview by Garda Edward Nolan, taken on May 4th, 1944.

Interview conducted in the Convent Parlour.

Mother Agnes present throughout, notes taken by Sister Catherine Cuddy.

Garda Nolan: Can you tell me your full name?

Evelyn: Evelyn Deirdre Phelan, Guard.

Garda Nolan: And your age?

Evelyn: I'm nearly twelve, Guard.

Mother Agnes: Evelyn, you don't have to address Garda Nolan by his title each time, there's a good child.

Evelyn: Sorry, Mother, sorry Garda Nolan.

Garda Nolan: That's alright, Evelyn. Can you tell me your address, please?

Evelyn: The Convent of Maria Goretti, Ballykeeran, County

Laois, Ireland, Guard.

Garda Nolan: And how long have you lived at this address, Evelyn?

Evelyn: All of sixth class.

Garda Nolan: So almost a year?

(Confirmed by Mother Agnes)

Garda Nolan: And do you go to school here yet?

Evelyn: Not yet. I still go to the primary in the village but I'll start in First Year in September.

Garda Nolan: So you don't go to school here but you live here? Where's your home?

Evelyn: It's on Devlin's Lane, Guard ... sorry, Guard ... out by the bog.

Garda Nolan: And why don't you live there, Evelyn?

Evelyn: Because Mammy and Dada didn't want me there anymore. Mammy got sick and couldn't take care of me and it's too hard for Dada.

Mother Agnes: The Phelans suffered a tragedy last year, Guard, and they sent Evelyn into our care. Her mother – also Evelyn – used to clean for us, before she ... fell ill.

Garda Nolan: I'm aware of that, Mother. Didn't something bad happen to your sister, Evelyn?

Evelyn: She got lost in the rain on the bog, and died.

Garda Nolan: I'm very sorry to hear that, Evelyn. Were you with her on the bog that day?

Evelyn: I was. Me and Dada.*

(Garda Nolan pauses to check notes.)

Garda Nolan: You and your dad, Evelyn?

(Evelyn nods in the affirmative.)

Evelyn: I didn't see what happened though. It was raining really hard – there was a thunderstorm and Dada went to find Frances and I had to go home by myself.

Garda Nolan: Your father said that he was at home with your mother, working around the house on the night that Frances went missing, Evelyn.

Evelyn: No, Guard. After dinner he said did me and Frances want to go for a walk up the bog to see the cutting machines, and we said yes. He was playing a game with us, getting Frances to run

205

off and him timing her on his watch, only Frances ran off and then it started to rain and he said we had to go home and that he'd go find Frances and I was to go ahead before I got soaked to the bone and caught my death.

Garda Nolan**: Are you sure, Evelyn? Only your mam and dad both said that you came home soaking wet without your sister – they said that only the two of you went to the bog to play that evening.

(Evelyn shrugs shoulders)

Garda Nolan: Did your father ever get cross and shout, Evelyn? Were you ever afraid of him? Did you and your sister get into trouble any times?

(Evelyn nods.)

Evelyn: Dada would get cross sometimes but Mammy said that it was because we were bold. Sometimes things would get broke in the house.

Garda Nolan: What things, Evelyn?

Evelyn: Cups and things. And plates, and the good china. And chairs and the table one time. The day I came here.

Garda Nolan: And did your father ever hit you, Evelyn?

Evelyn: Sometimes I'd get a beating from the belt, but only when I was very bold. He'd slap your hand sometimes, or cuff your ear but he wouldn't beat you up, like. Mammy said that's why he sometimes broke the stuff in the house and that it was better that he broke the stuff when he got cross, than us.***

Garda Nolan: And what about the night Frances went missing, Evelyn? When did your dad come home that night?

Evelyn: It was hours and hours, Guard. Mammy sent me to bed to warm up after the rain and hanged my clothes over the fireplace to dry them off. He woke me up coming in and I went to see if Frances was with him, but she wasn't.

Garda Nolan: And what did he say to you when he got home, Evelyn?

Evelyn: Nothing. When I didn't see Frances with him, I hid in the press so he wouldn't see me in case he was cross after being out in the rain so long and I should've been in bed. I thought she was hiding and he'd be very vexed.

Garda Nolan: What did he say to your mother, Evelyn?

Evelyn: She was gone to bed too. It was night-time when he got home.

Garda Nolan: So what did he do when he came in that night without your sister? What did you see him do from your hiding place?

Evelyn: Nothing, Guard. Nothing only wash his hands and go to bed.

Garda Nolan: That was all?

Evelyn: Well, he must have been tired cos it was so late. And he'd hurt himself out on the bog. He must have had a cut from a briar or something.

Garda Nolan: Why do you say that, Evelyn?

Evelyn: Because of the blood, Guard. When he washed his hands all, like, pink water came off them.

(Garda Nolan hesitates)

Evelyn: Are you finished asking me questions, Guard? Only I want to go to bed now. I'm tired.

Garda Nolan: Just one more, Evelyn. You're sure about that, are you? Sure that your dad was with you on the bog, and that when Frances went missing he was out of your sight too? And that you saw blood on him when he came home?

Evelyn: The water went all pink, Guard. He was grand the next day though cos he was able to make a fire out in the back field for some rubbish needed burning.

Garda Nolan: That'll do so, Evelyn.

Mother Agnes: Off to bed with you now, Evelyn.

(Interview concluded at 8.30pm.)

Mother Agnes's Notes:

The child has never before mentioned that her father was with her on the bog, either to me, any of the Sisters, or the Gardaí.

**Garda Nolan seems very confused by this testimony.*

***Evelyn has never revealed any of this information prior to this evening.*

Chapter thirty-seven

Ria
LONDON
May 2015

"You'll laugh at what I'm going to tell you next."

Jess took a swig from her gin and tonic and raised an eyebrow. "If it happened in that creepy place, then I'd doubt it very much. Curl my lip, make a sharp intake of breath or cover my mouth perhaps, but laugh? I don't think so."

We were sitting outside a wine bar near my house, the *Metro* thrown in the middle of the table, the sunshine beating down on us. I felt chilly, however, and pulled my light summer cardigan close over my chest.

I smiled and swirled the wine at the end of my glass, catching the eye of the waiter who came out of the restaurant to wipe down the outside tables and gesturing for a refill.

"Second-glass-worthy?" observed Jess drily. "And you downed your first in five seconds flat. I'd better drink up."

"I needed it."

I drained my own and decided to bite the bullet.

"Did you ever watch *The Waltons*?" I asked suddenly.

Jess burst out laughing. "You proved me wrong!" she explained, wiping liquid from her chin where she had accidentally spluttered her drink. "I wasn't expecting that!"

I nodded. I felt foolish, and didn't much want to join in.

"This is stupid," I said. "You'll think I'm talking absolute nonsense when I tell you this."

"No, no," Jess composed herself. "I'm sorry. It's just – you know – *The Waltons*! *Dah-dah-dah-dah-dee-daaaah!*" She swayed in time and waved her glass as she sang the theme music. "G'night, Mary Ellen!"

"Very good," I replied, dismissively. "Try Elizabeth."

"You've lost me."

"Well, there was this episode – in the late 70's, I think. It was so weird for *The Waltons* that it's always stuck in my head. Elizabeth – the little one with the red plaits –"

"Oh, I remember her! Come to think of it, you must have looked a bit like her when you were a kid?"

"Well, she was visited by a poltergeist in their home."

"*Goooood-niiiiight, Jeeeem-Bawb, Woo-ooooh!*"

Jess waved her hands in front of my face and cackled at her own spooky voice, stopping only when the waiter delivered our drinks.

I frowned. "Look, don't worry. I won't bother you with this," I growled as soon as he had left, and sat back in my chair to take a slug from my drink.

"Oh, come on, Ria! I'm sorry!" Jess smiled broadly but covered my hand with hers and squeezed. "It's just so – I mean – *The Waltons*!"

"Elizabeth was visited by the poltergeist because she was hitting puberty." I rushed the words out in case Jess interrupted me again. It felt foolish to tell her this, but I would have been frustrated if I hadn't finished. "I can't remember exactly but strange stuff happened, like pebbles being thrown about and a doll moving by itself and a rocking chair hovering off the ground. It was all quite spooky."

"And what's any of this got to do with the price of onions – not to mention what just caused you to turn white as a ghost yourself and demand to get to the nearest pub immediately?" asked Jess, prodding the copy of the freesheet with her forefinger.

"Lydia," I replied.

"The student who was with you when the place was broken into?" asked Jess.

I nodded.

"What ..." Jess began. "Oh – there's the connection with *The Waltons*."

"Yes. All the strange stuff that happened there – the wet footprints, the banging from the unused dorm, the lights going on and off – and there was other stuff too – footsteps, shuffling noises in the dark, that *humming* – it was all adding up, and getting too much, too unbelievable for there to be a logical reason every single time. And every single time anything happened, Lydia was there, or nearby, or had been there a few moments before. And my mind kept going back to that stupid episode of *The Waltons*."

Jess still grinned at me, but only half with mirth.

"I thought ... I came to the conclusion ... that it was all somehow connected to her, like Elizabeth Walton and her poltergeist. I thought that Lydia was ... perhaps ... somehow ... being *haunted*."

Jess stared at me in disbelief. "In all the years I've known you, Ria Driver, I never for a single second expected to hear you say something like that. A *poltergeist?*"

I looked away, unable to make eye contact for a moment. I hadn't expected to hear myself say it either. Not aloud. Because I had kept it locked up firmly inside for almost thirty years.

"I told you you'd laugh."

"Oh, I'm not laughing Ria – at *The Waltons*, yes – but at this poltergeist business? No. I'm thinking you need to talk to a professional."

I toyed with the stem of my glass, still avoiding Jess's shocked expression, trying to figure out a way to make her understand. I couldn't.

"What would you say it was, then? All of those strange things happening one after the other?"

"Just that – strange things happening one after the other? But all very ordinary things – intruders, electricity affected by high winds, a puddle of water on the floor that someone walked in – you said yourself that you were throwing your guts up in the toilet – you wouldn't have *heard* anyone walking about while you were doing that. Plus, you were under stress – you'd broken up with your bit of fluff, that nun was bat-shit crazy and coming down on your case, your whole future was gone all tits-up and you were stuck in the Holy House of Hell in the middle of nowhere, surrounded by god-bothering freaks! Of *course* you began to put it all down to ghosts

210

or the supernatural or whatever. It doesn't make it true. We can look for patterns in things all we like, but it doesn't mean there has to be any. Besides the kid was eighteen, well past puberty. *And* it simply couldn't have been a ghost ..." Jess leaned across the table, her expression veering between sincere and frightened, "because *they don't exist,* Ria."

She sat back and took a long drink from her glass.

It was a while before I replied. "Perhaps you're right."

She continued to study mc for a few moments, before changing the subject.

"The *Metro,*" she said. "All the ghost nonsense aside – what's all that about? Is it from that Matt? Has he sent you a message in a bottle after all of these years? Maybe he saw you? That day in Covent Garden when you said you saw him? Or some other time, if he's in London? And if he has reached out to you, what the hell is he on about?"

I touched the newspaper, warm from the sun, a little burst of newsprint smell wafting into the air as I moved it.

"Yes, it's Matt. It has to be. I think maybe he knows something ... maybe about what actually happened to Lydia. And I think he wants me to know."

"Why? What happened to Lydia?"

"I'll tell you about that. Yes, there's more ... much more."

Ria rolled her eyes, but didn't laugh or comment. "Are you going to reply?"

I thought for a moment, before nodding.

"Yes, I am," I said. "Because I need to know too. After all these years, I have to know what he knows. And besides which, I have something that he needs to know too."

Chapter thirty-eight

Ria
BALLYKEERAN
December 1987

There were no afternoon games to supervise in the fortnight leading up to the opening night of *Oklahoma*. All cast and crew were required, without exception, in the Assembly Hall for final rehearsals and preparation. It gave me time to work – to set the New Year exams or prepare for post-Christmas lessons. Instead, I told Benedicta that I wished to set a history project – I kept it vague – and requested permission to pay a visit to the library in the village. Surprisingly, she allowed me, although I suspect it was more because she couldn't think of a reason not to.

Still feeling ill, I would have preferred to retire to my room and nap under the pretence of working, but something in me felt that, despite how tired and run-down I was, I wouldn't – couldn't – rest, partly for fear of what I might hear or see along the Sisters' Corridor as the evening gloom of early December set in, partly because I couldn't stop thinking about everything that had happened – the noises, the bangs, the *attack* in the Study Hall that night – the footprints of a child that had no place being where I'd found them. None of this made any logical sense. My mind had started to turn in one direction, and one direction only. I had finally had to admit to myself that there was – could be – no reason other than supernatural for this series of events.

It wasn't that I didn't believe in ghosts, I had just always thought that they were something that happened to other people, to rare people with special powers or gifts, people who could 'see', or who were more in tune with the spiritual world. The fact that I had never encountered one meant that I just thought I wasn't that way inclined, in the same way that I was right-handed, and hated fried eggs. I had thought I would simply never have such an experience.

The events of the past weeks, however – how could I explain all of them? It hurt my brain to think about them – about how or why they were happening. And how could I protect myself – although, realistically, what could ghosts *do*?

Slam the doors, for instance. *Run around the upstairs floors* ... I shook my head, trying to shake the childish rhyme from my head, but it persisted in spinning around my mind over and over ... *The nuns are meant to keep her safe* ...

What if, somehow, that rhyme wasn't nonsense at all and was genuinely dark, like all the classics – 'Mary, Mary Quite Contrary?', for example; 'Ladybird, Ladybird'? What if it held more than a shred of truth? That someone – some*thing* – had been there for a long time – forty-five years, for example? – that child in the Nuns' Graveyard? Was it possible? Really and truly possible?

My mind reeled as I walked the chilly road into Ballykeeran on that Monday afternoon. A thick fog hung down over the fields around me and everything was grey. It was unnerving. Visibility was limited, and where the fog met the shorn fields, it hung and wisped in places like wraiths. I tried to concentrate on my steps, keeping my eyes on the road, fearful of what I might see in the gloom around me. *Keep trying to figure this out,* I urged myself. Is that damn place *really* haunted? On top of everything else?

And what is the link to Lydia Madigan?

Because she was almost always there, wasn't she? When things happened. In the Study Hall and the Dorm the night of the storm? On the Sisters' Corridor, where she shouldn't have been, the day of the wet footprints? That figure in the Study at four o'clock in the morning – I had thought that it *was* her, for heaven's sake!

A slow, misty drizzle had grown more persistent as I reached Ballykeeran library which sat on the outskirts of the village. The air inside was warm and dry and smelled of pages and print as I stepped in out of the miserable afternoon. I wiped my feet on the mat and took in the stillness and silence for a moment, the faint buzzing of the fluorescent lights overhead. I smiled at the librarian who poked her head out from behind some shelves and she frowned at me – a stranger. I made my way to a desk toward the rear of the room, took off my damp coat and gloves, hung my bag over the back of the chair, and immediately turned my attention toward the drawers of index cards in a filing cabinet next to me to see if I could find anything on my chosen subject.

The afternoon grew darker and wetter outside. Car headlights glided over the building as they passed on their way in and out of the village; the rain came in surges, heavy on the skylights one minute, silent mist another. Some Primary School children came and left, bringing with them the smell of wet hair and damp duffle, and the squeak of patent-leather shoes on the tiles that they smeared with muddy prints. For a good hour and a half, I barely registered any of it, instead cramming in what I could learn from the few books about the paranormal that I could find. I could have become a member, of course, and borrowed them, but I didn't think somehow that Benedicta would welcome such reading material in her House. As it was, I was trying to conceal my choices from the librarian who peered at me, the stranger, and at the books I had piled beside me. After the first time she had done it, I had returned to the shelves and selected a copy of *Hamlet* and another of *Wuthering Heights* and put them in a prominent position on the desk. Hopefully it was enough to help her to the conclusion that the copy of *Do Ghosts Exist?* and the tome of *True Irish Tales of the Supernatural*, were related to schoolwork. As an afterthought, I scribbled the heading '*Ghosts in English Literature*' on a sheet of A4 and casually threw it on the desk. I couldn't be sure if she'd notice it, or if she even cared, but I also couldn't be sure whether or not she knew Benedicta, whether or not it would get back to the nun once the librarian established who I was, and I had no doubt but that she would.

It was as I returned an Arthur C Clarke to the Science section that I spotted what I wanted. The copies of *Paranormal Times* were a good seven years old, but the magazine promised on its front cover to reveal the **Secrets of the Supernatural**, so I grabbed the few copies that were there and, with a glance at the curious librarian who was thankfully busy making herself a cup of tea in her small office, I returned to my desk and quickly began to pore over them. At first, my heart sank. With stories of UFO sightings, the Loch Ness Monster and the Cottingley Fairies, I felt sure that this would be as much use to me as the copy of *The Puca and other Stories* that I had left on the shelf. But three editions in, I stopped in my tracks as I discovered exactly what I was looking for: a long feature on a man called Maurice Grosse, and the story of The Enfield Poltergeist. A glance at the clock indicated that it was time I returned to school to supervise study, however, so I rummaged in my purse for a few ten-pence pieces and hastily photocopied the article. I tidied up quickly, and slipped out, back into the damp evening, and along the dark road back to Maria Goretti.

I read the notes by the light of my dim lamp much later when I was in bed. A part of me was sorry that I had, my blood chilled by the story of the London family whose lives had been torn apart – only ten years previously – by the malevolent entity that had inhabited their home. It had moved furniture, thrown bricks, and created noise and disturbance – a chill ran the length of my body as I read that the mother had thought burglars initially responsible, but the happenings accelerated, and while many were sceptical there were also many witnesses, including a police officer, who believed it was real. Chairs moved, beds shifted, an iron fireplace was ripped from a wall, coins would fall from nowhere – the list of activity was endless. But then the terrifying happened. The spirit began to *speak*, through the mouth of one of the children, Janet. The article contained transcripts of some of the tapes that were made, and I read some before I became too frightened to read more. I fell asleep with the light on, and dreamed of Lydia being thrown out of bed into the air by unseen forces and speaking in a gruff voice, swearing and floating in the air before me. I woke, terrified, but managed to sleep again, this time dreaming of someone else entirely. She was younger than Lydia, a thin, frail, child with long, wet hair, also speaking unintelligibly in a gravelly growl.

I woke again with a start, convinced that my bedroom door had just slammed shut, but there was no one there. After that, sleep evaded me. I lay there until five in the morning when I bolted to the bathroom, rigid with terror at whatever might be out in the corridor waiting for me, but unable to stop myself. I vomited deeply and for a long time before returning to bed, filled with dread, and waited for dawn.

Chapter thirty-nine

Ria
BALLYKEERAN
December 1987

It became so that I couldn't sleep, for fear of something happening; I couldn't concentrate because my mind was filled with possibilities and worry; I couldn't eat with the constant queasiness in my stomach – not that I could keep anything down either. I needed help, but not of the type that I sought. I was driving myself slowly mad.

Nicola Ryan was in Second Year. She was hard-working, diligent, curious, liked to ask questions in class, took on outside projects, had declared her interest in studying marine biology in college. Her classmates – and most of the staff, for that matter – called her a swot. I'd also heard 'lick-arse' bandied about from some of the girls. She was perfect for what I needed. And was possessed of an irrefutable disbelief in anything supernatural.

Asking her to post the letter to the Dublin Paranormal Society the previous week had been easy. It was making her the recipient of the reply that was difficult. I knew, however, that I couldn't have the information sent to the school address for fear of the nuns opening it and seeing it. In the end, I kept her after class and gave her a copy of *Wuthering Heights* as an "extra bit of reading" for the approaching Christmas holidays. I told her that we might do a small project on its supernatural elements in January, that her aptitude for science and logic made her perfect for what I had in

216

mind and that I'd speak to her more after the holidays and the exams. I told her that I'd have some additional information she needed sent to her house, for fear it might get lost in the school post, but if she could bring me the information when she received it so that I could make a copy for notes, that would be marvellous. I knew that Nicola would relish the prospect, and be happy with my vague explanation – so excited at the attention from the teacher that she'd do whatever I asked, without question. Including keeping it quiet.

"We don't want your classmates thinking that you're singled out for special attention," I told her. I felt horrible, manipulating her for my own ends, like a sleazy old man with a packet of sweets.

Poor, innocent Nicola lapped it up, however, and on the 14th of December I got what I needed. A prompt response from people who purported to be experts in the subject of the paranormal. I finally had what I needed to know about poltergeists. It had been placed on my desk, thankfully unobtrusive in a plain brown A4 envelope. Nicola sat, unflappable as always, in her habitual seat at the front of the room with a knowing smile on her face, and I nodded discreetly in acknowledgement. The collusion satisfied her, and would keep her silent, I was sure. I felt guilty, exploiting her, just as a means to satisfy this curiosity that burned inside me. I slid the envelope into my handbag, and decided that whatever work Nicola produced, I'd send it on her behalf to a couple of secondary school journals that I'd dealt with before in Dublin. At least if she were published, then something good could go on her CV out of my ruse. That was, however, a job for the New Year. In the meantime, I had more pressing matters to deal with.

I could hardly wait to get to the solitude of my room after lights out, locking the door behind me and ripping open the envelope before I even undressed for bed. It contained a brief letter, signed by a Frank Cross, thanking me for my interest in the paranormal and ending with a suggestion that I "keep an open mind". I laughed at the notion. Since I had allowed myself to believe that something ghostly was happening around me, my mind was a great gaping space where all sorts of theories and observations whirled as if in a vortex. I had gone from a world where everything was black and white, tangible and had substance, to one where life after death was more than a possibility – it was *real* – it was puddles of water on the floor, footsteps above my head. But how? And why?

In the dim light of my bedside lamp, I devoured the information that they had sent me. It included case studies, typical poltergeist or 'noisy ghost' behaviour. Cross had included a checklist of typical poltergeist activity:

Throwing or bombardments of projectiles
Opening, closing or banging of doors or windows
Movements (including levitation) of domestic objects
Sounds of raps or cracking
Imitative noises (e.g., sound of crying baby, or of barking dog, singing or humming)
Puddles, flooding
Outbreaks of fire
Pinching, scratching or biting of skin
Graffiti or writing (e.g. on walls)
Electrical disturbances and mechanical failures
Lights or luminous effects

I read and absorbed it all, knowing that it would most likely mean another sleepless night, but I had lost count of them at that stage.

I wondered if that, too, was connected – Frank Cross's information outlined that a poltergeist presence could mean "*a change in atmospherics, and an adjustment of energies which could induce physical symptoms such as feeling drained and tired, sadness, ennui and illness in susceptible persons*". Perhaps some of this 'adjustment of energies' had spread to me, too – that would explain the constant exhaustion, the feeling queasy, the inability to eat?

I read on, learning about thrown objects, things going missing or moving to unusual locations, items being witnessed hovering in the air. This was the harmless stuff, it seemed, however. Victims of poltergeist attacks, like the little girls in Enfield, reported being physically lifted and thrown, of being scratched and wounded, sometimes without their knowledge. Hair-pulling was a playful activity, being pinned down by an unseen force and strangled wasn't.

I read until the end, through the history of Borley Rectory in Essex – 'the most haunted house in England'; the Seaford Poltergeist, and an Irish example from what was called only a 'private residence' in Waterford, investigated by Frank Cross himself. Once finished, my mind raced to make connections, to think logically. But my thoughts led in only one direction: the one that led to Lydia being somehow central to all of this current activity. I couldn't shake the idea that Lydia was my Elizabeth Walton.

I rubbed my eyes with the heels of my hand as I sat on my bed, surrounded by photocopied sheets of paper, the originals somewhere in the files of sceptical Nicola Ryan, thinking so deeply that I lost any sense of time. Logically – I snorted quietly to myself at the context of the word – if Maria Goretti had been haunted by this 'Little Frances' entity, whatever that was, for years, then why would it have anything to do with Lydia? The rhyme had been created long before Lydia Madigan had come to the place, and would continue long after she was gone. But why was Lydia always – or almost always – around when these things happened? Was it because of who she was?

I tried to recall what I could from her file which I had studied in the Staffroom. Lydia Madigan had been shaped by her so-far short, tragic life. To start with, she was an orphan, under the guardianship of her Uncle Neville Cregan, her mother's younger brother – the feckless uncle who had disappeared on holiday without telling her, who left her alone to her own devices so much of the time. I had been surprised to discover that Sadie Madigan, then Cregan, was a past pupil of Maria Goretti herself, Leaving Cert 1964. A letter from Neville, sent in January 1981 mentioned this fact, along with his enquiry if there might be a place for Lydia when she was due to begin secondary school in 1983. I concluded that he had started to make his plans early, not long after the car accident which took Sadie and Mark Madigan. Even then, I surmised, he was looking for ways to relinquish responsibility for his niece, the burden he hadn't wanted or expected to carry.

The more I read, the more I felt for Lydia. Living in Dublin on a street of Georgian houses which were crumbling and many verging on derelict. It had been a street of tenements, a symbol of inner-city ruin and neglect, that was gradually being recovered as the decade progressed. I couldn't picture what it would be like to live in one of the houses – I pictured her life in my head – in a building that was crumbling, damp, dark. A young, innocent lost girl, whose guardian was an irresponsible fop. And now, here she was, banished to the depths of the countryside, life-shaping exams fast approaching, being victimised by a domineering nun – a loner, with very few friends and no one to stand up for her. Eighteen years old … 'Poltergeist cases often break out suddenly, triggered by trauma, or an event of significant transition, and not just during puberty …' Frank Cross had written.

It all seemed to fit – Lydia's life – the *energy* she must exude. Was I right? Was she the catalyst? The cause? Was she the reason that Little Frances ran around the upstairs floors so frequently lately? Was Little Frances a poltergeist? Or was she a lost soul making a connection with another? Reaching out the only way she knew how?

My head began to throb as I sat there in my bed, quietly ripping the pages of information into tiny, unreadable pieces in the small hours of the morning. Painstakingly, I shredded the sheets of paper as small as I could manage. In the morning, I would stuff them into the sanitary towel bins which were changed by an external sanitation company every couple of weeks. Even the nuns didn't look in there, I was sure. I couldn't be too careful, however. God knows I had learned a harsh lesson. I couldn't risk anything being found and taken from my room again.

Somewhere in the fields beyond, a fox shrieked, shrill and high-pitched. Almost human. Slowly I closed my eyes, in an attempt to block it out.

The following morning, I watched Lydia from my dais at breakfast, as I pushed Rice Krispies around my bowl. The prefect in charge of the Leaving Cert table had poured me a cup of tea, as was the custom, but the watery smell of it was making my stomach heave. I pushed it from me as far as I could, fretting, panicking, wishing that I knew what to do. My tired mind raced. What if she had been hurt, I wondered? What if she had been a victim of being thrown about, or scratched like those girls in Enfield? It's not as if she'd ever say, and she spent so much time alone that it was possible no one would notice.

She caught me staring again at Assembly and ignoring the playlet that the First Years had composed and were now performing about helping the poor at Christmas, one of them coming perilously close to knocking over the table on which the Advent Wreath stood, two candles lit for the two Sundays gone in December. With one eye, I saw Benedicta save it before it hit the ground and scowl at the child responsible, but with the other I was still watching Lydia, who had pulled up her sleeve and was scratching her arm in an absent-minded fashion. Could that be a physical symptom, I wondered. She saw me staring, however, and frowned again, puzzled, before pulling down her sleeve and crossing her arms.

By lunchtime, I felt that the exhaustion from the sleepless nights and the sheer effort of trying to process the information that I had gleaned was weighing heavily on me. Every footstep felt like wading through water and I set my afternoon classes essays to write for themselves. I didn't feel capable of active teaching – I had more going on in my mind than I could cope with. If I could just get some sleep, I thought, as I made my way down along the Green Corridor toward the stairs to the Language Rooms where my last class of the day was to be held, feeling as if I were in a dream already. Now that I had no supervision until teatime, perhaps I could manage an hour's sleep in my room – maybe that would keep me going? Although lately it felt as though there simply wasn't enough sleep in the world to be had.

I stood in closer to the wall as a crowd of people emerged around the corner from the Assembly Hall. It was the Stage Crew for *Oklahoma*, and they seemed to walk past me in slow motion. I saw Lydia look at me as she passed, her face filled with concern as she looked at me.

"Are you okay, Miss?" I heard her ask and I looked at her curiously, wondering why she'd ask such a thing.

I made to respond, to ask her what she meant, when suddenly my vision blurred, and my knees sagged. Behind Lydia, I saw Matt, and heard his voice call my name, until a rushing sound blocked it from my ears. I saw Lydia lunge toward me, as if to catch me, before everything went black.

Little did I know, it was the last time I'd see Lydia Madigan.

221

Chapter forty

BALLYKEERAN
1945

"This is a very bad business, Guard," the nun said, staring out of the window at a thick fog outside.

Behind her, seated at the polished round table of the Nuns' Parlour, Gerard Nolan nodded, his expression grave. He stared at the brown box that he had placed on the table in front of him when he had sat down, glad to be rid of it out of his pocket.

"That it is, Sister," he said. "I'm sorry to be the bearer of bad news."

"And after that business with the mother last Christmas, may God have mercy on her soul ..." Mother Agnes made the Sign of the Cross and shuddered. "Such a selfish act. Taking away the chance for herself to be received in Paradise, to see her poor young child again. And the little one on her own out there in the ground. We left enough room for her mother to one day go in with her, you know – an exception for the circumstances, of course. But who knew? Who knew that with today's news, more than ever, she should have been able to lie side by side with the child but, thanks to her own selfish hand, now she never will." The nun sighed and clutched her rosary to her breast. "The Devil is a hard worker, Guard."

"That he is, Mother, that he is," he replied, and blessed himself hurriedly, tapping his chest twice.

"What will happen to him now?" Her voice was cold as she turned to face the Chief Superintendent who shrugged.

"He'll most likely swing for it ... my apologies, Mother ... he will probably receive the death sentence and be hanged."

The nun's face filled with disgust. "That's no answer either, but what can you do when it's the law of the land?"

"It might be commuted to life, or, if the doctors see fit, they might judge him insane and he could spend his days in a mental hospital. The judge will make his decision carefully, although the man has no one to blame but himself, killing a defenceless child like that."

The nun sank down into a chair at the table opposite and thought for a moment. "Do you think that's really true, Guard?"

"Why would you say otherwise, Mother? Sure didn't the child's testimony in this very room incriminate him?"

There was silence.

"Did it though?"

The Guard spluttered. "Well, twelve good men and true thought so when they found him guilty in a court of law, under the supervision and guidance of God above!"

The nun pondered for a moment, gazing back out the window.

"You see, Garda Nolan, there were things that Evelyn said that day when you interviewed her that she hadn't said previously – I was with her at every interview, if you recall, at the request of her mother who was a trusted employee here."

"I'm aware of that, Mother."

"Like the fact that she said her father was with them on the bog on the evening that poor little Frances died, Lord have Mercy on her. And the stories of violence – of her father destroying the home, throwing things around, upturning tables and what have you."

"I saw the house in that state with my very own eyes, Mother," countered the Guard.

"That's as may be. But you see, Evelyn's parents ... when they spoke to me to ask me to take her in ... well, it was for their good, as much as her own. They told me they had begun to despair of her. And God knows she's a child with a temper – the *rages* that she used to have when she arrived here first, it was as though the Devil was in her."

"She must have witnessed terrible violence in that home, Mother. Monkey see, monkey do ..."

"But that's the thing, Guard. Her parents never wished it to go further than these four walls but it's only now that it resonates with me so I will share it with you. They told me that it was young *Evelyn* who would fly into these rages at their home, not her father."

"Ah now, Sister, knowing what we know now, do you not see that for what it is?"

"And what is it, Guard?"

"It's lower than the low, is what it is, Mother. That they'd blame an innocent, troubled child for their own destruction. Wasn't it bad enough bringing her up with such a lack of moral guidance in the first place? The child of what's now a – a convicted murderer and a madwoman who took her own life?"

The nun winced. "But why would she only tell us that information now? Those things that she said, that differed from her original account of what happened? The differences in her story when you interviewed her here after her mother's death from when she was interviewed after her sister's? Why change the story?"

"Because, Mother, that's what people do when they get courage. I've seen it time and again – with her mother gone, finally young Evelyn felt brave enough to tell the truth, felt safe enough under your good care to open her heart to God and listen to Him tell her to speak the truth and find justice."

The nun peered at him sceptically down her long nose.

"And I suppose it was God who told her to go and smash every plant pot in the whole convent the first week she was here, Guard? Is it God who tells her to run up and down the length of the junior dormitory at all hours of the night? I've had to move her to own room at the end of the Sisters' Corridor, where I lock her in at night and let her out in the morning and *still* she manages to cause havoc if she feels she's not getting enough attention. Is it God who told her to break things and rip things from other girls' lockers so that in turn *they all* have to lock things up during the day? Is it God who tells her the outlandish tales that she tells us in turn? Of imaginary fires that we rush to put out? Of cattle loose in the yard? Evelyn is a troubled child, Guard. And were I you, I might not have listened so quickly, nor been so convinced by her change of story."

The Guard snorted dismissively. "Sure that's children for you, Mother. Destructive, noisy. That's why we need a heavy hand like you to turn them into Greta's Girls. Good girls." He tapped the brown box with his forefinger as he made to stand up. "I won't keep you any longer, Mother. Will you tell her about her father? That's his watch in the box there. He asked for it to be brought to the child."

The nun set her lips in a thin line, and regarded the jewellery case.

"As a cautionary tale, Guard. Perhaps it will put her on the path to right. Although if God's the one with all the other messages, it might be better coming from Him. Seems she only listens to a higher power. Or a lower one."

Chapter forty-one

Ria
BALLYKEERAN
December 1987

The voice sounded as if it were coming from far away.

"*Maria.*"

It was business-like, verging on stern. I gasped as I woke, a sudden surge of fear running through me. I was in trouble. I blinked as bright daylight blinded me. I had no idea where I was.

"You had a big sleep, didn't you, Maria?"

The voice spoke to me like I was a child. I tried to sit up and take in my surroundings.

"Time for a little breakfast now. Do you think you could manage a bit of breakfast for me?"

I followed the voice and finally saw that it was a nurse, dressed in a pale blue uniform, a lapel watch hanging upside down on her chest.

"Sit up now," she instructed me, tugging at the pillows beneath my head as I tried to push myself into a sitting position.

The sun beamed in through a large window beside the bed where I lay. It was a low, winter-morning sun. I blinked and looked away, rubbing my eyes and focusing instead on the blue candlewick coverlet on the bed where I lay. My eyes travelled to my hand. Spotting the cannula that was inserted into one of veins, I registered that it hurt, and rubbed it gingerly, wondering why it was there. I followed the tube that led into it, to a bag hanging on a portable hook beside me.

226

"We had to put you on liquids, Maria." The nurse, a large lady who smelled faintly of onions, blocked some of the light as she rearranged me on the bed. She leaned over me to fetch something, and then wrapped a blood pressure band around my arm. "You were severely dehydrated, and exhausted too. You have to look after yourself a bit better from now on."

I felt the pressure belt tighten on my arm, uncomfortable for a few seconds, and then release again.

"That's coming down," she said, almost to herself. "Now. I'll get you a bit of tea and toast and we'll check you again after that."

I looked up at her as she smiled.

"You'll live," she joked. "This time anyway," and with that, bustled out of the room.

I sank back on the pillow and closed my eyes for a moment, disoriented and groggy and still blinded by the glaring sun through the window.

I had fainted, I remembered. At school. Matt was there ... so was Lydia ...

The second voice took me completely by surprise as I heard it from the end of my bed.

"So, the Lord won't take you this time, Miss Clancy," it said.

I gasped with fright and sat up straight to see. In a chair, at the end of the bed, was Mother Benedicta. She sat there, her hands on her lap, her brown rosary wound around them, her legs crossed, making her look as if someone had folded her into the chair. Her lips were thin, her eyes fixed on me.

"Mother," I replied, my voice sounding odd and cracked. "I didn't know you were there."

"I'm always there, Miss Clancy," she replied in a cold tone. "Myself and Jesus, we're always watching. We see everything."

I glanced around to see that I was alone with her in a small, private room. A bedside locker with a jug of water and a glass was on the same side as the drip, a tall wardrobe on the other side of the bed. A handbasin and, above it, a paper towel-dispenser were attached to the wall opposite. The nun occupied the only chair.

A familiar smell suddenly wafted in from the corridor outside and my stomach responded immediately with a loud gurgle. I was starving, I realised, as the nurse bustled back in the door with a tray carrying a silver teapot, a cup upturned on a saucer, a small jug of milk and a plate of toast.

"Now, Maria, get this into you and you'll be a new woman," she said, putting the tray down on an overbed table which she then slid from my feet up toward my chest. "If you keep that down then we might get the drip out today and get you back to your own bed tomorrow. Have to make sure the both of you are alright to go home first."

I frowned as she left the room, her uniform swishing efficiently. I glanced at Mother Benedicta, confused.

"Are you unwell too, Mother?" I asked.

I wondered what had happened to the nun? Had she hurt herself too, perhaps? Was it food poisoning maybe, that we were both unwell?

The nun shook her head slowly, and discomfort welled in me as I watched her eyes narrow. "Surely you can't think I am that stupid?" she said.

My right hand strayed to my left and I winced as I accidentally pushed too hard against the cannula. "Sorry, Mother, the nurse said that we … that both of us needed to be alright before we could go home …"

"And you think she was referring to me?"

"Sorry, Mother, I'm just confused … when did I … when was I brought here? I remember fainting …"

My voice trailed off, puzzled. It had been afternoon when I was on my way to my last class – which meant that it should be dark now – except it was glaringly bright, early to mid-morning bright … I racked my brain. There was a blurred memory there – more like a dream – of lights on a ceiling, one after another after another – and a man's voice – "*Can you hear me, Maria?*". Then, I seemed to recall opening my eyes to see a figure there, the shape of a woman leaning over me … busy at something … It was all so indistinct, so confused.

The nun frowned at me, and pushed herself forward in the chair. "You have been here – the County General Hospital – since Tuesday evening, Miss Clancy. It is now Thursday morning."

My eyes widened.

"The nurses say that you are suffering severe dehydration and are verging on malnourishment, and that you were exhausted to the point of collapse. It has not reflected well on the standard of care at Maria Goretti, Miss Clancy. A point I have been at pains to clarify since you got here."

I leaned back against my pillows, suddenly woozy again.

"Am I seriously ill?" I asked. "Is something wrong?"

Benedicta's lips curled back slowly. "Oh, there is most certainly something wrong, *Miss* Clancy."

I felt what little blood was there drain out of my face. I was sick. I was going to die …

"You are riddled with something, Miss Clancy. Sin, that is. *Mortal sin.* That is what is wrong with you. Do you know what a mortal sin is?"

The nun stood up. Instinctively, I recoiled, pushing back into the pillow.

"Mortal sin is a sin of grave matter," she began. "Mortal sin is committed with full knowledge of the sinner. Mortal sin is committed with deliberate consent of the sinner. When you chose to … fornicate … outside of the sacred vows of marriage, did you not fulfil these criteria, Miss Clancy? And by doing so *offend* God and reject his perfect love and justice? Do you know what St Paul said to the Galatians about mortal sin? He said: '*Now the works of the flesh are manifest, which are these: adultery, fornication, uncleanness, lasciviousness, idolatry, witchcraft, hatred, variance, emulations, wrath, strife, seditions, heresies, envyings, murders, drunkenness, revellings, and such like: of the which I tell you before, as I have also told you in time past, that they which do such things shall not inherit the kingdom of God.*' How many of these did you commit, Miss Clancy?"

I was frightened now, pressed back against the pillow as the nun paced slowly around my bed, and came to a stop by my side, where the nurse had stood to check my blood pressure. Her fingers worked agitatedly on the rosary in her hand, passing the beads rapidly through her fingers over and over again. I glanced up her face which had turned purple as she spoke, spittle gathered at the corners of her lips. I turned away from her, searching for the call button.

"*You will look at me when I address you,*" she said, her voice low and cold.

I twisted as far away from her as I could, but it wasn't far enough. I tried not to meet her eye, focusing instead on her hands.

"Why did you decide that you wanted to go to hell for all eternity? Why would you show the Lord Jesus such *contempt* in rejecting him? What sort of woman are you that you couldn't resist the weakness of the flesh – the *filthy* weakness – and end your chance of ever being drawn to heaven?"

"Mother, I'm sorry, but I don't understand…"

"You don't understand?"

Her tone had risen in anger, but it was terrifying now that it was quiet again.

I watched in horror as she lowered herself down over my face.

"Let me tell you a story, Miss Clancy. Or rather, retell you a story that you should be familiar with. A story that should guide you every day. It begins with a child, eleven years old, pure of heart, free of sin, the perfect vessel for Jesus. She sat on the steps outside of her home, sewing shirts and praying quietly, praising the Lord with her work. Until she was approached by sin – by a boy, a son of the family with whom her family shared their home. And what did he want? To violate her, to commit mortal sin, to take her purity. He threatened her with a knife and said that, if she did not surrender to him, that he would stab her. And do you know what she said, Miss Clancy?"

I was unable to move, to take my eyes away from hers. I knew the story, of course, but didn't know how to respond.

"She said what you should have said, Miss Clancy, you who share her name – she said '*No! No, I shall not. It is a sin! God does not want it!*' She warned her attacker that what he would do was a mortal sin, that he would go to hell and forever perish in the flames there. Even when he did as he threatened and stabbed her many times, she still stayed strong, saying 'no' all the way. She was pure, and would remain so for Jesus who took her to him two days later. She died from the wounds of the knife, but with her body clean. She died with forgiveness for her attacker on her lips. She died *pure*, Miss Clancy. And went into the arms of God. Her name *Maria Goretti*, our blessed martyr. She fought and resisted temptation. You too could have done that, Maria Clancy, but you chose not to. And now you are paying, paying with your eternal soul, and no entry to heaven – and a *bastard* in your belly on earth!"

I gasped, recoiled, finally realising what she was saying, what the nurse had said. I couldn't be …

The nun stood up straight again, her face a sneer of disgust. I thought by her expression for a moment that she might actually *spit* on me, such was her contempt. Instead she looked me up and down and stepped back, as if suddenly, physically disgusted. She leaned back against the windowsill for support, and watched me, silently.

"For two nights I have sat here – and for two months before that, begging God to show me why I made a mistake in selecting you to be the Guardian of our girls," she said quietly, glancing at the rosary beads before turning to look out the window. "'*How could I have got it so wrong, Jesus?*' I asked. '*What made me choose someone so unsuitable?*' – because I have known you were unsuitable since virtually the first day you walked into my office. Something about you felt *off*. But how could I, of all people, have made such an unwise choice?"

She turned to look at me again.

"And then I realised that I hadn't *picked* you. You were *sent* to me. But not by God. By the Devil himself …"

I gulped hard, unable to tear myself away from her face, her cold, white skin, her eyes which burned into me, the slight tilt of her neck as she calmly explained to me that I was from hell.

"You are my challenge. My test, to overcome, to show God that I walk in his path, to remind him of my promise that I always will, no matter what life has made me do. My life is reparation to my God and your soul is corrupt, Miss Clancy. My task is to stop you before you spread your poison among the innocent girls of whom I have charge, whose souls I protect for Jesus. Yes, you are corrupt, but I cannot – *will not* allow you to *become* corruption."

I winced, pulled back again as she approached the bed but stopped before she reached me. With her waxy, bony hands, she picked up the jug of water and poured some into the plastic glass beside it before setting it down again. She held it and looked at me.

"I have decided on the following arrangements," she announced, her voice calm and matter of fact. "It goes without saying that you will not be allowed to continue as a Guardian for the girls of Maria Goretti. You are now unfit for such a purpose. A

231

bad example, tainted by the sort of sin that we insist they avoid. You are unsuitable. However ..."

I leaned as far into the pillow as I could as she bent down over me again.

"As you fell while under our guidance, I have a moral responsibility to you and your burden of sin."

She looked down at my stomach, which I instinctively covered with my hands, and then back up to my face. She was so close that I could feel her breath.

"Jesus urged us to forgive, and I will continue to pray with all my might for the gift of that grace in order that I may do the right thing by you ..."

I watched as she raised the glass of water and brought it to my lips.

"... and pray with you for your own forgiveness. You will need to say sorry a thousand times and then a thousand more, you know, for offending God so greatly ..."

She tilted the glass against my closed mouth and began to pour. I mumbled, and tried to shake my head to say no, but she kept going. Water trickled cold down my chin, along my neck and onto my chest. I made a muffled noise of protest, but she didn't stop.

"You are technically homeless, am I correct?"

I moved my head away as she pressed the glass harder to my lips. Instead of stopping her, however, it merely resulted in the water trickling down my cheek. I could feel that the neck of the hospital gown was soaking now.

"So you can stay at Maria Goretti, in your room, throughout the holidays. I cannot put you out on the street – Luke, Chapter 3, Verse 10 and 11 tells us that John the Baptist said: 'Whoever has two tunics is to share with him who has none, and whoever has food is to do likewise.' However, you must be gone when the girls return from their break."

I turned my head further, unable to bear it any longer. With my left hand, I pushed the glass away, and felt the shock of cold as the last of the water landed with a splash on my chest. Desperate to get away from her, I tried to swing my legs out of the bed, but found myself trapped by the covers which were tucked in tightly.

"Stop!" I said, and, gripped with panic, I tried to force the covers out from under the mattress with my legs, convinced that she would try to stop me. She made no such move, however, instead calmly replacing the glass on the bedside table. I scrabbled at the covers with my feet and hands and eventually managed to free myself, half stepping, half sliding out of the bed, the cannula still in my hand, my head spinning and my legs feeling as if they might buckle as I stood out onto the floor. I turned to look at the nun, terrified.

"I have been able to make provision for you, once that needs to happen. In the meantime, we will take the opportunity of the time you have left at Maria Goretti to pray for forgiveness, to redeem what we can of your soul for the next life."

I felt faint, and leaned against the bed for support, watching with disbelief as she turned and calmly walked to the chair where she had been sitting to retrieve her coat which hung over the back.

"I will be back for you tomorrow. You must remain at prayer, Miss Clancy. At all times. Begging for forgiveness. Begging that the Devil casts himself from you."

She buttoned up the coat without looking at me, and then fixed me with her cold stare again. "But you are lucky, Miss Clancy. The most fortunate of sinners. Do you want to know why?"

I stared at her blankly, unable to believe what was happening. It had to be a dream of some sort, didn't it? A hallucination brought on by my illness.

"Because God and I are on your side," she said. "I have faced the Devil before, you know. In all his forms – sinner disguised as saint, demon disguised as angel. But he has never beaten me. I have always won, Miss Clancy. Always. And I will win this time too."

With that, she left, silently, gliding out the door of the small room, leaving me in complete silence. I watched her go, and then watched the door, anxious in case she would return, but she didn't. I was alone. I felt no relief, however. Instead, a tightness gripped my chest and a warm pool of fear spread from the pit of my stomach through my body. I felt it in my chest, and then my arms, and finally my legs which, without warning, began to tremble violently. A wave of despair suddenly washed over me, and, unable to support myself any longer, I sank to my knees beside the bed.

My mind was a jumble as I knelt there, bathed in bright light, my body shaking with shock and terror. And I did not know what to do. So, in the absence of knowing, I did the only thing I could think of – what Benedicta wanted me to do. I joined my hands, buried my face in the covers and began to pray.

Chapter forty-two

Ria
LONDON
May 2015

"Jesus Christ," Jess muttered under her breath. "*Je-sus Christ.*"

I knew that I could have made a joke there, should have, to lighten the mood. Warn Jess that He was not really the best guy to talk to under the circumstances, or assure her that she didn't need to start praying on my behalf.

But I couldn't.

Recalling it made me tremble. I had never verbalised it before, and hearing the story again reminded me sharply how it must sound, and of how it had felt.

"How far along were you?" she managed, taking a gulp from her glass.

"Eight weeks or so," I replied, glad that Jess's question had been a practical one. If she'd asked how the encounter had made me *feel*, I might never have been able to answer. "Of course, at the time, I didn't know that pregnancy was dated from your last period so when the nurses told me I was that far along, I panicked. Thought I'd had an immaculate conception or something. My imagination led me to all sorts of places – I knew absolutely nothing about being pregnant."

"But the baby was ..."

"Matt's," I nodded. "It was Matt's baby. Emma is Matt's daughter."

Jess's eyes widened again. "Does she know? Does *Joe* know?"

I nodded and shrugged, fiddling with the stem of my glass. "They do and they don't. They both know that it was someone in Ireland with whom I'd had a brief relationship. Joe was never bothered about who it was – he was just so ... *accepting* of everything. And he loved me so totally, and he loved Emma too when she came along."

"But what about Emma? She's twenty-seven years old. Surely she quizzed you up, down and sideways at some stage? Surely she wants to know who her real dad is?"

I shrugged. "I've always told her – and it's true – that *Joe* is her real dad. And he is – he did everything that ever counted, and still does. I explained that her biological dad wasn't all that important in the bigger scheme of things."

"But surely she must want to know who he is?"

"Maybe," I replied. "But she's never once asked outright. I don't know why."

Jess shook her head, her eyes wide. "I always said your kid was weird."

I smiled and gave a little snort of laughter. "Like mother, like daughter," I answered, and took a grateful drink from my glass, sighing as something inside me went free.

"That woman was insane," Jess said.

I responded with a humourless smile. "On that day, I wasn't so sure she was the only one," I said. "It was like an out-of-the-body experience. Finding out I was *pregnant* was big enough – what would I do? How would I manage? How could there be another human inside me? I felt shameful and afraid and alone. But add to that everything that had been going on back in the convent – remember, I had convinced myself that there was a poltergeist. I had been hearing things, seeing things – *ghosts*, for heaven's sake! In the brightness of the hospital all of that seemed far away – and completely implausible. I began to wonder if Benedicta was right?" I rubbed my eyes. "When she came back to collect me the following day, it was clear that everyone was in her thrall. The nurses couldn't do enough for her – three bags full, Mother. Even a doctor came to chat to her – it terrified me watching her huddled with him out in the corridor, both of them turning to gesture in my direction now and again. They were talking about me, like I was some sort of stray animal that they'd found and had to decide what to do with. Watching that exchange, I had never felt so powerless in my life. I was so confused and physically weak and I couldn't stop wondering what they were talking about, all the way back ..."

"Hold on, you went *back* there?" Jess eyes were wide in disbelief this time.

I nodded weakly. "She was right. I had nowhere else to go – I was technically homeless. And a clear-headed person would say that being homeless was better than what I was going back to, but I was confused and in shock, and under doctor's orders to rest. I was weak and tired, and still feeling ill – the morning sickness didn't just go away, even though I felt better able to deal with it. I allowed myself to be just led along, into the car with old Tom. Benedicta sat in the front seat, like a prison officer, and I was bundled into the back like a child. When we got there, I was almost smuggled inside while the girls were at classes and sent up to my room. I was to stay up there, and not be seen, like a shameful secret. And I complied. I was exhausted, and unwell, and I just wanted to sleep, and for it all to go away."

"You were vulnerable," said Jess.

I nodded in agreement, shivering as a cloud passed over the sun and the street darkened. "I was," I said. "But not as vulnerable as Lydia was. I just didn't know it."

Chapter forty-three

FILE OF MOTHER AGNES DE BRUIN
REGARDING THE CARE OF EVELYN PHELAN
CONVENT OF MARIA GORETTI, BALLYKEERAN, CO.
LAOIS
YEAR OF OUR LORD 1946

It is with regret, but also with much consideration, consultation, thought and prayer, that the decision has been taken to remove Evelyn Phelan from the Convent of Maria Goretti for the foreseeable future. Recent events have forced us to make this decision with heavy hearts in the hopes that a new arrangement will be for Evelyn's benefit, and for the safety of the other girls in our care.

Evelyn's behaviour has been constantly troubling since her arrival here. I have frequently documented outbursts of disobedience, wilful destruction of the property of others, answering back, disruption of the dormitories at night-time and even once of theft. An unfortunate recent incident, however, where Evelyn physically assaulted one of her classmates, the Day Pupil Maureen Kavanagh, has resulted in reflection on the matter from all of us who have responsibility for Evelyn's care and the decision that removing the child is best for all concerned.

For her part in the incident, Maureen Kavanagh is to be suspended for one week because her actions are deemed provocation. Unfortunately, she informed Evelyn that her father had been executed by hanging at Tullamore for the murder of her sister, which was not information that had been shared with Evelyn at that time.

Evelyn, however, in turn, reacted violently and while the exact details are unclear, she clearly attacked Maureen violently on the Great Stairs, threatening first to throw her from the highest point of the stairs down the stairwell which would have resulted in certain death. In the long run, she pushed Maureen down the final flight and Maureen has sustained a broken arm, bruised ribs, and severe bruising to her face and torso.

We, at Maria Goretti, assisted by our Parish Priest, Father Jeremiah Dunne, have reflected following the incident and conclude that, while under our roof, we did everything in our powers to assist Evelyn through our care and compassion, through thoughtful teaching, individual attention and appropriate discipline. We have sheltered her from information which could have distressed her and prayed in groups and one to one with her at every opportunity. Yet it seems that we have failed in our efforts and cannot continue, for her sake, and for that of the other girls in our care.

She will be moved, thereby vacating the single room at the end of the Sisters' Corridor this Thursday morning to her new residence. It is with hope and prayer that we place her into the trust of the staff of her next home.

Chapter forty-four

Lydia
BALLYKEERAN
December 1987

It's Opening Day! Or The Day Before Opening Night to give it its full title!

One week till Christmas, six days till we break for the holidays but, for now, it's showbiz all the way!

This day is always so magic – this year more than before, I think. Everyone is giddy with excitement – nervous too, of course – I think Ali Hakim was puking in the toilet outside the study earlier on – but there's this electricity in the air. It's like getting holidays a week early or something – everyone's messing about with each other, and it doesn't matter what year you're in – us Sixth Years are having the craic with the Inter Certs, and Second and Fifth are the best of pals all of a sudden.

The Assembly Hall looks deadly too – Stage Crew were excused classes this morning to set out all the audience chairs, and the stage curtains have been closed all day so that the final set is still a surprise for everyone. The whole place feels different – like it's somewhere else – there's even a different *smell* about it.

We've got a half day now so that they can set up make-up and costumes in the Sixth Year classroom behind the stage entrances off the Green Corridor. On my way down to the Ref for lunch, I saw a rack of dancers' costumes being wheeled in there, and Mr Flynn sellotaping the SILENCE! notices onto all the doors around the back of the Hall. It's going to be so much craic.

It's Friday too, so it's egg and chips and fish fingers for dinner, and the dessert trolley is parked outside already and if my eyes don't deceive me it's sponge pudding and custard – it absolutely couldn't get any better. In fairness to Sister Ruth, she can pull the odd treat out of the bag when it matters. Even she's a bit giddy today, and Mrs Treacy, the dinner lady who comes in from the village, is doing a little wiggle at something the Second Year table is saying to her – mad! Of course there's no Guardian here today – Miss Clancy has been missing since she fainted the other day in the Green Corridor which was a bit scary. Her eyes rolled back in her head and she went down like she was just a pile of clothes. Some of the girls are saying that she's been taken to hospital and she's in a coma or something but at the moment no one's thinking too much about her. I mean, everyone hopes she's okay, but we're still all laughing and in great form and tucking into our chips . . .

Until Benedicta's shadow suddenly swishes past the window and she storms into the Ref, something under her arm, and rings the bell for silence!

She gets it fast. She's got that look on her face that someone's in trouble, but surely not today? Surely she's just here to give us that lecture that we get every year to behave, that the eyes of the village and the world beyond are on us and that we must be exemplary *blah blah blah*. She ends some years by telling us to "break a leg" and we have to pretend to laugh because it's like her annual joke. The look on her face now pretty much says that there won't be any jokes this year, though. I steal a glance at Carmel who's sneaking a chip into her mouth.

Mother Dick stands up there in total silence, glaring at us all. She clears her throat.

"I have found something," she announces and you can feel the mood in the room drop. Seriously? Today of all days she's done a spot check? I glance around the room, wondering whose hairdryer she's got, or Walkman she's taken and feel sorry for the poor sod. At least it's not mine. She still has that from a couple of months ago.

"Time and time again, you are reminded of what is not permitted in school, that might be permitted at home or elsewhere," she carries on. "Rules have reasons, and reason is because of rules. This place operates because we keep to the rules. I thought you understood that."

I look back at her, and realise that she's a bit of a funny colour. Sort of purple, and there's spit at the corners of her mouth. And she's shaking a little bit. Normally when she gets cross with someone she does this cool, calm, collected and deadly thing. But this – this is like she's actually *raging* or something.

"But there is something that has been brought into this place that is so – so – *disgusting*, that I can barely bring myself to speak of it."

She looks a bit upset now, like she's going to be sick.

"Stand up, all of you," she says.

We get to our feet.

Then slowly she raises her right hand and pulls out what she has clamped under her left arm and holds it up.

My stomach drops, and I feel a burning spread through my cheeks and down my chest. No, I think to myself, *no*!

"Can the girl who is responsible for *this* remain standing. The rest of you will be seated."

She's holding the book high, so that everyone can see. Except it's not something that I want to see – that I *ever wanted* to see. A gentle rumble runs through the room as girls sit down and pull their seats in to their tables. The relieved ones. The ones who don't have to worry. I look at Carmel in panic, and blush redder as I see her join them. The traitor. I, on the other hand, remain standing. There's no point in not doing so, because Benedicta knows damn well who's responsible. After all, she's found the book where's it was slipped into the lining of my mattress, where I forgot about it. It seems that I'm to take responsibility for *The Passion of Sister Claude*.

I feel sick as Benedicta turns her head to catch me in her stare.

"Lydia Madigan," she says. "I should have known. Come with me now." She turns and storms out.

I give Carmel a final glare. She responds with a '*What can I do?*' face, and I call her a bitch in my mind. I'm in trouble now. And on opening day too. I turn quietly, helplessly, burning under the eyes of my silent schoolmates who are shocked and relieved in equal measure, and slowly follow Benedicta out of the Ref and onto the Brown Corridor where she's waiting for me.

And she marches me to her office, in complete silence, but it's like I can feel the sheer and utter rage coming off her.

I suddenly feel afraid.

Chapter forty-five

Ria
BALLYKEERAN
December 1987

The rising bell woke me with a start, directly outside the door of my room. I lay there, clutching my covers as I waited for the pounding in my chest to subside, listening as the bell was carried as usual, ringing all the way, up the stairs to the dormitory.

I heard the bustle of the girls rising almost immediately and tried to figure out what day it was. My bedside clock showed eight o'clock. But surely it should be seven? What about Mass? Maybe my clock was slow ... Whatever was going on, they were up and about very briskly this morning. Normally the sounds would come gradually, shuffling feet heading into the bathroom outside my door, the occasional groan, a loud yawn here and there. But this morning, movement seemed faster and there was the occasional surreptitious giggle which wasn't shushed vehemently by a cautious older sister or Eleanor Hanley, the prefect.

Then it hit me – of course – *Oklahoma*. It must be Friday. The musical opened tonight. The girls had an exciting day ahead of them, a half day to prepare, and then costumes and make-up from 6.30. Tonight was the night. It had all been leading to this. A thought of Matt half formed in my mind but I pushed it away. There was no point in even thinking about him. I couldn't deal with those thoughts – the sadness, the frustration.

I sat up. I still felt exhausted, even though I had been asleep since

I had climbed into bed the previous day. At least no one had come near me – thankfully, there was no sign of Benedicta. So far, anyway. At the thought of her, my stomach twisted in a knot, and it all came back to me – how she had been in the hospital, this talk of 'provision' for me … and the baby. The unbelievable, unthinkable, unplanned life that was starting to flutter inside me. The nurse had told me that it was no bigger than a kidney bean, but that it had a heartbeat and that soon, in the next month or so, should everything proceed as it should, the sickness and exhaustion should pass and I should begin to – in her words – *bloom*.

I couldn't imagine it. I would grow larger, and then give birth, and there would be a *baby*. A baby of my own. *My baby*. My hand strayed to my stomach. As if I might feel something. But there was nothing there. Not in my body, and not in my heart.

In my head, however, was fear. And anxiety. I glanced at the door, afraid that all of a sudden she might walk in, with her crisp veil and her waxy face and those cold eyes, preaching at me, reminding me of my sin. I sat up further and reached for my dressing gown which I had spread over my legs for added warmth. July, the nurse had said. Give or take a few weeks – I'd probably go over if it was my first. I suddenly gasped for air. *What in the name of God was I going to do?*

I grabbed the basin off my bedside locker and dry-heaved into it. When I was sure nothing else was coming, I reached for a dry cream cracker from the packet that had been left beside my bed the previous day. A bottle of Lucozade stood beside it – both things that the nurse had suggested I might keep down, provided for me in my absence. I reached for it, twisted the cap and felt it hiss against my hand. I grimaced as I drank straight from the bottle. I had always hated the taste, but it sparkled on my tongue which was pleasant against the dryness of the night's sleep, and it went down easily. It helped the cracker to go down too, and I sat there for a while, just concentrating on not being sick again.

I sat still, forcing my mind to stay blank, listening to the girls outside dress and wash, and to the sounds of their feet growing quieter and more distant as they headed off to breakfast, and their exciting day. I envied them fiercely. The excitement that they felt, the fun that they'd have, the challenge of the night ahead and the exhilaration of the applause afterwards. I envied them their togetherness, their friendships, the uncomplicated nature of what they had ahead of them today. I envied them their families and homes. As I heard the last of the footsteps grow fainter as they descended the stairs, I closed my eyes and allowed it all to wash over me. What had I done? And now, what would happen to me?

The sound of the door opening, and the sight of a dark shape through the opaque glass panels made me jump all of a sudden, and I instinctively slid out of the bed to my feet, ready to face whatever stood on the other side, be it some ghastly hallucination, or the cold face of Mother Benedicta. Instead, it was Sister Ruth, carrying a tray of cereal and toast and a pot of tea.

"Mother Benedicta said I was to bring you these," she said quietly, entering the room to place the tray on the desk.

"Thank you, Sister," I said, watching her. "And thank you for the Lucozade and crackers. I – I think they've helped a little."

The nun turned slowly from the desk and stood there, her hands joined. She studied the ground, nodding faintly while I studied her, neither of us saying anything. After a moment, she made to move toward the door. I felt panic rise in me. If she left, I'd be alone … with everything in my head. I didn't want to be alone.

"Wait!" I called.

She stopped in her tracks, still staring at the floor.

"Sorry, Sister," I said. "It's just … is everything set for curtain-up later?" I could think of nothing but small talk.

"I think so," she replied in her tiny voice.

"That's good," I replied. "Mr Flynn – the girls – they've all worked really hard. I'm looking forward to seeing it."

My words caused her to glance at me in horror.

"That'll be okay, won't it?" I frowned. "I'm sure I'll be well enough to get up for a couple of hours."

"You're not … Mother Benedicta says that you're to stay in your room."

Her voice sounded fearful. My shoulders slumped a little.

"Oh. I was looking forward to it – I assumed – I mean, I'd just be sitting there – I wouldn't be any trouble."

"Mother Benedicta says you're not to leave your room."

The nun's voice was a little more forceful that time.

I frowned. "But surely ... "

"*No!*"

I recoiled, as if she had smacked me. She flushed a deep red herself, her expression pained.

"Mother Benedicta has put me in charge of taking care of you," she said, her voice quiet again, but firm. "Until you're transferred, at least. Until then, you're to do what I say."

I stared at her, feeling the blood drain from my face. "Transferred?"

Sister Ruth glanced at me, worried. "Mother Benedicta said that she'd explained ..."

"Transferred where?"

"She said that she'd told you she'd made arrangements for what would happen to you ..."

"Transferred *where!*"

She jumped at my tone.

"To somewhere there would be people to look after you, before and after ... where the arrangements could be made for the ..."

She pointed in the direction of my stomach.

"Where's that? What arrangements?"

The nun took a step toward the door, visibly agitated now. Her breathing was shallow and fast, and she looked at me, then looked away again.

"What *arrangements*?"

I took a shaky step toward the nun. It was enough to make her bolt but I reached her side before she could leave. I felt my whole body tremble as I forced myself in between her and the door. We stood awkwardly close together. For a moment, I had a brief out-of-body sensation. *What was I doing? Body-blocking a nun from leaving a room? This wasn't me ...*

Sister Ruth froze. We stood there in silence for a moment, her staring at the floor, me blocking her way, neither of us able to move. I waited for her to speak.

"St Aidan's," she whispered suddenly.

"*What?*"

She paused.

"St Aidan's. You have a room in St Aidan's until the baby is born and then arrangements can be made for it."

She nudged me, very gently, but there was no doubt about what she was doing. Exerting dominance. Stunned, I allowed her.

"St Aidan's?" I repeated.

She didn't respond – didn't have to. The room suddenly lurched, and I stepped back, leaving her free to step out the door, pick something up that was out of my line of sight and then step in again.

I watched, unclear at first what it was, and then confused when I identified it.

Gently, the nun rested the white, enamel chamber pot on the floor just inside the door. Inside it was a roll of toilet paper.

"I'm sorry," she mumbled, and with that she stepped from the room, taking hold of the door-handle with one hand, and rummaging in her pocket with the other.

"*No!*" I cried, as I saw what she was about to do.

She looked at me in horror, and moved more quickly as I made for her.

"*No, you can't!*" I shouted. "*You can't do ... that ...*" My voice trailed off as she pulled the door shut behind her.

I watched in silent disbelief as she did what she had been ordered to do, as the lock clicked behind her. I was a prisoner.

I went to the door, in a state of disbelief, and jiggled the handle, and pulled the door, but to no avail. It would not budge. For an age, I stared at it, filled with disbelief, and anger, and outrage. And confusion. I glanced at the chamber pot and the toilet roll, at the breakfast tray. After a while, unable to think what I should do, I went back and sank onto the bed.

St Aidan's.

I had never seen it, but sometimes the local girls talked about it. "*If Desdemona was around here, Miss, they'd put her in St Aidan's*" ... "*If you give us any more essays, Miss, I'll end up in St Aidan's*". The Mental, they called it. Talked about padded cells and straitjackets. It was not a place that anyone wanted to go.

But they couldn't, could they? No one could lock me up just for being pregnant? It was 1987, not 1957!

I squirmed. But what if Benedicta could? I thought of the nurses and the doctor in the County hospital, kowtowing to her, nodding their heads deferentially, addressing her with respect. Mother

Superiors always commanded that extra estimation, just like Parish Priests and Bishops. What if she held the same respect – what if she held *authority* – at St Aidan's? What if all she had to do in this small town was snap her fingers and her bidding was done? It wasn't just possible, it was *likely*.

So, was I to be committed? My heart thudded behind my ribcage as my mind raced. But how could she do that? I was completely sane. An employee, a *teacher*. But not local ... no one around here knew me, could vouch for me. I had no family, no friends – I was a blow-in, a stranger. And the issue of my sanity... I gripped the side of the bed. *Was I sane?*

I had thought no one was watching – no one was paying attention, but what if they had been? What if Benedicta was been observing me all along? The last week or so – since I had figured out ... since I *thought* I had figured out what was happening with Lydia? I flushed, and felt my face burn – the library – the things I had researched – and the letter I had sent to the Dublin Paranormal Society – using that girl to carry my post – what had made me think that she would keep it secret? What had I been thinking? Of *course* Benedicta had read it, and the reply too – and now she knew about my theory – the haunting, the connection I thought it might have with a student ... And she thought – knew – that I was completely mad.

In the cold light of day it suddenly seemed so ridiculous to think that a *ghost* had somehow attached itself to a student and was making strange things happen – I thought back to watching Lydia closely – observing her every move. What if *she* had reported me to Benedicta for my odd behaviour? What if they were all in on it? What if they were all ... scared of me? My mind raced back to the damp footprints on the floor of the passage outside, how Benedicta had run from them – and from the ringing bell in the dormitory that day. What if I was completely delusional? What if I had imagined it all, and when she fled it was out of fear of *me?*

I realised that my entire body was trembling as I retraced my steps. She could have me committed – of *course* she could have me committed. What if I was having some sort of breakdown? Caused by splitting up with Leonard? Caused by having to abandon The Plan? Splitting up with Matt? Had it all been so stressful that I had started to imagine ghosts? Were they doing this for my own safety? For that of the baby? Was that why ... Were they going to take it away from me? Was that what Ruth had meant by *arrangements*? The horror of what she had actually meant suddenly dawned on me. Why was I so slow? I covered my face with my hands. This was too much.

I sat there for a long time, calming myself as best I could, trying my hardest to block it all out, make it go away, my hands pressed against my eyes, watching the different shapes and patterns that appeared there change and dissipate and transform in a psychedelic show. All around me was completely silent. I was alone.

A bolt of fear hit me.

I was, wasn't I? I was completely alone. I was in trouble, and I had literally no one. And they were going to take it away from me. They were going to commit me, and take my baby away.

They were going to send me to a mental hospital – what would that be like? Would it be like prison? Or worse? Would there be things like shock treatment or something that could harm the baby? What if all the talk of padded cells and straitjackets – all those things from the movies were true? What if it was worse? What if it hurt my baby?

Except it wasn't just my *baby.*

Matt.

I flew to the window, fully expecting to just see him walking past, but of course he wasn't there at all. He had to be told – maybe he was the only person who could save the baby. But then, what about me?

Outside, I heard an engine approach, and watched as the postman pulled up in his van outside. A normal, everyday occurrence that I had seen happen so many times since I started at Maria Goretti.

And suddenly, I was flooded with rage.

How dare they? How could they keep me a prisoner here – that was against the law surely? And then commit me to a mental hospital against my will? And take my freedom, my reputation, my livelihood? My *child*?

But I was an adult. A lay person. Not some waif or stray to be rescued by Mother Benedicta – not some helpless girl, stricken down by misfortune. No. That was not me. I was a grown woman.

She couldn't do this. I inhaled deeply. She *would not* have me, I decided. And she *would not* have my baby.

I began to pace the room. I couldn't stay there, I realised. I would have to do something, and something soon, before this went too far. What had seemed like an unlikely possibility on waking that morning had suddenly turned into an actual threat. Benedicta was going to carry out her plan, going to keep me locked up.

So I needed to get out – to tell Matt. To somehow stop this insanity that I found myself in. To ask for help.

Once again, I sat down on the bed quietly, but this time to think. It was time to stop feeling ill and helpless, to stop seeing ghosts and imagining things. I had to get real, as the students said. To think rationally and calmly but most of all to put an end to this. First, I needed to figure out how to get the hell out of that room, then as far away from Ballykeeran as I could.

Chapter forty-six

Ria
LONDON
May 2015

"I told you that you wouldn't believe me," I said.

Jess opened her mouth to say something, but nothing came out at first. Instead, she leaned across the table and poured herself a tall glass of iced water from the carafe that the waiter had placed there. Taking a deep draught, she composed herself.

"If I didn't know you for as long as I have," she began, her voice cracking, "then no. I wouldn't believe a word of it. Between *The Waltons*, and the poltergeists and then ... no. Not a word. But it's you, Ria. The world's most dependable, solid, straightforward woman ..."

"The Baroness of Banal," I smiled. "The Oracle of Ordinary, Csarina of Safe."

Jess smiled weakly in return. "I don't know what to say to you."

I shrugged. "This is all why – why I like things safe and ordinary and ordered and predictable."

Jess nodded. "So she was really going to put you in a nuthouse?"

"A psychiatric institution," I corrected her. "Except it wasn't really a *helping* sort of place at the time. They did accommodate short-term stays for people with alcohol or drug problems but, in retrospect, I don't think Benedicta would have booked me in for a mini-break, if you know what I mean. She wanted rid of me – I was a bad example – the *worst*. I was a slut, a sinner, something

252

shameful – and she was the moral guardian of all that she surveyed. Or so she liked to think. At first, I used to think she was just a bit old school, a bit extreme. It was only then I saw the beginnings of how insane she actually *was*."

"The *beginnings*?" Jess spluttered.

I suddenly felt tears pricking at my eyes and looked up to the sky in an effort to stop them from falling.

"Yes," I replied. "I thought that what she planned for me was the limit of what she was capable of, but I'm fairly sure I was wrong. I'll never know for certain, however."

I looked down, crossed and uncrossed my legs.

"So how did you get out?" asked Jess. "You *did* get out, didn't you? Did you shimmy down a drainpipe? Or break the lock or did your knight in shining armour suddenly dash up the stairs and carry you out of there, all sleeveless T-shirt and power ballads?"

I grinned, and thought for a moment.

"Lucky you know me as well as you do, Jess," I said.

She tilted her head to one side. "Why?"

"Because, as you said, if you didn't you wouldn't have believed what had happened so far ... and then you'd write me off as the world's biggest liar from here on in ..."

"Oh, come on!" Jess laughed. "How much stranger can all of this get?"

I looked her square in the eye. "A lot," I said. "By your standards. And that of normal, civilised human beings. Look at it this way – you might have believed me up until this point because of friendship and trust, but all that could change when I tell you what happened next. Because things were about to get serious. And weirder. So much weirder."

Chapter forty-seven

BALLYKEERAN
December 1987

The nun craved silence.

All day long, the wretched noises – shouting, giggling, unbecoming exuberance – it took every ounce of her restraint not to do to all of them what she had done to that dreadful child with the filthy book. The sooner that this musical was over the better. It was good for the school, but it brought chaos, and the nun couldn't abide chaos. Even the nuns were giddy and there was chatter all through the convent. Normally she could find some peace in her bedroom, but not this evening.

She shut herself into the Library and turned the key in the lock. She must not be disturbed. If she was to get through the rest of this night – greeting parents, smiling at people from the village, deflecting the looks and stares, although she was used to rising above all that by now, restraining herself from punishing giddy students as they deserved – then she needed solitude and calm, and the spiritual nourishment that she derived from praying alone. She would far rather have been in the Prayer Room downstairs, but it had been locked – on her orders. Tonight, the public would be in her Sacred House, wandering and straying – and the Prayer Room was private to her household, so she had ordered Ruth to lock it and bring her the key so that she might let herself in and lock the door behind her. Except Ruth was nowhere to be found, and time was marching on. Already tea was eaten, and the students dressed in their costumes – there was only an hour or so before the chaos of the evening began, so she had come to the Library instead – it was the quietest place she could think of with the students all milling about the school. She wouldn't stay for long, just enough to pray for strength to get her through a challenging evening.

She flicked on the light switch and tutted as she looked up and saw that two out of the three bulbs in the ceiling light were blown. Another minor thing that she'd have to take care of. Why was *everything* up to her? Why did she have to be in charge of absolutely every tiny thing?

The nun suddenly began to itch – first her shoulder, then the back of her neck, and around to her nose – she tried to chase it around her body to relieve it – arm, thigh, palm, shoulder blade … just where she couldn't reach. She wanted to scream – the *Devil* wanted her to scream. He wanted her to turn the tables upside down and throw the chairs as hard as she could, to smash the windows, and the TV that stood in the corner, to pull every single book off the shelves and scatter them with force around the room. She wanted to throw the Advent wreath, which was kept there while the Hall was being used for the show, against the wall, sending the three purple candles and one red flying, to break in pieces, then rip apart the fir that was wound into the circular oasis underneath with her hands. Instead, she closed her eyes against Him. She must not give in to Him. She must use the skills that she had acquired over her lifetime to stay in control. She stood still for a moment, to allow the rage to subside and calm to wash over her.

Once relaxed, she picked up the wreath and placed it down on the table nearest to her and looked at it, sighing. In the absence of the calm of the Prayer Room, she would make use of it. She slid the wreath along the table until it lay in front of a large painting of the Sacred Heart that hung on the wall between shelves, and, as she would at her usual private prayers in either the Prayer Room or the chapel, she took a box of matches from the pocket of her cardigan and lit two of the purple candles, leaving one for Sunday and the red for Christmas Day itself.

The nun then pulled out a chair from where it was tucked under one of the long study tables, turned it towards herself and placed it in front of her makeshift altar, kneeling down in front of it on the lino-covered floor, her elbows on the seat. Lowering her head into her hands, she began to pray immediately, silently and slowly, feeling a calm descend on her almost at once. She reached down and retrieved her rosary beads from her pocket and began to thread them through her fingers as she started to whisper the Rosary, picking up where she had left off the previous night. *"The First Sorrowful Mystery, The Agony in the Garden. Our Father, who art in Heaven ..."*

The rhythm of the prayers was so soothing, the feel of the wooden beads reassuring against her fingertips. She flew through the first decade, the second, the third ... It felt like no time and all the time in the world had passed by the time she reached The Fatima Prayer: *"Oh My Jesus, forgive us our sins, save us from the fires of hell, lead all souls to heaven, especially those in most need of Thy mercy. Amen."*

The words acted as a summons.

From behind her, the door clicked and she flinched, but didn't look up. On cue, it unlocked, opened and closed again with a squeak, and locked again. The nun pressed her hands tighter to her face and gripped the beads, the volume of the prayers rising from a whisper to a low tone. *"Hail Holy Queen, Mother of Mercy, Hail our life, our sweetness and our hope ..."*

She jumped, suddenly interrupted by a loud thud that rang out across the room. The book that fell came from the shelf nearest the door and it hit the floor heavily.

"Not now," she said crossly. *"I'm praying ..."*

She was cut off by a second thud, and a third.

"To thee do we cry, poor banished children of Eve ..." she spoke louder now, but it was pointless.

Books from all around the room began to hit the floor, one after the other, from one side and then the other, from high shelves and low shelves. They rained down on the floor at first, and then on the nun herself who put her hands up to shield herself.

"Stop, Frances!" she barked suddenly. *"In the name of God, stop!"*

The nun exclaimed as an encyclopaedia glanced off her raised hand, followed immediately by a paperback which whacked the back of her head. That was it. The nun growled, and stood up, keeping her head bent against the attack.

"*Am I never to have peace?*" she yelled, shielding herself. "*Why don't you go back to hell, eh? Back to Satan and your mother!*"

And with that, she abandoned her prayers, and ran to the door. Going out, she slammed it behind her, just as a *Book of Irish Birds* hit the table where the Advent Calendar was still lit.

And then, once she was gone, silence.

Chapter forty-eight

Ria
BALLYKEERAN
December 1987

I had fallen asleep at some point of the day, worn out from my emotions which veered from terror to fury, from despair to urgency. I had gone through everything I could think of to get out of there and, shy of breaking one of the glass panels in my bedroom door and making a run for it, I could think of nothing further. But it was a plan. If nothing happened between now and eight o'clock, then that would be my course of action. I couldn't stay there any longer.

I woke from a heavy sleep to voices – panicked voices – and running along the corridor outside my room. I was startled, and sat up quickly to listen, terrified of what might be there. But there was nothing there, was there? It was all in my head. After a moment, I realised that the voices were those of students. I crept to the door and listened. They were looking for someone.

"Have you seen her today?"

"Not since dinnertime. She got into trouble for some book or something and Mother Dick marched her out of the Ref and no one has seen her since."

"Jesus! Was she expelled or something?"

"No – her stuff is all still in her cubicle upstairs."

"So why are you looking down here?"

"Long shot. Mr Flynn said to try everything – c'mere, you'll be killed if you're found up here – Day Girls aren't allowed in the

258

dorms at all."

"I know – but Mr Flynn is going mental down there – he sent me to find you."

"She's not here anyway – I'll try the Study one more time ..."

The voices faded down the corridor. Too late, it struck me that I should have called out to them – but to say what? To tell them that I was being held against my will and I needed help? And then what would they do? Go and find a nun. That's what they'd do.

I sank back down on my bed and glanced at the clock on my bedside table – half past seven. I had been asleep for over two hours, I reckoned, and was angry with myself for that. I should have stayed awake – I might already have missed a chance to get out unnoticed. But maybe I still had a chance – soon the place would bustle with cars and parents, and people from the village coming for the opening night of the show. Maybe that could be a way out? Maybe someone would come to my aid if I told them I was trapped – I didn't have to tell them it was deliberate? I walked to the window and tugged at it, but of course it didn't budge. "*Dammit!*" I whispered. Maybe when there were more people around, I could just bang on the window until someone saw me? Although then what? What if they, too, went and found a nun who would tell them God-knows-what, and I'd still be in here when they'd all gone home for the night, with only the wrath of Mother Dick for company.

A surge of frustration ran through me. Maybe I could overpower Sister Ruth when she came with a meal tray? That's what they'd do on TV, wouldn't they? I shook my head at how ludicrous an idea that was, even if I had been in the whole of my health. Me, physically attacking some poor nun. It had felt bad enough just to stand in her way earlier. After all, she was merely doing someone else's bidding – although wasn't that the Nuremberg Defence?

I leaned my head against the cool glass of the window in despair.

The first of the cars arrived ten minutes later. In through the main gate and through to the Playing Courts where all nets had been removed to facilitate car parking. I watched them as they drove by, lights sweeping across the side of the church, and over the Nuns' Graveyard. As the car park filled, I could hear doors closing, distant, muffled conversation. All of those people just going to see their kids in a show and then home again. Simple. Uncomplicated.

Meanwhile inside, it was quiet. There were no girls to bustle along the corridor. No shuffling from the Study Hall below me. All of the life the building contained was now concentrated around the Assembly Hall, and it would stay that way until the final curtain. No one would come near me until the last encore was sung, the last ticket drawn in the raffle.

Somewhere, not too far away, a door was slammed – it sounded like the Library – but apart from that, nothing.

I pictured the Assembly Hall, which I knew right now would be warm and bright and filling gradually with parents and locals. It was where the life was – and where Matt was. I squeezed my eyes firmly shut against the tears I felt pricking them. Why couldn't it be like it was before? Why couldn't I just be *there* in the front row, watching, or backstage, helping? Why couldn't it be that he'd see me across a room full of costumed students and give me that smile that he did? Why was I in this terrible mess? And when would I tell him about the pregnancy? *How* would I tell him? Would he even believe me, or would he accuse me of lying about that too, and be convinced that Leonard was the father of this baby? And whether he believed me or not, what would happen then? A sob escaped me, and I pressed the heels of my palms into my eyes. I was in such a *mess*. How had this happened?

For a few moments, I allowed myself to wallow in the tears. And then, suddenly, the tears were replaced by something else. Determination. What the hell was I sitting there for, crying, when my employer – because that's all she was, not my parent, or moral guardian or *anything*, in fact, except my boss – had threatened to have me involuntarily admitted to a psychiatric hospital and have my unborn baby taken away. "Who the *hell* does she think she is?" I asked out loud. And with that, I turned, glancing around the room and heading straight for my wardrobe where I hurriedly threw on a pair of jeans and a jumper and my runners, before turning and surveying the wardrobe again. I pulled on my coat and, on second thoughts, my gloves to protect my hands. I glanced at my handbag, into which I had placed my purse and the photograph of my parents, where it rested on the bed, ready for me to grab when I had done what I needed to do. Then, with my teeth gritted, I wrapped a towel around my right hand and wrist and stormed over to the locked door of the bedroom. I didn't *have* to be there. No one could keep me prisoner against my will. And with the crowds arriving, it would be easy for me to slip out unnoticed and get myself to a bus or train or something and just leave in the night. Sure, they'd probably send the local Guards after me, but if I could just get myself home, get to Dublin, talk to someone who wasn't connected with this stupid town, someone who wasn't a Goretti Girl, or didn't know one, or who had never heard of this goddamn place – then I could explain everything and she'd have to back off, and maybe *she'd* get in trouble and ... and ...

I pulled my arm back, and was just about to drive it through the frosted glass with as much force as I could, when something unexpected happened.

The lock on the door clicked from the outside.

I jumped, and stepped back, startled. The handle turned, slowly, and the door squeaked gently open, just the smallest crack.

I watched it, frozen. It must be Sister Ruth, I thought. With another tray, or a new chamber pot or something? The door remained completely still, however. I pulled the towel off my hand and hurriedly dragged my coat and gloves off in full expectation of getting caught.

When she didn't appear, I pulled the door open.

There was, in fact, no one there.

I pulled it wider and peered out into the passage. It was dark, the only light at the opposite end coming up the stairs from the lobby below. I took a step, peered into the bathroom to my left, and craned my head to look into the bedroom on my right. There was no one. Then I looked down along the corridor.

There was a child there that hadn't been before.

My entire body jolted with a massive start. The child that stood there, in the half-light, staring at me, was small – six, seven years of age? She stood there, her bony arms hanging by her sides and her equally bony legs emerging from the frayed hem of a nondescript grey dress – a summer dress, I noted. Sleeveless. Entirely unsuitable for a December night.

And she was watching me intently. Somehow, even though she stood with her back to the light, I could see that – or perhaps I could sense it? Somehow, I knew that her eyes were dark, deep pools, and her mouth thin and straight, all of her face framed by lank, dark hair. And somehow, with the same sense, I suddenly knew who she was. The same child that I had seen in the graveyard that morning back in October. I shuddered. She wasn't in her grave, as the rhyme said, nor was she dead. At least not properly.

"Frances," I whispered.

My entire body turned to ice as she raised her hand, ever so slowly, and beckoned to me. It was terrifying. Yet mixed with the fear and alarm at seeing such a thing was a fascination, a burning curiosity. *Was she really there, or was it a hallucination? What was she made of? Was this really happening to me?* I felt my legs begin to give way with shock and I grabbed the doorpost as, soundlessly, she turned and began to walk away. As if hypnotised, I followed down the dark passageway, everything else a distant blur as I pursued her out toward the landing until she disappeared from view.

I began to make my way down the stairs, grasping the bannister firmly and peering over the side in the dim light to see where the child had gone, expecting to see nothing. I gasped, however, as I met her eyes again, those black pools set deep in her young face. She looked up at me from the stairwell below, already descended. I swallowed hard, my skin alive with a thousand pinpricks, a cold chill running the length of my spine, and carried on behind her.

When I reached the bottom step and turned, there she stood in front of me, at the door to the Boarders' Locker Room, but only for a moment. As if she were made of smoke, she suddenly vanished. I stopped in my tracks, staring at the spot where she had been, gripped with disbelief, still unsure that I had actually just seen what I was so sure I was seeing moments before. Then I felt the icy draught snake its way around my legs. But, unlike the child, it was nothing supernatural. Instead, it was a cold breeze from the doors beyond where she had stood, the door that opened out to the Playing Courts and The Walk. The door that led outside, to freedom. And it was wide open.

It was as if the bracing air suddenly woke me from a dream. For a second, I stood there, trying to understand what had happened, but only for a second. A smell of cold night hit my nostrils and I suddenly snapped back into reality. Without hesitation, I rushed toward it, outside and into the already bitter night.

Directly outside lay the gravel courtyard – the space between the back of the main school building which was overlooked by the Assembly Hall, where the disused prefabs stood. I stopped there, behind one of them, and shivered before taking a few steps forward, dazed. It was freezing. I glanced above me, into the night sky which was scattered with thousands of stars, clear as the eye could see. I wrapped my arms around my chest, glad that I was dressed at all, but only too aware that it was too cold to be without a coat. And I had forgotten my bag – with my money and passport. I swore in the darkness. I would have to go back inside for them – I couldn't go far without warm clothes, and I would get nowhere without money. I turned and looked back at the door, suddenly terrified to step back through it lest it should lock again.

The air suddenly filled with noise as, from my left, the opening notes of *Oklahoma* played out on Sister Cecilia's Steinway from inside the Assembly Hall. It was that time, then, already, I realised, and stood there for a moment, contemplating whether I should go into the warmth of the Hall and mingle with the crowds. Or I could head to the backstage entrance along the Green Corridor and see if I could find Matt? *That's* what I'd do – I'd try to talk to him now, or at least ask him to meet me afterwards?

A new confidence rose up in me. Even if she saw me, Benedicta wouldn't dare stop me in front of so many other people – she wouldn't allow me to show myself for the 'disgrace' that I was, lest I show her up. And if I could just talk to Matt – just explain to him that I needed help, and that I needed him to get me away from the convent, then surely he'd do that, wouldn't he?

Then I saw her again.

There was a flicker of *something* in the corner of my eye, coming from the direction of the Nuns' Graveyard which lay ahead of me in the distance. I stopped, and looked again. There she was. The thin little figure, in her summer dress, just standing there, grey against the headstones. Any normal child would be shivering, crying in the dark. Any real child, that was. Any live child.

Except this time, she wasn't looking back at me. Instead, her eyes were focused upwards. I stared at her for a moment, torn between my urge to go inside and find Matt, and complete disbelief at seeing her again. But then she slowly raised her arm and pointed upwards at the front of the House, and I turned to see what she was looking at.

At first, I saw nothing amiss, just the cold, grey edifice of the building, still and silent against the night. In the background, a snatch of 'Oh, What a Beautiful Mornin' caught the air.

I glanced back at the child, only to see that she still was pointing upward. She was *showing* me something, something that I couldn't see. What I wish I *hadn't* seen was the look on her face. It was clearer out here, despite the fact that she was further away – I couldn't understand it. The eyes were still dark and hollow – were they there at all, in fact? – and the complexion still ghastly grey. But instead of the serious expression on the face that I had seen upstairs, there was something far more sinister. I shuddered with fright at what I saw there. It was a face that haunted my dreams for many years: a grimace – a broad, humourless, *bitter* sneer.

The child was smiling.

Panicked, I turned again to look at the building, terrified of her, terrified of what I would see there. What horror, what supernatural nightmare could she be pointing to that pleased her so much? I staggered forward a step, unwilling to get any closer to her but simultaneously desperate to see what she was pointing at. My breath coming in short gasps, I studied the building. Again, for a few moments, nothing looked out of place, until a glimmer of light from the Library window caught my eye. I looked back at the child, horrified, only to see that she was gone.

At first, I managed only a whisper. But the word grew louder as I said it over and over, stumbling across the courtyard toward the door of the Assembly Hall. I had to warn them.

Heat and the smell of greasepaint enveloped me as I flung open the inner doors of the Hall, and heads turned as I tried to tell them.

"*Fire!*" I gasped at first, my voice growing louder as I repeated it. "*Fire! The school is on fire!*"

Chapter forty-nine

Ria
LONDON
2015

"Coffee, please," I mouthed at the waiter before turning back to Jess.

"Don't stop now!" she said drily.

"It was total and utter chaos," I said. "People started panicking, rushing out from the Hall past me to have a look, and then just pelting to their cars and trying to get the hell out of there – except everyone had parked without the slightest idea that they'd have to leave in a hurry, and it was madness, some cars blocking other cars – parents rushed back inside to grab their kids and get them out of there – everyone was screaming and stopping to have a good look up at the fire and getting in each other's way. People parked on the Courts had to drive out past the school building to get out the front gate so they were trying to do that as fast as they could. Then a window on the first floor blew out, and suddenly everyone was trying to reverse back onto the Courts – someone was screaming for the back gate to be opened, which it was eventually and then we had people trying to drive out in two directions – of course once people got off the convent grounds, there was only one road – a narrow little country road leading back to the village – cars were bumping and scraping each other, people were screaming. Matt and some of the teachers and nuns were trying to keep order, to create some sort of system to get everyone out quicker, but no one was listening – it was just utter hysteria.

The fire, meanwhile, got out of control very quickly. It started in the Library, they told us afterwards, so that explained why it caught hold right away – the room was full of old, dry books, wooden floors and shelving, wooden tables. It spread from there upwards, up through the ceiling to the Dorm – and up through there to the disused rooms above – they were full of old furniture, apparently, and all the bed fittings up there in the disused dorm were plywood and pine – next thing we knew, more windows started blowing out, and that made the consternation below worse. Great billowing clouds of black smoke were just being belched out through the broken windows, and then there was dreadful crashing as the floors of the attic dorms started to collapse down into the Big Dorm and then that went up – it was all so *fast*.

"Couldn't the emergency services do anything?"

"That was a disaster too – they couldn't get there fast enough. The Fire Brigade was completely delayed by everyone who was trying to *leave* the place – it could barely make it along the narrow roads with the way the traffic was backed up, and then get past the chaos in the school grounds. By the time they eventually made it through, the fire had spread completely through the whole place, the new school wing and convent quarters included."

"And what did you do? Surely it provided perfect cover to get the hell out of there?"

I shook my head. "I thought about that – very briefly, mind. But in the end I couldn't go ... the students ... I had to make sure that they were safe, that everyone got out. Some of the girls – a couple of them – foolishly tried to get back in to rescue stuff – they all had precious things that they kept – diaries, photos, stuffed toys, even money – stuff that was important to them. Myself – and the other teachers and nuns – we had to make sure that no one got hurt, and that we got everyone out of there as fast and as safely as we could. It was still bitterly cold outside too, of course, although none of us could feel it with the heat of the fire, and the adrenaline rushing through us. Then word came through in the chaos that the chapel doors had been opened so that became our gathering point. A group of us adults – some of the other teachers, Matt, myself, and a couple of parents, formed a chain to guide anyone who was still there safely inside through the Goretti Door – at least we could keep track of where everyone was once they were inside. I can't recall how many people filed past us as we stood there, talking to them all, urging them to stay calm – some of the girls were distraught, and so were a few of the parents. None of us were entirely sure that the chapel was even safe – if the wind changed, for example, and sent a spark across the grounds then couldn't that start to burn too? But it was the best we had, and in they went in what felt like this endless crocodile. And all the while, I watched the fire spread through Maria Goretti – through the Study Hall and the Prayer Room downstairs, all along the upstairs, down through the Sisters' Corridor – I couldn't see it, but I knew when my own room was alight. My every possession gone, I remember thinking. My books, photographs of my parents, my clothes – in an instant, I was left with literally nothing. And all the time, there was the dreadful sound of it, roaring like a huge beast in the night – and the smell, of course, the dreadful thick stench of the smoke. The fire crew battled it with hoses but... have you ever watched a house burn?"

Jess shook her head.

"It's like a living *thing*, the fire – after a while, if you stare at it long enough, it even stops looking like fire, and begins to look liquid, like a great wave, changing direction willy-nilly, sweeping over everything, engulfing it. It was so completely out of control, yet it was the only thing that *held* control, if you know what I mean. It was like watching hell in front of our eyes."

Jess was silent for a moment, her face grey.

"If you'd still been in your room ..."

I shook my own head. "I wouldn't be here today," I said quietly. "I'd have died from smoke inhalation. I hope."

"And Emma along with you ..."

I nodded. "You'd never have known me. I was lucky – mostly everyone was – it was a complete blessing that it happened when it did, when the whole school was gathered together in the new section, when they had time to get out."

Jess stared at me. "But you only got out of your room because the door ... unlocked itself?"

"It didn't unlock *itself*, Jess," I said quietly, lowering my tone as my coffee arrived.

"You're telling me that a ghost – the spirit of a little girl," said Jess, ignoring the waiter who gave us a strange look, "unlocked the door to that room and let you free, thereby saving your life?"

I nodded. "I know it seems unbelievable, but it's true – it *has* to be. I'd tried that lock twenty times during the day, twisting and turning it until I'd exhausted all possibilities."

"Oh, come on, Ria. You said yourself you'd been delusional – you were having some sort of breakdown. Couldn't it have been that nun – the kind one – the one who locked you in but brought you the nice snacks? Sister Swings and Roundabouts?"

I burst out laughing at the description. Jess joined me, the tension between us eased for a moment.

"She'd never have made it to the end of the corridor and down the stairs by the time I opened the door and looked out."

"She could have hidden in one of the rooms along the way."

"It wasn't her, Jess."

"Or maybe it was her that you saw standing at the end of the corridor – you said yourself the light was bad, and you were exhausted – you'd just woken up out of a deep sleep, you were just out of hospital, dehydrated, barfing your guts up every five minutes – surely you could have been seeing things?"

I sighed. "For years, I told myself all that stuff, Jess," I said quietly. "That it was a hallucination, that the door hadn't actually been locked properly – that it couldn't have been anything but my imagination, or mistaken identity, or maybe smoke already coming from the Library, or a trick of the light or whatever. And I can continue to tell myself that stuff. And I can agree with you, just to end this conversation – I mean, I don't relish the prospect of you looking at me forever more and seeing a stark, raving loony instead of your friend. But the truth of the matter is, I've lived that day over and over and over in my head for almost thirty years. And I know what happened. And I know what I saw. And *nothing* will change the knowledge that something … supernatural, or paranormal, or ghostly happened to me in that place. That I'm alive because of someone who came back from the dead to save me."

"But why *you*? Hadn't you concluded the ghost haunting that kid – Lilian, or whatever her name was? Why did it save *you*?"

It felt at that moment like a huge bubble welled up inside me suddenly, a bubble that threatened to burst, and bring me with it. I swallowed hard against it, and went back to watching the traffic go by for a minute to compose myself. Eventually, I felt ready to tell her.

"Because, Jess, on that night – whatever about the other stuff that happened – I don't think that the ghost was haunting Lydia."

"Why?"

"Because that night, I don't think Lydia was … *there* anymore."

Jess fell silent, staring at me, while I bit back tears at the memory. This. This had stayed with me all this time, despite my best efforts to banish it to the back of my mind, to tell myself that it never happened, to lock it all away in a safe box and never take it out.

"What?"

I blinked, and looked directly at her.

"Because after that day before the fire, no one saw Lydia ever again."

"What … what happened to her? Was it the fire?"

I cleared my throat and shook my head. "Maybe. Maybe not. No one ever found out."

"But surely … wouldn't they have found her remains in the fire if she had died in it?"

"Lydia was never found – no remains in the fire, no trace anywhere else. It was all kept very quiet for some reason – too quiet."

"And why, do you think?"

"Because of Benedicta. Because of who she was, and *how* she was. No one dared accuse or implicate her, but as sure as I'm sitting here with you, I'm convinced that she was connected to it. That no one ever saw Lydia Madigan again because of her. Until now. Because I feel in my heart that they've finally found her … that she's that body in the bog …"

Chapter fifty

Ria
BALLYKEERAN
December 1987

The fire crews fought on through the night. The Gardaí arrived, and managed to clear the roads in order to make way for reinforcement fire crews which arrived from some of the bigger towns around Ballykeeran.

At some point in the early hours, some people from the village got through with flasks of tea and trays of sandwiches and served them from trestle tables set up at the back of the chapel. We were grateful for them – exhausted firefighters, students, teachers, nuns and people from the village alike, all who had stayed to help or who simply couldn't get away. Every now and then, terrified-looking parents would burst in the door to be gratefully reunited with their daughter or daughters, Day Girls and Boarders alike. Gradually, the numbers of people in the chapel were going down. I would stay until the last of them were gone, I told myself. But then? I was completely unsure of what would happen then.

The atmosphere in the chapel grew quieter as the night progressed and people received sustenance. At first, the air had been charged electric with panic and uncertainty, but eventually, as people were accounted for, the initial adrenaline rush was replaced by a nervous exhaustion. In the dim light of the place, many people were silent as they stood nursing steaming mugs of hot liquid – others chatted quietly in huddles. Everyone looked exhausted and grey. The orange glow still raged through the stained-glass windows and the smell of the smoke encased us all – clothes, hair, skin – it was trapped up our nostrils too. I wondered if I would ever smell anything else again.

I poured myself a cup of tea and made my way halfway up the main aisle, sinking onto a pew, alone. All was quiet at last and I was suddenly exhausted. I sipped the tea, into which I had put two sugars, to try to keep me awake. At least I didn't feel nauseous, surprisingly enough. Small mercies. I closed my eyes and leaned against the back of the seat, clutching the cup to my chest to warm me through.

"Are you alright?"

The voice was gruff. I opened my eyes, and was startled to see Matt standing in the aisle, towering over me, his hands in his pockets, his hair wild, his face grubby from the smoke.

I glanced around and nodded.

"I didn't know you were out of hospital …"

My eyes widened with alarm.

"It was a virus, was it?"

I glanced around again before looking back at him. So, he hadn't been told by Benedicta. "That's … that's right," I replied nervously, looking down at my tea. It wasn't the time or place.

"When did you get back?" he persisted. "Nobody saw you round the place."

"No," I agreed. "I was told to stay in bed."

And there. I had missed an opportunity to tell him the truth. But I was so tired. And unsure of what to do next.

"So we got everyone out, it seems," he continued.

I glanced up at him, saw his tired eyes, and the expression of concern on his face as he, in turn, looked at the few remaining students, many of whom were still in costume and make-up from *Oklahoma*. A couple of them had curled up on pews and were nodding off, or trying to. One Second Year was still sobbing into a cup of tea, comforted by a couple of older girls.

I followed his gaze and shrugged slightly.

"Yes," I said, "but it's hard to account for everyone when all that scramble happened immediately after everyone fled the Hall … hard to know who's gone home, or who's gone with a friend."

"Everyone will have to be telephoned," he said. "It's just a mess."

His voice trailed off and he looked back at me, a semblance of kindness fleeting on his face. My heart contracted at the sight of it, and I looked away hurriedly, partly in case I might cry, and partly in case a look between us might be seen. I glanced back toward the trestle table and my stomach dropped. Benedicta was there, but thankfully she wasn't watching. Instead, she was scurrying intently between groups of students and teachers, speaking *at* them rather than to them. She looked extremely agitated.

"Why do you keep looking round like that?" Matt asked suddenly.

I looked at him, and saw his face turned to stone again.

I couldn't help myself, I glanced back toward Benedicta.

"I'm not ..." I started.

He looked in the same direction as me, not seeing what I saw. "It's like you don't want to be seen talking to me, but we're just ... oh hang on, it's your fiancé. He's coming to get you, isn't he?"

I frowned at him, flabbergasted.

"Don't be ridiculous!" I barked. "That's not – I don't –"

"That's exactly what it is." Matt stepped back, away from me. "Jesus Chri–" he lowered his tone to a whisper. "*Jesus Christ, Ria,*" he hissed, "you are unbelievable!"

"Matt, will you *stop!*" I hissed.

I couldn't bear it any more. The accusations and suppositions, the lecturing, the questioning of my moral character. Not from him, or from the nun behind us who was currently gripping a Leaving Cert tightly by the arms and shouting something into her face.

"I'm not having this discussion with you," I said. "It's nonsense. It's rubbish. I'm tired. I just want to sleep. And this isn't about any fiancé, or you – so can you just leave it out? *And leave me alone for five bloody minutes?*"

There was silence suddenly from the trestle-table area as a number of teachers and students fell silent and stared. I flushed red and stood up, barging out of the seat and pushing past Matt in the aisle.

And then a shout rang out around the chapel, bouncing off the hard marble and stone.

"She was inside!"

We watched, open-mouthed, as Mother Benedicta suddenly turned and flung open the chapel door, throwing herself out into the night. A scurry of people followed her out instantly, the remainder looking at each other in shock. Hands flew to mouths, girls clutched other girls. One of them sobbed loudly. My stomach flipped as I rushed toward them.

"What is it?" I asked then turned from one girl to her calmer companion when she wouldn't answer. "Miriam, what is it? What was Benedicta talking about? Who was inside where?"

The girl's face was ashen as she turned to me and replied. "It's Lydia, Miss. No one has seen her since lunchtime today – we thought she was sent home, but Mother Benedicta's just come in looking for her ... she said she was inside ... inside the school. Lydia's in the fire, Miss."

I turned to look at Matt. He was looking at me, the absolute horror on his face mirroring my own.

Chapter fifty-one

Ria
BALLYKEERAN
December 1987

"Any word?"

Matt shook his head. "No sign. The experts are still sifting through everything, but it could take weeks."

"And the Gardaí?"

"They're not saying much to anyone except Benedicta, but it seems that they're fairly satisfied she was in there. The unofficial word is that, apart from a few calls, they're not extending the search any further."

I swallowed hard, and silently took the news in. I wanted to be sick. And not because I was pregnant, but because the news made my stomach churn. So it all seemed to be true. Poor Lydia must have been in there. But where? And if everyone else had been able to get out, then why not Lydia?

I walked to the window of the room where we stood to see if my taxi had arrived yet. My train wasn't for another two hours, but I needed to do some things in Portlaoise. Withdraw money from the bank, buy myself a new coat – the owner of the B&B and had lent me hers for the past couple of days – and pick up some bits and pieces for my flight – a book, a snack, a small bag to carry them in. Everything else could be done in London when I landed there.

"I think it was Benedicta's fault she didn't get out," I began.

Matt sighed and got up from the armchair where he sat. "I have to go," he said. "I promised my mam I'd get the turkey and ham from the butcher's."

I bolted from my chair, over to him.

"How can you even think about Christmas? Why won't you listen to me, Matt? I've spoken to people, put things together and it doesn't add up – Lydia was last seen being frogmarched out of the Ref by Benedicta because of that stupid book, right? But she didn't turn up to do Stage Crew when she should have – and I mean she wouldn't have missed that for the *world*. No one saw her leave the building, and her belongings weren't touched – I heard those girls looking for her in the Sisters' Corridor just before the curtain went up, so she hadn't been sent home. So where was she? Where had Benedicta put her when she took her away at lunchtime? That woman is capable of things that no one seems to realise!"

He turned and glared at me.

"Like locking people up, Ria? Why? The woman has a hardline stance on discipline, but *locking someone up*? Why would you say that? You're being ridiculous."

"I'm not. It's true. She did it to me. She locked me up."

"But *why*? Why in this day and age … and how … can one human imprison another human in a public building? Tell me why?"

I blinked. I couldn't. Not yet. He'd never believe that it involved him. I couldn't find the words to tell him about the baby yet. Not now, not with the fire so fresh.

"And how did you get out if you were locked in?"

I looked away from him. He thought I was mad as it was, never mind if I told him the truth.

"The lock turned out to be faulty," I lied.

And he saw it as such.

"*Bullshit!*" he spat, shaking his head in disbelief at me.

"Why, Matt, don't you believe a word I say?"

"Because you're not capable of telling the truth! Remember, I don't need any further proof of that!"

I couldn't reply. He was right. If he only *knew* the truth, however, then he'd have me in St Aidan's too. I glanced up and down the road. Where was the damn taxi? I had to get out of there.

"Why did you come here?" I asked.

"I wanted to let you know that there was no sign of Lydia yet. I know you're worried."

"You could have phoned. The B&B has a phone, you know."

He sighed, calming down. "I wanted to tell you in person. I think we should be prepared for the worst. Her uncle is coming later today – I thought you might want to meet him."

"He found time in his busy schedule, two whole days after the fire that's probably killed his niece, to come and see what's happened?" My tone was icy.

"What could he do?"

I turned to the window as a car pulled up the driveway. "I won't be here later anyway," I said. "I'll be gone."

"Are you going into town to pick up some stuff?"

"No, I mean I'll be gone, gone."

I went to move past him toward the door, but he caught my arm. "Where are you going?"

"I'm leaving, Matt. There's no reason for me to stay here in this mess anymore. There's no job for me, everything I owned is destroyed, and if Benedicta has her way … look, I'm leaving. I don't belong here, and I can't stay another minute."

"But what about …"

"What about what? Lydia? *Us*? There can't be an 'us'. You don't believe a single thing that comes out of my mouth – you simply don't *want* to. And, much like her uncle, what can I do about Lydia? Not even you will believe me when I tell you that I think Benedicta did something awful to her. So what's here for me? I have to go, Matt – this place is poison – I have to get away from here."

He frowned as he looked at me. I released myself from his grip and went out of the sitting room. Then I raised the latch of the front door beyond. A gust of wind blew rain over the threshold, and I hunched over as I watched the taxi driver turn and reverse toward the front door. I had arranged to pay the owner by B&B by bank draft once I sorted my finances with the bank, and without coat, or luggage, I had nothing to do but run.

"You were going to go without saying goodbye?" Matt said from behind me.

I didn't turn. "Goodbye to what, Matt? There's too much bad stuff here. Ballykeeran has been a bad place for me … except for you, but even that went wrong."

"If you'd just told the truth …"

"I *did*." I turned to him, anger gone from me now, replaced by sadness. "But you won't … Look, there's no point in this conversation any more. Everything's gone – the convent, Lydia …" my voice wavered, "us. I want to be gone too – before Christmas. You go get your turkey and ham, and carry on with your life. I can't be here anymore. Not if you won't believe me." I stepped out into the downpour.

"But I loved you, Ria, I'm sorry …"

I couldn't be sure, but I thought that there were tears in his voice.

"Me too, Matt. But you didn't trust me. You couldn't give me a fair chance. I'll be in touch. Goodbye."

I ducked into the taxi and slammed the door behind me.

"Desperate day, love – Portlaoise, isn't it?" said the taxi driver.

I nodded into the rearview mirror where he could see me, and without any delay, he put the car in gear and slid away.

I turned, saw Matt step out the front door after me and shut it behind him, pulling up the hood of his parka. He looked sad, and lost. Which was exactly how I felt. I watched him for a moment, committed his face to memory, and then bit back tears as I looked away, just as the car pulled down the drive out of his sight, aware then that I'd never keep my promise, would never be in touch like I'd said.

But that was all he'd expect of me, of course. Lies.

I watched the rain fall in great sheets across the countryside as we drove away, the driver silent except for when he asked me if I'd "heard this yet" and turned the volume on the radio up. I listened to the sound of a melancholy piano giving away to traditional Irish instruments, followed by the growl of a man's voice. "It's called 'Fairytale of New York'," he told me. "That fellah with the teeth – MacGowan, and yer wan that sings that one about the chip shop and Elvis … mad stuff altogether."

And as I listened, the tears finally came. Of grief, and loss, and a broken heart. Tears of lost opportunity, lost *things*; tears of uncertainty and fear; tears of relief and exhaustion. I pressed one hand to my still-flat belly as we reached the outskirts of Portlaoise, and with the other wiped my eyes.

By the time I sank, exhausted, into bed in the cheap hotel in London that night, all the tears were gone. And I had already begun to suppress the memories, even though they would always be there.

PART 3

Chapter fifty-two

Ria
LONDON
May 2015

"*Ria.*"

I was in the process of folding my raincoat, ready to hang it over the back of the armchair when I heard him behind me.

I froze. This was too soon. I wasn't ready.

I had arrived at the trendy hotel in Bloomsbury early. I wanted to make sure that I could compose myself, and have at least a few sips of coffee with my trembling hands to try to settle me before he arrived. I wanted to fix my hair, apply a layer of lipstick. Relax myself as best I could. Yet I had done none of those things, and here he was.

I laid the coat across the chair, smoothed my skirt, and turned, unprepared for the great leap that my heart made when I saw him. It didn't feel real, seeing him like that. I had thought about this moment happening since I'd replied to the email address in *The Metro* and, in turn, he had emailed back with a date and time for us to meet. But I couldn't picture it exactly. As hard as I tried to conjure up the image of the man I saw striding across the piazza at Covent Garden Marketplace, it was Matt from almost thirty years ago that I kept seeing. I couldn't imagine him aged.

But he was still him. Still Matt. The hair was a distinguished grey all over, shorter, still a little unkempt. Despite a couple of lines, and the definite, indescribable, inevitable change that the passage of years made to a face, he still looked the same. A little tired, but still handsome. Time had suited him better than it had me, I realised, and I looked down, suddenly ashamed of my crow's feet and hollow cheeks. At least my roots weren't grey. The early morning trip to the hairdresser's had ensured that. Overkill, I was sure. But still. It had been a long time.

"I wasn't sure you'd turn up," he said softly.

I looked back at him, frowning. "Of course I did," I replied.

We looked at each other for a few seconds more, at a loss for what to say. It hit me sharply that if I hadn't turned up he'd most likely have just shrugged his shoulders in a gesture of 'I tried', as he went back to his life.

I had thought constantly about what exactly Matt might want to see me for since the day that Jess had brought me *The Metro* on the Common. My first conclusion had been that he had information on what had happened to Lydia, but I had jumped to conclusions before and it had almost driven me mad. He could want to see me for any reason – as part of some twelve-step programme, perhaps. Maybe I was merely a piece of a puzzle that needed to be put in place before he moved on to something, who knew what?

For me, however, I simply couldn't *not* have turned up. Because of Emma, he had been in my mind, every single day, since the last day I had seen him. He had no such link to me, however, and no idea of his importance to me. This meeting to him was old times. To me, it was a *lifetime*.

"Coffee?" he said suddenly, pointing at me in a decisive motion, relieved that he had thought of something to do.

"Yes, please," I blurted.

"Plain or *faaancy*?" he said, smiling.

I gulped at the sight of the smile. I thought I'd never forgotten it – but its effect had dimmed over time in my mind. Seeing it before me again was like a black-and-white picture colourised.

"Can I have a fancy?" I replied with mock timidity, smiling myself.

"Cappuccino? Latte? Mocha?" he asked.

"Cappuccino, please," I replied, and he gave me a thumbs-up before heading in the direction of the bar.

I let out a long, slow sigh of relief, and sank down into the chair nearest to me and took it all in. I was here. Matt was here. But why? What was I doing here? Was I wrong to be here? To dredge up the past like this? It didn't matter anyway. I was too far in. I could never have left without finding out what he wanted, without having a conversation with him, without looking at him at least for a little while longer.

He reappeared from the bar in minutes. I smiled awkwardly as he caught my eye, and looked down at my legs, picking an imaginary piece of lint from my black linen trousers which I'd ironed painstakingly that morning. He sat down opposite me, on the edge of the chair, and rested his arms on his knees, leaning over the table between us.

"The waiter will bring it out to us," he said. "There's a smoking terrace out the back – do you want to sit out there?"

I shook my head. "I don't smoke," I said. *Had he forgotten?* "Sorry – do you? Would you rather sit out there? I'm happy to …"

He shook his head and sat back a little. "No, no – me neither. It's just a nice day – I thought you might prefer to sit outside. The weather's been quite good, lately, hasn't it?"

I nodded in agreement. "Great weather for teachers, as they say," I replied. 'They' didn't, of course. I had just needed something to say.

"So you still teach?" he said.

I nodded again, feeling like a plastic dog on a dashboard. "Always have," I replied. "I've taught in London for years now."

"I can hear a little hint of it in your accent. Have you always lived in London, since …"

The waiter arriving with our coffees cut him short. I was relieved. It was difficult enough seeing him without getting into all of that straight away. It seemed like someone else's life, sitting there with the sunshine warm through the window.

"And do you still act?" I asked, as the waiter left us. I leaned forward in my seat and busied myself with adding sugar to the coffee.

"Not really," he began, reaching out a long arm and picking his Americano up off the saucer before leaning back into the chair and crossing his legs. "I do various things – at the moment I'm writing. I moved to Galway after … *then* … and I still live there. My mother died in '98 and ..."

His mother. *My daughter's grandmother.* I couldn't. Couldn't bear to hear any more about his life since. I thought I was, but I wasn't ready.

"I saw you," I blurted.

He frowned and leaned forward in the chair again.

"Last month. In Covent Garden. Was it you?"

Matt thought, and nodded. "It could have been," he said. "I came here then, trying ... it's been really hard to find you. Normally, in this day and age, you just look someone up on Facebook or Twitter and there they are. But you – it's like Ria Clancy doesn't exist."

I smiled. "She doesn't. Either does Maria Driver, mind. I haven't gone by Clancy in years – I've used my husband's – my ex-husband's – name professionally my whole life here. And I did think about using Facebook once, but, it wasn't really my thing ... my daughter's always telling me I should get a social media profile."

"Your daughter?"

I flushed again, and my hand holding the coffee started to tremble. I concentrated on trying to steady it.

"Emma," I said.

There she was, in the conversation now. The first time for him to hear of her, to hear her name.

"I was going to see my friend Jess the day I saw you. I was wandering through Covent Garden – it was a lovely sunny day, and I like to do touristy things sometimes ..." I let my voice trail off. I was babbling. It was becoming way too awkward.

"You look ... different," he said.

"Old?" I gave an awkward giggle.

"No. Far from it. Just – different – but still the same too."

I squirmed. "It's been a long time," I said.

"It has, and it hasn't," he replied, cryptically. "I'm having a hard time wrapping my head around the fact you've had a whole separate life since then. With a husband, and a child – or children? I mean, not that you shouldn't have ... but I just find it ... in my head, you've always been as you were then."

I stared at him and braced myself. "And you've had a whole life too. A wife? Children? A writing career?"

"Yes, I have. A life. A wife. Two boys – Thomas and Christopher. And, like I said, I've done lots of stuff – directing, couple of non-fiction books, bit of journalism, voiceover work. All a bit random. I live just outside Galway city –"

"You have two boys?"

"They're in their early twenties," he said. "Thomas is doing his Master's and Christopher is travelling. He's in Australia at the moment but ..."

I didn't hear any more. This was too much to process. Of all things, it shocked me the most. It meant that Emma had half-brothers. Thomas and Christopher had a half-sister. I stood up abruptly.

"I can't do this. I have to go," I blurted.

Matt stood up too, confused. "But why? We only just ... I haven't told you why I wanted to see you yet ..."

"I can't do this, Matt," I repeated, picking my raincoat up from the back of the chair. "Not now, anyway – this means something different to me than it does to you ... I can't explain..."

"Look, Ria, don't go yet," he pleaded, reaching out to touch my arm.

I turned sharply at the feel of his hand, tried to meet his eyes, but they were suddenly elsewhere.

"There's something I have to tell you ... someone ..."

His voice trailed off as he stared beyond me, toward the lobby lifts. I turned toward what he was looking at. And as I saw what he saw, my blood suddenly turned to ice in my veins and every hair on my body stood on end. The last thing – the last person – that I ever expected to see again.

"*Lydia.*"

The word came out in a breath, and my knees sagged. I felt the world start to spin slightly, and Matt's hand on my elbow as I sank back into the seat, seeing only her.

A look of concern crossed her face as she began to walk toward me, very slowly.

"It's fine, Lydia, don't rush," I heard Matt say.

Out of the three of us, she looked the most different – it was her eyes that I had recognised, those huge brown pools. But the closer I looked at her, I realised that there was something very, very wrong. They seemed bigger in her face than before, and were ringed in grey tinged with purple. Her skin was an odd, waxy colour, and her hair was obscured by a headscarf which trailed over her shoulder. As she moved, I could see the outline of thin legs against the silk of her wide pants, and her hands were bony where they emerged from the long-sleeved silk kaftan that she wore over them. She winced as she lowered herself into the last empty armchair at the table where we sat, helped by Matt who guided her gently, taking her straw handbag and setting it on the floor beside her. She smiled her thanks at him, looking up at him from under her eyelids. I saw the old Lydia then for a second, but in a flash she was gone again.

"Can I have a drink of water, please?" she asked him softly and he was gone again, back to the bar to get it for her.

Left alone with her, I continued to stare, the world finally stopping its spin.

"Miss Clancy ..." she began.

"Ria, Lydia," I corrected her. "*Lydia* ... you're ... *alive!*"

"Only just. I'm sorry I've given you such a shock," she said, her voice faint. She sounded nothing like she had when she was a teenager.

I could think of no reply, and shook my head to indicate that it was alright. But it wasn't, was it?

"I didn't mean to. Mr Flynn – Matt – was supposed to tell you I was coming but I got here early."

We both looked up at Matt as he returned with the large glass of water. He put the glass in front of Lydia and sat back down in his seat.

Lydia took a tiny sip of the water and then replaced the glass gingerly on the table, holding it with both hands, as a child might steady it.

"Did you sleep okay?" he asked her, concerned.

She nodded. "Oh yes," she smiled. "It's very comfy here. May as well treat myself to a little style when I'm up in town."

There was a hint of an English accent to her voice, too, I noticed.

"And are you feeling okay?"

She grimaced. "So-so. Sometimes the drugs don't work, sometimes they do. It's as good as I can expect." She turned to me.

"You're wondering why I'm here," she said, and gave a small smile again. "You look well. I'm so glad we found you."

"It was Lydia who asked for my help in finding you," added Matt.

I felt a sudden stab of disappointment. So it hadn't been him after all.

"The newspaper ad was Matt's idea," said Lydia. "We couldn't find any trace of you online so we went old-school. Matt thought it was a long shot, but I had a really powerful feeling that we were meant to find you."

"We tried a newspaper in Boston too," Matt interjected. "I remembered you'd mentioned wanting to go there a long time ago. It was Lydia who said to try London because of what ... anyway, it worked, obviously."

"Our next move would have been one of those Facebook campaigns," said Lydia. "Those things can go viral, especially when there's someone like me involved. And while that would achieve what we wanted quite quickly, it would also make things very public and I sort of want to keep this between ourselves, so I'm so relieved this all worked out." She looked from me to Matt.

"Why ..." I struggled for words. There were too many questions swirling around my mind, and I couldn't prioritise one. "The fire?" I managed.

"I should have gone looking for you years ago," Lydia replied. "To explain what happened."

"But the fire – everyone assumed you'd *died*? Though nothing conclusive was ever found in the ruins. I thought something horrible had happened to you. You just *vanished!*"

"I actually wasn't there when the fire happened," she began, tentatively. "In fact, I didn't know there had even been a fire until a while after it happened. I sort of got caught up in a bizarre snowball of events. At the time I just couldn't get out of there fast enough, and I kept going. And then when I realised there were questions about what happened to me and where I was – I felt then that I *couldn't* go back. It's all sorted now, mind – I've spoken to people – like I'm speaking to you. There's not much can be done about it all now, under the circumstances ..."

I leaned toward her. "What are the circumstances, Lydia?" I

asked softly, studying her face. She looked exhausted, frail.

"I don't have long left, Miss … *Ria*." Her voice was a whisper. "Maybe months, if I'm lucky. Or unlucky, as the case may be. That's why I need to get my house in order now – the Universe wants me to. And *I* want to. I can't go easy until I resolve certain things, and confront others. I bumped into Matt by chance last year – I'm fairly sure he was *sent* to me – just walking past the hospital door after I'd seen my consultant." They exchanged a glance, and a brief, wistful smile. "I was in a daze at the time and it never occurred to me to ask for contact details, but afterwards realised that it was meant to be, and I looked him up – thankfully *he* has a Facebook page. The meeting made it clear to me that it was possible to sort one last thing – and I wondered if you'd both help me do it."

"Of course," I said, focusing on her, pushing back the information that she had just given me. Months left. This girl, this child who had once, so briefly, been in my care but who I'd never forgotten. "What is it that you want us to do?"

Lydia looked at me, reaching out for my hand and grasping it weakly, then doing the same with Matt. The two of us sat there, awkwardly, linked by her, as she looked at us both.

"I need to go back there, one more time," she said. "I need to return something. But also, I need to see it, to confront it, to breathe it … to see if I can figure out what happened to me – to *us* – and to come to terms with all of the *energy* that it left behind inside me. And I want to know if you'll come with me? If you'll come back to Ballykeeran, before I die."

Chapter fifty-three

Ria
IRELAND
June 2015

The sun shone again on the day I returned to Ballykeeran.

I made my way by airport bus from Dublin Airport to Heuston Station, and from there to Portlaoise. The countryside which flew past the train window was the same as before, as was Portlaoise train station, for the most part, although I had seen so little of it so long ago I probably couldn't have told the difference. I carried my weekend case down the stone steps and out onto the road outside where, this time, a familiar face awaited me. Dressed in jeans, his shirt sleeves rolled up, Matt could have passed for someone in his thirties, but for his hair colour. My giddy girl's heart gave a little skip when I saw him, chastised by the serious grown-up that I knew I ought to be. He smiled when he saw me, and I returned it – a smile that lasted a little too long.

His hire car was small, but clean, and smelled pleasant, nothing like the first vehicle that had picked me up at this very same spot all those years before. The temperature on the dash read 28 Celsius as we set off, and he rolled down the window as he negotiated the streets of the town which seemed familiar and unfamiliar at the same time – I had never spent much time there, after all. Matt quizzed me as we drove – had my flight been okay? Was the train down from Dublin a nightmare? Was I hungry?

"I've booked dinner for six thirty," he told me. "I hope you don't mind, but Lydia gets tired easily and she wants to talk to us both. This – what we're doing tomorrow – is a really big deal for her."

"Not just for her," I replied.

It was strange and awkward to sit there beside him, unsure of what to say. We had so much to talk about – but should we talk about any of it? Where could I begin?

"How is Lydia?" I asked. "Did her flight go okay?"

Matt grimaced. "It was tough going for her. Ideally she could have done with an overnight in Dublin before getting the train down here, but she was keen to get this far and rest. She's very ill, you know. You'll probably even see a change in her since we met two weeks ago. I'm not sure what tomorrow is going to take out of her."

I stared out the window as he spoke, a picture of Lydia in my head as she was now, switching to her as she was then. Matt remained silent as he drove, but it wasn't for long. Within moments we pulled into the car park of a small hotel, where we would spend the night. It had all been arranged by e-mail over the past couple of weeks: that we would meet to regroup after our travels – Lydia and I from separate airports in the UK – to let her rest up for what was ahead – her final return to Ballykeeran.

She was dressed in red when we met for dinner. Sitting in a high-backed armchair at a low table in the quiet hotel bar, pillar-box silk hanging loosely over her frail body, and a headscarf patterned with cheerful strawberries. Large gold hoops hung from her ears and her lips were a slash of crimson against her pale face. She smiled broadly when she saw us, and held her cheek up for a kiss as I reached the table. I sank down into the seat beside her and held her hand for a few moments, studying her face as we exchanged pleasantries about flights and train trips. Matt settled himself opposite me.

Then she turned to Matt and said that he and I should go ahead and order.

"I'm running on low fuel," she smiled. "Only trouble is, I'm not sure what I want to use the reserve tank for – to tell you what happened to me, or to hear what's happened to you."

"There's no question, Lydia," I jumped in. "I have to know – if you can manage – please tell me what happened to you. I've worried, you see, all this time."

"I'm sorry," she replied, her eyes misting over. "Like I said, I should have let you know, but ... once I left there, once I got away, something *kept* me away. It was like the Universe protected me from it, and innocent people were hurt in the process – but not on purpose."

"You mustn't blame yourself for anything," I said, glancing at Matt, who was looking at the menu.

Lydia shrugged. "I don't. And I don't mean that to sound uncaring, but over time I've changed from the cynical kid I was and I've realised that we are all merely puppets to a higher power." She broke into a grin as I frowned.

"*Jee-sus* – not Jesus," she giggled, a trace of the schoolgirl visible again. "No. I didn't catch a dose of the holies. But I did realise that the Universe – fate, destiny and all that – you're probably poo-poohing the notion – is a powerful force. I'm sure you think I'm all hippy-dippy and slightly bonkers, but ... well, that's the understanding the world and I came to, and it's worked well for me. It helps me see clearly, helps me understand stuff and has helped me immeasurably to come to terms with things. Some people look on it as surrendering choice, and self-determination and will – they see it as copping out – but to me it's the only lens that I can look through that shows me a clear picture, and it's brought me great peace. I'm not scared, do you understand? And my view of things – having the Universe as my guide, fate as my companion, gives me enormous comfort and strength, and it's given me a clear path that I've needed to take to make everything right for me, to reconcile things, to balance my chequebook."

I studied her earnest expression in silence. She sipped from a glass of water and shifted slightly in her chair.

"So where did you go, Lydia?" I probed. "What happened after ... after that day?"

"Would you like a drink, Ria?" Matt interjected politely. "And I'm just going to get some pizza from the bar menu – does that suit? Lydia, are you sure you don't want anything?"

She hesitated and then said she'd try a bowl of soup, if it was vegetable.

"Just a sparkling water, please," I said, "and pizza sounds great. Veggie, if they have it."

I turned back to Lydia and looked at her expectantly, keen for her not to lose momentum.

"That day. That bloody strange day. I was in terrible trouble with Benedicta," she began. "She'd found a book that I'd hidden in my bed – this awful, trashy thing that Carmel – do you remember Carmel? – had foisted on me as a joke. She'd insisted I read it – it was all about a nun getting it on with a priest, you can only imagine how that went down in Benedicta-land – but I'd hidden it out of sight, with the aim of getting rid of it altogether. I forgot it, of course, and naturally Benedicta found it, drawn like a fly to you-know-what. She was livid with me, I had never seen her so angry – and she'd always hated me, for some reason. But that day she behaved in such a way – so *monstrously* – that something snapped inside me, and when I eventually got outside and away from her, I decided that enough was enough. And I walked. I didn't care who saw me, or who tried to stop me – I was having absolutely none of it. I just strode out the gate, on that dark December evening, and off down that country road in the direction of the village. I had ten pounds in my pocket, and I was getting out of there – by bus, train, Shanks's pony – I didn't care."

The memory stirred in me. The same feeling, on that same day – the same plan, even.

"As it happened, I didn't have to go very far on foot. About half a mile up the road, I heard an engine coming behind me and, on impulse, stuck my thumb out. I didn't think the driver would even spot me in the dark – I was dressed in my Stage Crew gear – all in black – but he did, and pulled in a little way ahead and I ran on up to him – only to discover that it was Tom Gorman, the old fellow who often picked up teachers and girls from the train or the bus if it was needed – I'm sure he'd have driven you a couple of times, am I right? I was sure the jig was up. I contemplated making a run for it across the fields – very Richard Kimball – but something made me get into that car with him ..."

Chapter fifty-four

Lydia

December 1987

I cop that it's Tom Gorman too late. He's slowed to a stop and I'm alongside the car. I've never thumbed a lift before but the Day Girls who live a way out of town do it all the time. No one should bat an eyelid at a young girl hitching a lift into town on a Friday night. But Tom Gorman, of all people. I'm screwed. Being caught off school premises is only the start of it … I start to sweat. He'll take me straight back to Benedicta. What will she do to me then? I panic. It flashes across my mind that I should run – I could clear the ditch by the time he'd get out of the car – and I'm younger and faster and fitter than him. Surely if I legged it off across the field in the dark he wouldn't come after me – and even if he did, then I'd lose him fast enough.

In my mind, this plan takes form at lightning speed, but my body is frozen stiff. And I'm sore, and tired – in too much pain to achieve what I'd need to do. It would never work. I watch as he leans across the passenger seat and opens the door for me to get in. And, somehow, I don't run – it crosses my mind that I am as insane as Mother Dick as slowly my legs propel me to the open car door of their own volition and I climb in.

The stink of booze hits me the second I lower myself onto the passenger seat, and I look across in alarm, expecting to see him – I dunno – *cross-eyed* or something, with his tongue hanging out and a big red nose, but he looks normal. Mind you, he's sitting down, holding on to his steering wheel. It might be a different story if he was on his feet. I contemplate running again, but something refuses to let me move. It's some animal instinct inside me, I reckon, the one that's seduced by the heat of the car. It's bitterly cold outside, and even though I've been moving as quick as I can, I know that my jeans and sweatshirt top won't keep me warm for long. So what's it to be, then? Death by hypothermia or drunk driver? I decide in an instant to take my chances with old Tom.

The smell in the car is rotten. I've only been in it a few times before – he's driven everyone somewhere at one point or another – and the stink of stew and sweat and animal feed and dirty tweed and whatever else he's got going on in there is vile. It always comes in waves – just as you think you're getting used to it, something seems to disturb another layer of his great cake of stink and a fresh waft floats up your nostrils and down your throat, and you think you're going to pass out. Tonight, though, the stink of booze overrides everything, it's so strong. I say a little, silent prayer to St Jude, Patron of Hopeless Cases.

"'Tis a fresh one out," he mumbles, as I reach for the seatbelt.

"Yeah," I say, looking away from him, terrified of the moment when he figures out I'm from Maria Goretti. But then I'm not in uniform – a flash of hope – he may not realise I'm a schoolgirl at all.

But he doesn't look at me – instead, he glances in his rearview mirror, and accelerates, sending the car into spasms as it jerks violently and then cuts out.

He sniggers. "Kangaroo Petrol," he slurs, and slowly fumbles with the gearstick while simultaneously turning the key in the engine.

Somehow, he pulls it all together, and we slide off again – smoother this time. I hold my breath, and grab the door handle with one hand, and the side of my seat with the other and hang on for dear life. But after a while, it becomes clear that there's no need for me to do this. Hunched over the wheel, there is no difference between Tom Gorman's driving sober or drunk as a lord. I conclude that it's probably not the first time he's done this. It doesn't make it right, but it does make me relax about his driving the tiniest bit.

We drive on in silence for a little while. My breathing is shallow as I am suddenly overwhelmed and exhausted – the adrenaline of my flight, and the terror of this car ride suddenly giving way to a flashback of what happened back at Maria Goretti. But that couldn't have happened, could it? I must have imagined it ... but that face ...

I shake my head to try to blot it from memory. I am almost grateful when Tom Gorman speaks again, his voice thick with porter.

"Are you not up above at the show?" he asks.

Shit, shit, shit. He knows who – or, at least, *what* I am. I look at him sideways and frantically think about what I should say. Thankfully, he takes the responsibility from me.

"Should have shown my face myself," he says, concentrating hard over the wheel, "But tonight's me Christmas night out. I don't take a drop often, but I'll toast the season that's in it alright. And I'll be honest with you, I can't bear the feckin' singin' and leppin' around. I like a bit of *Murder She Wrote* on the telly, not oul' choirs and all that oul' shite."

I can't help myself. I smile at his disgusted tone. Wonder what Benedicta would think of him saying that. Then the thought of her wipes the smile from my face again, and I peer earnestly out at the road to check our progress.

"But sure the whole town will be up there come eight o'clock. Licking the holes off the nuns – pardon me French, miss. Jaysus, if they only knew who they were lickin' up to, and her father hanged for murder and her mother buried in unconsecrated ground. I could never understand how people couldn't *see* that."

I frowned and looked over at Tom, but he was just rambling on.

"It's like no one remembers who she is, but the whole town was talkin' about her back when it happened. There was rumours that he never did it, of course. My brother Ned, God Rest Him, swore till the day he died that that woman's father couldn't have laid a hand to hurt a hair on the head of that child, and that he swung without knowing where she'd ended up. And he swore that if they dug that coffin up, they'd find bones but no child. 'Twas a funny business – I was too young to know what was going on, of course, being around the same age as her, but I know she got sent away.

And I remember the day she came back because I drove her from the train station."

I stare at him, completely mystified – it could just be the ramblings of a drunk – but if it isn't – then is he talking about who I think he's talking about?

He goes quiet again. I'm dying to ask him but I'm afraid to speak. If I can just stay quiet then maybe he won't begin to wonder where I'm going and what I'm doing – won't realise he should do a U-turn and take me back. My mind starts to race at a mile a minute again. What would I do if he did that? I just can't go back there.

The first of the orange street lights of the village suddenly come into view and my heart jumps a little. If I can just get him to let me off in the village, then I know that there's a bus at eight o'clock – I'll have a bit of a wait, but maybe I can hide somewhere till then. A gateway or an alley? Eight fifty from my tenner – one of the things that I took off Benedicta's desk – will get me to O'Connell Bridge, and I can walk home from there. But ... oh God ... what if Tom expects me to pay for the lift? Usually he charges the Day Girls about two pounds from the school to the village – but of course he hasn't actually driven me the whole way and he's not really, officially, a taxi. But still ...

And then the car slows down, and I have to focus on now. We have reached the diamond at the centre of the village, deserted, except for a few cars parked outside the pub. Tom Gorman aims in the general direction of it too, and doesn't so much park as get the car as close as he can outside and let the engine die. He opens the driver's door and heaves himself out. I scramble for my own door, nervous that he has forgotten me and is about to lock me in.

I slam the passenger door shut, and wait for him to lock his door, but he doesn't. Instead, he aims a feeble salute in my general direction over the car, mutters "God Bless", and gives a little stagger before swaying in the door. A spill of voices and light and hubbub empties out onto the street for an instant and then grows muffled again behind the closing door.

I stare after him, relieved. He hasn't charged me.

I begin to believe that luck is with me. Firstly, I am alive – secondly, I am not back in Maria Goretti – and, thirdly, I managed to get out of there in the first place. And now Tom has forgotten to charge me – or has just decided not to, out of the goodness of his heart.

This day – it feels entirely like an out-of-the-body experience. How can any of this actually be happening?

I'm soon snapped back to reality by the bitter cold of the Laois night. I glance at my watch. Still a bit of a wait, which is a concern in this temperature, but I'm pretty sure I can tolerate that wait, I tell myself. As long as it means that every minute I am a minute closer to getting away from here, from *her*. I can figure out what happens next once I'm out of here, and safe.

I plunge my hands into my pockets, and immediately feel ill as I encounter again the brown box in there. I should return it – shouldn't have taken it in the first place – but equally, I can't go back there, not after what she did to me. I'll think about that later too. Resolutely, I step into the shadows around the side of the house next door to the pub, where I might not be seen, and pray for that time to go quickly.

Chapter fifty-five

Ria
IRELAND
June 2015

"Tom Gorman got me out of that place." Lydia smiled and rolled her eyes to heaven. "Rural Ireland in the 80's, eh? But it got me out of there under the radar. He must have had no recollection of me being in the car that night. Not that I think he'd have presented himself to the Gardaí to say that he'd given me a lift – it might have proven a bit tricky for him, all the same."

She looked up as the waiter arrived.

"Here's the food," she remarked, shifting in her chair and wincing.

I stole a look at Matt, who was watching her, his face pulled downwards with sadness. I wondered if there had maybe been more between them since she had found him? Against my better judgement, I stiffened at the thought.

Lydia closed her eyes and rested her head against the back of her chair while the waiter served our food. She opened them again long enough to acknowledge the bowl of soup that he placed in front of her, but made no effort to pick up her spoon.

"So what became of you, Ria?" she asked me, smiling.

I was keen to hear more about her story, but realised that she needed the breather and took her up on her cue.

I filled them in as we ate. All about my life. My safe life, safe career – safe marriage which had ended, but amicably. I mentioned

Emma once, glancing at Matt as I did, but there was no reaction. He simply nodded and shook his head where appropriate.

It was Matt's turn next – but his story was short, most of it told to us already. Again, he named his sons, and made a cursory mention of his former wife. I hadn't known that she was 'former', and wondered what had become of her, where she had gone, who had ended the marriage … but he didn't dwell on it.

"What happened when you left Ballykeeran, Lydia?" I asked then.

She had rallied a little, I noticed, having nibbled on some brown bread.

"The last I heard, you hadn't been found but when investigations turned up nothing, they came to the conclusion you had died in the fire. So how did no one spot you leaving? How did you get away without encountering people – apart from the drunken Tom – who were able to say they'd seen you? How did you become entirely invisible?"

"And why did they give up looking when it was only *assumed* that I was dead?" she added, asking my next question for me.

I nodded.

"Quite simply, no one I encountered *remembered* me," she began. "Like I said, Tom Gorman could barely remember his own name, and if he did recall giving someone a lift, then he certainly never said anything to the Gardaí about it – I could have vouched for how drunk he actually was driving around the back roads of Ballykeeran, remember. Then the bus driver going to Dublin just looked at the money in my hand and not my face when I boarded, and I sat near the back all the way to Dublin. I mustn't have registered on his radar at all. I disembarked at O'Connell Street, through the doors midway down the bus, in the middle of all the passengers that had got on along the way in Portlaoise, Monasterevin, Kildare, Newbridge – so many people at so many stops. I was hidden in plain sight, and, once off the bus, I simply made the short walk to the house on George's Street, expecting to have a battle with Uncle Neville on my hands – what was I doing, home like this? Where was my stuff? What about my schooling? Isn't that what my mother would have wanted and so on. What he would have meant was: 'What are you doing, cramping my style?

Don't expect me to look after you!'

He wasn't there, of course. It was a Friday night. Plus, I wasn't due back to Dublin until the following week for Christmas hols. The house was completely empty and I was alone and cold and exhausted and, to all intents and purposes, on the run. I sat down on the sofa in the dilapidated old living room, my bruised body aching all over at this point, and I cried and cried and cried. And then I took a slug from the bottle of brandy that was sitting in the middle of the coffee table, amidst foil cartons of god-knows-how-old Chinese takeaways. And then I took another, and another – it went straight to my head, and I was hit with a terrible, terrible fear. It was some sort of reaction to all the stress I'd endured that day – I know that now – but back then, I thought it was that I deserved it – that I had reason to be frightened, because of what I'd done."

"Which was?" I asked.

Matt and I watched in silence, as Lydia leaned over the side of her seat, and pulled her handbag up on to her lap and rummaged in it. She placed a brown box in the centre of the table, and looked at both of us, her eyes fearful.

"I'm a very different person now than I was then," she said. "But the truth is, when I was a kid, I did some bad things, and I've never been truly able to forgive myself for them."

Matt leaned forward. "What's in the box, Lydia?" he asked.

"It was the last thing I ever took," she said. "I swear. And before that it had only been tapes or videos here and there, or a packet of biscuits, or maybe a bar of chocolate from someone else's locker – I've donated to charities my whole life since, to try to make it up to the Universe."

"So you're saying you …"

"Stole stuff," Lydia sighed. "I was light-fingered. A shoplifter – but I never took anything big, anything of significant value."

"So, you were a teenager who shoplifted a couple of times," I smiled. "In the school where I teach, there are kids who deal drugs, who are involved in gangs – we've even had knives and guns on the premises – I wouldn't think you should beat yourself up too much over a couple of videos."

"It was *wrong*!" Lydia barked, with a strength I hadn't expected. "Stealing is wrong. It's unkind, it deprives others. My mother would been so ashamed of me. But still I did it. I don't know why – whether it was the thrill of getting away with it, or some deep-down hope that I'd get caught and someone would pay attention to me in a way that didn't mean I had to get up at four in the morning, or spend an hour in the chapel saying the Rosary, or sit completely alone, night after night, in a wreck of a mansion on the wrong side of town." She paused for breath, grimacing at some pain from somewhere.

Matt knelt down beside her chair and grasped her arm, concerned. A pang of jealousy hit me and, in order to cover up my reaction, I reached out and opened the box.

The physical sensation that rippled up my arm as I touched what was inside gave me a shock – such a strong one that I fumbled and dropped the box, but not the watch that lay inside which I'd slipped out from its discoloured cream silk bed and into my hand. It was a man's watch – old, and stopped – at four o'clock exactly. The brown leather strap was worn, but intact, and the gold surrounding the off-white face was tarnished and dull. I turned it over, and strained to read the inscription on the back by the light of the small candle in the middle of the table.

"*To William Francis Phelan on our wedding day, from Evelyn Mary Flood, June 1930,*" it read. It triggered something in my memory. "*William Francis Phelan,*" I whispered, racking my brain. William Francis Phelan ... Francis ... Frances ... Frances Phelan ... Prionsias Ní Faolain ... Little Frances ...

My eyes shot up to look at Lydia.

"Where did you get this?" I asked, my heart beating loudly.

She sighed heavily again. "After Benedicta marched me out of the Ref carrying that stupid book, she brought me to her office. She was fuming – I'd seen her lose her temper before – but this time she was *cold,* and her eyes were sort of glazed over ..."

I nodded, my mind suddenly flashing back to the hospital room that sunny day in December. I shuddered.

"She just ushered me in, without saying a word, but she didn't have to – and then she closed the door behind her and disappeared for ages – I don't know what she went to do, but I was on my own in there and ... I don't know why – I never *planned* to take it – I never actually *planned* to take anything – but I saw a ten-pound note on her desk, sitting under this box, and I just couldn't fight the urge. I grabbed them both and stuffed them into my pocket. I don't know what I was thinking. Anyway, I didn't know what was in the box until I got home to George's Street – and then I saw it, half out of my head on Uncle Neville's Hennessy – the engraving. And I could hear Tom Gorman's voice rambling in the car – *'her father hanged for murder, her mother buried in unconsecrated ground'* – and I figured that I'd done something really, really bad this time, that I'd taken something really important."

Lydia's shoulders slumped, and her expression darkened, as she looked back into the past.

"Now, there was no way I was going back with that thing – she'd done what she did, I was *never* going back, and no one could have made me. But I'd stolen from her, so she *had* to be coming after me – after me with the *Guards*, I figured. So I panicked. Threw a few things into a rucksack, raided the housekeeping tin, grabbed a coat and hat and let myself out of the house. And I ran, and ran, as fast as my aching body would allow – head down, taking stupid, dangerous routes so I wouldn't be seen. Down alleyways, all the way down the *bad* part of the Quays – there was nothing there then, not even the Point Depot – I didn't even really know where I was going, to be honest. I ended up at Dublin Port. Alone, out of breath, frightened – I had no ID, no ticket to go anywhere – I didn't even know if I had enough money to get one, or if I did, where I'd go. But, once again, the Universe stepped in for me. It was three girls from Westmeath in a car this time. They approached me, wondering if I'd take a lift with them. They'd got a deal with one of the ferry companies, you see – a car and four passengers for ninety-nine pounds to Holyhead, except their fourth passenger had backed out at the last minute and the driver – Siobhán – poor, nervous Siobhán – she was terrified that if they didn't do things by the letter, they'd have to pay more, and none of them had much money. I boarded that ferry crammed into the back seat of a Citroen Diane that was carrying more people and luggage than could possibly have been safe – the boot was tied shut with baling twine, for God's sake – and I stuck with all three of them for four years afterwards, when we all finally went our separate ways. We lived in Manchester for a while, and then Warwick, then

Siobhán and I went to Kent. I ended up in Somerset – where I live now – near Wells. But those girls … they were the family that I'd never had. I love them to this day, as much for who they are as for what they did for me."

Matt drained his pint glass. "So you were out of the country before anyone even noticed you apparently hadn't made it out of the fire?"

Lydia nodded. "And I was oblivious to the fact that the place had gone up in flames. I was clueless, until about six months later when one of the girls heard something on the grapevine from an Irish person who knew another Irish person and so on. It was just a juicy bit of goss from home – this convent down the country that had gone on fire, and the girl who had vanished without a trace afterwards. I never said anything, of course, and no one ever put two and two together. In fact, I resolutely avoided learning anything about it. Just in case. Eventually, in about 1998, life had moved on, and it was good. I had just opened my shop and healing centre – Willow Holistic. I had done a lot of studying, a lot of alternative therapy, a lot of healing myself – I was in a good place, or so I told myself. But deep down, something was niggling at me. I realised that I just couldn't carry on living the lie and so I decided to come clean. I wrote to Uncle Neville, told him that I was alive and that I was ready to come home if needed, whatever that meant I had to face."

"And what happened?" asked Matt.

"Nothing," replied Lydia. "It was a very cold case at that stage – truth be told, they'd never pursued it very avidly. Even though there was no real evidence, the Guards always thought that my remains were just never found in the debris of the fire – it was too big, or the local services had overlooked them or something – with no family really on their case, they literally let it lie and assumed they knew the truth. It was a shock for them to find I was alive, but when it transpired that I was over eighteen at the time I disappeared, and appeared to have left of my own volition, then there was no case to pursue. Obviously the watch and the money had never been noticed missing, presumed destroyed in the fire, a bit like me, so had never been reported stolen. Uncle Neville used some of his contacts to make sure that the story never got into the press, and I was a free woman. Except I wasn't, not really. I put that …" she pointed at the watch which I still held, "somewhere safe, and tried to forget about it – facing Benedicta was the one thing I just could not bring myself to do – but it niggled at me ever since. Sometimes I feel that it's watching me, pardon the pun. And I feel like it's stopped because a part of my life is always going to be December 18th 1987. So that's why I've come here – because I have to let that day go. So I can put that thing back where it came from – give it back to the Order, bury it in the ground – I'll know when I get there – and finally set myself free of the hold it's had over me – so *I* can finally let go."

We were silent. I turned the watch over and over in my hands. So much information, so many threads to string together. It was all a jumble in my brain, and I felt I simply had to make sense of it all. But there was still a part of the story missing. Something that Lydia had said, that had grabbed my gut and wouldn't let go.

"Lydia," I said softly, "I'll understand if you're too tired. But if you can manage it at all, can you explain something to me?"

She nodded weakly. Her face was drawn and exhausted.

"Only, you said that Benedicta had 'done what she had done' to you?"

Lydia nodded again, and rearranged herself in her chair, leaning over to sip from her glass.

"What did she do to you, Lydia? And how did you actually get out of there?"

Lydia sniffed, smiled weakly, and looked at me.

"I've never told anyone what happened that day – not in full," she began. "But that's why I wanted you here so desperately, Ria. I need, of all people, to tell you. Because if you think that I've forgotten a single thing that happened to us there, then you're very wrong."

"I haven't forgotten either," I responded quickly, my heart pounding.

Matt looked at us from under furrowed brows.

"Good," Lydia replied. "Because this is something else I have to get off my chest before my time. And I think that – because of what happened to us there – in the storm that night – the shutters and the lights, the running in the attics, those wet footprints that time – do you remember? Well, I reckon you're the only person who won't think I'm mad."

Chapter fifty-six

Lydia

December 18th 1987

When she comes back, she has this big bunch of keys in her hand, and she doesn't even look at me, just keeps looking at the keys, one by one, separating them, studying them, and then moving on to the next one, until she finds the one she wants. *Then* she turns her attention to me. I want to crawl in under her desk away from her to get rid of the pure *hatred* that I feel coming from her eyes. She stares at me for a while – until the noise of some people passing her office goes away – and then she tells me to follow her.

We go up the stairs and I think to myself that she's taking me up there to supervise me packing up my stuff. It's the worst possible punishment – expulsion. But why am I surprised? Benedicta has hated me from the moment I set foot inside that convent. I'll never forget what she said to me on that first night, when I arrived by myself, thirteen years old and broken-hearted. "So *you're* the orphan," she said, looking me up and down, and from that moment she just picked on me. If my uniform was slightly imperfect, if I was talking too loudly, or not enough, or my hair was *distracting*, as she called it once, or my cardigan was frayed, or my hands were in my pockets or whatever she chose to pick on that day. The older I got, the more she persecuted me – I've spent more time sitting at my desk at four o'clock in the morning than anyone else in the whole school, for stuff that other people wouldn't get into trouble for.

Once, it was for dropping a cup while I was washing up. It didn't even break.

And now, she's kicking me out, just when there's only six months before I can *leave*. I groan inside as I begin to think it through – I won't be able to sit my exams in June now – it's too late in the school year to get a place anywhere else. I'll have to sit this year out, and go back to school somewhere else in September and start my Leaving Cert year all over again. I'll be a schoolkid until I'm nineteen years old – and I was so close!

And the musical. I'll miss it now. I've looked forward to opening night so damn much – and I really wanted to just have this for my last year – my life is full of shit things, and the musical is a *good* thing but she won't even let me have that.

I think about getting Carmel into trouble – telling Benedicta that the book is hers. After all, I didn't exactly see Carmel standing up for me in the Ref when Benedicta stormed in and held it up for everyone to see. It's so embarrassing that people would think I'd read a book like that, never mind keep it in my mattress. Why didn't I put the damn thing back in Carmel's locker before now? Let her take the bloody blame for it. In the long run, however, I decide against dobbing her in it. It wouldn't work anyway. Benedicta would just twist it, make me look the bad person – disloyal to my friend, selfish. Just because I'm an orphan doesn't make me special. That's always one of her favourites. It's never once made any sense in any argument or punishment she's picked or doled out, but it's what she always comes back to.

I follow her into the Dorm, and turn right to go to my cubicle to get my stuff, but that's not the direction she goes in. I stop, and watch as she goes left, and yanks the uniform rack in front of the disused door to the Baby Dorm out of the way.

And then I understand what the key was for.

And *then*, things start to get really weird. And I start to panic a little, because I don't know what she's doing, but she's reached a level of seething fury that really scares me. And I'm right to be scared, because once she has the door to the stairs up to the Baby Dorm unlocked and open, she stands back and just points up there. I freeze.

Her voice, when she speaks, is low and quiet. *"Get up those stairs,"* she commands me.

So I do. I walk hesitantly over to where she stands and stop for a second, looking up into the dark. I'm petrified. I think back to that Friday night all of a sudden, that weird night with Miss Clancy and the noises up there, someone running about. I grab the door frame and start to protest. "There's someone – something – it's not safe up there!" But next thing I know, she's *pushed* me, and I land on my hands and knees on the bottom and second steps up. I'm stunned for a moment, until she growls at me again; "*Get up there!*" I turn and look at her before I do. Her eyes are wide and her nostrils flared, her lips pursed together so that I can't even see them anymore. She's breathing like she's about to have a heart attack and her whole body sort of *judders*, like electricity is surging through it or something. I can't figure out which is scarier – her, or what's upstairs. It seems I have no choice, however, but to take my chances with the dark.

I scramble to my feet, and walk slowly up the old wooden stairs, feeling my way along the cold, stone wall as it gets darker. The windows – there should be light up there – they must be boarded up, or something, I reason, as I take the turn in the stairs, and look up into pitch blackness. I daren't look down, for fear of losing my footing – I remember the stairs well from when I used to sleep up here – they're worn at the edges, and slippy from years of use.

I hear Benedicta close and lock the door at the bottom of the stairs, plunging us into total darkness, and begin to mount them. Her trademark soft shoes make no sound, but I can *feel* her, and hear her fast breathing, and the rustle of her skirt.

I grope my way along the wall, knowing that I'm coming to the wooden railings at the top – there to provide protection around what is essentially an open trap door, still there from when this room was an attic long, long ago. I know I'm almost at the top when I get to them. I take the last three steps, gripping the plywood bannister, and reach the top, stepping onto the wooden floor of the room. I stand there, staring into the darkness, trying to see if I can pick anything out, but I can't. For a moment, I fancy that I'm standing at the edge of a great black hole, as if space itself is in front of me. I clutch the top of the railings, terrified to take another step, to go any further.

The choice is soon taken from me.

Benedicta is closer to me that I thought, and when she shoves me I go flying into the darkness with a squeal, my arms out before me to break my fall – for a second, I am sure that it's true, that I'm falling into space – but the pain at my temple as I connect with something hard comes just before I hit the floor. I have fallen against one of the unused bed frames, I realise. They're all built-in – a permanent wooden bedframe unit attached to the floor, with wooden slats across the top of each, where the mattress should go. I push myself up on my hands and knees, stunned and disoriented. I try to focus, to ascertain where the nun has gone, whether she's behind me or in front of me. I realise that it's the latter when I feel the stinging smack against the side of my head. I cry out in pain.

It's immediately followed by a second slap with her other hand, and then another to the top of my head. I try to stand up, but can't, and instead I try to protect myself, try to get my hands up over my head and face. She showers me in slaps and blows, some with the flat of her hand, some with her fist – she connects with my ear, and I lose my balance, falling sideways, terrified that I might hit my head again off the sharp wooden corner of a bedframe. I cannot tell where I am in the room, or where the next blow is going to come from. Come to think of it, she can't see either, so she's just aiming at random, hoping to connect. She kicks me at one point, when my hands are back raised over my face, and my stomach is exposed. I grunt, as sparkles of pain explode just under my ribs, and hunch down to prevent it hurting so much, should it happen again.

The attack seems endless. She pushes me, and I sprawl backwards, suddenly worried that I will fall through the open trapdoor and down the stairs – I am completely, and terrifyingly disoriented. I find my voice eventually – it emerges from my silent shock and disbelief that this is actually happening, pleading with her to stop, but she ignores it. I'm sure she can't hear me. Her breathing is fast and thick, and the attack grows more frenzied, the slaps, and punches, and pushes and shoves. She manages to get me wedged against one of the bed frames, so that I cannot stop, and pummels me repeatedly on my shoulders and back. I scream, hoping that someone will hear me – but knowing that it is early afternoon and, that everyone is in the school wing, far below me, and that my cries are wasted.

I am sobbing by the time she stops. Cowering against the end of one of the beds, my hands thrown over my head, and my body curled as tightly into a ball as I can manage. I curl myself closer to the floor, try to protect myself as best I can. I can hear her breathing in the darkness, panting with the exertion of the beating. It seems as though she has stepped back from me. I pray that it's not for her to just take a rest, and brace myself again, as I hear her take a deep breath, and then hold it. The room falls into complete silence.

I whimper. I have no idea where she's gone – my heart won't stop pounding loud enough for me to listen to anything that might give her away. In the pitch blackness of the room, the wait is unbearable. Is she still here, I wonder, or is she simply regrouping to start again? Does she mean to kill me?

And then she reveals herself.

She is right beside my ear.

Her face, beside my face. Suddenly, I can smell her – the stale smell of her breath right up against me. When she hisses at me, right into my ear drum, I scream as loudly as I can, suddenly possessed by a wave of fear that electrifies me. She hisses that I am a *filthy orphan*, a *slut*. I scream so loud and so long that I don't hear her retreat. I stop myself from screaming – it takes everything that I have in me – and I listen. Then I hear the clicks of the door to the Dorm below opening, closing, and locking.

Is she really gone? It takes me an age to trust that she is. To slowly move my arms away from my head, to look around, to listen, to try to sense her presence. But she is really not there. I am completely and utterly alone.

It takes me a while to realise that this is not a good thing.

Better than being pummeled and beaten, at risk of hitting my head or falling down an open staircase, however. I curl my body into a seated position, wrapping my arms around my legs which are pulled under my chin, and taking a moment to rest my head on my knees. I must try to think, must try to focus.

Now what?

I have no idea what is to happen next. Will she come back? Will she let me out or … what? Leave me to starve? Come back for another beating? Expel me? Keep me here? I contemplate going down the stairs and testing the door, but I'm not brave enough for that yet. What if she's on the other side of it? I rub my eyes, and try to think, to calm myself down.

I try to place myself in the room, but I can only guess – I think I am leaning against the first bed on the right-hand side, although in the frenzy of the struggle with Benedicta I may have moved further along the room, away from the stairs – it's impossible to tell. I turn my thoughts to the skylights and look up at the ceiling. They had blinds on them when I slept here – I remembered the Guardian each night closing them with a long pole, because they were too high in the roof to reach even by standing on a bed. Now, there's no trace of even a window's shape, no outline of light even barely discernible. I can't even attempt to guess where the windows are – or were. I shudder. There seems something terribly final about the idea of them being sealed up against the daylight. It feels coffin-like, even though the room is big. My breathing grows faster as I scare myself even more. My eyes stray toward the back of the room, where the locked door through to the storage attic next door should be, and I shiver again. They were dormitories once too, long long ago. The thought of those running feet – the *sound* of them – come into my mind again, and a fresh fear strikes me. I cannot think about that, now, I tell myself. I simply can't.

And after a while, I lose track of time.

I know that she brought me up here after lunch, but then there was that time I spent waiting in her office … my hand flies to my pocket as I remember. I am amazed that the box and the money are still in there.

Then it occurs to me. If she doesn't let me out before this evening, then I can draw attention to myself when the boarders come up to the Dorm to get changed into their costumes for the Show. I know that movement up here can be heard downstairs – so if I jump up and down, and shout, maybe – then someone will hear me, and maybe, just maybe, Miss Clancy will be back at work this evening, in time for the show? She's sure to come investigate if she hears sounds from up here again? And even if she goes and gets Benedicta, then I'll just tell them that she's beaten me up, and locked me up here? That's against the law, surely? And I have to have bruises, don't I? I check my face for any lumps or bumps –

surprisingly, nothing – but sure enough, the side of my head smarts where I hit it against the bed. There must be bruises on my body too. The more I think of them, the more I begin to ache all over. Surely someone would have to ask questions if they saw that I had been attacked?

But what if Benedicta has spotted the box and the money missing? What if she's gone to get the Guards? What if that's why she's locked me up here? To keep me safe until they arrive? And I can't prove that she beat me up, can I? No one's seen me, and it's just her word against mine. I could have just fallen … down a stairs, for example. Who'll believe me? Miss Clancy might, but that won't count – Benedicta is the all-powerful, almighty Queen Bitch around this stupid backwater. I start to cry as my plan unravels. I am so very alone here, and so very scared.

I start to rock back and forth in the blackness, questions tumbling through my head, before it is overtaken by a blankness. I am not even sure if I am conscious or not. It feels as if I have left my body.

When I come back to it, the fear rushes through me over again. Time has passed. How much? I don't know. I have no idea whether it's day or night, today or tomorrow, if the girls have already been up to the Dormitory and are gone again – if it's Showtime, or if it's the middle of the night. My head starts to spin – what if Benedicta never comes back to find me? What if I make all the noise in the world but it's dismissed as just rats in the attic, like Miss Clancy tried to say that time we were here on our own?

What if they think I'm just Little Frances up to mischief?

Then real terror grips me. What if … what if I'm not *alone* up here? I can feel the tears start again – tears of panic this time. I want to scream and run and claw the walls and … and …

There's a click from below as the door to the Dorm opens. Every hair on my body stands on end – I feel my back *fizzle* as goosebumps erupt all over me, up my neck and into my hairline. I grip my knees tighter to me – *she's coming back*. I look in the direction of where I've heard the sound, and brace myself.

She's left the door open down below this time, and a shaft of dim light is cast up the stairs. It takes a moment for my eyes to focus, having been in total darkness for … how long? So when I see the small girl standing there, I'm at first sure that it's one of the First Years, already in costume ... but, hang on, there are no First Year boarders anymore ... and no First Year Day Girls signed up for *Oklahoma* ...

So I look again. And this time, I see her more clearly.

And I grow light-headed with terror, and shock and disbelief.

Because she's not ... *all there*. I rub my eyes, sure that I'm seeing things, but I'm not. There's a small girl there, alright – she can only be seven or eight years old – in a grey rag of a dress, and with lank, wet hair. And through her, I can *see* the wooden railing erected around the trap door. It's blurry – as though a thick cloud obscures it – but I can definitely see it. I gasp. *I can see through her.*

I whimper, and jump to my feet as more details register – her pale, almost grey skin, her huge dark eyes, the thin slit where her mouth should be. I try to back away from her, convinced that she is coming toward me – convinced that something truly terrible is going to happen to me this time. It makes no sense, there's no reason to this ...

But she stays where she is, staring at me, her expression unchanging.

And I stare back at her, my mind blank with sheer terror, until a single thought suddenly enters it.

Frances ... Little Frances ... you're real.

I'm not sure if I speak it or just think it – I'm sure it's the latter. But somehow, it's like she *hears* me, and she moves her head in some sort of acknowledgement – I can still see the post *through* her head, behind those ghastly features of hers, as she nods once, and then steps – no, not steps – *glides* – *floats?* – to her left, and lifts her right arm to point down the stairs. She still stares at me, then looks down the length of her arm, and then back at me. My heart lurches again as I realise what is happening. *She's telling me to leave.* She's left the door open for me.

And with that, she fades, growing dimmer and dimmer before my eyes, until she's not there. I blink, stare at the space where she's been, rub my eyes, and look back. She's definitely gone. Was she really ever there?

I take a few hesitant steps – registering pains in my head and body from the attack as I move for the first time since Benedicta left me alone – and peer anxiously down the steps to the Dorm below, glancing back, checking all the time, to see if the child has come back, or if she's just moved a distance away and is watching me from the darkness. And the thought of that is enough. The idea that if I peered into a dark corner of the room, that I might see that face peer back. I start down the stairs, almost tripping myself in the process, half sliding, half climbing to get down, to get into the light and out of that stairwell before the door suddenly slams shut. And then I'm down. I'm in the Dorm. I contemplate for a second running to my cubicle and getting some stuff, but I decide against it, and instead I run, as hard and as fast as I can down the stairs, through the lobbies below, past the Study Hall, past Brock's Piano, past Benedicta's office – as silently and as quickly as I can manage. I fear, as I flee, that I'll bump into someone – anyone – a student, or a nun – God forbid that Benedicta catches me, but for once luck is on my side. When I reach the dimly lit Brown Corridor, I realise why – the hubbub from the direction of the Ref means that they are all at tea. *I have a chance*, I think, and duck down the Green Corridor into the School Wing, away from the noise. Three quarters of the way down, I dive to my left, through the glass double doors and there, beyond them, is freedom. The Assembly Hall door. The entrance for the Day Girls, and later tonight for the audience to opening night of *Oklahoma*.

I won't be there, I realise, as I pull the door too hard and it swings back, slamming noisily off the wall outside as it does. But suddenly I don't care. I'm out, and I have to get away.

I run as fast as I can, despite my aching body, through the shadows outside, out through the chapel gardens to avoid being seen from windows at the front of the convent, and onto the road. I cannot get far enough, fast enough, I realise, as I keep running, out into the starlit, bitterly cold night. Running as if eyes are still watching me.

Chapter fifty-seven

Ria
BALLYKEERAN
June 2015

When she finished, myself and Lydia didn't speak.

Instead, our eyes were locked – somehow, it was as if she *knew* that I understood her exactly. I took the frail hand that she extended toward me, and I clasped it gently, for fear of breaking it. And she smiled at me. A smile of gratitude, of release. I mirrored it, and rubbed her hand.

"You understand, don't you, Ria?"

I nodded, my eyes wide as I tried to take it all in. "It's the same as what happened to me … the same thing. *Frances*. She was real. And Benedicta … she locked *me* up too …"

Lydia replied by closing her eyes and shaking her head.

"I *felt* it," she said, then yawned deeply. "Please tell me tomorrow," she said softly, releasing her hand and patting mine with it. "I want to take it in and I'm too tired now."

She looked at Matt, who was watching us, his face a picture of shock and confusion.

"Will you help me to my room, Matt," she said hoarsely.

Silently, he obeyed, taking her by the arm, and gently guiding her away from the table and toward the lift. I watched them go, half expecting her to turn again, but she didn't. When they had gone, I sat there at the table, alone, numb, trying to take it all in.

Matt returned about ten minutes later, walking briskly past the table, his hand held up in a 'wait' gesture. He returned to our table minutes later, carrying two glasses of golden liquid. "There's a fire in the bar," he said. "Would you mind if we sat by it for a bit? Only I'm really cold ..."

I nodded without hesitation. I was cold myself, my whole body chilled enough to want to sit by a fire in June. I followed him, and sank gratefully into the armchair that was positioned to the side of the small solid-fuel stove. He sank his Bushmills in one, and I followed suit, smiling as he looked at me with a shocked expression. I smiled back as I swirled the last drop of the liquid in the light of the flames and drained the glass thoroughly. Matt signalled to the waiter for two more.

"Is she okay?" I asked.

He nodded, settling himself into his own chair.

"Exhausted," he observed, "but in strangely good humour – like she's just – *purged* herself of something."

I nodded. "She has," I replied. "And I know how she feels. Sort of ... *elated*."

"Exactly," he agreed, pausing to allow the waiter to place the two glasses on the table.

We made a silent *sláinte* in each other's direction, and sipped our second glass delicately.

"You take very good care of her," I said. "I'm just going to come right out and ask if you're ... you know, *involved*?" The whiskey was making me bold already, I realised. There was no point in beating around the bush all the same, though. Too much had been revealed tonight to be coy about something so straightforward.

"*Jesus*, no," Matt replied, staring into the flames. "Lydia has a partner, Rick – they're devoted to each other, but she didn't want him to come with her this time, wanted to do this alone. She basically ordered him to stay at home, to keep the business running, and she'd come back to him when she'd done this one last thing. I met him in London the first time she came up, the poor sod. He's broken-hearted. I fucking know how he feels."

Matt took another slug from his whiskey and stared into the flames.

"How?" I asked.

He glanced at me, then back to the flames again.

"I lost my wife, Sam, to the same damn thing ten years ago," he said, his voice wavering. "Watching Lydia … it's hell. But I can't not help her. She sought me out … sought *us* out so deliberately. Sam never got to carry out any final wishes – it was quick at the end – so I feel I owe it to *her* to help Lydia … I'm sorry …"

He held his hand firmly over his eyes for a few moments, the slightest shudder of his shoulders the only indication that he was crying. His eyes were red when he took his hand away and took another slug of his drink for fortitude. I reached out and gently touched his arm.

"I'm truly sorry, Matt – I had no idea."

He shook his head. "Don't be. Honestly. Mostly I'm fine, but I'm finding this business with Lydia tough going, especially when she gets weak like that. Did you understand all that, by the way? Was she speaking in metaphors again? Is there any chance it was some sort of – *holistic-speak*, or something – the child pointing her way to freedom? Do you think Benedicta really beat her? I mean, I know she was a tough old hatchet, but that's insane."

I stared at him. "*She* was insane," I stated. "I told you then but you wouldn't listen. Benedicta. Stone cold mad. She was the reason I ran as fast as I could away from there – and clearly the reason that Lydia ran too."

"Are you saying that Lydia was telling the truth there? At times I thought it was her drugs making her ramble … it used to happen to Sam …"

"That *wasn't* her drugs, Matt," I said. "I swear she was telling the truth. And you can choose to believe me now or not, because I've only ever told my best friend this story and, to be honest, I sort of regret doing that because now she thinks I'm slightly touched. But I swear to you that every word Lydia just told us is true. Bad things, strange things happened in that place – I know for a fact because they happened to me too …"

And so I began to talk. Late into the night, by the fireside, until the residents' bar closed and beyond. Like Lydia, I purged myself of the burden that I had carried around for the last twenty-eight years.

There were traces of daylight in the sky when I slipped into my room, exhausted, but I didn't care. It was all out there now. Matt knew. Everything that had ever happened. Everything I had never told him. Well, mostly everything.

316

Chapter fifty-eight

BALLYKEERAN
June 2015

They bickered about 80's films in the car on the way there.

As the wipers swooshed away the heavy summer downpours, Matt and Lydia pitted *Stand by Me* against *The Princess Bride*, fought over which was worse – *Mannequin* or *Cocktail*, and which was sadder – *Sophie's Choice* or *Terms of Endearment*. Matt declared *Ferris Bueller's Day Off* as his absolute favourite of the decade, Lydia spoke passionately about her love for *The Breakfast Club*.

"I loved Judd Nelson so much. How about you, Ria?" she asked me, turning as best she could to see me in the back seat.

I smiled and nodded. "Me too, Lydia," I said. We laughed.

Looking at her, re-energised that morning, considering how weak she had been the night before, I felt that strange protectiveness creep over me again, as it had back at Maria Goretti – a feeling I had only ever experienced again with Emma. I glanced at Matt, who knew now – but didn't know quite what to make of what I had gone through back in '87, and still unaware of his daughter. The timing was still wrong, I told myself. And it wouldn't be fair to take his focus off helping Lydia, not when he had tied it up so much with the memory of his wife and her unfulfilled wishes. He was full of life and laughter as he argued with Lydia on the drive in the rain, but underneath … what sadness he must have known.

I felt protective toward him, too, suddenly. I was lucky, I realised, with the life I had. I'd got off so lightly by comparison with these two people, all three of us thrown back together again after so long.

We fell silent as we drove through the village of Ballykeeran – the same, but different: new names over the doors, a modern Centra, even a chain coffee shop where The Copper Kettle had once been. I felt sad for it – not because I felt any affection for the place, but for the changes that time had brought, taking some of the soul away from the little shops and cafés, stealing away the individualism of every town, making every high street the same. The atmosphere in the car began to feel absolutely gloomy as we left the village again, and drove along the familiar roads toward where Maria Goretti had once been.

"How's your Auntie Cecilia, Matt, by the way?" I asked out of the blue.

Lydia looked at him, puzzled. "Auntie Cecilia?"

"Oh yes," I chimed in. "Didn't you know? Someone got his job as the director of the school musical through nepotism."

Lydia squealed in delight all of a sudden. "She was your *aunt*? Sister Cecilia?"

Matt joined in the laughter. "Auntie Eileen. My mother's cousin, actually. So what? She left the nuns, actually – packed it all in, and went off to America to become a piano teacher."

A thought flashed into my mind – that it could have been *me* who went to America and became a teacher. That could have been *my* life.

"Met – wait for it – an ex-priest," Matt continued; "and they got married back in the noughties. They formed one of those show choirs – you know, like *Glee?* – and take part in competitions all over the Midwest. She's ecstatically happy."

"That's so lovely, Matt," I responded, with genuine feeling. I thought of her that day, playing the Bowie riff on the piano and realised that I wasn't surprised.

Lydia's response was to start singing 'Don't Stop Believin'', by Journey, at the top of her voice, tunelessly, reducing us all to laughter.

The laughter faded, however, as we took the final turn, and the road grew even more familiar. To my left a low wall ran, but instead of the grey stone that I remembered, it was painted white, bordered with nodding purple Agapanthus, and with neat gold lettering affixed along it: *St Anthony of Padua Care Home*.

"Oh look, the *Arbeit Macht Frei* sign is gone," remarked Lydia, peering out the front windscreen and pointing to where the blue metal arch had been, holding the original tall gateposts together. "Didn't anyone else feel like they were coming back to a concentration camp coming through that gate?" she asked, only half in jest.

Now, there were two simple, low gateposts, topped with plaster urns containing pink and purple petunias. It was almost welcoming.

My stomach felt uneasy as Matt turned in the gate. It was a turning I had taken in my head so many times. And some of it was the same. To my left stood the old chapel, where I had endured so many freezing cold morning Masses, where we had sheltered from the fire. It stood now behind a fence which kept it and its grounds separate from what was on our right-hand side, where in my mind's eye and memory stood the grey stone building of Maria Goretti. What stood there now couldn't have been more different. A modern, white, multi-level building, flat-roofed and elegant.

Matt glided slowly by its exterior, opening his window for a better look, and we all peered out. It was easier to see, now that the heavy shower that had hampered our journey had stopped. Above us, the clouds were being blown away, and traces of blue had started to appear in the sky. A typical Irish summer's day.

The new building was set further back than the original one had been, and now, along the front, roughly running from the Ref to the Study Hall's original location, I reckoned, was a long, low pool which contained three water jets that shot up into the air and sprinkled back down making a soothing gurgling and splashing.

We carried on straight toward the car park ahead, passing well-kept flower beds where the top pitch had been, bordered by saplings. The grass was neat and lush, edged with flourishes of floral colour. The car park was where the rest of the Playing Courts used to be, freshly tarmacked and marked out in white paint. We carried on toward the rear, and pulled in where the Rounders Pitch had been, parking close to the where the fir had grown, where Matt and I had kissed that day. All three of us were silent as we stepped from the car, studying our surroundings.

"Well, this is different," observed Matt.

"You don't say," replied Lydia.

"Did you know this was here, Matt?" I asked.

He shrugged. "Yes and no – I haven't been back to Ballykeeran much since my mother died and I sold the house. I knew that there was some sort of retirement home here, but I assumed it was still in the hands of the Order of Maria Goretti – I didn't know that the name had changed, or all of this."

We started to walk toward the entrance, automatically moving to the edge of the car park, where a path was marked out, along the route of The Walk.

"Everything's changed," whispered Lydia.

"Not everything," I replied, a couple of steps behind her and Matt. She turned to look at me, and I nodded over the low yew hedge to my right. The small Nuns' Graveyard was still there, exactly as it had always been and, behind it, the Goretti Door.

Lydia gasped.

"Is she still there?" she asked, breathless.

I searched the space until I saw it. "She is," I replied, spotting the small incongruous rock among the crosses. We exchanged a glance, and slowly resumed our pace, Lydia taking my arm instead of Matt's and we huddled together. He fell into step behind us and we carried on in silence, past where the Study Hall had once stood and the gravel courtyard behind had begun.

The entrance to the St Anthony of Padua Care Home was now where the gable end of the Assembly Hall had been. A ramp led up to wide automatic doors, which swooshed open for us, and we stepped into a cool, clean, open lobby. Sudden sunlight flooded it from a large atrium, and we paused to take it all in.

The wall to our left was glass, overlooking a sprawling green lawn, which spread out over an area where, in our time, farmer's fields had just been visible through the Leyland cypresses, It was now bordered with newly planted trees, and marked out with wide paths around the edges and through the centre.

The floor of the lobby was white marble, and in the middle was a round reception desk, where two women and a man sat, wearing headsets and dealing with paperwork. Throughout the space were occasional seats, comfortable chairs and benches, some of them occupied by elderly people, or nurses in pale pink tunics and white pants. After a moment, I realised that all of the patients were either priests or nuns, marked out by veils and dog collars or pins of a particular Order. Vases of fresh flowers were dotted about on stands, religious iconography was hung on the walls, but only stylish pieces that fitted in with the modern feel of the place; a large silver Brigid's Cross, a contemporary wooden carving of St Anthony, a cross made from bog oak. Gentle music was being piped from somewhere. I cocked my ear and recognised it as *Pie Jesu* on pan pipes.

Toward the far end of the lobby, where the stage would have been, and running behind it the Green Corridor, a marble staircase swept gracefully upward to a second level, doors leading into a number of rooms visible through a glass-fronted balcony. Signs suspended from the ceiling showed arrows pointing in the direction of Treatment Rooms, Residents' Rooms, a Prayer Room, the Refectory, the Mortuary. But there were also signs for a Dialysis Unit, Physiotherapy, Occupational Therapy, Triage and Emergency. A doctor swept past us, wearing a white coat and a stethoscope, and I realised that the place was as much a well-equipped, private hospital for religious orders as a retirement facility.

We made our way to the reception desk, where Matt introduced us. "I spoke with someone last week," he explained. "This is Lydia Madigan – she was a student here in the 1980's and wanted to visit ..."

"That was me," the man piped up, leaning over his colleague and extending a hand to Matt. "Delighted to finally meet you in person. I had a chat with the staff, and our administrator, Sister Irene, will be able to see you – would you like to take a seat and I'll let her know you're here?"

Moments later, a woman, dressed in a navy skirt and white blouse appeared. She wore no veil, but the birthmark on her face identified her immediately as someone we had known – a nun.

I stiffened. "Sister Ruth," I said as she approached us, her hand extended.

She flushed and stopped in her tracks, a deep red rising from her neck up to her face. "*You!*" she managed, before checking herself, and shaking hands with Matt and Lydia before hesitantly taking mine. "You'd better come with me," she said.

She took us to a small, bright room, marked Consulting Room 3, overlooking the green lawn. With a sweep of her hand, she indicated that we should sit down in three brightly upholstered armchairs. She herself took a small stool and perched on it, looking at us in silence for a few moments.

"So it *is* really you," she said to Lydia. "We thought … we weren't sure what had happened to you after the fire …" She turned her attention to me, and studied me, wide-eyed. "And *you* …"

I, in turn, watched her nervously.

"You … *left* … were you alright?" She glanced from me to Matt, and I felt panic rise in me. She knew, of course. Knew that I had been pregnant, knew that it was Matt's.

I glared at her as if to warn her off. "Everything turned out *fine*," I said firmly. Discomfort spread through me, and I hoped that I had conveyed enough with my look to make her say no more.

"We didn't think that we'd meet anyone we knew," Matt said. He seemed happy to see her, and completely oblivious to my discomfort.

The nun looked at him. "And I certainly didn't think I'd come to work this morning and meet *all* of you," she replied.

"You're Sister Irene now?" I said, and she nodded.

"Yes. I reverted to my given name some years ago. Ruth was simply one that I took when I joined the Order back in the early 1980's – we all had to, at the time. A lot has changed since then, of course."

"This place is really fantastic," said Matt. "I haven't been in Ballykeeran for a long time – I had no idea this was here."

"It's literally a phoenix from the flames," replied Ruth – Irene. "It took a long time to come about, but it's a fitting replacement for what was originally here. And Ballykeeran is a lovely, tranquil spot – central too, convenient for anywhere in the country. We have residents from Donegal to Dingle. It's a wonderful place to retire to and be cared for. I was honoured to get the job as administrator here. All of the Maria Goretti Sisters were scattered to the four winds after that terrible event in 1987. No more than yourselves, of course." She eyed me again, with curiosity.

I didn't reply, however, just continued to study her. She had aged well. Nuns often did, I observed, without the stresses and strains of family, and careers, and the big bad world in general. Their sheltered environments and lifestyles seemed to be good for the skin, if nothing else.

"And you, Lydia. I thank God as I sit here to be looking at you. How are you?"

"Well, truth be told, Sister, I'm a bit fucked."

Matt snorted, and I couldn't prevent a broad smile from spreading across my features, as Lydia looked at the nun, the picture of innocence.

Sister Irene winced, and shut her eyes for a moment, as if hoping the offence would be gone when she opened them.

"I apologise," continued Lydia. "But I think that you could probably tell by looking at me that I might not be in the whole of my health. I'm quite short on time, actually, so I wanted to come here for a couple of reasons. To tie things up, to get some answers. Because my time here has completely marked my entire life, and Ria's too ..." She glanced at me, and I caught her eye for a second. "So I think we were hoping that maybe the Universe, or God or whoever floats your belief boat, might give us some answers by coming here. And it seems that as you're here, you're our best bet to get them. So maybe you can shed some light on some things for us?"

Sister Irene shifted on the stool, uncomfortably. "I'm more than happy to try," she said. "What was it that you wanted to know?"

Lydia leaned forward in her armchair and fixed the nun with a stare.

"I won't beat around the bush. One word. *Benedicta*," she said. "You knew her, we knew her, but what I've never known, what I've never been able to figure out, is exactly why that woman hated me so much? Why she *beat* me, and why she locked me up?"

Sister Irene's eyes widened, and her eyes flicked toward me, her expression worried. "You ... as well ..." she blurted.

Lydia nodded calmly, her mouth set and determined.

"I'm not looking for retribution or anything," she said. "But I've been doing some reflection over my life – for obvious reasons – and

I just have this need to know. How someone who preached Christianity could treat another human like she did. A kid – a kid whose parents had died, a kid who had a screwed-up home life. And she *did* physically assault me, and keep me locked against my will – *that's* why I left, by the way, as if it wasn't obvious. I didn't die in the fire because I missed it by a matter of hours, running as fast as I could away from here. But why? Why would she do that?"

Sister Irene looked sad as she listened to Lydia. She turned and looked out the window for a moment, at the shadows of clouds scudding across the grass. "You're right, you know," she said eventually. "You're owed an explanation. And an apology."

"I think we both are," I chimed in, my voice cold. "But for starters, the explanation would be just fine."

"Maybe you should follow me to my office, then," Sister Irene said, standing. "We'll have more privacy there."

Chapter fifty-nine

BALLYKEERAN
June 2015

The nun placed the old, russet-coloured journal on her desk and folded her hands together on top of its faded cover.

"Her birth name was Evelyn Phelan," she said. "When she joined the community, she took the name Benedicta. At first, I thought it was because she saw her vocation as a blessing. But as time went on, I began to suspect that, in fact, she believed that *she* was the blessing, and that the world was a better place because of her presence." She smiled a little at my wide eyes. "Speaking candidly within these four walls, I wasn't a fan. She ruled with an iron fist, had unreasonable expectations, was controlling, punitive, and vengeful. We nuns were as afraid of her as the students – except for a few of the older ones, who had never known anything other than hardline Catholicism and discipline. But us younger arrivals had been trained in a different way – a softer, more Christian approach. We were fans of Taize chanting, folk Masses, forgiveness and acts of kindness. I was very naïve when I was sent to Maria Goretti – I thought everyone was like me. So my first few years turned out to be a very difficult transition period. The hardliners were a dying breed, however. Thankfully things have changed. After the fire, everything was thrown into disarray. We were all displaced. A new school had to be found for the students, so the local Technical School expanded to take them in, and the two schools ultimately amalgamated to form the Community School that still exists now. I was sent away to a convent in Wicklow – a lovely place, with lovely people – but I often wondered about here, and when I heard about Anthony of Padua being built – he's the Patron Saint of the Elderly, by the way – I felt a calling – a calling as strong as the call to my vocation, and I applied immediately. When I got the job, I truly felt as if God needed me to be here. I still see it as an extraordinary honour.

I hit the ground running in my job as administrator, my first task to sort through what was left from Maria Goretti. Boxes of files had been found, miraculously undamaged in a shed way out the back, and it was in them that I found the records from a previous Mother Superior. And a picture of Mother Benedicta began to emerge, a worrying one.

We had all known that she was from somewhere in the locality – which was unusual, as nuns from the Order tended not to be stationed near their homes. We knew that she had been a missionary, and had worked among unmarried mothers in Dublin, but as she was so unapproachable, we never would have dared to ask her any more. She didn't chat to us, and we were too terrified to look her in the eye, so we knew little or nothing about her.

My study of the files revealed that Mother Benedicta, or Evelyn Phelan as she was –"

"Of course – her surname was Phelan too," I said.

The nun simply looked at me, and carried on.

"… had a very disturbed childhood. Her father was hanged for murder, and her mother took her own life – though not necessarily in that order, I believe. Evelyn was actually sent away from home to live at Maria Goretti, where her mother had worked as a cleaner. And by the age of thirteen, she was an orphan, who lived with the local nuns, with the shadow of her father's crime and her mother's so-called sin over her. It must have been very disturbing, indeed."

"And who was it that her father murdered?" asked Lydia.

Sister Irene took a deep breath, and touched the journal on the desk.

"Allegedly, her father murdered Evelyn's younger sister. Who is, unusually, buried outside in the Nuns' Graveyard."

"*Frances.*"

Lydia and I said it together. The name hung in the room. It felt almost like an invocation.

Sister Irene nodded. "Frances Phelan. Murdered on Ballykeeran Bog in 1942 at seven years of age. Evelyn was ten. Her father went to the gallows on testimony that Evelyn provided."

"But?" prompted Matt.

"But indeed," sighed Sister Irene. "According to what I can piece together from this journal, he was a wronged man."

"How?" I asked.

"Because Evelyn's final sworn testimony to her father's guilt was provided only *after* she was sent here – to Maria Goretti. But it was different from what she had originally told the authorities. The Mother Superior at the time, Mother Agnes de Bruin, kept extensive notes on the case. Originally, you see, young Evelyn Phelan came home and told everyone that she had lost her sister in a storm on the bog – that they had quarrelled, as kids do, and Frances stormed off, to teach her sister a lesson. Except she never returned. It was assumed, initially, that she had got lost on the bog, perhaps fallen in a boghole, or injured herself in some other way and died out there – possibly of exposure. At least that was the story based on what Evelyn originally said had happened. A few days later, the body was found by Evelyn's own father, the poor man, and the broken-hearted family arranged her funeral privately. Because she was the daughter of their valued cleaner, the nuns at Maria Goretti responded to the unusual request that she be buried in their private cemetery, which was usually reserved for members of the Order. She had always had aspirations for her children to be Goretti Girls, apparently, and the nuns agreed as a kindness in the exceptional circumstances.

Her mother became very ill after that – couldn't leave the house, fell into a deep depression, apparently. She couldn't take care of Evelyn, and the father, I suppose, found it too difficult to take care of her either, so the child was taken to the convent and left in the care of the nuns there. There's no mention of whether it was a permanent or temporary thing at the time, but the fact that her mother killed herself shortly afterwards certainly sealed the deal. The next thing, the father was arrested for murder based on an interview that Evelyn had with the Guards right here. She told them a whole new story – that her father had been *with* the girls on the bog that evening, and that she had later seen him washing blood off his hands. She also described a home life where he was prone to violent rages and anger, often directed at the children. Two and two made five, of course, and he was deemed too dangerous, and the crime too heinous for it to be commuted to life imprisonment. He was executed at Tullamore Gaol. Their troubled child was now a ward of the Sisters of Maria Goretti."

"But you don't buy that," I said. The nun's cynical tone had been very much in evidence throughout the telling of her story.

"Neither did Mother Agnes back in the 40's. This is her journal – it was mixed in with the stuff that was brought from the shed – all old stuff, probably moved to make way for more modern files and documents. Benedicta can't ever have found it or else it wouldn't be sitting on my desk now. But Mother Agnes kept meticulous notes on Evelyn's behaviour – destructive outbursts that just came from nowhere, complete lack of discipline. She literally ran wild around the place, if the mood took her. Broke and smashed things, attacked other students, verbally and physically. She showed no sorrow over her mother's death – in fact, when the news was broken to her, her response was something like, 'Oh good, she can be with precious Baby Frances now' – I'm paraphrasing, of course. But if the subject of Frances herself came up, it could cause displays of grief on a biblical level – pulling at her hair, rending her clothes and so on. And then snap, back she'd go to being a perfectly normal child in a rather abnormal situation. She was unpredictable though – had to be given her own private room that could be locked at night – that one at the end of the Sisters' Corridor – your room."

I shivered violently as someone walked over my grave.

"And then she had to be told that her father was to be executed. There was trouble over that too – one of the students at Maria Goretti told Evelyn before the nuns could, and Evelyn assaulted her by pushing her down the stairs. Eventually, things were sorted and Mother Agnes describes sitting her down and explaining to her what was to happen, advising her that it was so important that she always told the truth, and that even if she hadn't told the truth in the past, that there was still time to do so. Evelyn remained resolute, however, and the execution went ahead. Mother Agnes describes her as changing afterward, but in an odd way. Like she became more confident, *powerful* even."

"She was clearly a very disturbed little girl," I said.

"So do you think she did it on purpose, then?" Lydia asked. "That she ... *framed* her own father for the murder of her sister? That she was sick enough at what – ten, eleven years of age to do that? And why? And who really killed Frances, then?"

Sister Irene shrugged. "I draw the line – as did Mother Agnes – at stating that as a fact. There *was*, however, something very unusual about the whole situation. There were also rumours locally, you see ... rumours that the body was never found, and that the little girl Frances isn't actually in the coffin that's buried on the grounds here. But also rumours that Liam Phelan didn't kill the child, and that he was hanged because he refused to reveal who did. Nothing is clear-cut. And we can all surmise, but none of us have any proof of anything. And I don't suppose we ever will now."

We digested what Sister Irene told us in silence for a moment. None of us, offering any conclusion or theories about what we had just been told, and what we knew from the past.

It took Matt to break the silence.

"So how did Evelyn Phelan become Mother Benedicta, then?" he said. "You said she went away for a number of years?"

"She did missionary and charity work for a number of years. She returned to Maria Goretti in 1978, and took over as Mother Superior in 1980, with a very strict agenda. There was no one left, at that stage, at the convent itself who knew her from her time here as a child and she tried her best not to mix with the locals. She kept herself aloof, and always in control. Anyone who might have had an inkling that she was Evelyn Phelan, was never quite sure, because of how she conducted herself. No one would dare confront her on it. Of course some people *must* have known, but if they did they said nothing. And the rest of the story you know – what she was like."

"So what happened, do you think, that turned her from that violent child into the contained adult that we knew?" pondered Matt aloud, only to be interrupted by Lydia, who snorted disdainfully.

"Yeah. *Contained.*" She side-eyed him and, in a Spanish accent, quoted one of her favourite films. "'*You keep using this word, but I do not think it means what you think it means.*'"

Matt smiled weakly.

"Contained," she went on. "That's exactly the word I was thinking of as she slapped the crap out of me in a pitch-black attic, and I'm sure it was what Ria thought when Mother Dick informed her she was going to be committed."

"Well, she didn't pluck that idea from thin air," said Sister Irene.

"What do you mean?"

"Well, that's what happened to *her*. Mother Agnes's notes describe how she became completely unmanageable and they had to make a decision about her future. So they sent her away ..."

She caught my eye as she spoke.

"... to St Aidan's hospital. Evelyn Phelan spent her teenage years and young adulthood committed – involuntarily – to a psychiatric institution. It changed her completely. By the time she returned to Ballykeeran in 1978, whatever they did to her, there was no trace of Evelyn left. It was entirely Benedicta. We had no idea that Evelyn was still in there."

I heard Lydia open her mouth and take a breath, and waited for the word 'nut' or 'headcase' or 'cuckoo' to come out, based on her form so far since we had arrived. I was wrong, however.

"I have something belonging to her," she said softly. "Something that I shouldn't have. And I won't be able to rest easy if I don't in some way return it to where it came from. Can I leave it with you, Sister Irene? Or is there a grave that I can place it on, or a memorial spot of some sort – maybe in the chapel, I'm not sure how it works?"

Sister Irene looked somewhat taken aback.

"None of the above, I'm afraid," she said.

Lydia looked momentarily crestfallen.

"But you could give it to her yourself."

It was our turn to be disconcerted. Lydia looked at me, her eyes wide.

"She's ... still alive?" she managed.

Irene nodded. "Eighty-three years old, frail, but physically fit. And upstairs in her room as we speak. I mean, I can understand if

330

you don't want to see her, but … under the circumstances for you, Lydia … it might … I mean, she doesn't talk much sense anymore. She's harmless, really. In fact, she spends most of the day talking to her sister, Frances."

I couldn't help it – I gasped, and reached out for Lydia's arm.

Irene looked at me, puzzled. "Her mind comes and goes a little – sometimes she's sharp as a die, and then the next she's back when they were kids. She had an enormous breakdown after the fire and never recovered fully. So do you want to go up, Lydia? Ria? It's entirely up to you."

The thought terrified me, but then again, the day wasn't about me, was it?

As for Lydia, she had no such hesitation. As agilely as she could manage on her spindle-thin legs, she jumped to her feet. "Show me the way," she said, in true Lydia fashion. *"Show. Me. The. Way."*

Chapter sixty

BALLYKEERAN
August 1942

"Come *on*, Frances. Don't be such a sucky babby. Where were you hiding?"

"I wasn't. Mammy will kill us, Evelyn. We need to go home now. She'll be wondering where we are."

"She won't wonder where *I* am – just her precious little angel, Baby Frances. Now we're late and it's *your* fault. Why did you run away? Tell me or I'll pinch you!"

"I didn't want to go as far as where the men are cutting the turf with the machines."

"You're such a silly baby! You think they're bad because the machines are from Germany, so you think they're like the fellahs from the War that you seen at the pictures – but it was you who wanted to come anyway, hanging out of me like a bad smell!"

"*Noooo*, Evelyn – it's getting dark and I want to go home to Mammy!"

"You didn't want to go home to Mammy when you disappeared on me just now and me soaking wet now. I didn't know where you were gone. Never mind Mammy. You have to stick with me when I say so. Mammy won't be around forever, do you know that? What if Mammy was gone in the morning? What if she died stone dead and was buried and gone? What would little sucky babby Franny do then?"

"Stop, Evelyn!"

"Well, *what? What would you do? Answer me!*"

"Dada would look after us."

"*No! No, he would not, Frances.* Dada would look after *me,* but not you, because I'm his special girl, his pet. Not you. I used to be Mammy's pet, but then you came along and you took all the love and now she has nothing left for me. So that's how you're Mammy's pet now. Because you're a thief. But if Mammy died and was gone then there'd be no one to love you, Frances. You wouldn't be anyone's pet. Except maybe, if you were very good and did everything I tell you to, and became my servant, then maybe I'd give you some of what's left on my plate sometimes, and give you my old clothes, and then you'd have to thank me and say that I'm great. Say that now, Frances!"

"Please, Evelyn, it's lashing rain – I want to go home!"

"Say I'm great, Frances, or so help me God, I'll slap you!"

"*No, Evelyn!* Stop, you're being stupid. I'm going home now and I'm going to tell Mammy on you!"

"*Say. It. Frances!*"

"You're great. Now, can we go home?"

"No. I've changed my mind. We're not going yet. Because I want to go see the machines and you have to come with me or else I won't give you my scraps and my old clothes when Mammy's dead."

"Stop saying that, Evelyn. *Stop!* Mammy's not going to die."

"She is. When I bring home this big bit of bogwood here – look – and hit her on the head with it ... like *this* ... then she'll be stone dead. How will you like that, Frances? You could stop that happening though, if you just do what I say. You can save Mammy if you do exactly what you're told. You just have to stop crying like a little babby. Stop it, Frances ... stop your whinging and come with me *now ... or I'll hurt you ... like I'll hurt Mammy ... like this ...*

Chapter sixty-one

BALLYKEERAN
June 2015

It seemed entirely fascinating to me that she wasn't wearing a veil.

At first sight, from the doorway, she was just an old lady, sitting in silhouette against a picture window which overlooked the chapel, over the new fence and into the gardens, and the small graveyard which were the same as they had always been. An oatmeal-coloured fleecy blanket was arranged over her legs, and a walking stick lay across her knees. Her back was still straight, with no trace of a slump in her rigid posture, and she was as thin as ever.

But it was seeing her hair. White, thin, cut short and close to her head, parted to the side. That fascinated me. It was as if she had removed her armour, as if she were somehow diminished. There was something about her that still frightened me, even after all this time, but seeing her head bare made me a little braver.

She didn't look at us at first. Just continued to watch out of the window, glancing up at the gathering black clouds which blocked out the earlier sunshine. We were in for another summer shower. Emboldened by her fragile appearance, I crossed the room and stood in front of her chair. When she turned to look at me directly, my stomach contracted, however. I wasn't as brave as I thought I was, after all.

Her face had obviously aged, the eyes deeper in their sockets, the skin papery, the lips set in a thin line, but it was still the woman that I saw in the occasional recurring nightmare. I glanced at Lydia, who still stood in the doorway, to see how she was coping. It was just the two of us who would see Benedicta. We had asked Matt to stay outside.

The eyes narrowed when she turned and saw me and she looked at me for a moment, leaving me to wonder if she recognised me at all. Maybe she didn't. Maybe I was a short chapter in her life that had been forgotten in the intervening years. She studied me thoroughly, her eyes darting from my face, down to my shoes and back again. And then the lips curled back in a familiar sneer.

"So, you came back, did you?" she said.

I felt my cheeks and chest redden immediately, and my throat grow dry.

"Good morning, Mother," I croaked, before clearing my throat.

She snorted, turned her head back to the window. "Is it now," she mumbled.

I crossed my arms and looked out the window myself.

"Looks like we're in for another shower," I remarked. I wasn't surprised when she didn't reply. "This is a lovely place now."

I continued with the chatter, purely because I could think of nothing else to say. Despite everything, I had no desire to confront her, or to accuse her, or to look for an apology – because I knew I'd never get one – but when Sister Irene had said that she was *here* – *still alive* – I had been filled with such an urge just to *look* at her, like an exhibit at a museum of the weird and wonderful that I just couldn't miss the opportunity. I was in her room for nothing more than curiosity. To see what the witch had become in her old age. To link the present and the past, and to hope that somehow it would draw a line underneath it for me. It crossed my mind that it was like being at a wake. Like paying my respects by the open coffin and then leaving.

The idea that, as much as I had wanted to ... *view* ... her, the fact that I didn't have to stay gave me a delicious sense of release. I could simply walk out of there and leave her to it. I didn't have to wait through an admonishment, or stay still until permission was granted to leave. I was *free* to just walk away from her – I didn't have to plot, or fret or worry how I might make my exit. Because she was nothing but an old woman in a chair, who was nothing to me. What harm could she do to me now? I took what felt like a cleansing breath, and a step toward the door.

Then she spoke.

"You had somewhere you were meant to be, you know," she growled.

I stopped dead in my tracks.

"There was a place for you, where you might have redeemed your life and your soul. But you followed your own path anyway," she continued. "What did you do with the *bastard* in the long run?"

I was suddenly flooded with anger. No one had ever referred to Emma in that way before. My beautiful, adored little girl. I turned slowly, back to where she sat, still staring out the window.

"My *daughter* is well, not that it's any of your concern. She is healthy, happy, university-educated, gainfully-employed, kind and loving. She was wanted and adored and cared for by her mother her entire life, and she loves me in return. Something that you'd have ripped away from both of us if you'd got your way and forced me – *against my will* – into a psychiatric hospital."

She sneered again. "Who told you? Was it Ruth? With her à la carte faith? Folk songs and guitars? I knew what was best for you then, and it would have been best for that infant as well. I always know what's best. The Devil snuck you past me, Miss Clancy, and no mistake."

"And what about me? Did he sneak me past you as well?"

Lydia spoke from the doorway. Immediately the nun's demeanour changed as she searched her mind to place the voice. She looked a little like a robot, searching for information in its internal memory. Slowly, Lydia walked in to the room past me, stopping when she had positioned herself directly in front of Benedicta. The nun looked at her in alarm, her face echoing a look I had seen twice on it during my time at Maria Goretti. A look of fear.

"Ria – would you mind awfully shoving that over here?" Lydia asked, pointing to a plastic chair which was beside the single bed that was behind me. I obliged, and she sank down into it.

Benedicta watched the whole exchange with horror.

"You'll have to forgive me, Mother," Lydia sighed as she arranged herself. "Only the old legs don't hold me up like they used to. You probably know how that feels yourself, though."

The nun opened and closed her mouth, but no words came for a moment.

"You ... *you* ... you were..."

"Still locked in an attic covered in bruises? Burned to a toasty crisp? Is that where you wanted me to be, Sister? Out of your way? Not *disrupting* you anymore?"

"But you're *dead?*"

"Yes. Well. Not the first person you know to come back to life, am I, Mother? Am I right about that?"

The nun was trembling now, as she did when she was filled with rage. "Who ... who let you out? Was it Ruth? But I had the key!"

"Poor Sister Ruth is getting the blame for everything today, isn't she, Ria?" Lydia seemed to be almost enjoying herself.

"It wasn't Ruth, as it happens. You should look a little closer to home, Mother. Let me gast your flabber a little more. I believe that my liberator – and Ria's if you're interested – was none other than your own, darling, dearly departed sister Frances. How do you like them apples?"

Benedicta held Lydia's gaze for a moment and then, out of the blue, suddenly burst out laughing. "*Do you hear that, Frances?*" she shouted.

Lydia turned, quickly, half-expecting to see something behind her.

"*You're able to open locked doors now, as well as knock over candles and start infernos. Aren't you only mighty! Shame you couldn't be as useful when you were alive!*"

Lydia glanced at me, and we exchanged a brief glance. Were we losing her to some sort of reverie? Had she lapsed into one of the delusional moments that Irene had mentioned?

Then again, based on what Lydia and I knew, who said they were delusional?

"That's long over. And neither forgiven nor forgotten, but it's not why I'm here," continued Lydia. "When I left, Mother, I took something belonging to you, something that I shouldn't have."

"Always knew that there was something *evil* about you, child," the nun hissed at her. "*Thou shalt not steal!*"

"*And forgive us our trespasses, as we forgive those who trespass against us. Judge not lest ye be judged*, et cetera!" Lydia fired back. "I'm here today to give it back to you. To do the right thing by you – who couldn't do the right thing by me. Or Miss Clancy, for that matter." She fumbled in her handbag, first pulling out her purse and withdrawing cash. "I checked, and ten pounds in 1987 is worth in the region of twenty-four euro today so let me return that first." She held the money out to the nun, who looked at it as if it were a filthy cloth, and made no effort to accept it. After a few moments of holding it out, Lydia turned, looked around the room, and handed me the money, indicating that I should put it on the bedside table beside a jug of water, a rosary, and a small statue of a praying Virgin.

"I don't know if it will be any use to you, Mother, but I need it off my conscience before I go to meet my Maker."

"The Devil?" the nun quipped.

Lydia tilted her head to one side and shook it, tutting loudly. "The devil thing is getting very old, Mother, and it's not very helpful so I'd like it if you could just stop. Now, where is this box …"

Lydia turned her attention back to her bag, while Benedicta watched her.

"Here it is – this is yours, Mother. I didn't know what it was when I took it, and I failed to return it to you out of – understandable, I should think – fear over the years since I left here. That doesn't make it right, though, so I want to return this to you with my humble apology, a sincere one, from my heart."

The nun's hands trembled as she reached out and took the box from Lydia. "It was you … not the fire …" she managed, before taking it from Lydia, and holding it in her hands as if it were the most precious, most delicate thing that she had ever seen. "You've had this … all along … Do you know what this is? You stupid, evil girl? Do you *know* what this is? You *stole* my father's watch? The only thing I had left of him? All this time … you *thief*!"

The nun had leaned forward in the chair, her face red and spittle gathering at the corner of her lips.

Unnerved by the sudden change in her, Lydia sat back in her chair. "I said I was sorry, Mother, and I meant it. Arguably, you can look at it as my having stolen it, but I also saved it from the fire so that you might have it again – that's the way the Universe might see the situation."

Lydia flinched as the nun suddenly, and without warning, stood up, gripping the watch in one hand, and the walking stick in the other.

"This was all I had left of him," she repeated. "My father! The kindest, most loving man who ever walked! He *loved* me! And he was taken from me!"

"In fairness, Mother, he was arrested for murder."

I winced. It was probably not the best time for Facetious Lydia to make an appearance.

"Not by *them*, by *her!*"

"By who? Frances? Did he love her more than you? Were you jealous?"

"Not that sniveling, whining brat either! She was *her* child. There was no interest in me once she came along. *She* never cared for me one iota, she was jealous of me because my father loved me so much. She wanted me dead instead of Frances – she said so herself, I heard her with my own ears!"

The nun was ranting now, standing over Lydia in her chair, shouting at her, becoming more furious by the second.

"And he, the fool, did everything to make her happy – he arranged *that*, for the love of God!"

She was pointing out the window, in the direction of the chapel gardens. I registered that it was the Nuns' Graveyard that she pointed to.

"It was your mother who wanted Frances buried there, Evelyn," I said, in an effort to turn her attention away from Lydia.

It worked. She turned, glaring at me.

"What did you call me?" she snarled.

The sight of her ... her lips pulled back over her teeth.

"*I asked what you called me?*"

And there it was. 1987 again. Her voice, her demeanour, everything about her was suddenly energised again, as if she were possessed by the spirit of her younger self.

"*Evelyn*, Mother. I'm sorry ..."

"Don't *ever* call me by that name. My name is Mother Benedicta. That name you called me was *her* name. They called me after her, you see, because I was the only one, the blessed one. Until that little brat arrived and ruined everything. Didn't you, Frances?"

I couldn't help myself. I looked around behind me this time, sure that there would be someone there, but there was no one. Was it because she was mad? Or was she really ... could Benedicta see her?

"And while it might have been my mother wanted her out *there*," she pointed out the window again. "it was my father who fixed it all so that my poor, broken-hearted *mother* would be consoled. But I knew he couldn't have done what she wanted, what everyone believed he did ..."

"How did you know, Mother?" I said, trying to remain calm.

"Was that why you told them he did it?" Lydia said.

The nun swung around to glare at her.

"Why you changed your story and told the Guards that your father killed Frances? Did you want to hurt him because he dared to make someone happy that wasn't *you*?"

The nun's nostrils flared as she looked down at Lydia. "How dare you!" she hissed. "How dare you assume to know anything of my private life, my childhood. How *dare* you accuse me of lying!"

"But you did lie, didn't you, Mother?" Lydia continued. "Why was that? Why did you suddenly hate your father so much that you did that to him? You must have known that he'd go to prison?"

Suddenly, the nun's expression changed. A flash of something that looked vaguely like regret crossed it. "I thought we were just going to see the nuns," she said, as if she were disappearing into a memory. "But he didn't come in the door. He just left me. He could easily have taken me home. And there was nothing *wrong* with *her*. She could have taken care of me, like she did when I was small, before Frances came. There was only one child left. It had to be easier than two. It had to make her feel better, make her head work right again. It had to help. One less mouth to feed, one less set of worries. And Frances was safe – the nuns had her, like Mammy wanted ... but still, he *left* me, and went back to *her* – she was *useless*, for God's sake. Couldn't even get out of bed. But when Frances was gone, it would have been easier – I had *made* it easier for them – Jesus, Mary and Joseph, could they not have seen that? But he walked away ... and left me there, by myself ... left me there with Frances ..."

I looked at Lydia, and she looked back, her face filled with concern. She slid forward to the edge of the chair, and spoke to the nun in a calm voice.

"What do you mean that you had made it easier for them? What did you do, Mother? Am I wrong when I say that I think *you* killed your sister?"

"Dada put on the whole show for Mammy, so that she wouldn't get her special feelings hurt. Crying in her room all day, and praying, and cursing me and wishing that I was dead instead of *her*. He arranged the whole thing for Mammy's sake. But he couldn't have ever found what he was looking for. I hid it too well ... I was good at hiding ..."

"Do you mean Frances' body?" Lydia continued. "Is that why, if we dug up her little coffin there would be nothing there, like the rumours in the village said? Like Tom Gorman told me? Like the nursery rhyme that was made up about her? Was your father protecting you, Evelyn? Did he take the blame for what you did? *Thou shalt not kill, Evelyn.*"

The nun began to shake violently.

"Lydia, I think we should get Sister Irene," I interrupted.

She ignored me. "And is that why Frances is still around? Or at least *was*? Is that why she was running about the attics, and walking around with her little damp feet? Because she didn't want you to have any peace for what you did to her? Is that why she let me and Ria free that day? To stop you getting *pleasure* out of what you were doing to us? Was Frances *haunting* Maria Goretti to get at you, Evelyn? To get her own back? Was that it? At least that's what I think."

Suddenly, the nun stiffened again. Where her shoulders had slumped a little while she was lost in the earlier memory, they suddenly straightened, and she turned back to Lydia, her eyes filled with anger.

"Who are you to *think* anything at all, Miss Madigan, especially in relation to me? I should call the Guards on you, you thieving little madam! And *you* ..." she turned and glared at me, "you were relieved of your position here a long time ago, Miss Clancy. You are an unsuitable role model for my students. It's no surprise that Miss Madigan here is such a thieving little maggot, with you for an example. You were always fond of her. Leading her down the path to evil."

She turned back to Lydia.

"Well, I can see by the look of you, Miss Madigan, that God has had the last laugh. It brings me joy – even more after today – to know that you are suffering, like you deserve. I'm glad I left you to Satan. I'd have saved you, you know, if you'd let me."

A surge of fury ran through me. "How dare you!" I began, taking a step closer to the nun, but Lydia interrupted me.

"You left me to Satan, then did you?" she said, her voice low and calm. "So that's why I'm getting the ending I'm getting? And what sort of an ending do *you* deserve then? A murdering, lying bully who killed her own sister and saw her own father hanged because he didn't pander to her every need? If I deserve *this*, then what ending is ahead of you, you malicious old *cow*? I've longed to call you that, and more, for years now. The way I see it, at least my suffering will be done by the time I'm called to whatever's next on the other side, if anything is. But you? You're the reason *hell* exists."

The nun's age and apparent frailty belied the speed at which she could move. It took her a nanosecond to raise the walking stick as high as she could, and to strike Lydia with it, directly on the temple, with great force. Her scream brought Matt running to the open doorway from where he had been waiting outside. He crossed the room in a flash and grabbed the stick, just as the nun was about to strike down on her former pupil's head one more time. Seconds later, he was followed by two of the staff in the pink tunics, who grabbed Benedicta to restrain her.

I didn't care what they did. I was too intent on getting Lydia out of there, and getting out of there myself. We had heard enough.

Sister Irene was dashing up the stairs as we got to the top, Matt and I supporting Lydia either side. "My God!" she cried. "Are you alright? I saw her on the internal cameras – I'm so sorry! I'd never have left you in there with her if I'd thought for a second –"

"It's fine, it's fine." Lydia flapped her arm, signalling that the administrator should calm down.

"It's *not* fine," said Matt angrily. "Can we get her some medical attention? She's not well."

"Of course," said Irene. "We'll take her to a treatment room downstairs – here, let me take your arm, Lydia – I can't apologise enough."

I stood back, and let her bustle in, grabbing Lydia by the arm, and shouting instructions to a waiting doctor who stood at the bottom step of the stairs, who in turn rallied more nursing staff below. I fell behind a step and watched it unfold below me, as if all in slow motion.

And then I stopped, stood still on the step I had reached, and listened, very hard, because it was difficult to hear clearly through all the hubbub. No ... I was mistaken, it seemed.

Until I started to move again, and I heard it *again* – at least I thought I heard it. I stopped once more, and there was nothing.

I reached the bottom step, behind a protesting Lydia, and a babbling Sister Irene, and a grumpy Matt.

But there it was again. I was sure of it this time.

I shivered, and looked behind me. To see if whoever was humming was close by me on the stairs.

Instead, I saw something that I'll never forget for the rest of my life – along with everyone else who was on the concourse of St Anthony of Padua Care Home that day.

An elderly nun, alone, charging as fast as her frail legs would take her, away from two nurses who were trying to coax her back into her room, shouting unintelligibly, her face red and distorted with fury.

And as she got to the top step of the wide marble staircase, I watched as the walking stick she leaned on heavily gave way.

As if someone had kicked it.

And I saw her fall. Except there was something unnatural about the way that she fell, the way that her chest was suddenly thrust forward first, followed by the rest of her body as she lost her balance, her expression one of pure shock.

As if someone had pushed her.

And I watched, in horror, in frozen disbelief, as she plummeted down those marble stairs, her limbs flailing as she rolled and slid. And I heard the crack as her neck broke, and the slow sound her limp body made as it slowed to a halt, broken, three steps from the bottom.

Everyone there saw that.

But what they didn't see – what only Lydia and I saw – because she had turned back to watch with intense dread, slipping her hand in mine to grip it with a strength I didn't think she had left – was the small, almost transparent child that stood at the stop of the stairs for an instant. Thin and with wet hair, her arms bare in a filthy summer dress. Smiling.

Frances had had her revenge.

Chapter sixty-two

ENGLAND
June 2016

The formal apology, signed by the head of what remained of the Order of Maria Goretti in Ireland arrived too late for Lydia.

Rick told Matt that she had passed on a morning in August, in her own bed, at home in Somerset. Her last request was for him to open the window, so that her soul might fly free, and a gentle puff of wind ruffled her hair just at the moment that she took her last breath. He swore that it was her mum, come to take her safely away.

And I cried.

I cried because Lydia wasn't here anymore and I missed her, even though and because I hadn't known her as well as I could have, and as much as I wanted. I cried for all the years that my life had been without her, and I cried for what we'd gone through in those few short months in Ballykeeran all those years ago. And I tried to console myself with the fact that she wasn't in pain any longer, and that if we hadn't gone through all that strangeness – if she had been just a student who had gone on and done her Leaving Cert and left, and I had been just her teacher, then we would never have crossed paths again anyway. But it didn't work. I couldn't find any sense or meaning or good in her passing. I cried for poor, broken-hearted Rick, who had to be held up by his friends at the crematorium. I cried for all the pain she had endured, the lonely upbringing she'd had, the loss of her parents, and I cried for the future that could never happen now.

I cried for Benedicta, believe it or not. Arguably the most damaged of all of us. I cried for Frances – more of which later – and I cried for that great, stupid hulk of grey stone that had gone down in flames a week before Christmas, 1987. It hadn't been the convent's fault. It hadn't been anyone's, except a very, very sick woman who had lied and manipulated her way into a position of power. After she died, words such as Narcissism and Borderline Personality Disorder were bandied about. Not that it mattered anymore. She'd done her damage.

And I cried for myself. For the life that I might have had if she hadn't … what? If she hadn't just plain hated me because of something she saw in me? If she hadn't been deranged? If she hadn't seen Matt kiss me by the fir tree that day? If I'd worn tights the first time I met her? Who bloody knew?

I finally allowed myself to cry for the maybe that was Matt and me. For Emma, who had gone her whole life without knowing a father who may well have loved her as much as the one she did know. I cried so much, in fact, that she and Jess staged an intervention one Saturday afternoon, and threatened to call my doctor. And Jess nudged me quietly to just tell Emma, to finally let her know everything. And she was right. And so I told my daughter about an odd job that I'd held once, about a very mentally ill lady, and about the fact that ghosts were real. I told her who her father was, that she had brothers, literally from another mother, as the kids say, and that my life had been very different from what it had set out to be. And her reply? "But that's what life's supposed to do, Mum." And I wondered where she got her wisdom from.

And what of Ballykeeran, and the mysterious death of Frances Phelan, seven years old, in the summer of 1942? The human remains in Ballykeeran bog? *Of course* they were Frances, Lydia said. Or at least what was left of her after seventy-three years on an active bog at the mercy of machinery and animals and the elements, which amounted to a jawbone and a fragment of finger, hastily identified using DNA taken from her recently departed sister's hairbrush.

"What were you expecting, the Tollund Man?" Lydia scoffed on hearing the news in her own dying days. And when I asked why 'of course', she snorted, as if I were an idiot. "Because that's how the Universe works," she said. "Why do you think we're having this conversation? Why do you think we're all back in each other's lives, why we went to Ballykeeran? Because she *wanted* to set all of that in motion. Frances *wanted* to be found. She decided it was time. That's why it happened now."

And, do you know what? Hard as I try, and as long as Matt and I talked about it after Lydia was gone, I simply couldn't think of a better reason, one that made more sense. I'm sorry that I never said that to Lydia, mind. Sorry that I called her Dirk Gently, even though we'd both laughed.

Lydia never knew, of course, that my story slowly grew an ending.

That on finding Frances Phelan's remains they exhumed her coffin and found, instead of a child, the bones of a medium-sized animal. A dog, they said. The family pet. There's no official line why, but the oldsters around Ballykeeran, according to Matt's schoolfriend, the local Guard – because everyone knows everyone in the countryside – pretty much laughed at the police and more or less said, "But that's what we've been telling you for years." So the story that started the rhyme the local students used to chant was, after all, true. Putting two and two together, and carrying four and a half, it seems that Liam Phelan, unable to find his younger daughter's body, and becoming increasingly worried about his wife's long-term mental illness, decided to lie to her and say that he had found Frances, in order that they might hold a funeral and be done with it, in the hope that his adored wife might rally and leave her sickbed. Only one other person was in on the secret, apparently, one Ned Gorman, the local undertaker. Ned, who told his younger brother Tom some years later, although Tom Gorman wasn't available for comment, having been killed by a drunk driver in 1994. How I wished I could have been the one to tell Lydia that! She'd have laughed herself sick at the irony.

So why was Frances' 'body' not exhumed back then, when murder most foul was in the offing and local tongues were wagging?

Well, because she was a Greta's Girl. And no one, not even the

Chief Justice of Ireland would have obtained permission from the Order to dig up someone from their sacred ground. A fact that Liam Phelan had counted on when he carried out his desperate act of deceit to placate his wife. How torn that poor man must have been! Grieving for his little girl – seven years old and missing – he can't even have known for certain if she were alive or dead. And then going through the pain of a funeral – had he *killed* the dog in order to have something to add weight to the little white coffin, by the way? And then made sure that it was closed – Ned Gorman would have seen to that, of course.

But why did Liam Phelan hang?

Why did he never refute the charges of murder laid at his feet in the months after his daughter's disappearance? Why did he calmly go to the gallows, when he could have just told the truth? That he didn't know if Frances were actually dead – although it was likely at that stage, but still not certain with no actual body – and that he'd buried the dog to keep his wife happy?

That part – that explanation was most obvious of all to me. Because somewhere, between Frances going missing, and Evelyn Junior being packed off to live at the convent, he must have figured it out. That his younger daughter's killer was his elder daughter. And, because he loved her, he said nothing, to keep her from getting into trouble – ultimately taking the rap for murder. But he still loved his wife too, and that was why he sent Evelyn to live at Maria Goretti, in order that Evelyn Senior wouldn't be left at the mercy of her remaining daughter and her rages in the house.

Except Evelyn Senior couldn't bear life without little Frances and killed herself, and Evelyn Junior couldn't bear the notion that her father had betrayed her and sent her away when – as she said herself – she'd arranged for life to get a whole lot easier for the family. So she put her twisted little mind to best use and got her own back. A family trait it seemed. Revenge.

She was right about a couple of things, mind, Evelyn-turned-Benedicta. She was right that her father loved her. He never told anyone the truth, whatever he had found out about the night Frances died – and ultimately he died for his daughter, to protect her. Which was a shame because, had he told the truth, then she might have got some help. Although on second thoughts, I'm not sure that women's prisons provided the necessary psychiatric support in those days and, besides that, who am I kidding? Benedicta was beyond help.

Oh, and the other thing she was right about? Yes. She was very good at hiding things. Because no one ever figured out where she had put little Frances' body on that night in 1942, or how she actually killed her. That was one secret – probably one of many – that went with Benedicta to her grave – in the Nuns' Graveyard in Ballykeeran, but around the rear of the chapel, where no one was likely to see her or visit. And as far away as possible from the grave where Frances' remains were eventually re-interred. It was inconceivable that the sisters should be together for all eternity.

There are plans afoot now for a posthumous pardon for Liam Phelan, a local committee who are going through the appropriate steps. And with Benedicta's confession of sorts recorded by the internal cameras in her room, and the evidence both circumstantial and otherwise, they're in with a good chance of it being granted. Shame that there's not a single soul left, however, who might derive comfort from it. Other than myself, I guess.

And so, a year later, after it all came to a literal crashing end at the St Anthony of Padua Care Home, what of me? Ria Driver, née Clancy, now fifty-four years old, still a teacher, still living alone in London. No alarms and no surprises. Well. The occasional surprise is alright, I suppose.

I have a ... a 'friend' now. Called Matt ... I might have mentioned him ... who lives in Ireland, but comes to the UK to catch up with his son who attends college here, and who detours to London now and again. He has apologised for not listening to me all those years ago, when we might have had a chance at a future together if he hadn't jumped to stupid conclusions and "been such an arsehole", as he says himself. And I have accepted it.

Matt has been there as I've cried, and I've been there as he cried over our mutual friend Lydia. And we've talked long hours about whether it's possible, because of what I saw, she saw, and what he now thoroughly *believes* I saw, thankfully – because one delusional party is never a good basis for a relationship – that something of Lydia is still with us? That she has somehow become part of her beloved Universe and that her energy has remained, in some way, tangled with our energies, and that of other people who forged her and loved her and hated her in all sums and measures?

It was he who came up with this theory a few months ago, on the drive back from scattering her ashes into the sea, in fact, when, stuck on the M5 in traffic, I asked him if he actually believed in ghosts and, in the silence as he thought about his answer, suddenly Simple Minds came on the radio. And as we listened in silence to Jim Kerr sing 'Don't You Forget About Me' in that deep voice of his, we looked at each other wide-eyed, and burst out laughing because that had to be her, didn't it?

"She just loved Judd Nelson," I laughed, and he nodded.

"*The Breakfast Club* though," he replied. "It's still not a patch on *Bueller*."

He smirked, and we both laughed again. And I was suddenly struck that it wasn't only a message or a reminder, it was a … *prompt*, a *nudge*. The timing, at last, was right. *Thank you, Lydia.*

"I have something to tell you," I said suddenly, thankful that we were stopped. "You have a daughter …"

That was a little strange, I have to admit. And there was silence for a few weeks when he went back to Galway. And I thought for a moment that it was all gone again, all over. But then, a surprise. Which is why I like them now. A little. An email, followed by a Facetime – get me and my technology – followed by a kiss outside The Ivy after dinner one Saturday night when he was in town. Just a kiss, mind. I do still stand by my 'no alarms' rule. Although I might be ready to let that slide a little when we travel to Cornwall next month for Jess's wedding. To a thirty-five-year-old restaurateur, no less. Her 'Swipe Right Angel Delight', as she calls him. I've no idea where her adventure will take her, but I'll gladly hold her bouquet as she says her vows, and root for her every step of the way. And maybe I'll book a double room at the country hotel, and bring a spare toothbrush, just in case. And, as Jess persists in reminding me, I'm only fifty-four. Still younger than Madonna, and of an age with Meg Ryan, and Enya and Heather Locklear. And Susan Boyle, she adds, but only because she doesn't want me to get too big-headed.

Her wedding is a big deal to me, actually. Not only do I get to see my best friend and confidante – the person who forced me to confront My Story – have a chance at fun and happiness and, who knows, true love, but I will also get to see my daughter and her father meet for the first time. If that goes well, then I will be with her when she meets her brothers when they are both in Ireland in October. And if all *that* goes well, then who knows?

And if it doesn't? Well, I still have what I have. My own flat, a job, my health, no cats. And My Story. Except now it has an ending. It has come full circle and closed. And while there is still much to think about, and wonder about, and remember, it is so much easier to fit it back into the box where I keep it now, and keep that box closed until I *choose* to open it again. Mind you, I still don't tell anyone about it. Apart from Emma and Jess, and Matt of course. But no one else. They'd never believe a word of it. Sometimes I don't believe it myself, and I lived it.

But I'm no longer defined by it.

I didn't even realise that I *was,* but it was something that Lydia said made me realise that it did. That somehow, somewhere inside me, it was always December 18th 1987. And now, for better or for worse, it isn't any more.

It's now.

And that'll do me just fine.

The End

351

If you enjoyed this book from
Poolbeg why not visit our website

www.poolbeg.com

and get another book delivered straight
to your home or to a friend's home.

All books despatched within 24 hours.

Free postage on orders over €20*

Why not join our mailing list at
www.poolbeg.com and get some
fantastic offers, competitions,
author interviews, new releases
and much more?

@PoolbegBooks

www.facebook.com/poolbegpress

*Free postage over €20 applies to Ireland only

THEY ALL FALL DOWN

CAT HOGAN

Ring-a-ring o' Roses . . . How far would you go?

Jen Harper likes to play it safe. She is settling into life on the outskirts of a sleepy fishing village with her little boy, Danny. Life by the sea – just how she wanted it.

When she meets Andy, she feels the time has come to put her baggage and the scars of the past behind her. Then she is introduced to Scott, Andy's best friend, and is stung by his obvious
disdain for her. Why is Scott so protective of his best friend? What is the dark secret that threatens all of them?

In her attempt to find answers, Jen must confront her demons and push her relationships to their limits. By digging up the past, she puts Danny and herself in danger. Will she succeed in uncovering the truth before they all fall down?

Raw and energetic, They All Fall Down *is a fast-paced and addictive novel exploring the depths of flawed human nature, the thin line between love and obsession and the destructive nature of addiction.*

ISBN 978-178199-864-9

POOLBEG
CRIMS●N

THERE WAS A CROOKED MAN

CAT HOGAN

Scott makes enemies everywhere. Powerful people want him dead. He's coming back to Ireland to finish what he started. But first, he must make it out of Marrakech alive.

Jen knows Scott will come back. Every day, she waits. He almost killed her last time and, fuelled by hate and arrogance, he's not a man to ever just move on. He will kill her and he will kill her young son. But her husband and friends believe she has spiralled into paranoia.

So she knows, when he returns, she'll face the psychopath alone.

In this powerful thriller, Hogan plunges us into the world and mind of her psychopathic killer from the first line and relentlessly tightens the tension until the very last page.

'Hogan writes vividly and unflinchingly.
Scott Carluccio Randall
is an anti-hero to reckon with'
AIDAN GILLEN

ISBN 978-178199-850-2

ALSO AVAILABLE FROM

POOLBEG
CRIMSON

THE OTHER SIDE OF THE WALL

ANDREA MARA

When Sylvia looks out her bedroom window at night and sees a child face down in the pond next door, she races into her neighbour's garden. But the pond is empty, and no-one is answering the door.

Wondering if night feeds and sleep deprivation are getting to her, she hurriedly retreats. Besides, the fact that a local child has gone missing must be preying on her mind. Then, a week later, she hears the sound of a man crying through her bedroom wall.

The man living next door, Sam, has recently moved in. His wife and children are away for the summer and he joins them at weekends. Sylvia finds him friendly and helpful, yet she becomes increasingly uneasy about him.

Then Sylvia's little daughter wakes one night, screaming that there's a man in her room. This is followed by a series of bizarre disturbances in the house.

Sylvia's husband insists it's all in her mind, but she is certain it's not – there's something very wrong on the other side of the wall.

ISBN 978-178199-8328

THE LAST
LOST GIRL

MARY HOEY

Unravelling the past can be dangerous . . .

On a perfect July evening in the sizzling Irish summer of 1976, fifteen-year-old Festival Queen Lilly Brennan disappears. Thirty-seven years later, as the anniversary of Lilly's disappearance approaches, her sister Jacqueline returns to their childhood home in Blackberry Lane. There she stumbles upon something that reopens the mystery, setting her on a search for the truth – a search that leads her to surprising places and challenging encounters.

Jacqueline feels increasingly compelled to find the answer to what happened to Lilly all those years ago and finally lay her ghost to rest. But at what cost? For unravelling the past proves to be a dangerous and painful thing, and her path to the truth leads her ever closer to a dark secret she may not wish to know.

'A haunting, mesmerising first novel with a chilling secret at its core. It will grip and surprise you to the very last page' *RTÉ Guide*

ISBN 978-178199-8311